YET TO COME

YET TO COME

A NOVEL BY
CRIS MAZZA

BLAZEVOX[BOOKS]
Buffalo, New York

publisher of weird little books

BlazeVOX [books]

blazevox.org

21 20 19 18 17 16 15 14 13 12 01 02 03 04 05 06 07 08 09 10

BlazeVOX

Acknowledgements

Acknowledgements made to the following publications in which portions of this novel first appeared:

Trickle-Down Timeline (Red Hen Press)
Coachella Review
Ella @ 100
LitBreak
Big Other

The following works are quoted in this work:

> "They will say to themselves, 'I was heartless, because I was young and strong and wanted things so much. But now I know.'"
> Willa Cather, "Old Mrs. Harris"

> "The world just goes along. Nothing much matters, you know? I mean really matters. But then sometimes, just for a second, you get this grace, this belief that it does matter, a whole lot."
> Lucia Berlin, *A Manual for Cleaning Women*

> "People's lives... were dull, simple, amazing and unfathomable—deep caves paved with kitchen linoleum."
> Alice Munro, *Lives of Girls and Women*

> "She thought of being launched out on a gray, deep, baleful, magnificent sea. Love."
> Alice Munro, "Differently"

> "... two people who love each other can be saved from madness only by the things that come between them—children, duties, visits, bores, relations—the things that protect married people from each other."
> Edith Wharton, *Souls Belated*

I'd like to express a lifetime of thanks to everyone who ever bought or read one of my books or attended a reading where I shared my work.

Especially on the publication of this novel, deepest gratitude for support-beyond-workshop:

Diane Goodman
Gina Frangello
Christopher Grimes

YET TO COME

YET TO COME

She doesn't like her name and never wanted to think of herself as someone who would go around answering to it. She does, of course. Go around and answer to it. At least she has to turn her head or turn around when someone calls out or addresses her. She hasn't successfully come up with a replacement name, and how effective would that be without a lot of bullshit aggravation? It's already on her social security card, credit cards and tax forms.

As girls, her sisters claimed their grandfather—for whom English was not his first language—couldn't remember their names and called them, in order, *Lily*, *Girly* and *Hey You*. That made her *Hey You*. Not bad, and better than *Girly*, because if there was one thing she isn't, it's *girly*, at least not in the makeup, nails, skirts and heels departments. For a brief time in the late 80s she tried that, but of course the shallow appliqué wasn't a difference-making transformation. Perhaps it's not a *renovation* that's needed, but a do-over, several do-overs. Not to *be* 18, or 20, or 24 again, but maybe to be able to get a few things right that at one time came out so very wrong. Profoundly, when it comes to a boy named Cal. A boy who must be now, somewhere (she *knows* where), a man. Depending on your definition of *man*. Or was he a man already the last time she saw him? 30 years ago when she was still a girl, even though they're almost the same age, him older by a mere 16 days.

/s/ X

Chapter One

One Night, Two Perspectives, Three Screwdrivers

March 1, 1980, San Diego, California

They'd known each other long enough, Cal maybe could've just turned the knob and walked in, since she expected him. But he didn't. He knocked. She answered by opening the door and walking away without looking at him or saying hello. "You ready?" he said.

"No." She was already in the bathroom, then came out holding a comb and glanced at him quickly. "Well, at least it isn't a *date*."

"What's that supposed to mean?"

"You look better in jeans. Why d'you wear those disco pants?"

"These?" Cal looked at his legs. Marcello had said black pants, and these were what the store had in the category of *pants* and *black*. He wore them to every gig, just about every weekend. "What's wrong with 'em?"

"They're repulsive. We're not going to a *disco*, are we?" She was still in a bathrobe.

"You don't *have* to come with me." He tried to look somewhere else. Mail on the kitchen table. Albums left on top of a speaker.

She went back to the bathroom and started to brush her teeth, then came back to the bathroom doorway. "D'you think anything will happen?" A trickle of toothpaste ran down her chin. He moved slowly toward the bathroom, until he could see half the sink.

"Maybe. Things don't just *happen*, though, you've got to make them happen."

"I know that. Is it anything like where Rudy works?"

He put his fists in his pockets. "Oh, I forgot your Mr. Big works in a bar."

"A fancy one, with an expensive restaurant." The toothbrush in her mouth made her words blurry.

"Then don't expect it to be the same."

"What kind of people will be there?"

"Whadda ya think ... a club called *Macho's*."

"Gays?" Then she laughed and sprayed toothpaste, not quite far enough to hit him.

"You wanna go to a gay bar?"

"Once was enough." She turned back to the sink and spit her mouthful of toothpaste. "If something doesn't happen tonight, *dang* I'll go crazy, I swear I will, sitting at home and *thinking*."

"Don't think you're the only one who ever sat at home thinking," he said.

She looked over her shoulder, out the bathroom door, at him, then turned back to the mirror.

"Well, you could've *done* something, like I am tonight." She rinsed her mouth again and spit. "So who'm I gonna find at this place?"

"A lot of sailors go there."

"Thanks loads."

"A lot of people. I never took a census."

"But I bet you counted all the babes under sixteen."

"Just the ones with long dark hair."

"Good," she said. She shook her head and her hair landed back in place. They'd both had long hair, in high school. After that hers was frizzy for a while. It was straighter now, and shorter. Now it was shorter than his.

She went into her bedroom, then called, "Do I need a purse?"

"You'll hafta buy drinks."

"Dang." She closed the bedroom door most of the way. "Rudy always makes my drinks. He only lets me have three. Screwdrivers."

See, Cal, if I could ever someday explain to you ... about that night in 1980 ... and also that time when we were sixteen. I know I was a mopey teenager, and even tried to tell you why, having to do with not liking things I was supposed to want. And you <u>listened</u>. And usually tried to joke me out of it. Then that one time, you ... well, you tried something different than a joke. And you wanted to call it love. A 16-year-old human male can't <u>love</u> any more than a feral wolf. And if love is expressed by jamming your finger inside someone– Dang, Cal, I

know one of the ten-thousand times you apologized, you said you knew it must be wrong cuz I wouldn't stop bawling. I don't remember crying, before or after. But if I was, it was because it was the same day, or the day after, my dog was mashed by a car. I'd had Shep since I was FIVE. Anyway, understandably, our friendship had been getting more and more awkward since that time. But I always needed someone to talk to after my pointless non-relationships. With men, I mean, not dogs. A few men. Very few. Two. The real relationships with dogs so outnumber the men. The night in 1980 in that club with you ... I hadn't yet gotten another dog. I needed to talk to someone who already knew me, but how sick is this: I hoped you didn't know I was still a virgin.

She came back into the living room wearing gray slacks and a loose summer top with very thin straps across her shoulders, which were already brown, and it was only March. "But I can make one drink last a long time." She rubbed lotion on her hands, hesitated, then took more lotion and rubbed it up both arms and shoulders, under the straps. Cal turned away.

"I just sit and watch him work. Everybody likes him best of the bartenders."

Cal stood with his back to her, looking at his feet, where the bottom of his pants hid his shoes. She was right, the material was thin and shiny, clinging to his thighs, flaring at the ankles.

"They all talk to him like they know him, and it gave me this funny feeling in my chest because only *I* knew him. Or so I thought." She stood right beside Cal, but he didn't move. "I just sat there watching him, then he would come down to where I was, lean over the bar and whisper something, usually about one of the customers, but so everyone knew I was with him." She moved in front of Cal and picked up a silver bracelet from the coffee table, put it on one arm and pushed it all the way up, almost to her armpit, then shook her arm until it fell back to her wrist. Cal was watching, but she didn't meet his eyes. "They all told me I was lucky because Rudy was such a great guy." Cal headed for the door. "Rudy hates that job. He can't wait to finish accounting school. Maybe the church-thing will make him bookkeeper for everyone's doorbell-hours, so he won't have to associate with *worldly* things like money … and perverts like me." Something clanked. Cal turned. The silver bracelet on the coffee table. And she'd picked up a framed snapshot of a dog. "You know, that dog loved me more than … well, than anyone deserves to be loved."

Cal was already holding the doorknob, looking back at her. "You finished? Did that help?"

"No. Let's make like a goalie and get the puck out of here."

It was early. The parking lot was empty. He took his saxophone case out of the trunk but she still hadn't gotten out of the car. "C'mon, hurry up."

"Do I hafta go in *now?*"

"Unless you wanna pay the cover charge."

"*Dang*, I don't want it to look like I'm coming *with* you." She was staring straight out the front windshield.

"Look," he said, "after we get through that door, you're on your own. I'm not gonna come to your table or even *look* at you. I'll be looking out for myself, and I don't wanna hafta worry about getting *you* home."

She turned and met his eyes. A shuddering moment. And he thought maybe she shivered too. "Good. I just don't want anyone to think I'm with the band."

"Yeah, you'll never get that funny feeling in your chest if people know you're here with the skinny sax player."

"The one in disco pants, that's for sure." She got out of the car.

They stopped at the service door where the employees and band members went in. He knocked. "You sure you wanna do this?"

This time she didn't look at him. "I have to. I'll go crazy otherwise." A waitress opened the door. "Otherwise I might end up like *you*, dragging around, just getting older."

"Thanks. I can always count on you to define my life." He joined the other band members, setting up on a small stage.

All I know is it was too damn early for me to be ordering my first drink. I nursed it a long time, sipping it through the plastic straw that's meant for stirring. Rudy had warned me not to drink through the straw

because I would be affected by the alcohol faster. Could that asshole have been right? I sucked each ice cube, taking turns, letting them all shrink at the same pace, until each was a sliver, and yet your damn band was <u>still</u> setting up, saying "test" into microphones, twanging metallic notes, moving the drums around to make room for still more amplifiers.

☯

He watched her. Nothing new about that. Whenever she was around. Even if she was throwing barbs. Sometimes she seemed to have no sense, no judgement, like the religious-nut she was nuts over. And now, as he watched, she actually left her purse on her seat and left her table. Cal's mic and monitor were already set up, he was waiting for the final sound-check, seated on a stool at the back of the stage, his sax on a floor stand, his legs stretched out in front, heels on the floor, feet rocking slowly side-to-side. His glass of tequila in both hands, between his knees. He was carefully sloshing the contents in circles without spilling over the rim. Staring at that, but aware of her. She was coming toward the stage, then went around the side and stood on the floor, below Cal's stool.

"When's this damn thing gonna start?"

"What's your hurry?"

"I've already had a drink. Three's my limit."

"What happens after three—you turn into a pumpkin?"

"Rudy told me three was enough."

"For him maybe, so he wouldn't lose control and find himself in bed with you."

"Har-de-har."

Another band member edged past the drums and brought Cal a jigger of tequila and a glass of beer. Cal finished what was left in his glass, then took the jigger.

"*Dang*, Cal." She turned away while he emptied the jigger. He watched her lower one strap and rub her shoulder, slowly, squinting at her skin. "Hope I'm not peeling."

"You're not."

She turned back toward Cal. He sipped his beer then wiped the foam from his beard with his palm.

"Know what? If you ever go bald—and it's a good bet—you can just turn your head upside down."

"Har-de-har back atcha."

"Okay, then," she said, "I guess I'll fill my glass with water so it looks like a drink."

When Cal laughed, she glared.

"What's so damn funny?"

"Little Miss Sophisticated. And he called *you* a pervert?"

"Shut *up*. He never said that word. Just that it wasn't right to *be* with me."

"I think he was gay. A puritanical queer."

She started to walk away, then turned around. "What about *your* excuses, Cal? How long has it been for you—what're *you* waiting for?"

He watched her until she was back at her original table. She picked up her purse and, with her usual absurdity, the empty glass. When she came out of the restroom, sure enough, the glass was full again. Then she moved to a table even farther from the stage.

Was <u>alone</u> the only way I thought I could function in a crowd? Alone, and yet not-alone because I knew you were watching me? And, somehow, therefore, <u>safe</u> ... because of it? I had no intention of leaving that club with a stranger! But no other intentions either. I don't think. Which, at best, is coy. At worst ... well, dang, <u>coy</u> is bad enough. I couldn't admit I thought it might be cool, you playing in a steady-gigging band with (what turned out to be) a big crowd dancing. You smoking and drinking which was so different than when we were teenagers. (Weren't we wide-eyed bumpkins?)

When you guys finally started playing, there were still only about fifty people in the club, and only half of them dancing, a bunch of empty tables between where I was and them. It's hard to remember but maybe I can picture it cuz it's when I had to order my 2nd screwdriver. I was going to wait longer, but this waitress picked up my glass of water and stood waiting for something. Sorry, one of those jobs-you-do-in-college that I never did, I don't have the proper reverence, and probably don't tip enough. That night, did I tip at all? Did I ever pay?

Who picked up my tab? You? If so … dang, Cal, I am such a weasel. I won't say bitch, that's a female dog, and dogs are honest about … well, love and such.

Anyway, you were right, Marines and young Latina girls. They had exaggerated eye makeup and flipped their long hair and kept it flying around like silky flags while they danced. The men didn't have any hair to flip around. I remember, and probably also remembered it right then, at a gig in high school, when you jumped off the stage to dance and play the cowbell, how your long air … well, didn't exact flip, but was wild. Wild in the way tall dry grasses are wild. Is that an insult? I mean natural. Jeans and a T-shirt. You were so frank and instinctive— that kind of wild. Your band in high school played Chicago, Tower of Power, Blood Sweat and Tears, and The Doobies—which you always sang. But that band that night in 1980 … yes, I was disappointed. The trumpet was out of tune, the drums too loud, so was the bass, and that singer attacked every note flat, then slurped up to find the pitch. They all sounded the same, even the pop songs I should've recognized, plus you didn't sing anything. What were you doing in that crappy group? Maybe what I felt was helpless—powerless to get you back into something better. But I got that second drink to last through the first set.

When the band took its break, pre-recorded top-forty music came through the speakers. "Turn it up!" the girls called from the dance floor. There were a couple hundred people in the club, but she was still alone, blocked by 4 or 5 empty tables. She was staring at the tabletop, drawing something with her straw, as Cal made his way toward her, stumbling over a few chairs, but even that didn't make her look up. So he said, "Hey," when he was still ten feet away.

"What now? I thought you weren't going to talk to me." Then she glanced up, briefly, "they'll think I'm *with* you." Her eyes darted elsewhere.

"*They* don't even know you're here. Nothing'll happen if you stay way back here."

She leaned back in her chair but kept both hands on her empty glass, tipping it and tapping it on the table. "What d'*you* care?" She lifted the glass to drain a few remaining drops. Even the ice cubes were gone. "I mean, you trying to be my pimp?"

"Good idea." He pulled a chair from behind him and sat backwards, accidentally rapping the chair's back against her table. She grabbed her glass as though it was going to blast off. "Maybe I wanna see it happen. I wanna *watch* you leave with someone." Or he *needed* to. If he could keep himself from jumping the guy and stomping his ass before …

"You've known I've been with lots of guys." She was looking down again, her fingers twirling the glass. When a waitress hovered beside the table, she wrapped her hands around the glass. So Cal ordered a beer and the waitress left. "You knew I've been with Rudy for … these few months…" She raised her face and probably caught him staring.

"Otherwise known as six weeks," he said, "and I knew nothing was going on."

"You wish."

"So why'd you break up? What happened, you had to ask if he had a prick?"

"Shut up. I keep telling you, he was in this kind-of church …"

"What were the commandments? He couldn't lay any pipe 'til you converted?"

"He might've married me if I had."

"So why *didn't* you? Convert, that is."

"It was … I wanted him to see … we could've been okay together, without *that*. That religion thing … It was icky."

"You *are* a pervert." He stood, trying to laugh, and maybe he succeeded. "Trying to seduce a man away from church. Have you no decency?"

"A *weird* church, they didn't even call it *church* … But at least I'm not as wretched as *you*."

He turned and walked back toward the stage, but stopped several tables away, started to go back toward her while he yelled over the music, "You're crazy if you think I've gone this long without wetting my wick."

"You bragging or complaining?"

The top-forty music faded. Cal wheeled and ran toward the stage.

Maybe someday we'll be trading stories and get it straight, or maybe it doesn't matter. Maybe we'll both forget it and get on with our lives. I mean, it wasn't <u>that</u> big a deal, was it? So, I honestly didn't know where I was going or what I was going to do after I took a leak, then sat at a different table, this time in the middle of a lot of other crowded, noisy tables. There were even several empty glasses at the new table, and an ashtray full of cigarette butts ... and why didn't I even care or wonder? I think I lay my head on the table for a second, but the smell of the cigarettes made me even more dizzy. Cuz by then I was already whirling a little, and I'd never felt like that at Rudy's bar. Like <u>there</u>, I was always more sharp than ever, keeping my eyes on Rudy as he laughed with the customers. His fingers never even touched the waitress's hand when he took change from her or handed her the drinks she needed. That's how much I observed and remembered. Not like what I remember from that night with you ... my head likely going back and forth from down on the stinky table to propped up in my hands. When someone asked me to dance, I might have just stared at him, but I can't remember what the hell he might have looked like or how long he stood there til he gave up and moved on. Marines, they all look alike, right? Amazing that a waitress even asked me if I wanted anything, but somehow I had another screwdriver. I didn't think I ever actually slept, but had a suddenly-woken-up feeling when the band stopped playing. Everyone seemed to be talking very loud, then they must've realized they didn't have to anymore, and the throbbing conversation settled. When the slurpy singer sat across the table from me, I couldn't figure out where I'd seen him before. Duh! It was the band's table! But ... did I do it on purpose, move to that table on purpose? I still wonder, and can't answer.

Between sets, a waitress was always standing at their table to get their orders. As usual they were all having beer and tequila. Hunched up and clutching her glass, she almost looked like a frightened monkey. Cal lifted one of her drooping straps and put it back on her shoulder, then sat beside her.

"What're you doing here?" he asked. "Why didn't you dance with that guy?"

"I dunno. He didn't give me a chance to answer."

The trumpet player sat in the last empty seat, on her other side. He was wearing jeans, a white shirt and a red tie. Cal smoked and drank. He had a sax reed in his mouth along with a cigarette, then he crushed the reed in the ashtray and everyone at the table cheered. Everyone except her, of course. She leaned toward Cal. "Can I tell you something?" She giggled, suddenly even closer. "Can I tell you something personal?"

"It's a free country."

"I mean, I hate your pants. I knew I could tell you, though, I mean, I figured you'd wanna know. What're friends for?"

"Good question."

"But it's a two-way street, y'know. You can tell me something personal. C'mon, ask me anything."

Cal put his cigarette out. No longer a monkey, more like an 8-year-old, she pointed her straw at the rising smoke and blew at it, then coughed.

"Okay," he said, "why *did* you go to that gay bar?"

She was batting at the air as though smoke still lingered. "A girl in accounting class thought it would solve my problems." She rubbed her eyes. "With men. She thought my problem with men *was* men."

"So she thought you should be boffing women instead?"

"I don't think a girl can *boff* another girl."

"Whadd-ya think lezzies do together, sing campfire songs?"

"No, I jus' mean it's not, like … *boff* sounds so hard, like a fight or something. With girls it's … softer."

"How'd *you* know?"

"I'm a girl."

"That doesn't mean … it can be soft with a guy."

"Dang, didja hear what you jus' said? Bragging about being *soft?*"

"You know I meant it different." He finished his beer. "When it's something that means something … I mean it *should* mean more than... That's when it's … better."

"What're you talking about … please?"

The waitress was already putting down another beer. He pulled down half of it before speaking again. "That really is a good question," he said, "what're friends for."

"Yeah. A miracle we've been friends so long."

"Have we?"

"Haven't we?"

He drummed on the table. "Except one time when we were more than friends."

"*That* time?" Her lips tightened. "We were less than friends. Why doncha wear jeans or something?"

I probably couldn't even tell you, it was the first time I got drunk. Rudy sure made sure I didn't. My head felt like a brick balancing on a toothpick. Did I ever say that out loud? I planned to, whenever I felt like talking again. I remember I could hear the other band guys talking but couldn't tell how many different conversations. Thought I was still laughing at the last thing I said but was also drooling on my arm. You smelled of tobacco and liquor and sweat–the smoking and drinking were new. And you looked serious and exhausted. Where was that boy I'd known with the crazy grin? I probably didn't say that either. What I <u>did</u> say was probably a pile of sassy-ass bullshit. Why'd you like me so damn much?

"If you were in a different band, like a *better* one, maybe you could wear different pants."

Someone said, "Hey, wa'chit." The table jolted. Ice cubes rattled.

"I don't care what you think of my pants."

"Well ... if you were wondering why you never score—"

"It's nothing to do with my pants."

"Okay." She closed her eyes and drained what was left in her glass through the straw.

He said, "We already established your love life isn't a raging success either."

She pushed her glass away, stacked her fists end-to-end on the table and rested her forehead on the top fist. "That much I know. He wouldn't even hold my hand in public. His church, or whatever it was, said it was a sin to be with someone *worldly*. Anyone not in this church-thing was *worldly*."

"Asshole."

"Yeah. This is weird."

"What is?"

"I think Rudy was making my screwdrivers a little weaker than these."

"What was a churchy-asshole doing as a *bar*tender?"

"It was where he worked."

"You sure he put *any*thing in your drinks?"

"Maybe not." Her fists collapsed and her head fell to the tabletop. Everyone's drinks jumped. "But at least they were free."

I think I'll send you a postcard. Cuz I know someday, and someday soon I think, I should explain. A person's first time drunk at 22? Pathetic. The whole thing wasn't tragic or anything, just pathetic, and if I could explain ... It's just that right now I don't know <u>what</u> I would explain. Everyone always wants to explain. "Let me explain!" Don't they mean justify? Don't they mean "I didn't listen to you but now you have to listen to <u>me</u>"? But I'll send you a postcard. Maybe I can tell a whole story on postcards. One or two a year. The story of my life (if I ever have one) since the story of that night.

2008, El Centro, California

He's been a man for a lot of years now. In 1980 a younger one who hadn't yet acted out of wretched acquiescence and got himself married to someone else. (*Wretched* in 1980 was jargon for *horny*, by 2008 had returned to its original meaning.)

Spring came in February in the lower California desert. A bird pecked at the windows of his house, sitting on the sill, tap-tap-tapping, painting the sill with purple shit. Two, three, four different windows, all day, rat-a-tatting. One morning, Cal was cleaning window screens, because the major form of precipitation here was dust. He also washed the sills, a job not tacitly included in the screen-cleaning task that had been not-so-tacitly requested of him (admittedly, when he asked for a chore). But it would have been difficult to ignore the plum-and-black splats of shit and pretend the duty was complete. The screens were drying propped against the garage door, the windows cranked open, so the bird achieved its life's wish. It was finally in the house. And, inside, realized this was not what it wanted at all.

Cal caught the bird in a sheet, put it in a cardboard box. He drove it 20 miles away, into a state park in the desert. When he opened the box, the bird, wings somewhat tattered from its hours up against the window glass, flew instantly, gone in a fluttering second, the force of its departure knocking the box out of Cal's hand. Gone so fast he barely could follow the directional line of flight. But thought, perhaps, it was—by accident, just fluke—the route back to town.

Later, the screens back in place, the windows shut, the bird returned, tapping, not knowing why it so fixatedly wanted this thing it wanted, this thing that has frayed its feathers and bewildered its instinct, this thing that upon achieving led to imprisonment, darkness, and miles of flight, only to return and want it again.

He looked it up. It was a male brown-headed cowbird. Instead of spending its time with a mate, building a nest and making hundreds of trips back and forth with bugs to stuff down the pre-fledglings' throats, the male cowbird had time to spend pecking at windows because the female, producing up to a dozen eggs a season, laid them into the nests of other, usually smaller, birds. Industrious sparrows, dove, towhees, catbirds. The cowbird hatchlings grew faster, frequently crowded the bio-kids out of the nest and occupied the step-parents' time and resources. Why wasn't it the duped, dutiful sparrow or dove pecking with aberrant wretchedness at his window?

In the extra room where his step-daughter, and later step-grandson, used to sleep, Cal got his saxophone out, sat on the bed fingering the keys, but didn't put the mouthpiece between his lips.

☯

Yeah, I'll send a postcard, everything out in the open, even the mailman can read it. Nothing to hide. I was a silly messy stew and slopped it over onto you. (Dang, could I write the whole thing as poetry

23

like that?) I actually think you probably won't even remember. We were stupid kids. Weren't you kind of blitzed too?

☯

March 1, 1980, San Diego

"Well …," he said, looking into his glass, like maybe some black-and-white guy in a movie, or a vodka ad, "free drinks are good, but being strong enough … that makes all the difference." His hand, his left hand, was on the table between them. When had she sat up again? He only knew the warmth, the buzz, the jump of energy, the neon, the flash of heat into his gut, and lower, when she put her hand on his. It was a feeling that said he needed to be, and could be, even *would* be more than he was, if he was with her.

"I know, Cal. I know how you feel. See, once I was waiting for him in the bar's entry, after his shift, and he came out and put his hand on the back of my neck, under my hair …"

"Like this?" Cal slid his hand up her neck.

"No." She went even more limp. "But that feels good."

He stroked her neck. It felt so thin. Then slid his hand around to the other side of her face, used both hands to turn her so he could kiss her. She leaned against him. He lowered one of her straps and groaned as he pressed his open mouth on her shoulder. His mouth moved up her neck, buzzing against her when he said, "I shouldn't be doing this. Why am I?" Then she opened her mouth as he kissed her again. He hoped the beer had washed most of the cigarette taste from his mouth. His hands slid over her shoulders and down her arms.

"Good question. And why aren't I minding?" she laughed, holding onto the table with one arm as he was pulling her closer. "It must be the booze," she gasped, maybe still laughing, "That's what Rudy said once when … things started to … get going, so to speak. I'd stayed at the bar till he was off, then he had a drink. When he kissed me, when he unbuttoned my shirt … he blamed the booze. Very flattering … doncha think?"

Cal moaned, his face against her neck, his hands under her blouse, moving up her back. "Oh baby," he mouthed her earlobe, "Shut up." She

24

was warm and soft and supple, but he took his hands out of her blouse, held her head and kissed her again, then kissed her cheek, one eye, and her temple, holding her face next to his.

"But'cha know what?" she said. "I always seem to find guys who give me just the opposite of what I want … or think I should want."

His mouth against her ear, he said, not too loud, "I was always ready to give you what he wouldn't." He put his tongue in her ear. She giggled, then shivered.

"But, you didn't listen, … when you wanted to, I *didn't*—" She lifted her chin, her head falling back, stretching her throat as he kissed it.

He held her neck in both hands, stroked her cheeks with his thumbs. "But I always wanted to. And you stayed friends with me. Just to torture me? What *did* you want? *Any*thing?"

"That's what I dunno."

They looked at each other. "Maybe now you've figured it out?"

"The thing is … it's something I'm sposta want. And I don't. Not enough. But maybe—"

He pulled her close again, her chair tilted, almost fell over. Someone was laughing. "Showtime." That asshole Marcello. "Save some for later, man." The other guys were finishing their beers and leaving the table. Cal moaned, more like a whimper, and stood.

I know one last thing, one last thing I think I know, that waitress, the last time she wanted me to order something, all I said was something like "Get them to play some Doobies."

And I was probably laying full out, the top part of my body flat on the table. I know by then the dance floor was packed, the last set and all they wanted to do was dance … dance the night away … How many songs have that line anyway, and did you play one of them? Van Halen, Leo Sayer … could your band's singer do that disco-mouse voice? How could anyone tell? The girls shrieked and the men shouted out the lyrics. They stomped their feet and seemed to move faster than the music's tempo. Many of them dancing with beer mugs in one hand. So that must mean I had at least one eye opened. The speakers and the dancing feet made the room rattle so the table actually shook and my head vibrated, along with the ashtray and a few pennies left scattered near the edge. One fell and rolled away. It seemed to roll slowly, for a long time, in a wavy line ... maybe it would go straight across the dance floor and out the door, across the parking lot—

She sat up when Cal stood behind her chair. "How're you doing?" He put his hands on her shoulders. The singer was speaking into the microphone, his voice boomy and incoherent. "C'mon, I asked him to play something with no horns so we could dance."

"No ... everyone'll think I'm here with you." She turned and leaned against him.

Yeah, I know more than just one more thing. There are a few more things. Like your shirt was that slippery nylon. And a few more things than that. Did I stand on your feet while we danced? I can't remember touching the floor. No, it's not one of those you-lifted-me-off-my-feet moments. Just that how could I have been dancing? Cuz it's not something I do, or ever did. You were strong and solid. And smelled real.

The only tune left in the band's repertoire that didn't have any horn parts was "After the Lovin'." It wasn't even scheduled in the last set til Cal asked for it. Not that he thought she'd like it (actually he knew damn well what she would think of it) but it was the only way to get out there with her. The dancing couples stood pressed together, rocking back and forth. Cal held onto her wrist and tightened one arm around her shoulders, working his way to a clear spot on the dance floor, right below the stage. The loudest part of the song was the bass. She practically stood on Cal's feet and held onto him while he did all the dancing.

"Our *parents* would like this song," she said into his shirt. "Get a new band." Her head, her face, came only to the middle of his chest. "You're better than this."

His arms tightened. "Nothing's better than this."

"No, this band, it sucks. You should be playing, I dunno, with what's's'name ... Maynard ... Mangione ... who is it you like so much?"

"Yeah ... Basie hasn't called me yet." One of his hands pressed her head against his chest. "Right now that's okay."

That last chord ... a long shimmering out-of-tune noise. And yet people clapped. You were moaning and groaning–or muttering–you said something, but I couldn't hear it cuz another song started. Did I fall down when you let go of me? Cuz you suddenly jumped onto the stage. What did I do? Maybe that one was the last song, or else it took me an awful long time to get off the dance floor and back to the table, cuz why do I remember that by the time I got there, the trumpet guy was already sitting on his instrument case drinking a beer, the drummer lighting a cigarette, and silly you standing there holding my purse, looking around, your eyes watery blue.

She walked, or staggered, into his embrace. "I was afraid you'd gone home with someone else," he murmured.

"Don't remind me what a failure I am. A big zero. An X-ed out name on the living-it-up roster." Her words muffled but hot against his shoulder.

He picked up his case but kept one arm around her, heading for the exit, then he put his mouth against her head and mumbled into her hair, "What should we do about this?"

"*This?*"

"You know, what're we gonna do now?" He opened the door and the air was surprisingly cool. The breeze was slightly salty and a low fog was drifting in from the coast.

They stopped at the car. "*Now?*" she said. "Now ...? I guess we go home ... and on with our plans ... you know, for our booming-with-potential lives. Becoming a famous sax player for you … For me … a dork at a desk."

He was listening, but his mind flying … not *that* far ahead, just to the next minute, or hour, or tomorrow. He unlocked her door then hurried around the back of the car, and he'd gotten into his seat by the time she sort of crumpled into hers. As soon as she was there, he tried to gather her in his arms, pulling her halfway across the stick shift, kissing her throat, her ears, her mouth. She relaxed, sighed, parted her lips, closed her eyes. He could feel a hum from her throat buzz against his mouth. Wasn't everything exactly right, exactly in-tune, in rhythm, in sync, mellow and harmonious, sweet and rich and overflowing yet still swelling … shouldn't he have just left it the fuck alone? But no, then he did it, popped it, broke it, ruined it … he should've kicked his own damn reckless ass for always having to blabbidy-blab *everything* …

He spoke against the side of her head, into her hair, "How's this for a plan… why don't we move somewhere else. There's this jazz combo that wants to add me, out in the desert. I could get some other job too. You can do anything you want. You can have a dog, two dogs, however many dogs … we would … it could be … Oh damn, it's what my life should *be* …" He lifted her over the stick shift into his lap, his face buried against her neck, his voice refusing to shut up. "Oh god, I love you, I love … I've always loved you." His hands and arms were shaking. "Let's go away together and start *over*, forget everything else, we could be anything, do anything—oh please, I've wanted to ever since … I love you …."

You even thought to add the dogs … Don't think I didn't notice.

Okay, yes, I remember the other parts too, what you said … I hope you didn't mean you couldn't succeed without me. That's absurd.

I don't remember if I bumped my head on your car's ceiling, but it felt like it when I sat up–suddenly enough to make my brain spin even more. But, spinning, how the hell was I able to notice my feet, in sandals, with my toenails painted pink? When had I done that, and why? I'd never done it before, and won't again.

She rose, straddling the gearshift. Then moved back to the passenger seat. "Let's go home."

"Wha's wrong? You feeling sick?"

"No. Yes. I dunno."

"Hey, wha's wrong? Did I do something wrong?"

She sighed. "You *should* join that jazz combo. You're better than this shit."

"But what about …"

"Lemme go home and wake up yesterday so I can … I dunno … change my mind?"

In the next silence, the car began to feel too warm. "About what?"

"I dunno. Something, everything…what I thought I wuz doing …"

"You mean … that's *it*?"

She didn't look up, didn't move except to clench her toes, her voice steady enough but suddenly soft, and not as slurred. "No one ever said stuff like that to me. Not even you, way back when … Why can't I … Why couldn't we be meeting for the first time right *now* … tonight … What I mean … Why can't this be the first time I ever saw you? Cuz you might be—" Sweat trickled down her temples. "Dang. Let's just go."

What was she going to say he might be? The *answer*? while Cal drove she had her feet pulled up, her arms wrapped around her shins and her forehead on her knees. Several times he almost reached to touch her, then pulled back. Would it have made a difference? He eased up to the curb a few doors down from her apartment, then did reach for her while he shifted to neutral. But despite having remained motionless the whole way there, by the time the parking break rasped, she already had the door open and was halfway out. He was wrestling with his seatbelt, but when the fuck had he even decided to strap himself down?

Not yet all the way out of the car, she hesitated, looked back at him. "See ya."

"Wait, can't I come in? I won't … Please, can't I just come in and stay …? I'll just hold you, I promise." He caught her wrist. He was lying sideways across the gearshift halfway into the passenger seat, still holding her wrist, and she was on the curb. He couldn't see her face. Then she yanked her hand away.

I'd never seen my neighborhood when it was that quiet. I hadn't lived there long before that night. That kind of quiet, it amplified the sound of my footsteps, made it sound like I was hurrying down the sidewalk. Maybe I was. Maybe I should admit I was. And I could hear you getting out of the car, slamming the door, and then behind me saying, "Please ... please ...."

But I didn't turn around until my door was unlocked and I was inside. You were still on the porch. Nothing between us but a half-closed door. That's when. Yes, I saw it. Your disco pants making it more explicit. And I'd never seen an erection before. Not even that time when we were 16. But ... it didn't make me feel anything. As the door closed a little more, you leaned against the jamb. I know it seemed that the door lingered still partway open for a moment, or more than that.

September 2009, El Centro, California

When the cops got there, they found the TV room furniture a little askew with dirty dishes and food scattered on the carpet. In the kitchen, carnage of the turkey was strewn on the floor, with more dishes, even one of the crystal goblets—from broken to chipped to downright rubble—and the poultry-knife standing upright, its point buried in the wooden serving platter. They also found Cal on the front lawn, locked out of the house. The officers, male and female, took turns, one inside, one outside, asking the same questions. "Are you okay? Are you hurt anywhere? Do you want her arrested?"

Yes, no, and no.

"How'd she get a 200 pound man out the door against his will?"

"I didn't fight back."

"Good idea."

"Yeah, I just went the direction she was pushing me. I knew she'd calm down."

"What was the fight about, sir?"

"I won't send any more money to the … kids."

"You can decide not to press charges, but if it got worse, you can't stop us from arresting her."

"It was just food, and … I moved my horns down to the shop."

The cops, of course, didn't understand that.

He walked around the block, 8 p.m., temperature still in the 90s. When he got home, the kitchen was cleaned, the garbage taken out to the cans at the side of the house. Virginia was making ice cream sundaes with root beer.

"A mother's instinct is fierce," she said, "but I don't mean the things I called you."

"Yeah."

☯

I said I'm sorry, didn't I? If not, I meant to. Before I shut the door.

☯

March 2, 1980, San Diego

She was sunbathing before noon on the courtyard, a textbook over her eyes. How long had she been outside? He'd called at eight, let it ring ten or fifteen times. Same thing at nine, and again around ten. He cleared his throat before he was within twenty feet of her. She didn't move. His heartbeat was as thick as his throat when he swallowed. "Imagine meeting you here," she said from underneath the book, and he cleared his throat again.

"I wanted to make sure you were okay."

She sat up and reached for her robe. "I wasn't that drunk."

He was staring at her flowerboxes. Or trying to. "Oh." He rolled a pebble under his foot. He was wearing white tennis shoes. "But maybe *I* was drunker than I thought."

"Oh?" She moved into the shade after tying her robe around her waist.

"Yeah." His whisper was raspy.

It would have been a quiet morning, except the birds, lots of them, squawking, screaming and singing.

"But don't worry about it or think that we can't even be friends anymore," he said, "… 'cause … I didn't mean it."

"Didn't mean what?"

He could see that she shivered. The shade was considerably cooler than the sunshine.

"You know."

He put his fists in the pockets of his jeans. Their eyes only touched once, then they looked away again.

And before I was ready to send the first postcard, you beat me to the whole get-on-with-your-life thing. Maybe I'm still not ready, but I'll give it a try.

Dang, Cal !   May 7, 1981
Good talking to you. Almost like old times. And <u>that</u> was a quick change of plan -- a whole new family!(??)
My plan, for now, keep my nose in the accounting books and don't think about tomorrow ... or yesterday. Cards like this are a great idea, only enough room for what needs to be said. Maybe just tell a joke. Try this one: A girl and a jazz sax player walk into a bar ... signed X

PLACE
POST CARD
POSTAGE
HERE

D23422

Post Card

Cal Tonnessen
7512 W San Diego Ave
El Centro CA 92243

There's still a dog … a shell of her former self, but still a bigger heart than …

There had been a boy whose heart spoke in music …

Too many clichés … start over.

There had been a husband, but he's not important. Perhaps his leaving is important, but, face it, he's not the only one who left. That is, abandoned the pairing. Which couldn't be called a *relationship*. She needed health insurance. He needed … what? To not be alone? Which he was anyway, every night, in a separate bed and separate bedroom. Which she didn't mind. So what was lost? Maybe just the anchor, the mooring. Some kind of safety to not have to wonder who she should be looking for, or what should come next. She was a beard for herself. She had lived there with him, so she lived there. It was where she had lived. She had done her living there.

After almost 20 years, *why* he left, why *he* was the one who made the first move, maybe not important either. He played the oboe and had daytime employment as an insurance underwriter (thus the health insurance for both). They'd met because his wire fox terrier needed frequent grooming. Ten years into the marriage-of-convenience, the Colorado Symphony hired a 22-year-old Phenom principal oboist right out of Curtis—a position for which the husband had auditioned and hadn't made it out of the first round. Now with three in the narrative, the husband needs his name: Blaine. He begged the 22-year-old oboe sensation for lessons and was taken on. Did they have an affair, Blaine and the principal oboist? Depends on your definition of *affair*. Blaine was madly agog over the life of a 22-year-old double-reed virtuoso who had an agent and traveled to Europe for solo competitions and sometimes won; who went to New York on long weekends for lessons and recitals, to attend concerts, operas and plays, and wouldn't be in this cow-town long.

That the 22-year-old was a man, or barely out of boyhood, makes no difference either. Blaine had never asked his wife to be *his* beard. She doesn't know what he'd needed or expected from her (maybe needed and expected and never got, how about *that*?). And whatever-it-was with the 22-year-old hadn't been technically consummated, unless you counted one night holding onto the 22-year-old body before it could get any further away. The 22-year-old had consented to the night in bed together when it appeared Blaine might be breaking down or cracking up or just splintering sideways. And his wife no help, comfort or support, nor was she asked to be, but she had eyes, didn't she? Couldn't she see what was happening?

Yes, she could: smoldering wreckage. Sleeping, crying, losing his job. Valium, Prozac, marijuana (twelve years away from becoming legalized), nothing helped. Except maybe walking away and trying to hide.

Back in 1980-something, a dog-groomer who trained and showed her own dogs could give training advice to clients. Advice could be paid for. Thus her dog-training business had followed the same basic trajectory as the Dog Whisperer, except a slower growth, with a lower angle of rise. That is, she didn't write books or star in a TV show. She'd made some low budget videos once, but had very little distribution. She'd appeared on local TV news occasionally, which helped. But mostly, with more than three nationally ranked dogs of her own, her weekend seminars had netted 3 to 5 K, and she'd scheduled four to six a year. Private lessons $100 an hour. (Yes, people had paid for that, just to win at performance shows where there was seldom a cash prize for winning.) Boarding and training a client's dog, $150 a day. It had worked. So why has she let it become a flaccid, pale version of itself that barely paid the bills? Just because she now lives alone? Which isn't all that different, except the unfolding drama of recent years in the *other* bedroom has been eradicated.

Wide-angle to zoom: February 2008, TV documentary: *American Sex in the 21ˢᵗ Century*.

What she learned: Everybody loves sex. Everybody is shedding their workday facades and frolicking in their bare-animal selves, enjoying the hell out of the primal joy of visceral ecstasy. Passing it back and forth. Everybody is having (giving *and* getting) it orally. With orgasms. Of course they are. *Every*one is (are) having orgasms. In books, magazines, movies, television dramas, blog postings, Facebook and Twitter updates. And getting there by themselves if no one else is around. Her bedside drawer of books had already told her she was supposed to. Or if she hadn't learned how by herself, very young, maybe she wouldn't. Ever. Maybe that would explain why she hadn't, ever.

Watching TV in her one-bedroom apartment where she runs her one-employee (herself) dog-training business. A dog still seemingly serene on the floor, no outward sign of pain, during her owner's "research." Formerly done on her computer—for a week or two or three at a time, before letting it go again for months—searching for manifestos from women who hadn't, ever. Every health or medical or psychological or sex-advice site flickering in the ether explained the causes of "anorgasmia." Not very many (as in *none*) of them included a person, as in a case study or volunteer; nothing in first-person; not even a name offered to typify a person who appeared, otherwise, in physical health and built normally—and of course psychologically & emotionally "okay"—but who'd never had one. Everyone is spraying their intimacies on this cybernetic wall expecting everyone else to care, to oooh and ahhh, to tag them as the cool girl, the complete girl. But no one revealing (or bragging) that they never come. That they never have.

This girl with a crippled dog named *Climax*.

A few times since moving to this apartment she'd returned to her drawer full of books, where she'd researched during years before her first computer. Books about sexual fantasies and the conclusions drawn by the psychologist (or sexologist) who compiled them. "In college," one anonymous subject wrote on her survey form for the psychologist-author, "there was this girl in my dorm that hadn't, so we locked her in her room with a vibrator and told her she couldn't come out until she had one."

What would they have done if she was still in there three days later? Or three weeks? Or she might have faked it so she could go get something to eat (and them off her back). *Warning: there will be no victorious orgasm at the end.*

Nevertheless, that particular term of research managed to get her into the car to find a sex store, to shop for a vibrator. Then … in her room with the door closed …

Why bother with the door *now*? There's nobody out there.

She and Blaine had never shared a bedroom. In those days, splitting space in a whole house, behind the other bedroom door, no telling whether it was damp with weeping, blue-lit with email, or radioactive with cellphone usage. (She could've used that second bedroom as an office, but what use did they have for a living room anyway, so the home office—for scheduling dog-training sessions, planning and booking seminars—had taken most of that.)

So, she was in her apartment bedroom with the vibrator, but not locked inside, and no one outside the door saying she couldn't come out until she completed the task. The buzzing was loud. The vibrator pale beige, hard plastic. The lifelike models were too expensive. (Business was barely okay, and this was not something she could write-off.) She held it against where she knew she was supposed to, on the side, and it felt good, it did. But it didn't go anywhere from there. It sounded like she was drilling something. And she was doing it to herself. She couldn't even begin to imagine the buzzing plastic phallus was part of a phantom person who loved her.

The dog, Climax, disabled by a decade-old dog-attack injury, slept beside the bed. Slept undaunted by the mechanical drone. It sounded a little like grooming clippers, but dogs are situational, so, since this moment has none of the other accouterments of a grooming session, no fear response.

No other response either.

She went outside to the common area's garden. Straight to the somewhat ugly, shaggy bee balm with its musky, spicy, potent odor, like a boy's sweat.

Chapter Two

Two Backyard Parties

December 2, 1981
Now a new plan for me:
ditched accounting college.
As well as anyone met there
(guess who!) Back to the
dogs, so to speak. Starting
with grooming school (and
to do that I'm moving.) Step
2 (or 1A): *get another dog.*
Then (2) train my ass off. (I
mean the dog's ass.) Maybe
a dog is my ax. Like your
horn, your ax. Don't
abandon it, Cal.
X

PLACE
POST CARD
POSTAGE
HERE

D23422

Post Card

Cal Tonnessen
7512 W San Diego Ave
El Centro CA 92243

1983

It. What she didn't want him to abandon. Of course clearly she meant the sax. Otherwise, if *it* was something else—the *it* containing everything he felt about her—she would have provided her new address. That *it*, the real *it* refused to be abandoned. Maybe if he got a dog, took it to every groomer in San Diego— How many weekends would that take? Weekends and evenings were needed to build up his instrument repair shop, housed 100 miles away from her (if she was still there), inside a music store, while he accepted as many weekday hours he could get in the store itself, plus teach as many private students as he could schedule in the store's lesson-studios, weekdays after school.

He'd explained his plan on the phone back in 1981, after she'd briefly taken his calls again, a plan that had actually partially started before that night they were together at Macho's. The brass guy in that band had a trumpet-playing friend out in the Imperial Valley—the fucking pointless desert, in El Centro—who had a five-piece jazz combo. A jazz combo out there with all those *mariachis*. That desert-guy's sax player was quitting and moving. Probably moving and therefore quitting. It was a difficult place to decide to continue living. So in 1981 Cal had already started filling in at the desert jazz combo's gigs, driving two hours each way for a $75 gig. But the trumpet player in El Centro also owned a music store and offered Cal a job there, so he could stay, stop the driving. Plus the store's instrument technician was a retiring band teacher who would stay another year and teach Cal wind instrument repair. It could be a life. That's what he told her.

The time of that last phone call, he'd been full time in the Imperial Valley for only a few months. And not alone. The woman he'd brought with him had two kids. A boy in high school, after that hopefully the army. A girl six months past nine. Make-up and her own phone were scheduled for 12, according to the woman— her plans for the girl's $200 monthly child support.

The woman with the kids was someone who'd just started hanging around at his gigs in San Diego, the last six months before he made the move. She was a friend of a friend of the band's brother-sister singers. Hanging around the gigs, then the rehearsals, then started hanging around *him*. Made it easy. Or better put, he just didn't say no.

"To what?"

"You know."

"Oh. To wetting your wick." The scratchy laugh.

"I guess."

It was supposed to be just once. But she came back for more. There was no reason to shake her off, avoid her, hide from her. She was always there. She didn't seem to have anywhere to go after a gig. He didn't know yet about the two kids she'd left at her brother's house. She was 8 or 9 years older.

"*Dang*, Cal."

"Yeah. So I figured … why not give her a place she can live with her kids."

And give me some reason to be doing anything – he didn't say – *some reason to keep a job, keep a car running, stay away from weed and coke. Give me something else to think about, someone else's problems to solve, something I'm responsible for.*

After that, her phone rang with no answer until it was disconnected. He'd given her his El Centro address but didn't know if she wrote it down. Until he got that first postcard. Two years ago, now.

1983

The girl child's name was Trinity. She was having her 12th birthday party, the first one to have boys. It was early September and still damn hot. But she wanted a piñata out in the yard, and Twister in the living room, with music. No other baby games, and *good* candy in the piñata. She nixed Cal's idea of including small school items like new pencils or pens.

"Hey Trin, how about some movie tickets, or McDonalds gift-certificates?" Her mother called her Trin. Her girlfriends called her T. Cal could guess where the boys would take that.

"Why not just put a whole stereo and a couple of records inside?" he said.

"You can butt out," the girl said.

"We'll need you to swing the piñata," the woman said. Her name was Virginia. *Her* girlfriends called her *Virge* or *Virgie*. Cal used her whole name, to emphasize something he was trying to get her to understand, or if there was any reason he needed to get her attention during her dueling idiocy with the girl—at this age mostly in harmony—instead of (what he usually did) just butting out.

When he'd first learned the girl child's name, sometime after the supposed-to-be-a-one-night-stand with her mother but before moving together out to the desert, maybe even when Virginia was introducing her daughter to him, he'd said, "Trinity. That's interesting." He wasn't sure if maybe there was a church reason, but didn't know if he cared enough to ask.

"It's because when she arrived, we became a Trinity, a threesome."

"I thought there's an older brother," he'd said.

"Yes, Angel, so with Trinity we became three."

"What about …" Then he'd decided not to ask. And by the time he knew about the man, Pete, who sent the child-support checks for the girl, it was no longer in his head to ask about the trio thing. At least Pete was the same man who the boy went to visit in Las Vegas every weekend. Cal wasn't sure where the bus fare came from. But he wasn't looking too closely at the bank statement in those days.

Virginia had had a job. He'd thought she'd had one when she was hanging around his gigs, but it turned out that was an assumption based on, well, people had jobs. At first, living with him in the Imperial Valley, she'd worked at Kmart for about a month. They let her go, she said, because the other women talked about her in Spanish behind her back and she wasn't going to take it. Did that mean she quit? He didn't ask. But he did inquire, "How do you know they were talking about you if they were speaking Spanish?"

"That's how they are," she said. "They also run into me with grocery carts in the store. On purpose, I know it."

Cal's friend who owned the music store got his brother's catering company to hire her as a freelance party waitress. She was too slow, Cal's friend said, and she tried to tell the bartender he was making the drinks wrong. When she applied to be a teacher's aide at Trinity's school, Cal discovered she hadn't finished high school. But in those days school districts actually paid parents or retired people as the crosswalk guards or playground proctors. Then she suddenly stopped doing that after a few weeks. "Trin didn't want me there," she said.

At her party, Trinity wore the tight designer jeans she'd requested for her birthday. Neither Trinity or Virginia responded to his inquiry: had she sat down in a bathtub of blue paint? Trinity had a two-page magazine spread of Brooke Shields, wearing those same jeans, taped to the wall of her room. But instead of the flowing silk-looking blouse Shields wore— buttoned only between her smallish breasts, falling away to show her flat suntanned stomach—Trinity chose to wear a halter top. Some of the other girls wore tanks or sleeveless tops, one of them with leg warmers and a miniskirt, but none of them were as physically developed as Trinity.

"Are you letting her wear that?" he'd whispered to Virginia in the kitchen.

Virginia shrugged. "She's old enough to dress herself."

Virginia had fixed Trinity's long hair so her face looked small in the middle of a big ratty mess. It was one of Virginia's styles, except she wore wigs (she'd been almost bald since her first pregnancy). That was probably why Virginia's hair-do didn't change much, but after the piñata Trinity's had become a messy, sweaty ponytail. Cal had executed his assignment manning the rope, raising, lowering and swinging the smiling black-and-red bull-shaped piñata while each blindfolded kid took three or four swings with the souvenir bat Cal had gotten at the ballpark in San Diego when he was 12 but had never used. All three boys, Black, Latino, and white, were skinny shrimps compared to Trinity, but as quick as her with cliché kid-talk, *awesome* and *radical, killer* and *badass.* They each wore a T-shirt with some big words or nasty-looking cartoon. One of them—the Black one, or maybe Latino/Black—had a cap like a cab driver mashed onto wet-looking curls and big aviator sunglasses he had to take off when he was blindfolded. While the kid whaled away, Cal could smell whatever goop had been used to make those wet-looking curls. No one touched the piñata (a few almost clobbered Cal or each other).

"Let them *hit* it," Virginia shouted. So they all had another turn without the blindfold, and in 5 or 6 swings, the bull was tufts all over the yard, the kids scrambling together on the ground on hands and knees, greedy bastards trying to get the most for themselves. One seemingly younger little girl with short dark hair who'd come in a dress with a sailor collar—maybe someone's little sister or one who hadn't kept up with her classmates—stood to the side of the jumble of arms and legs, hair and feet and hands. So Cal went inside (taking his now scuffed bat), grabbed the last box of the chocolate bars he'd hidden away after loading the piñata, and dropped it whole and unopened into the dark-haired girl's sack.

When Twister started, Trinity said, "We don't need you for this," then turned the stereo up. Kool and the Gang. Now Trinity was wearing the cab driver cap. Cal went to the kitchen for a beer. At some point, when 4 or 5 kids were snarled up on the Twister mat, Cal happened to look through the kitchen's pass-through window and saw a boy sink his teeth into the bulge of trinity's halter top.

Cal went down the hall to his bedroom. The bedroom he shared with Virginia. In a ritual he used to do at gigs, he peed, holding his dick with one hand while his other hand held the beer bottle to his mouth, trying to pee as long as it took to swallow the rest of the beer. What a boor he'd been then. A dirtball. No *wonder* ...

He was almost back down the hall bringing the beer bottle to the kitchen when the Twister game broke up, apparently because the cabbie hat fell off Trinity's upside-down head so another girl picked it up and put it on her own head. Some names were called. *Bitch* and *Ho.* Hands slapping at each other's faces in girl-fight posture he'd seen too many times at club gigs, bodies so far apart only their upper arms can reach each other. "Where's Trinity's mom?" he asked the dark-haired girl with the sailor collar, sitting at the kitchen table with 4 or 5 plates of smashed goo and the eviscerated 3-layer cake Virginia had baked and decorated.

"She said she was getting something she forgot from the car."

In a junk tray on the pass-through windowsill, Cal kept an old sax mouthpiece still holding a frayed reed, specifically for times like this, although usually for bouts between Trinity and Angel, or Trinity and her mother. (Virginia and He's-My-Angel never fought.) Cal tongued five pig-squeal bleats. A burst of laughter, hoots and exclamations. Maybe the fight was already over anyway. Someone turned the music up. Hall and Oats. Two of the boys came into the kitchen for more cake. The bathroom door slammed. One of the boys said, "She tweakin," then slid his eyes sideways toward Cal, ducked his head. The dark-haired girl was no longer at the table. When Cal went back to the bedroom to get away from the thumping funk, one of the other girls was in there, looking at the dresser, the top of it where boxes and bottles sat. Not his shit.

"You lost?" Cal asked.

"Uh, where's T at?"

From the living room Virginia called, "Kids, Cal brought some new records from the store."

Like hell he had.

But Virginia had 6 or 8 albums fanned out on the floor, the Twister mat kicked aside. Journey, Foreigner, Styx, Genesis, The Go-Gos, Duran Duran, Motley Crue, Black Sabbath ... Maybe the whole top-sellers rack. Four or five of the kids were on hands-and-knees sliding the albums around on the carpet, flipping them over to see the photos and songs listed on the backs. Cal couldn't see Trinity out there. "Let's have a dance, I can still shake-it-up," Virginia said, over the top of the Hall and Oats still playing. She ripped the cellophane off an album and stopped Private Eyes with a screech of the needle across the grooves.

The dancing started, Virginia bumping hips with some of the girls, and Trinity literally leaped back into the room – from her bedroom? The bathroom? – the cabbie hat perched on her back-to-big-and-loose ratty hair, and now also the aviator glasses screening her eyes. The wet-curled boy, who'd arrived wearing both, danced tentatively, while Trinity boogied in a circle around him. Maybe if he had his hat and glasses back he'd start to get down, but was an undressed Superman without them.

In the kitchen, Cal started throwing away paper plates, plastic cups and spoons. The plates and cups had pictures of E.T. riding a bike, thick and waxed, used once and piling up in the trashcan. He looked through cupboards to put the rest of the unused ones away and found two different drawers plus a cupboard crammed with paper plates and cups, from a stack of 1000 plain white ones, to Valentine, Christmas, Easter and Halloween themed plates, plus sets with pictures of balloons or stars, some not opened. While looking, he also found a cupboard with no less than a dozen boxes of prepared cake mix.

A car passing in the street rattled the manhole cover. On reflex Cal looked out the window and saw the dark-haired girl sitting on the raised brick garden box that separated the front porch from the driveway. The garden box had one bird-of-paradise plant, most of its fronds dead or broken. Cal was only renting this house and had asked the owner to pay half the water bill if he took care of the lawn. He hadn't had a chance to do anything with the gardens, but maybe fixing them up would be another way to stay out of the house an extra hour or two on weekend mornings before he went to the shop.

The dark haired girl was picking tiny weeds out of the garden box, making a little pile of them on the brick edge where she sat, her bag from the piñata beside her. Cal had bundled the trash and come out the front door. "Dancing not your thing?" He put the trash bag down on the porch, on a bench that was there with two other trash bags waiting for a trip to the container around the side of the house. The porch area, tucked between the house and the garden box, also collected blowing trash from the sidewalk and street.

"I guess not," the girl said, not looking up from plucking the spindly weeds. From the house, either thumping of the bass or feet on the floor. The screeching, whooping voices inside were all female-pitched, but then again, these boys hadn't started changing.

Cal cleared his throat. "You're a friend of Trinity's?"

"I guess."

"Well, she invited you, didn't she?"

"I guess so."

"How do you know Trinity?"

"I help her with math."

"That's nice, how's she doing?"

"Okay I guess."

A breeze hit Cal's face, cooling his sweat. Over his head, a sign Virginia had hung there squeaked a little. The sign said *Cal & Virgie*. In script, cut into wood, then varnished. When the dark-haired girl turned and looked at him, for the first time since he'd come onto the porch, she likely wasn't looking at that fucking sign, but said, "You're not her dad."

"No, I'm not." Then he wondered if she'd said that to mean he shouldn't be asking questions about Trinity. But, *dang Cal*, she's all of what, 11 years old? He picked up the trash again, then picked up the other two bags. "Guess I'll get these where they belong." And who was he explaining his actions to?

When he came back, the girl was just sitting there, as though waiting for him. She smiled a little. Didn't she? Cal said, "Trinity's copying your math homework, isn't she?" The girl's smile faded. Cal almost touched the top of her head with his index finger as he passed to go back into the house, but stopped his hand at the last second. He paused in the doorway, then turned back, went back. Cleared his throat again. "Did she say she would hurt you if you didn't let her use your homework?" He noticed the girl was holding the little heap of weeds in one cupped hand. She didn't close her fist. She also didn't answer and wasn't really looking at him, although she'd turned to face him when he'd spoken. "If she did," he said, "tell your parents, or the principal. Tell someone." He waited, but she didn't move. "Do you need a ride home?"

"My mom's coming. I called from inside."

"Here," he said, extending his hand beneath hers. She tipped her palm and dumped the snarl of wilting weeds into his.

By the time the last kid was gone, the indestructible Twister mat was torn and three records were in 5 or more pieces. "We didn't want to dance to them so we danced *on* them," Trinity gasped. She'd seemed to be laughing or hiccupping for an hour, still wearing the wet-curled boy's hat.

Cal got his car keys from the kitchen so he could go to his repair shop. "Can you take these back to the store and say they were broken when we opened them?" Virginia asked. He pretended he hadn't heard and kept going into the garage where he'd squeezed his car into a slot between boxes of shit that had suddenly accumulated. Maybe Virginia had mentioned something about having a yard sale when he hadn't really been listening.

He was glad for the excuse to spend a Saturday evening at the repair shop, because he'd given up the daytime hours for the party. He'd more than once told Virginia (usually when she asked why they didn't go out dancing anymore, as if they ever had, unless she counted hanging around at his gigs) that, since he worked day hours in the store, nights and weekends were when he had time to devote to his business. Even if he was really just sitting there listening to his records (most of which he kept there) on the music store's stereo system. And thinking. He took care of himself there. It was nice if he didn't have too much of a backlog of instruments to repair, so could focus on just the right image. He didn't keep a picture of X there. It wasn't *that* private. But sometimes, just seeing a short boyish-but-not-really young woman of about their age— their age back in 1980, if that looked any different now, which it *must*— scratching her bare shoulder while she looked at something in the display case... Or if he'd spotted a couple dancing at one of his gigs, and the girl was a lot shorter than the guy, and sort of draped against him like a ribbon (he never saw one stand on the guy's feet)... Even, rarely, one of the models they used in *Playboy* might appear more vigorous than languid, have a wry smile, austere eyes that impaled him, short dark hair. He'd kept a photo series from *Hustler*, a pair going at it in an empty movie theatre—you were probably supposed to imagine there were other

45

people in seats toward the front while the couple guzzled each other. It was not necessarily if a girl or model *looked* similar, but the way she looked *at* whatever she was looking at, some glint of expression, a sharpness that hid something deeper and heavier, maybe about to cork him with a zinger. Admittedly, in *Hustler* a girl might be looking with layers of deep meditation at a guy's cock, or over her shoulder with smoky complexity, locking eyes as he fucked her ass (that one was probably in something more illicit than *Hustler*). But, really, once Cal closed his eyes, he didn't need the staged bare genitals.

Sometimes he did both, fixed a few instruments, then had his "alone-time." And was able to not be back home until Virginia was already in bed, on her side against the wall. He could steal in and lie still, and sometimes even have another session of alone-time when he woke, somewhere after midnight, and began the wake-doze slide toward 5 a.m. Daytime was much too busy, even if he was home, the kids were usually around, phone ringing, music playing. Hell yeah, he made thin excuses— the kids would hear, he was tired, he didn't feel well—until the thinness was on the verge of transparency and he had to give it a go, often faking a finale if he knew he was losing it, or after he'd figured it had been long enough to be enough.

No he didn't pretend Virginia was *her* (self-named X). How would that even be possible? The basic ingredients weren't just a wet place to put it. He knew other guys really got off fucking anything who would fuck, the anonymity or the variety putting the fencepost in their dicks. Maybe he'd already had the biggest hardon he would ever have— how many years ago now, almost three?—and it wasn't novelty or big tits or contortionist positions that stimulated it.

Now it was only this: Turrentine or Coltrane or Brecker on the stereo in his shop. An oscillating fan passed by his face in slow rhythm, cooling sweat that prickled between passes, until later when the sweat would run crooked rivulets through his chest hair. Not a reverie just to see himself with the saxophone, himself on the stage or in the spotlight, himself speaking the mood with his reed, his horn, his breath and body. If it's him playing, he plays for her. She comes into the club. She feels it in the way the horn phrases the tune into emptiness and longing. In subtone or with a hard core, burbling runs or sharp tonguing, vibrato growing wider, slower, or a deathcry scream. She would stop, framed for a moment in the open door, only a silhouette, except the sax player can't see, plays with his eyes closed. The door gently shuts, like an eyelid dropping before sleep. In darkness, she can see the sax player in the low floods on the tiny stage. Stars occasionally glint from the sax's bell. Dark backs of heads between her and him. Sometimes someone gets up, a black human shape blocking the sax player from her for a moment. But laughing, talking, glasses clinking don't cover what his horn is saying. She's still there by the door during the last two or three block chord changes, when his playout utters his ultimate plea. His last note is held, throbbing, and he opens his eyes and meets hers.

So he took care of himself. But that night after the Twister party, almost midnight when he got home, Virginia was awake.

It was dark, but he could tell Virginia was sitting up. He turned away, pretended to be feeling for the light just inside the bathroom door. The dim bathroom light was the only one he used, mornings getting up before dawn and coming to bed after her in darkness. If she was asleep, he didn't even worry about how loud his pee hit the water or the toilet's flush, but tonight tried to do both more softly. Just before he turned out the bathroom light, he saw Virginia was not wearing the soft cap she usually wore to bed. She had a wig on. That usually meant …

Cal sat on the side of the bed, his body in the shape of a question mark. From behind him, Virginia asked, "What're you doing?"

"Taking off my socks." His socks still on his feet, his feet on the floor, his hands on either side of his legs on the mattress.

Virginia shifted, maybe getting closer to him. "Didn't today make you think?"

Cal couldn't think of an answer.

"Babes, what's wrong?"

"Nothing. Six or seven horns came into the shop today."

"Oh. But didn't today just make you *think*?"

"Okay, what was today supposed to make me think?"

She *was* closer behind him. "Birthday parties! I wish we could have a birthday party every week, but that would mean Trin is growing up too fast. Girls are such sweet wild things."

His sudden intake of breath might have sounded like a sigh. He cleared his throat to cover.

"Babes, don't you think … I think you need a child of your own."

Cal hadn't moved, and she hadn't touched him yet. He swallowed, clutched the edge of the mattress a little harder. When she shifted even closer, the old box-spring groaned and the mattress noticeably sank in the spot where he sat, which would help her to slide against him. He could stabilize it by lying down on his back, but didn't think there was room now.

All the furniture had been Virginia's, taken when she'd moved out of her husband's house. She'd wanted new stuff and said, "You shouldn't have to use that asshole Pete's dresser, Pete's sofa, even Pete's *bed*." Cal had said if they still worked, then why throw them away? He didn't say that whatever Pete had done in this bed meant nothing to him, but Virginia seemed to believe it should, because she'd said, "I'm a different person now, I'm not the woman who slept in this bed before, I'm like that goose who's been born into a whole new world." Yesterday Cal had told her about a music lesson he'd been giving where the kid came in using the same bad embouchure every week, and Cal taught him how to do it right, and every week he came back doing it wrong again, "like a goose who learns where the food is and every day can't find it again because he's born into a whole new world."

He realized her bizarre suggestion was still hanging in the air, as though he were considering it. "Let's just raise the two who are here."

"No, Cal, you really need a child of your own. Every man needs his own child."

"Can't every man decide for himself what he needs?" Cal tapped his socks on the shabby shag carpet. Virginia also wanted new carpet, and he knew it wasn't unreasonable. Every room was a different disheveled color, with stains and decades of dirt.

"Sometimes you don't know until you have it that it's what you need. Let's start trying. Let's—"

Cal stood before she could drape herself over his shoulders. "I think Trinity needs your full attention. Did you know she makes other girls—"

"Cal, this would be for *us*."

He propped himself against the wall with one hand and stripped his socks off his feet. "I don't think anything needs to be changed. We've got enough to deal with as it is."

"I just feel it's right, Babes, I just know it's what you need, I just ... *do*."

He held his socks in one hand. The clothes hamper was at the foot of the bed, beside the dresser. He thought his walking over there, lifting the lid, placing the socks in the hamper, and taking the four steps back to where he'd been standing probably seemed like acting. But when he got back to where he'd started, he said, "I'm not sure you're able to be objective about this kind of decision."

"It's easy for me to be objectionable."

Cal was standing in the dark beside his bed, still wearing jeans and a t-shirt. He felt himself nodding. He imagined a burst of brittle laughter. *Dang, Cal.*

Virginia was half reclining on her hip just about where he would have to lie down if he were going to sleep tonight. "Really, trust me, a child in your hand is worth ... Well, you don't know because you haven't ... you *need* your own, Cal, you just do." Virginia rolled a little more to her back, one knee still bent. She lifted the wig's longish curly hair out from under her shoulder and lay it on the pillow. "C'mon, Babes, c'mon, trust me, come here with me, let's ... tonight."

"I'm tired, Virginia. Horns have stacked up at the shop while I was playing around here today. Move over."

He was lying down, covered up, open eyes staring at the closed bedroom door, with Virginia back on her side of the bed. He could feel the telltale vibration, hear the occasional sniffle. He realized he was still dressed in jeans and t-shirt. A monster, a piece of shit, still fully dressed, lying in bed beside a woman he'd asked to come live here with him.

Jan 1983
What happened to my 2-cards-
a-year plan? Over a year since I
quit accounting. Learned
grooming instead. Moved, got a
job. Grooming = designated job
for anyone who only wants to
hang out with dogs. Got a mess
of free picture cards –
serendipitous cuz only ¼ card to
tell a life story. Real story might
suck as much as the truncated.
Hope yours has been better but
I guess I'm not letting you tell
me. Still no *I show mine if you
show yours.*   X

Post Card

Cal Tonnessen
7512 W San Diego Ave
El Centro CA 92243

So why are you sending these? He wanted to ask. *It's like cutting me off except this time no door closing in my face.*

What would she say to that? Probably something like, *Dang, smarty, go ahead, let's have us a talk—you always thought you knew what I would say.*

The landlord would not buy new carpet, claimed he'd had it cleaned when the last renter moved out. Now with Trinity's and Angel's friends in and out every day (and night), there was no way to prove it wasn't the truth. Cal checked the cost to replace the carpet himself. Too much, his business too new, his intake from the two jobs barely now covering rent, bills and food. He checked commercial carpet cleaning costs and told Virginia they could start saving to do that. Virginia responded that she was looking into getting a job at the Christian store on Main Street, in the storefront right beside the music store.

"Christian store?" he said, smiling, "Do people go there when their pet lions get hungry?"

Virginia, squinted a little, looking back at him. "What?"

"Never mind." He took a bite of oatmeal. It was 5:30 a.m., the kids both still in bed before school. He usually got to his repair shop by six to work 4 hours before the music store opened (unfortunately not before the guy who opened would have the stereo playing heavy metal). Virginia made oatmeal in a double-boiler, topped it with a pat of butter and brown sugar. It was really good, and most days kept him from an Egg McMuffin. "What makes you think they'll hire you, what qualifications do you have for a *Christian* store?"

"I've been talking to her, I go down there a lot."

"Why? What are you buying there?"

"Nothing, mister skintight."

Cal swallowed, drank some juice, then said, "I think that designation is for the clothes you've been buying Trinity."

"Big words don't make you smarter." She scraped the ring of remaining oatmeal from the pot into the trash. The kids never ate oatmeal, thus the six or seven boxes of sweet cereal in the pantry. "Okay, Babes, I just miss you and want to see you. You're at the store so long every day."

"How are you seeing me from the Christian store?"

"I usually see you in there when I walk past." She was filling the sink with soapy water to wash the one pot. "But sometimes I don't see you. Where do you go?"

"I don't know, back into the shop, to the restroom, the guitar wall, checking sheet music." He got up to fill his thermos with coffee. The coffee pot was beside the sink, and his wallet and keys sat with the junk tray on the ledge of the pass-through window where a person washing dishes could watch the TV in the living room. The TV was on now, the sound down to almost nothing, people sitting around a coffee table with matching coffee mugs.

She said, "Who do you talk to on the phone so much?"

"Customers. Stores have phones so customers can call and ask if you have something."

"I know *that*. I've worked in *stores*." The pot clanked into the dish drainer, and the drain started sucking the hot water out of the sink. "If I work in the Christian store, we could have lunch every day."

When he finished fastening the two lids on his thermos, put his wallet into his pocket, hooked his wad of keys to his belt loop, picked up the sack lunch she'd made for him, and then looked at her, he realized he hadn't really seen her this morning. She wasn't dressed yet, but had leg warmers over sweat pants. It was probably already 80 degrees. "Are you cold?" he asked.

"I have to stay in shape."

His mouth opened, then shut. Best not to ask.

As Cal expected, the Christian store job never happened, but Virginia joined the church the Christian store owner went to.

Fridays the older kid, Angel, started appearing in the kitchen even before Cal came in for his oatmeal. Then he went back to bed for an hour. Friday afternoon was when he would take the bus to Las Vegas to visit his dad. But it took until Cal's wallet was left flopped open after Angel went back to his bedroom (likely Cal coming down the hall a little earlier than usual) for Cal to realize he never had much cash left at the end of the week if he had to buy something on Friday afternoon or Saturday.

He mentioned this to Virginia. She said, "No, my Angel doesn't steal, he's not an animal."

Cal said he was going to start keeping his wallet locked in the file cabinet but it was going to be a pain in the ass to go lock it up every time he got home and then unlock it every morning before he left. Virginia said, "Angel needed his allowance. I told him to get it."

"Doesn't Pete pay his allowance when he's there—his child support?"

"Maybe it's not enough. Maybe Pete came up short this week."

"Why are you covering for him, he needs to be taught—"

"I'm his mother, you don't know anything about raising kids." Her wooden spoon broke in half when she slammed it on the counter.

No more than one or two weeks later, one morning just after the clock radio-alarm came onto the country station at 5 a.m., Virginia fell out of bed instead of getting up. Then, still curled on the floor, she vomited. She couldn't stand up straight to get from the floor to the car. Cal pulled on his t-shirt and jeans, stepped into his tennis shoes, threw the blanket over her and half carried her out the door, then had to leave her sitting on the brick planter to go back into the house to unlock his wallet and get his keys. Down the hall in the bedroom, the clock radio was playing "Blue Eyes Crying in the Rain."

Hours later, in the waiting room, a doctor came to sit beside Cal and let him know that Virginia had an ectopic pregnancy and they would have to remove one of her ovaries, as well as the embryo. He knew how hard this was, the doctor said, but ectopic pregnancies were life-threatening and suddenly turn what should be a happy, hopeful time of discovering there was a new baby into a sad time of loss that Virginia would need help and support to recover from. And Cal too, the doctor said, would feel it.

When the hospital learned Virginia was divorced and had no job, a social worker helped her apply for Medicaid. Trinity stayed with a friend and Angel went to Las Vegas (and missed school) while Virginia was in the hospital for 3 days. She cried the first time Cal saw her, after the surgery. She clutched his hand and he patted her shoulder. He wasn't sure if it would count as help-and-support if he asked her what had happened to her birth control, so he didn't. But wasn't she on the pill? He didn't know if he should have known rather than assuming.

The day she came home, Virginia had a small bouquet in her lap when the nurse wheeled her out the front door where Cal had brought the car. Actually, Cal didn't notice the bouquet until Virginia was in the car, lifted it from her lap and said, "Isn't it pretty?"

"Very nice," Cal said.

"Want to know who sent it?"

"Your parents?"

"My new church." She leaned forward to smell the bouquet so Cal couldn't see to the right before making his left turn out of the lot. "The woman in the other bed, they must have brought flowers in for her five times. For an appendix, not for losing a baby."

She was silent, they both were, the rest of the short drive. She wiped her eyes before getting out of the car in the driveway, carried the bouquet to the bedroom and put it on her nightstand, then lay down. Cal went down the block to the grocery store and bought a cellophane-wrapped cluster of 3 roses. Virginia teared-up again when he returned, walked around the bed to her, holding the packaged roses. In one motion she took them and reached up to his face with both hands, so he bent closer and their lips met. Yes, it was a kiss. The kind they did.

"We can try again, Cal. I still have the other side."

"Maybe this was serendipity."

"Where'd you get that word, who've you been talking to the past three days?"

"It means … never mind. Maybe this was … for the best."

"How can you say that, we lost our *child*." She sat up abruptly, whipped off her shirt and threw it toward the hamper.

"Let's just talk about this later." When Cal picked the shirt up on his way out of the room — one he'd brought to the hospital yesterday for her to wear home — he found the 3 cellophaned roses had been caught inside it when she'd pulled it over her head. He brought them to the kitchen and put them into a juice glass. Trinity was in the kitchen writing in a notebook, which she'd slapped shut as soon as he walked in.

"Homework?"

"My personal, private journal, not for your eyes."

"I'm sure I'll survive the disappointment." Cal put the three roses on the pass-through ledge above the sink. His wallet was there too. He'd gotten lax with Angel gone.

"Hey, Cal?" Trinity switched to her precocious-wisdom voice. "Don't sweat it. She's, like, baby-crazy. She tried to sucker my dad into having another one after me."

By the time he turned around, Trinity had left the kitchen to go to her room.

Prior to going to the shop on Saturdays, Cal mowed and trimmed the yard before 7 a.m. He would do it even earlier, but running a mower and edger earlier than 6 seemed rude. (No one having thumping parties with their stereo speakers outdoors seemed to worry about being rude on Friday and Saturday nights.) Through October, by the time he swept the sidewalk, driveway and front porch, it was over 80, maybe even nearing 90. November through January he really didn't need to mow and trim, but he did it anyway, and could take longer, if he wanted, because the temperature only got into the 80s. He'd been finding cigarette butts on the front porch for several months. Virginia opened the front door and asked through the security screen if he would like a fried egg sandwich and coffee. The kids were still in bed, the air conditioner already on. A fan blowing from the pass-through ledge across the kitchen made the egg sandwich cold by the time it was in front of him at the table, but it was still good, the egg crackly brown at the edges, cheese melted over the top, the toast light brown, not too hard. Way better than the Denny's Grand Slam he'd been planning on.

"Trin and me'll be coming downtown to get some shoes for her. Maybe we can meet you at the store and get lunch?"

"She needs shoes already?"

"There's a new style of high-top tennies. I might get me a pair too and start jogging again." She wiped the congealed bacon grease from the pan with a wad of paper towels.

"Did her check come?"

"Money money money, it's all you think about." Virginia whirled back to the sink. The fry pan clanked against the already-chipped enamel.

"Someone has to."

"How about think about me, *my* needs for a change?"

"Okay, what do you need, we'll go later … together."

"Some needs can't be bought. How about when are you going to make me be an honest woman?"

The mouthful he chewed, as good as it tasted, was cold fried egg. "It's up to me to help you be honest? What happened to your new church—"

"It's not about them, but yes, since you asked, they do agree."

"Okay." He tore off two more bites before chewing. Through a full mouth, "What is their agreement about dishonesty?"

"That we're living together like a man and a woman."

"You mean one of us is pretending?" *Dang, Cal.* He wished he hadn't said that. He stuffed the last big piece of egg sandwich into his mouth before he'd swallowed the last two bites, stood with his coffee.

"Are you really this dense?" She slapped the counter with a towel. He looked, but she'd evidently been killing a fly.

"Well, apparently I don't know what we're talking about. Maybe you can catch me up to speed later."

"Later, always *later*. You need to make me out to be an honest woman."

"Why don't you tell me what you want?"

"We should be *married*."

He didn't say anything, watching another fly creep toward a grease spot on the stove, then pause to rub its hands together.

"It takes two to say I do. Think about it, Cal, you have a job, I keep the home and raise the kids, it's like seren-pity."

"It *is*?" He retrieved his ballcap from the table beside his plate, put it back on. But his keys were across the kitchen on the pass-through ledge, and his wallet locked in the file cabinet. "So if you had a job, it would be a different story?"

"You're purposely twisting everything upside the head." With a butter knife she tapped on the counter, like a rim shot emphasizing every downbeat: "I'm sleeping in your bed. You should take me there to be your wife."

He put his hand on her shoulder as he went behind her to get his keys. "We're doing okay, let's just keep it this way."

1984

Six months later, just when the short months of mild winter temperatures were climbing back into the spring 90's, the wedding ceremony took place in the backyard, under a chicken wire canopy covered with tissue-paper carnations. Trinity wore a miniskirt and midriff off-the-shoulder top. Angel wore stonewashed jeans and a t-shirt with a suit coat. Cal asked him if he'd found the coat in the hall closet where some of his clothes had been moved, but Angel said, "Dude, no, I don't do handed-downs." Angel brought the stereo speakers outside and spent a week making mix tapes for continuous music. He asked Cal what he wanted to contribute to the playlist, but, besides the fact that Dexter, Pharoah or Coltrane should never just be mood music, Cal couldn't imagine them in the vibe for *this*.

Virginia wore white. At least not down to the floor, full, swooshy or trailing. But definitely lacey. Cal had asked, when she showed it to him, "White? What's that all about? You've been married before."

"I *feel* like it's my first time."

"Then that flower girl and best man you've got lined up were immaculate conception."

"At least they're supporting me."

"Okay, maybe they can take over with the rent and electricity."

"Don't be a dufus, it's my *wedding*."

He'd let her set the date when she'd told him she was pregnant again, in January. He wasn't sure how it would have happened, with how seldom he relented and how careful he was when he did. He knew enough to know it *could*. But in February, after the invitations had gone out and the caterer paid half (more than wiping out the carpet-cleaning savings), she said it had been a false alarm. The next one, two years later, wasn't, but was another ectopic, and, being married, the hospital bill put him into another hole just after emerging from what the wedding had hollowed out.

September 21, 1984
So the plan is developing:
Working in a grooming shop takes care of basics, and helps find clients for the private dog training biz. But starting to realize I might need to move again to make this work. Someplace progressive, and big enough, but not too big, and the percentage of yuppies over the "service class" pretty high. Hope you're well and still blowin' thru the changes.
X

PLACE
POST CARD
POSTAGE
HERE

D23422

Post Card

Cal Tonnessen
7512 W San Diego Ave
El Centro CA 92243

Starting over, this sputtering life-story. Why did you decide to mix up the timeline?

All of her dogs have been bitches, and spayed. The business was training, not breeding. Of course 25 years ago there were no on-line dog-trainer/behaviorist schools. You just went out and did it. Or it happened like evolution: You trained and showed your own dogs and did your share of winning. You took a dog grooming course, you had to handle a lot of big, severely untrained—stubborn, lazy, stupid, or aggressive—dogs. You had a natural knack you can't explain. The grooming shop owner turned all problem dogs over to you. Customers started referring friends with problem dogs to you. You started giving customers advice on how to make their dogs easier to handle. Someone asks you to come to their house to show them. You do it free for a while. Then there's a book, *The Accidental Tourist*, that becomes a movie, where a depressed guy with a difficult dog hires a private dog trainer. They fall in love, of course, but it's the training set-up that's important to you. That this can be done. It can be what you do. *The Accidental Dog Trainer.*

Some accidents are also mistakes, but many mistakes were not accidents. In 1980 … *Rudy*. He had soon been history. He chose his church-thing, and probably, if he rang enough doorbells, the church-thing elders overlooked or forgave Rudy for having ever slid his hand up her neck or squeezed behind her on the stool at the bar's piano with his arms around hers for four-handed chopsticks. A calculated temptation, perhaps, was what she was to him. A wicked fantasy to test himself against. A game, a ritual. His weird-church's version of how native Americans sent young men into the wilderness to test their acumen, cunning, bravery and resolve. Eventually he married a woman he'd pointed out to her once—when she actually attended the church-thing's Sunday "meeting" (never called "worship" or "service")—a woman he hadn't yet met but whom the church-thing elders would like him to marry. Maybe accounting was just another temptation-test he'd given himself (her for *lust*, accounting for *greed*). He became a math tutor, then manager of one of those after-school-help-with-homework semi-scams.

At the first grooming shop she worked in after moving to Boulder in 1983, before the germination of her private training business, she met Blaine Barkley, the oboist with a day job, reed thin with fragile-looking wrists, thinning blond hair and doe eyes. She hadn't even been aware she was flirting with him when she'd said, taking the leash of his wire fox terrier, "I always had a thing for musicians."

She lost her virginity. There was some difficulty. Maybe more than some. It hurt. They tried it less and less often. Her hair grew, she got another perm, moved with him to a rental house with a backyard. She did all the outside maintenance, where she also exercised and trained her dogs. He practiced his oboe, played an Asian game called *Go*, watched *Kung Fu* reruns, and fairly faithfully went to work. She kept *The Hite Report on Men and Male Sexuality* in her nightstand drawer, not even realizing that Shere Hite made her real mark studying *female* sexuality.

Five, maybe more, years went by.

Chapter Three
Three or Four More Fights

Jan 1985,
Happy New Year, three weeks late. Visited my parents in CA over the holidays and passed through El Centro. On the drive home, I remembered how I first got to Colorado: through the Virgin River Gorge, past Mussentuchet UTAH — *get it?* — and stopped to rest at Noname Rest Stop in the Rocky Mt foothills before the climb to the summit. Which was an anti-climax. HA-HA
X

PLACE
POST CARD
POSTAGE
HERE

D23422

Post Card

Cal Tonnessen
7512 W San Diego Ave
El Centro CA 92243

Girl, I know you're not inviting me to make any comeback except a pretend one … so … as you once said: you bragging or complaining?

And her retort, imagined well enough to cause him an unimagined wince. *Dang, didn't you once say it's easier to laugh than cry? Do you even know what I'm supposedly joking about?*

I think so, I guess. Something that's my fault?

1985

If there was one thing that brought Cal home from the music store for dinner, it was tacos dorados, the thick oily peppery meaty smell wafting from the open kitchen window to the front porch. In a burst of olfactory endorphins, he might have even said aloud that it was like perfume luring him home. Which may have put tacos dorados on the menu more often.

As did the phone calls to the music store at 4 or 5 with dinner announcements, left as messages if he wasn't available.

Cal, tacos for dinner tonight! And, when the calls increased to three or four per week, spaghetti, pot roast, and bar-be-cued chicken might be the broadcasts.

One afternoon in April he came home around 4, after his floor shift and before his private students. A taco call had come earlier than usual. The aroma was already opaque, meat and onions browning, fresh chilies sliced so their spice spritzed and hung in the air. His eyes watered and nose ran. She'd learned to make tacos dorados the real way, the right way (instead of those pre-formed shells and packaged seasonings) from someone at her church. One good thing had come from that membership. Also quiet Sunday mornings.

"You have a church meeting tonight?" he asked, then started reading the newspaper he'd left on the table at 6 when he'd departed, so was still was not sure if church was the reason for the early dinner. The sizzling white noise was some kind of peace.

When he finished skimming an article about the new geothermal plant, he asked, "Did Angel ever get up?"

"Are you deaf as a doorbell?" She shook the frypan on the burner so its contents hissed louder for a second.

Cal looked up from the paper. Virginia banged a second frypan on another burner—the pan that would fry the tacos after the tortillas were loaded. He said, "I noticed this newspaper hasn't been touched, which means no one's looked at the job classifieds, so—"

"I *just* told you I'm making this for Angel's *breakfast* too, if you could maybe pay attention to an answer when you ask so many questions."

"I just asked one— Wait, breakfast? He's not up yet? What the hell—?"

Virginia's hand came down on the empty pan's handle. The frypan was in the air, somersaulting, then clanging on the floor. Thankfully still empty and not scattering his tacos across the linoleum.

"It's when he *sleeps*. Can't you let sleeping dogs lie?"

Cal waited until she picked up the pan and it made a second bang onto the burner. "By that, you mean I should be afraid of the consequences if I drag him out of bed and say he's not living free under this roof anymore?"

"He just graduated."

"Wasn't that almost a year ago?"

"You know he had to finish credits in summer school, why are you always asking. He's been thinking about what he wants. He deserves a little rest after finishing school."

"Is that why—" ... *you're still not working.* He didn't say it, of course. He cleared his throat. He'd already, more than once, brought up the GED evening classes at the high school. The last time, just a few weeks ago, she'd said she was still thinking about it. Now the tacos were being fried, so he kept his mouth shut and went back to the newspaper, a photo of a celebration of newly naturalized citizens. Once Blue Sand, the jazz combo, had been hired for a citizenship swear-in party, so Cal had written the arrangements for a list of Mexican folk standards. Those tunes were still included on their playlists for banquets, weddings, retirement parties, and any other excuse for middle-aged people to talk, laugh and drink over the sound of real (or formerly real) musicians playing their hearts out (or at least Cal did, on his featured tunes, if they reminded him of X, and played them *for* X, imagining she could hear him). He quietly hummed *Sabor a Mi*. It didn't take long for the guys in the combo, of course, to start calling it *Taste of Me*, then the handwritten playlists started to say *Taste Me*. And recently *Eat Me*.

The tacos were, thankfully, done before Angel made an appearance. The table loaded with individual bowls of grated cheese, salsa, cilantro, guacamole, onions, tomatoes, and olives, along with the platter of tacos and three plates, there was no longer room for the newspaper. Virginia took a taco and sat down across from him.

Cal was loading his first three tacos with the condiments but could tell Virginia was looking at him as she chewed, so he asked, "Is Trinity having dinner tonight?"

"She's on a date." Virginia chuckled, covering her mouth with her hand, then swallowed. "His name is B-base. I think a musician. Maybe you know him. He has a corvette."

"She's with a guy who drives?" He finally took his first bite.

"How're they gonna get anywhere?" Virginia's chair screeched backwards on the linoleum and she left the table. She got two glasses from the dish drainer. "Speaking of which, maybe we could drive Angel to his Dad's and go on a little vacation ourselves? Just us."

"What're you going to do with Trinity?"

"She has friends to stay with." Ice clattered into the glasses. "C'mon, how about it?"

"In Las Vegas?"

"Well, naturally, that's where we'd be after dropping Angel off." She filled the glasses with soda from a big plastic bottle and pushed one across the table to Cal.

"Thanks. I actually wasn't going to take any time off ... If I did ... How about, I don't know ... Colorado?"

"What's there?"

"Something other than desert ... what's in Vegas? Except maybe a house where Angel could go to live for a while? If we're driving, we could pack his stuff."

Jars in the refrigerator rattled when she shoved the door closed. "Why would you say that? *This* is his home."

"Maybe he needs his father's influence, a strong male—"

"And you're not up for that?"

"Not when you don't let me."

"You don't know anything about raising kids." Her chair clonked the table leg as she resumed her place. "Would you like to try with one of your own?"

"Let's concentrate on him for a minute. Vegas is a big city, there's so little here ... unless he goes to technical college. Even then, the opportunities here are limited, you have to see that, you've been having trouble yourself finding—"

A fork clanged onto a plate. "Yeah yeah yeah yeah. Put me down cuz I'm raising my kids."

"Letting a 13-year-old date a guy with a car is hardly—"

"You can butt-out on that one. When was the last time *you* were a teenaged girl."

Music started somewhere else in the house, actually mostly bass thumping the floor. Cal put three more tacos on his plate and

64

concentrated on stuffing them with the fixings. The avocado was going to run out first. "Did you make beans?" he asked. He could smell them.

"Darn, yes, I forgot." She got up again, pulled a pot from a burner then clinked it on her plate, the only place available on the table. Fragrant beany steam enveloped him for a serene moment of nirvana while she spooned a pile onto his plate.

"Have you thought about the house, Babes?"

"Well … the house … I think about what kind of insulation it doesn't have when I write the electricity check, and I guess I think about it when I write the rent check."

"Exactly. Rent. We can stop paying rent."

"Oh—" His mouth was full. He didn't want to rush savoring the greasy blend of flavors, but swallowed a little too soon. Then needed a big drink of soda. "*We* can?" His voice had that thin, scratchy thing that happens when a bit of chili touches a vocal cord.

"Like I've been saying. Do you ever listen to me? *Buy* the house." Virginia refilled the cheese bowl then left the package of grated cheese on the table.

Cal put two more tacos onto his plate. There were still five or six on the platter.

"Leave some for Angel and me. I'll eat with him. Anyway, he's willing to sell. I asked. It's a doggy-dog world, you gotta go for it."

"How many dogs are fighting over this house?" He tried to sprinkle cheese from the bag into a taco. It spilled as much around as into the shell.

Virginia pushed the cheese bowl so it clanked against his plate. "But, babes, wouldn't it make a nice anniversary present?"

"What is the first anniversary theme, brick-and-plaster?"

"*Your* version would be biscuits and gravy." She got up and dropped her plate into the sink. It splashed into something so probably didn't break. Then she started adding more water.

"Hell yeah, a perfect gift."

"One you get almost every week ."

"Really? Thanks. My dreams have come true." The faucet was still running. When he brought his plate to the sink, he reached past her and turned it off. Sudsy dishwater was inches from the top of the sink. "Remember? Conserving?"

Virginia tipped her cheek onto her shoulder. "Don't you know I have dreams too? And shouldn't we have dreams together?"

Cal stepped back but she was already turning around. She grabbed both his biceps and pulled on him. His body didn't move, but hers did, forward, up against him, releasing his elbows to slip her arms around him.

The same moment Angel shambled into the kitchen. "God, get a room."

Virginia laughed, squeezed Cal's ass, then broke away to fill a plate of tacos for Angel. Cal went back to the music store.

Eww, ick (hear her squeaky laugh).

Just going along, keep the boat from rocking.

Dang, Cal ... how can you?

Easier than caring.

Jeez, too many things are easier than what's real. Man overboard.

It was soon afterwards, the phone call and unusual visit both coming to the music store. First a smell of onions. The onion fields were harvested in April, so driving to the store before dawn with windows down to try to enjoy fresh air that wasn't yet in the upper 90s became problematic because the odor of onions wafted everywhere. But people started to smell of onions too, if they worked in the fields. He knew several guys whose wives, usually second wives, had come from field-working families, and they had continued working the seasonal harvests because sisters and mothers were out there, they could spend all day with family. The UFW contract not even a decade ago had made harvesting a better job than minimum-wage fast-food, and it wasn't easy to be hired onto a crew. Cal had mentioned it once to Virginia, especially since winter produce was harvested in moderate temperatures. Armies of harvesters weren't needed as much in the months of 110°, so a great many pickers worked only part of the year. From mid-December through March— Broccoli, cabbage, lettuce, cauliflower—no one could tell which field the picker had worked. But the April onions soaked into clothes, skin, hair, auto interiors and bedrooms.

But it was unusual to smell it inside the music store. Cal was in the back, in his repair shop. The onion scent had barely registered, except maybe to stimulate noontime hunger, when Cliff, store-owner slash trumpet-player, came to the back to tell Cal someone was there to see him. "I'm going to send her back here, okay? The store's kinda starting to reek. Just like Marty says, you know? Reeks like leeks."

Cal was changing springs on an alto sax. A few keys were removed, the tiny screws set aside in a dirty saucer that had once been his ashtray. If he'd still smoked in the shop, there'd be no other smells: pizza brought in by the afternoon-shift or Cliff having a tray of tamales delivered.

The oniony waft got stronger and a short woman around 50-years-old stood in his shop doorway, a cotton light blue workshirt tucked into jeans, jeans tucked into boots. "'Scuse, sir?"

"Yeah, hi, how can I help you?"

She could be the parent of a kid whose horn was in the shop, or a horn that needed to come in. Parents didn't usually need to talk to him, but sometimes an uncle had an old clarinet in the garage and they wanted to use it for junior in 5th grade band and had to ask if the repairs would be worth it (because the kid might quit in 3 months). But that was usually September, not April.

"Sir, you the parent of Treenty?"

"Trinity? Yes. Well … step-parent. Do you need to talk to her mom?"

"The mama don't answer door. I know you work here. Mí cuñado, very much younger, husband's baby brother. Treenty tell him you work here."

"Okay, how can I help you?" He worked the sax's remaining keys, like drumming his fingers. The pads made a percolator sound on the open holes.

"Bobby live with us sometime. Sometime not working."

"I don't do the hiring here."

"No-no, not that. He dating with Treenty."

"Oh." He lay the sax across his knees. "I don't know the right way to say this, ma'am, but Trinity … she doesn't go for … um, Chicanos? Sorry, not sure what word … um …"

"I know, sir, Bobby es negro. Black. I marry brother."

"Oh. Well. That makes sense, at least. What grade is he in?"

"Grade? No-no. No grade. Thirty-three years."

"Really? *I'm* not even … I mean …" He wasn't yet 30.

"I have to go back. I came at lunch. Tell her mama. They sometime   — Daytime, in our house while we at work."

"You mean after school?"

"All day, all day. He so old for her."

He tapped his foot, staring at the minuscule screws he would have to use a magnifying light to replace in the saxophone.

"I have to go. My husband know I come here. He tell Bobby too. No listen. I say *tell papa. He make stop.*"

"Well, *Papa* is …" His fingers drummed the saxophone keys again, then he gingerly placed the instrument onto his work table, on top of some invoices but careful not to disturb the removed keys and ashtray of screws. *Papa is what?…impotent? …someone else …somewhere else?* He pushed his stool back and turned to put a hand on her shoulder. She seemed to know the dance: she turned to leave, and he walked with her, through the store to the front door, his fingertips remaining on her shoulder blade while he said, "Thank you for coming to tell me, ma'am. We'll certainly talk to her about this. I mean, we'll … we'll do something. We surely will."

And then the phone call. Not Cal to Virginia regarding Trinity with the 30-something-year-old man. He would make that call (better over the phone), but hadn't yet before the other call came.

Cal was finishing a clarinet re-pad, just about to check for leaks. Cliff popped in to say, "Phone for you," and was gone again. He would've said so if the call was from Virginia. If it wasn't her, usually a band director wanting to know when a horn would be ready, big parade or concert this weekend and of course some kid waited until the week before to notice the valves were stuck or flute was tweaked. If he wasn't busy, Cliff gave stopgap answers or took messages. Cal had considered having his own phone number just for the repair shop, but then who would run interference on the interrupting calls?

"How can I help?" was Cal's unidentified-caller answer.

"Hey, buddy, working hard or hardly working?"

"Uh ... somewhere in the middle." It could be one of the guys from Blue Sand. Although Cliff would have said so, and would've mock-insulted Cal before turning the phone over to him.

"Pete Steuben here. Virgie's ex. She told me where you work." The guy paused longer than he would need to take a breath, long enough to take a drink or drag on a cigarette, not long enough to be eating. "I thought it wouldn't hurt to, you know, trade notes. On the kids, I mean."

Tradin'-eights was a jazz expression for alternating improvised solos, communicating with each other with riffs on a theme. But Cal didn't feel like trying to make some kind of pun, and certainly Virgie's ex wasn't a jazz guy, what were the odds on *that*?

"You still there? I call at a bad time?" The guy's voice had no quality that pictured him: age, fat or skinny, tall, short. smoker or non, heavy drinker or just beer, hotshot, lowlife, executive, hunter, military, weekend warrior ... nothing.

"Oh, sorry." Cal put the clarinet on a stand on his workbench. "Yeah, the kids. I don't know if I can tell you anything that Virginia hasn't..."

"Matter of fact, Virgie mentioned you wanted to boot Angel to come live with me." Not even an accent to indicate where he was from. And Cal couldn't remember Virginia ever even telling him what Pete did for a living.

"I only suggested, maybe Angel would have more opportunity in a bigger city, and maybe you have contacts—"

"Know what? I even believe you. Virgie constantly gets things wrong. I'm sure you know that by now." The guy chuckled. "She said you were trying to get rid of him."

"Well, maybe she misunderstood." Cal was staring at the flame on his Bunsen burner. He closed his eyes and watched spots flare.

The guy blew out a big breath, for sure he was smoking. Cal only smoked outside and made Angel do likewise but was pretty sure when he wasn't home, which was more than half the day, Virginia let Angel smoke in his room. Cal felt a cigarette break calling.

"Between you and me, I'm gonna tell you now, I don't want him back, even to visit ... for a while. Maybe a long while. He took my car without permission, smashed the front fender. Then claims the car was hit in a parking lot. Parking lot my ass. I could *smell* what was going on in there. From cracking the cap all the way to the puke. Not to mention a rip in the leather seat. Like he's stupid enough to put a knife in his back pocket blade *out*."

"Wow, that must be—"

"It's more than that, it's a lot of things. Sorry to dump this on you like an unsuspecting dupe—no offense there. I feel for you, man. Maybe I should give you a head's up. There's something weird about Virgie's relationship with Angel."

Cal's turn to let out a breath, but not like the relief of a first draw on a cigarette—more like a toke he'd been holding in.

"I don't mean *that* way," the man continued.

"No, I didn't—"

"See, my mother is Mexican—my name's actually Pedro, but my mother wouldn't allow talking in Spanish at home, plus it wasn't cool to be ethnic in the 60s, by junior high I was Pete. Anyway the kids are barely at all Chicano and aren't into that—but Virgie got the name Angel from some of the cousins on my mom's side. From what I seen, there's never been a kid named Angel who *was* one. Moms of the so-called angels ... well, name him Angel and he not only can do no wrong, he's like God's gift to them to serve ... it's hard to describe without sounding like ... Like for some reason giving their Angel everything he wants is everything *she* wants."

"That's ... well ..." Cal finally turned his Bunsen burner off.

"Yeah, then the rest of the world has to deal with the monster she makes."

"What do you think about the Army?"

"For Angel? Great idea. Coming from a Boomer draft-dodger, of course. But hell, yeah."

The draft had been gone by the time Cal was 17. But Virginia was 9 years older, so this man likely at least that much.

"I thought he might have mentioned it to you," Cal said. "I thought he was considering it."

"Angel don't talk to me. Unless I have my wallet out." The front door bell chimed as a customer came in or left. As though he'd heard it, the guy said, "Hey, good talking to you, pal. We'll hafta do it again."

70

"Can I talk to you about Trin—"

"I really gotta run, late for work."

"Okay, can I get your num—" The call ended.

The rest of '85, Angel was hired and let go from two—or a stretch to say three—part-time positions. One of them apparently cash-only, so no unemployment insurance, which had lasted two or three weeks after the other two terminations. Virginia tried making Angel one of her salesmen in a multi-level direct-sales enterprise for a hair-growth product. Virginia had to give a cut of *her* sales to whoever had recruited her, but she wouldn't tell Cal who that was. To make better money she had to recruit her own string of dupes. She'd made a photo book of before and after shots, illustrating negligible results, using her own scalp. Again, his question about who took the photos was met with, "Always asking so many questions, you're such a questionable person."

Still, she invited a viewing of the photo book, along with her brochures and order forms, before she began packing them into a brand new attaché case she'd told Cal she needed for her new business. Cal took note that the case was real leather, but only pretended to look at the photos. He sort of knew what Virginia looked like without a wig, but even that had been a mistake, coming into the bedroom at the wrong time.

Leaning over the photo book, Trinity said, "Shit-damn, Mom, you grew about as much hair as Yoda. You aren't thinking that goo is making you able to go without a wig, are you?"

"Your opinion will be welcome when you tell us who's the grown-up adult you're spreading yourself for."

"Like I'm going to help you try to harass him. You're the one who isn't acting *grown-up adult* going out looking like someone yanked out half your hair in a bitch-fight."

Then Trinity leaped away as Virginia coiled to backhand her. Virginia abandoned the slap and said, "It's something that sometimes happens to pregnant women, which I'm sure you're going to find out sooner and later." She turned to Cal who was slouching against the kitchen doorway waiting for an opportunity to back out of the room.

Trinity muttered *crazy bitch* under her breath, while Virginia said, "I was pregnant with Angel." Cal already knew that.

Trinity slammed the refrigerator door, a soda in her hand. "Yeah, she gave her all to Angel and he's *still* sucking all he can get."

After trinity's bedroom door banged, Virginia finished packing her attaché, picked it up and smiled at Cal. "A real business woman!"

Before she left for wherever she was going, she said, "By the way, I gave your name to Angel when I gave him half of my qualified leads – that's a sales term I learned, better than cold calling. So I call it hot-calling. I mean, not only do you already have a relationship, you're an obvious discographic, what with *your* hairline. Make him do the whole pitch before you buy."

This spared Cal the need to buy anything, because Angel never made a pitch.

1986

Technically, of course, he knew how it had happened. Again. That is, he knew how it happens when it happens. But he couldn't remember actually doing what was necessary to make it happen. His abstinence wasn't an exercise in birth control or discipline, self-denial as some sort of cleansing. It wasn't even a statement of his enduring longing for X (his "statement" on *that* was made more than a couple times a week, in the bathroom, at his shop after-hours, even in bed long past midnight). With Virginia, he just couldn't stay interested long enough to keep a hardon long enough to come inside her. So he must have leaked, one of those times he couldn't talk his way out of even starting. Like one recent afternoon when Virginia pointed out to him—with some kind of applied coyness he at first thought was just an illusion caused by a new wig with bangs—that the house was empty of kids. It *was* unusual that an empty daytime house didn't happen often, considering the kids were untethered teenagers, but one seemed to sleep all day. *Not when the kids could hear them*, had been used so often to postpone or just dodge the deed, Virginia no longer made suggestive invitations if either of the kids was home. And Cal's early rising was his reason to preclude the activity after-retiring at night. So that day after lunch when she pointed out the house was empty, Cal had responded with enthusiasm, "Hey, great, let's go to the movies!"

With as few as there were to remember, he didn't remember anything from two months ago that could have led to it. A second tubal pregnancy, the same or similar emergency drama, this time Virginia doubling over in a crunch of cramping while they shopped together in a grocery store, one of the intervals when he'd taken away her checkbook and accompanied her for all shopping due to expenses scraping the bottom of his income every month. After her two nights in the hospital this time, the joint checkbook was returned to her.

The two nights in the hospital included the tying off of the second tube. After a doctor came to sit beside Cal in the emergency waiting room to explain the situation and remind Cal that it was okay to feel grief for losing what might have been a son or daughter, as well as losing any further opportunity for Virginia to have another baby, there was (again) no moment at any time to wonder aloud hadn't she been using birth control and how had it failed.

The tubal pregnancy was in August, after the pyramid scheme had ended, after Virginia had opened her own business checking account and Cal had supplemented to pay her expenses every month for the 3 or 4 months it lasted, until she finally agreed to close it down, having lost plenty, he didn't bother keeping track. She'd probably even bought some product for Angel to sell and he'd pocketed whatever money he'd taken in, the week or so he actually made calls, usually to people on Virginia's customer lists as he never had his own. Cal tried not to hear about it when Virginia inadvertently let it drop while trying to explain why her business checking account was too low again to pay her bills.

June 1986
I see I still have all these
cards from the Zoo! And that
I've not kept to any kind of
schedule in writing on them.
Chalk it up to long hours and
new friends. Really? _Me_?
Friends? Maybe just one. Not
counting the dog(s). Really,
grooming 40 hours a week,
then clients on the side (like
teaching private music
lessons). Weekends for dog
shows. SOUNDS EXCITING!
(???)   X

PLACE
POST CARD
POSTAGE
HERE

D23422

Post Card

Cal Tonnessen
7512 W San Diego Ave
El Centro CA 92243

I wish I'd known you when we were 10 — the zoo was free then, we could've ridden our bikes there, walk the downhill path through the rainforest, sat on a peanut-shaped bench for lunch. I'd pay their blood-money prices now if I could go with you.

You finished? Did that help?

Okay, I deserved that.

Overall it seemed a dream-like year—a trance or daze—when suddenly it was December and they hadn't done a damn thing about Trinity running around with a guy twice her age for more than a year. In Christmas cards, Virginia told her parents and siblings and friends that Cal had bought her the house as a gift. The paperwork *was* done, the mortgage payments *had* started. It had taken weeks of copying documents, one more always needed, scheduling inspections, wrangling with the former owner over what he wouldn't fix, which turned out to be everything when, unexpectedly, there was a document signed by Virginia that agreed to buy the house as-is.

1987

What else Angel did the previous year, Cal wasn't sure. He hadn't ever had another conversation with the father. But finally Angel enlisted in the Army. He'd spent one night in jail for something Cal wasn't sure of and Virginia didn't expound upon, but she did tell Cal that she thought someone had told Angel if he got any more of a record than that, he'd never be able to enlist in the Army, something Angel had talked about since high school, as in "If I *need* a job, there's the army."

So there would be a party. Catered, with a band.

"You could pay *me* to cater it," Virginia suggested.

"I'll give you $200 to order pizza and soda."

"*Soda*! If he's old enough to kill, he's old enough to drink."

There were a few trumpets and a clarinet Cal had repaired over a year ago and had never been picked up, so he let Cliff sell them and used the $600 to help pay the $700 catering bill and $200 for the band, a 4-piece garage hair-band, inciting three visits from the cops the night of the party. Which also could have meant hauling Cal off for supplying liquor to underage partiers, but as soon as the street pulsed with the police lights, the keg, as well as Trinity and her crew of party-crashers disappeared, temporarily. Trinity had been barred from the party by Virginia unless she provided the name of the man she was still seeing, but one of her girlfriends arrived with four guys, all too young to have been the one, and they stayed in a far corner of the yard, behind the band, except to periodically venture to the keg. Cal kept an eye on the dark corner where sometimes there appeared to be more like five guys, and once he thought he saw someone jump down from the cinderblock wall at the back of his yard. The wall, he realized, must have been the escape route when the blue and red lights suddenly hushed the shouting and the band's thumping ground to a guitar growl before ending, so Cal had to go contend with the increasingly testy uniforms while whoever needed to was over the wall, likely crouching just below it on the other side, although after the last visit, when Cal threw a breaker switch to quiet the band for good, Trinity, trailing a pot smell heady enough to make Cal crave a toke, came sauntering through the house alone, asking if there was any more pizza.

Angel slept the next day while, for the 4th or 5th time since they'd lived there, Cal rented a rug cleaner, and Virginia wept, with periodic outright wailing, while she cleaned the kitchen. At first Cal thought it was over broken dishes or the dent in the refrigerator, but he realized long before she had sobbed through dinner and cyclically all night—vibrating the mattress the way he sometimes feared he did with his brazen alone-time lying right next to her—it was for Angel's departure the next day. That he'd used her sob-induced mattress pulsation to camouflage a session with X did make him feel like shit—even more than the shit he always felt after coming then coming back down to earth to the rude reality that it was just his hand, and *now* what?

So, feeling like shit was maybe why—it was exactly why—he went down to the police station and tried to file a complaint. He'd actually tried to tell one of the cops who came to bust-up the party, but realized—when his request for help concerning his teenaged step-daughter sleeping with a man in his mid-thirties was brushed aside by the 20-something patrolman—that he sounded just like someone who would be hosting a raucous drunken party resulting in trash, vomit and urine on the sidewalk and front lawn. So he went to the station and asked if he could report statutory rape of his step-daughter.

"You the legal guardian?"

"I …" He almost said *pay the bills*. Is that really what he cared about? "Not really."

"Yes or no."

"No."

1988

Now it had been over two years, and Virginia was still demanding that Trinity either stop seeing or supply the name of her boyfriend (who could be 35 or 36 by now, older than Cal), using it as an ultimatum in every unrelated spat, even the one over quitting school. But the child support money still disappeared somewhere besides the food budget. There'd been a time, years ago, Cal had suggested Virginia bank the support check so Trinity would have a college fund. Put away $1200 a year, even for 8 years, and she would have had $9600. She wasn't going to go to Yale, after all.

"Sorry for casting aspirations at you," Virginia had said, "but I didn't suppose Mr. Miser wants to be paying for the clothes, shoes, lingerie, make-up and skin products a girl needs."

Whether or not the $200 a month even paid for what Trinity was wearing, especially on her face, Cal didn't inquire. He actually didn't see much of Trinity at all, as though she planned her comings and goings (and brawls with Virginia) to avoid him.

It was Virginia's brief, expensive stint in a summer school bartender class that finally tilted the standoff with Trinity, still 16 the first half of 1988. Bartender classes were 3 to 6, so there would be no dinner until after 6:30, but quietly watching the news with a beer, or alone-time in his room under a ceiling fan, lured him home. Monday of that week, home at 5:30, a pong lingering in the house, tobacco for sure, but also weed, flowery air-freshener, body odor, something similar to the smell in the bathroom when Virginia didn't empty the trash enough during her or Trinity's periods (which, he supposed, could have been happening that week anyway), and musk cologne. Still, the house was empty. He had an hour to spend on the bed, wondering for the first time if he ever left some smell behind.

But he decided to come home Tuesday at 5. As he approached the house, a car was pulling away—a corvette—and Trinity was on the front porch. As Cal's car slowed to turn into the driveway, Trinity returned inside the house, and by the time Cal gathered his keys and small satchel and got out of his car, the house was empty, the front door even locked.

So Wednesday, Cal drove home at home at 4, parked on the street behind the corvette, wrote the license number in the gas mileage record notebook he kept in the glove compartment. He went around the block, drove by the house 3 more times, picturing himself going inside and confronting them. Every scenario included dodging a fist, or worse, which sent him back to the music store where he told Cliff what was going on. Cliff, an established business owner, knew people—lawyers, even judges. By Friday at noon, Cal had a name and address.

Friday Virginia was home when Cal arrived at 5. Spaghetti sauce was cooking, and she had quit bartender school. Cal handed her the notepad sheet with the name, Robert Saunders.

"What's this, a job? Already? I just quit that racket this afternoon."

"It's the guy. Trinity's … guy."

"That *bitch*." When she slammed her spoon back into the spaghetti sauce, splattering the paper, Cal managed to get it back into his hand while Virginia was sputtering something about jail and cutting balls off and sending Trinity to military school.

"Just a second, Virginia. We have to do this right. Here's what I found out: *you* can make the criminal complaint." He realized he was holding Virginia's wrist and gently removing the spoon from her hand. "She's a minor, so even though they like having a victim help with prosecution, they can file charges without Trinity making the complaint." His arm around her, he guided Virginia to the table. They both sat and he continued to hold Virginia's hand. "She doesn't even need to know you did it. Not right away. Can you imagine the mess if you tell her first and *then* try to do it?"

She clutched his hand with both of hers. "Will you go with me, Babes?"

"Of course."

Then stroking his left hand third finger, "Will you wear your wedding ring?"

"It's at the shop, it gets in the way… Okay, if it will help."

Although Cal wondered if they should wait until Monday during normal business hours, Virginia signed the complaint that evening around 8. No one could tell them when a squad car might arrive at the man's address or locate the car via its license plate. Cal suggested the police could come to their house Monday between 3 and 6, and he would take Virginia to the movies. He did that anyway, but couldn't tell when it had actually happened.

Dang, you really did it, bud? I thought you didn't want to care?

It's just, from the start, I thought I could keep myself from thinking too much about what I didn't get by solving problems for them. A place to live, stability …

Ah, the martyr. Can't say you've done a bang-up job.

'Cause I floated with the tide—look how long it took for me to do anything.

Why do you stay? Wish I could say I get it.

Of course you don't—or better put: you still don't.

He heard it from down the hall. Grunts and gasps and shrieks, it had already gone beyond words. He hurried toward the sound of combat, screams and thumps and ripping and more thumps. Immediately saw the gang-style writing on Trinity's bedroom closet door when he stopped in the doorway. Then the pile of clothes torn out of the closet and strewn around, currently being stomped and kicked by Virginia despite both her arms pinned behind her back by Trinity. Posters likewise ripped from walls and puckered underfoot. A portable TV he'd been unaware existed was on its side with a cracked screen.

Both began using words again as soon as Cal was in the room.

"She's visiting that pervert in jail. *Visiting* him!"

"She's tearing up my clothes, wrecking my room, *she snitched, got him busted, no one cares if I'm happy.*"

Both still locked together, Virginia with arms pinned, Trinity's hands occupied with holding her mother's arms, their feet still shambling around the small space … Virginia back-kicking at Trinity and Trinity forward-kicking her mother, until, just as Cal moved to try to get between them, Virginia fell, Trinity still holding her arms, the twisting mess of bodies continued on the debris-strewn floor. Virginia now screeching "Get out, get out, you're dead to me," and Trinity, "I hate you, you loser bitch, owww, let go, fuckhead."

Cal had managed to take Trinity's wrists and extricate her hands from Virginia's arms. She was a tall girl, and not a lightweight—her hips and figure had more than a little filled out the past few years—but Cal just backed her up by walking forward, until Trinity's back was against a wall. Virginia was on her feet again and resumed kicking the clothes around, even picking items up and attempting to shred them. "Go ahead, go on, go run to that dirtball loser, see how many outfits and shoes he buys for you, see if you like your private room at juvie."

"Anywhere's better than this, you and your asswipe gumby, *I'd rather sleep in pig shit*, I know where somebody loves me for *me*."

Something crashed in the kitchen before Trinity's voice, wailing curses, was outside, then began fading down the sidewalk. Easy to hear because she'd left the front door open. Virginia put her foot in the neck hole of a rock-band t-shirt Cal recognized from the music store, and, kicking and pulling simultaneously, ripped it in half.

Later, dry-eyed and without either make-up or expression, Virginia put a grilled cheese sandwich in front of Cal, who wasn't even sitting at the table yet. She left the kitchen. Cal took the sandwich with him to the shop and straightened the slide on a trombone. Virginia was in bed with the lights out when he got home. Trinity had not returned. He stayed up, made popcorn and watched a nature documentary on TV with the sound so low he couldn't hear the narration, but wondered if any of it involved adolescents being forced to leave—or instinctively leaving—family units (packs, prides, troops). He let his eyes shut and continued to listen. The manhole cover in the street rattled, five, six, ten, eleven times. Was he counting? He dozed, woke with an infomercial flickering and Virginia snoring in the bedroom.

Instead of going straight to the shop in the morning, Cal took his once-a-month circuitous path, putting all the utility bills in drop boxes to save on stamps. But he changed the route slightly so he would go by the downtown park next to the hospital. It was early enough that walkers and joggers were using the path before the summer scorch took charge. He spotted Trinity at a picnic table with two other people, one standing. At least one besides Trinity was a girl. Fast food paper sacks were on the ground under and beside the table. Noticeable because the standing figure kicked one, discharging wadded garbage when the sack burst.

The highest heat was between 3 and 5 o'clock. It didn't really cool enough for exercise before midnight. So Cal was the only one on the jogging path when he returned at 6 p.m. with a hamburger and soda in a sack. Trinity was still at the same picnic table, shaded by an acacia tree. The path came within 30 feet of the table. Cal left the path at an angle, set the sack on the table, and angled back to the path, without stopping. Trinity hadn't raised her head as he approached, and he didn't know if she looked up after he put the sack down. It was at least 95 degrees.

Virginia never said a word, if she even noticed, when Cal loaded his saxophone into the car before dawn. He gathered up his checkbook, any ATM cards—defunct or new—all the credit cards, even the checkbook for Virginia's old business account that had been closed for 2 years. He told Virginia he was going to go over everything while at the shop and simplify them down to only what was working and necessary. He couldn't tell if she agreed or even heard him. The water was running in the sink where she was standing. He took an ATM from her wallet in clear view. Even held it up between two fingers when he said what he was doing. He stuffed all of it into an old nylon backpack Angel had used for school. Into his pocket, he put the spare set of house keys and one of Virginia's old watches, after he made sure the battery was still good.

There were about a dozen walkers on the path at 6 a.m. The sun already up, still low but sunlight was starting to extend across the grassy areas. The acacia tree's shade was nowhere near the picnic table that sat beneath it, nor any of the others in the vicinity. No one was at the table. But he saw her, alone, in shade cast by the restroom building, sitting on the concrete, her back to the stucco wall, her forehead against her knees. His fast-food bag had a breakfast sandwich and orange juice. After he placed it beside her feet, he didn't leave. He saw her forehead roll enough that she could have seen the bag. Her hair was either utterly greasy or she had wet it in the restroom, although the last time he'd been in the men's room here, no one could have put their head between the sink bowl and rusty faucet with its trickle of tepid water. A paper soda cup could allow for collecting and pouring. There were red blotches on her neck.

"If you're waiting for me to say thanks, you can just go." She didn't lift her head.

Cal put the watch and key on the pavement between Trinity's feet. She was wearing clear blue sandals that looked like they were made from gummie candy. Her feet looked grey and dusty.

"Around noon, I'm taking your mother to Yuma. We'll see a movie, then stay for dinner." The shade was shrinking so quickly, he already felt sun on his back, already a trickle of sweat. "Go clean up your room. Put your clothes away. Hide that gang shit on the closet somehow." He cleared his throat before saying *There's nothing in the house to steal.* And then never said it.

"Who says I want to go back?"

But she was there, in her room, when Cal and Virginia returned around 8. He never did get the extra house key back, but changed the locks one day when Virginia and Trinity went shopping for new clothes. Another day, when Trinity and Virginia were out somewhere all day, he painted Trinity's closet door. It took 3 coats of primer to cover the ink marker that had been used to write there, then he added a coat of dark brown. Despite the lingering paint smell, Trinity stayed in bed for a few days, a new Walkman playing cassettes into her ears. He suspected, but did not ask, Virginia had taken Trinity for an abortion. He didn't know who would have paid for it.

Oct 1988
I'm not a beard, I just play one on TV. Or he's the beard, for insurance. Did I need it this badly? (My business Ins. would only pay for dog bites!) Guess what: a musician. But I am on TV! Monthly spot on local yakkada so-called news, "Living With Our Pets," much easier to simplify in 3 minutes than living with humans, eh?
   Without a church, without flowers or cake, even without rings. Who needs all that crap?
X

PLACE
POST CARD
POSTAGE
HERE

D23422

Post Card

Cal Tonnessen
7512 W San Diego Ave
El Centro CA 92243

Oh, girl, I don't know if this will make it harder or easier to go on.
      What other choice is there? I mean besides going on.
      Right.

Back to now and *American Sex in the 21st Century*, watching last month's television documentary on DVR. Someone's research gets made into entertainment.

About time, they say, since Kinsey's landmark reports were over 50 years ago. Wanted to write *seminal* instead of *landmark*, but the computer's thesaurus didn't offer that word. (A client was chastised for using *seminal* in a meeting. When he told the story, the first taken-aback response from the listener: how could anyone object to using the Seminole Nation as a metaphor for *highest significance*?) But would *seminal* fit a study of sex? Maybe Kinsey's reports were not just *seminal* but *orgasmic*. Someone even believes Kinsey's studies "helped usher in the 'sexual revolution' of the 1960s and 1970s." Although some people didn't get the invitation, weren't *ushered*. That's a good new name: *Some People*. Shortened sometimes to *Someone*. (Passive-voiced, but is the story now mine instead of an anonymous *she*?)

Kinsey endeavored to replace the long-standing Puritan orthodoxy of what constitutes *normal* (or the more notorious category of *abnormal*) in sexual behavior with a scientific one: "Nearly all the so-called sexual perversions fall within the range of biological normality." Some people still fall outside the parameters. Usually this deviation is blamed on the far reach of that old societal orthodoxy, still making a stand in cultural politics and even public policy in 2008. Some of us—liberals, Progressives, from a non-religious upbringing—still don't fit *that* explanation either. We just don't understand. *Someone* here is trying to figure it out.

On Kinsey: "His great accomplishment was to take his pain and suffering and use it to transform himself into an instrument of social reform, a secular evangelist who proclaimed a new sensibility about human sexuality." (T. M. Brown and E. Fee, American Journal of Public Health. 2003 June; 93(6): 896–897.) The name *Kinsey* wouldn't be a bad adoption, if it were still (or was ever) possible to attain *that* template. But sometimes "pain and suffering" is nothing more than selfish whining. What's so defective in having food, clothes, housing, a car, fulfilling work and absorbing hobbies?

Kinsey's second book, like the first, two years earlier, was a media   sensation,   and   with   a   savage   counter-offensive.   A congressional investigation of the grants funding his research. And we think this tea party bullshit is new? Keep people from knowing anything and they won't *do* anything, is that the theory? Well, some people have been reading all of it—well, a lot of what came after Kinsey's 800-page tome—and more, including *The Happy Hooker* (didn't <u>she</u> do a study too?)—and still didn't *do* …much. Didn't, or couldn't? Tried, or stopped trying? *Someone* has to accept culpability. And no, you shouldn't be thinking about Cal when you say that. Why are you thinking about Cal? Especially with your spurious marriage's 20th anniversary somewhere around here.

Back in 1989 to whenever … those early years of that coupling, did anything happen? (Not just *that*. That didn't happen, why would it have happened *then*?) Putting together a business, a one-person gig, doing everything including learning the skill, making a name, having a reputation… the days slide away, ruminating on other shit isn't conducive, there's always a critical something on a list that's not yet crossed off.

Some life story. Maybe one that was better told on postcards.

Chapter Four
Four (or Four Hundred) Orgasms

March 1989,

It's an art, like one of your 8-bar solos, to get my life compressed to a postcard. Just wanted to say I'm still kick'n along. Not kicking the dogs! But new stuff to learn every day. A self-trained profession (despite the many books), and no union to collectively bargain my take-home or working conditions, aka my house. Do you know why zoos pair a dog with a cheetah? (If they plan to use a cheetah for PR). Because the wild animal cues off the domestic friend for stress. If the *dog* isn't nervous with an audience or traveling, the cheetah more apt to relax. Good method for some kinds of human anxiety? (Hasn't worked yet.) X

PLACE
POST CARD
POSTAGE
HERE

D23422

Post Card

Cal Tonnessen
7512 W San Diego Ave
El Centro CA 92243

1990

One good thing about being the one to drop Trinity off for afternoon GED classes at the high school was that he picked up the mail and put it in his satchel on the way to the car, before Trinity flounced out of the house and into her seat. It was difficult to tell if her body language was to display exasperation at having to do this or some kind of swagger at pulling this off: An agreement between Virginia and Trinity, brokered in some so-called therapy they went to together, that Trinity could quit high school if she completed the GED. No caveat that she would need to get a job or even help around the house. From waking (11? 12?) until she left in Cal's car at 2:50 p.m., she occupied herself in her bedroom. There were three things Cal knew she did in there: 1. experimented with make-up (based on how different she appeared—her skin tone ranging from copper to alabaster, her eyeshadow in tones of purple and red, her eyebrows shifting from arch anger to clownish surprise—each time she emerged from her thumping room for a meal or to make brownies, from which she'd packed on at least 20 pounds). 2. Drugs, a variety, probably not heroin, but enough of the rest that she hadn't even really finished 8th grade and going to high school in the first place was a sham. And 3. writing letters to B-Bass, or Bobby Saunders who had turned into Berto-SD in prison. He'd gone not for statutory rape but for leaving the state while on probation for statutory rape, which had been a plea deal, probably assisted by Trinity, as soon as she turned 16, asserting on an affidavit that they were going to get married. True, she'd been with him when he was picked up, returning to California from Nevada, but she'd been smart enough to waylay a marriage because her support checks, such as they were, wouldn't stop until she was 18, six months away. These days she just cashed the checks herself.

As to the mail, the postcards didn't come any less frequently after the one informing him of the marriage, and there was no discernable timetable, so he could *imagine* the frequency might be increasing. At first, after the marriage news, he'd hoped, begged her silently, that there wouldn't be any more. For a week he'd spent the first twenty minutes every day at the shop, until Cliff arrived, sitting in the dark listening to Dexter Gordon's "Where Are You?" and Coltrane's "Why Was I Born?" *Why do I want a thing I daren't hope for? / What can I hope for? I wish I knew.* (He knew the wallowing lyrics from the Ella Fitzgerald version.) But … he started to think …would she have told him she did it because of medical insurance just to spare him? And, if so, did it mean she cared? Why bother telling him at all? Was it a cosmic signal that they were in parallel perditions—of their own making—and shared knowledge was how they could go through life together? How would she answer if he asked her, he hadn't been able to conjure.

It was because of the postcards that it was best if he got to the mail first. Not that Virginia had ever particularly noticed one of them. Her increasing scrutiny of his dealings with any woman, anywhere, likely had nothing to do with 1 or 2 postcards a year. He was fairly certain he had, by some miracle, managed to get them out of the pile of mail before she saw them (probably because until Angel went to Kuwait, Virginia had little interest in the mail except when the support checks were due, and when she searched through the pile of junk and bills for the military envelopes, she cast aside everything else equally).

He wasn't sure what had ignited Virginia's mistrust, not that he didn't deserve it, considering his new thoughts about the postcards had increased the frequency of his alone-times at 2 or 3 a.m., as well as finding opportunity at the music store after-hours, even occasionally in the bathroom if he let Virginia go grocery shopping alone (which was a trade-off, accepting the danger of Virginia solo with an ATM card so he could be secluded with whatever the last postcard had said, which might take weeks to fully appreciate the nature of, but he was starting to get it).

Interesting, when he thought about it, that the first noticeable jealousy flare-up was during a make-over attempt. A make-over of *him* attempt. It sure seemed Virginia was trying to snuff out any sex appeal he might've still had, when she brought home parachute pants. On first sight, he realized they didn't get their name because they were baggy (like the pleated pants she'd tried to get him to wear a few years before), but because the material was a shiny, thin, nylon resembling what people thought parachutes might be made of. They also had seams in unusual places, and zippers everywhere, replicating the apparent complication of a parachute. And indeed they looked like they'd been packed away and sprung out of a little pouch for wearing because the material was naturally full of wrinkles and creases. The pair Virginia bought were metallic silver, more like the thin veneer of an astronaut suit than a parachute. The zippers were all red. One zipper looked like it would sever the pants at the knee. Some had no purpose other than to accentuate the crotch, three on each thigh, set at angles all pointing up and in. She was holding the pants by each side of the waist, extended toward him, as though putting them onto a paper doll.

He said, "I'm not wearing those. Take them back."

"But they were on sale. And they're in style, Trinity has them too, and as soon as I lose a few pounds, I'm—"

"Then you can have these."

"I might want red ones. We'd be so styl'n, Babes. Hit the clubs together."

"Clubs?"

"C'mon, let's liven things up. Maybe I can help shape your hair—you can grow a mullet."

"Weren't you worried about how soon I'll be bald?"

"But that's exactly *why*, you still have thick hair in back."

"So you want me to look like Benjamin Franklin?"

"Is that what you're saying *I* look like without—?" She dropped her arms, thrashing the pants downward, as though cracking a whip.

"I didn't mean that."

She probably didn't hear him. If she had, it couldn't deter what was brewing. "Oooo, all the little chicanas, dancing for the *sax*man, you have your pick of the flock, don't you?" When she threw the parachute pants, they did actually seem to float a little longer than jeans would have.

"What are you talking about?"

"I saw that slutty girl dancing in front of you at the last gig." Virginia put both hands at the sides of her head—holding still the long, dark hairdo of her wig—closed her eyes, pursed her lips into an inflated kiss and started a boom-chicka motion with her hips. "You likey the chicana girls to dance for you? Dey jiggle dey hips and bounce dey boobies. All for the *sax*man." She was trying to use some kind of accent, which sounded like what people might think was Caribbean.

He said, "My last gig was a retirement— Wait, How did we get from kids' pants to *this*?"

At once her voice was a screech. "Admit it, you don't *want* to look good for me!" The pants weren't so far away—they'd landed on the sofa as though sitting there watching the show—that she couldn't reach them in one motion and use them to start whipping. "It's exactly like they said, if you don't want it at home, exposed facto: you must be getting it somewhere else." The zippers stung like shotgun pellets on his arms. (Not that he'd ever been shot.) He caught the flailing pants and hung on. He'd seen this enough times happening in Trinity's bedroom, he knew the kicks came next, not aimed, but just because her arms were occupied trying to wrestle the pants away from him. He pulled her closer, managed to get his hands onto her upper arms, feeling the thuds against his legs, but willed himself to collapse onto the sofa—it was like he weighed 300 pounds and was having a seizure while trying to lower his body into a sit—but when he got there, Virginia was there beside him, the pants a wad between them, his hands now holding her wrists, her breath coarse. This was pre-tears.

"I seen them dancing for you. I seen them looking at you."

"But doesn't it matter that I haven't noticed *them*?" If it even took place the way Virginia had assumed and concluded.

"You play with your eyes shut."

"Yes. I know." And he knew who he was 'noticing,' behind his eyelids, as *she* made her way through darkness, around silhouettes of heads at tables, shadowy clumps of people with clinking glasses or smoke rising in empty dialogue bubbles above their heads.

"*I* used to dance in front. You noticed *me*. But now …" Virginia tipped her neck over the back of the sofa—the impending tears would pool in her eyes, and then a mascara disaster.

"C'mon," he tried to rouse her. "Is all this because your birthday is coming up?"

Well, it did rouse her. "Right, bring up my age." She lifted her head, and he felt her jerk, trying to lift one or both arms, but he was still holding her hands, that is her balled fists, his fingers in a ring around each wrist. "Is that what you're telling me? That you're still in your early 30s and I'm over … That I've gotten so old, you can't …"

He watched the red blotches fade from her cheeks and neck before he tried an answer. "Virginia, it's not … Life gets … you know, so full of what you have to do to just keep going."

"You're telling *me*. Sometimes I just want to spend all day in bed in the feeble position."

Sometimes Cal felt like a straight man, not supposed to laugh when the audience does. But he understood how she felt, more than she knew, or would ever know if he could help it. "If you feel that way, then do it."

"Who's going to cook your dinner, make your lunch, do your laundry?"

"I can do them myself."

"That's a bad-faced lie. When have you ever— You just said your plate's half empty."

"Half *empty*?" Cal felt a smile. "Not with your cooking. I *want* it piled high." True, cooking for himself was a lie. Why would he replace what she put on his plate with bowls of cereal or bologna sandwiches? He assessed it was okay to let go of her hands.

"You know what I *mean*." Virginia pulled the pants out from where they had become twisted between them, held them up by the waist. "Trinity might fit these. She might like new ones when she goes on family day next month."

Even though this was the first he was hearing about Trinity going to a visitor day at Susanville, a good 700 miles away, Cal didn't answer. Virginia had revved up and he gladly let her go. A chatter phase usually knocked out any (or any more) pending hysterics. "I swear, Babe, she's so excited, like it's Christmas eve. And making so many plans for being together when he gets out. Lists of ways to make herself better, schedules of how long to exercise, take care of her skin, study for her GED, what kinds of food to eat and not eat, jobs she could get or businesses she could start, lists, all kinds of lists, I saw them when I straightened up her room. She didn't move on to someone else when he was gone, she's sticking by him, no matter how far apart. Maybe it *is* true love." And then she sighed, as though spent.

"I guess we have no choice but to wait and see."

"Negative, always negative." Virginia stood and left the room, taking the pants. In a minute, he could hear her shaking them out, and it did sound like a flag—or a parachute—flapping in the wind.

He never saw Trinity wear the silver parachute pants, but that doesn't mean she didn't. It only means she didn't wear them to GED classes, which was almost the only time Cal saw her, when she got into the car, when she got out, and when he watched to make sure she walked through the gate and onto school property. Doors to the portable classrooms parked in two rows on a former dirt playing field all faced each other, so he couldn't see her actually enter a building. On her trek through the gate, toward the buildings, until she went out of sight between them, she never met up with or even talked to another person. Of course it was close to 3 in the afternoon, the flood of regular high school students who'd left school for the day was over, only those with after-school clubs or rehearsals remained, and they were busy.

(Sometimes Cal parked and went into the band room to pick up or deliver a few horns that had needed to be or had been repaired.)

He asked Trinity if she was going to finish in time and would she be allowed to march in graduation. Virginia had mentioned saving the date so they could go.

"It's not the *same* as graduating." The snotty lilt had become familiar, but usually succeeded to cutting a conversation short. "But, no," she added. "I won't have it by then."

"Isn't it a test that you get ready for and then take? Not credits you have to finish."

"Okay, so I *won't* be ready. You don't have to pretend like you care."

"Got it. I won't be someone who cares, I'll just play one on TV."

"Lame." Timed perfectly with her exit from the car, and walking away with the door still hanging open.

Cal let a hunch grow for a few days, maybe a week. Then, after Trinity disappeared between the buildings, he drove around the block to the other side of campus, slowly, next to the curb, and pulled up to the other gate just as Trinity was coming through and turning down the sidewalk, not in the direction of home. Could it be she didn't even notice? She didn't look and stop until Cal backed up in order to stay parallel with her. And at that point, instead of pausing, glaring, or cursing, she simply opened the door and got into the car.

"Busted." She was the one who said it. "Take me to jail."

"I'm taking you back to school."

"Don't bother. They don't even know I exist in there."

"I see." His foot pulsed on the throttle, letting the motor rev and wane, rev and subside.

"You can skip the lecture about did I look even a day into the future. I got it covered."

"Then why sneak around? Be brave enough to just quit without hiding."

"Haven't you learned anything yet? Why cause an inferno if I don't have to?"

The blather and exploding-laughter of a group of kids was approaching. Cal kept both hands on the wheel, looking straight ahead during the crescendo and culmination, suddenly curiously aware he appeared to be a 33-year-old man parked in a car with an unrelated 17-year-old, even though the current circumstances made him feel twice his age. Then the group passed and their voices dwindled. He said, "I would think she'll get over you not finishing high school easier than you trying to trick her into believing you did."

"Come *off* it, if she thinks it's such a big deal, she can go finish her own."

"She knows the mistakes she made. She doesn't want you making the same ones."

"Are you on crack? I can't believe you're trying the *it'll break your mother's heart* routine. Cuz it won't. Not since Angel got the boot."

Cal turned to look at her for the first time since she'd gotten back in the car. She was wearing overall shorts with one of the straps unhooked, making the top flap hang down at an angle, exposing the tube top she was wearing as a blouse. He looked away when he said, "What?"

"Oh, always last to know? *Dis*-honorable *dis*-charge." She made it a chant. "How's that for popp'n shit?"

Cal looked back at his hands and let them slip down around to the lower part of the wheel, then took and turned the keys, making the already-idling car screech. "Fuck." He didn't realize he said it out loud until Trinity laughed. Sitting still, windows up, it was getting hot, despite the thin stream of air conditioning. "Do you know why?"

"All's you have to do is know *him* and you know it's bad. And I don't think you ever did know the real Angel. What can they kick you out for? Drugs? Rape? Murder? Nothing would surprise *me*. But it also won't surprise me when Mom's party to welcome him home gets crank'n." It was the most she'd said to him at one time for months.

"No. No party." As though Trinity had asked if she could have one.

"If she does have one, can you take me to Susanville? We'll both get out of there."

He checked his mirror and pulled away from the curb. "We'll see."

Uncharacteristically, Virginia was at the open door, still behind the screen, as Cal walked toward the house. Naturally he wasn't expected home at 3:20. "You came early for din—" Then she must have seen Trinity, for some reason taking a long time to get out of the car. "Is she sick?" Virginia barely moved aside as Cal opened the screen and edged past into the house.

He didn't come up with an answer until he was already around the corner in the kitchen. "Ask her."

The screen rattled, then slapped, Trinity must have been in the foyer. Virginia said, "I'll call and get an extinction for your homework."

Even though out of their sight in the kitchen, Cal still turned away to hide a smile. Trinity, having gone the opposite direction, down the hall toward her room, called back, "All homework is extinct for me, Momsie."

"You finished!"

"Yay, let's have a party." Then the bedroom door slammed.

"I didn't know the test was today," Virginia came into the kitchen. "Or I guess must have been yesterday. Did she forget and think she had to go again today?"

Cal was looking at several days mail strewn on the table, which reminded him he'd forgotten to get today's before leaving with Trinity. He didn't see anything in any way related to the military. But why would they officially inform a discharged soldier's mother?

She touched his arm on her way to the sink. "Cal?"

"Oh, yeah. Something like that."

She ran some water, then turned it off. There were no dishes to be washed nor to be put away. The only things on the counter that didn't always live there were 5 or 6 liter bottles of soda. There was likely no room for them in the refrigerator or kitchen. She'd recently put a set of storage shelves in Angel's room to store supplies of food she bought on sale. Cartons of ramen soup mixes; flats of canned beans, tomato sauce, more soup; large boxes of cheese crackers and granola bars.

She pushed the soda bottles to the back of the counter. "So, what're you doing here?"

"I'm … tired." He slid the mail aside, spotting a department store bill as he did so. "I'm tired. Let's go to Yuma. Get some pie." He dropped his keys on the table and sat, taking the salt and pepper shaker in each hand.

"At 3:30?"

"By the time you get ready and we get there, it'll be after 5." After sprinkling some salt onto the table, then adding pepper, he swept it together, licked one finger, dabbed the pile, then put it into his mouth. He wondered if it might be a method to help him stop smoking. "We can get dinner first. Then pie."

She crossed her arms, then uncrossed them and put a hand on her hip. "Yuma isn't the only place we can get pie."

"But Yuma's not here. I think maybe we should be … not here. For a while."

"What? Why? Is something going to happen?" Then she made a strange squeal. "Is Trin's fiancé getting out and coming here?" She even clapped her hands twice before clasping them in front of her chest.

"Now he's a *fiancé?*"

"Is he coming?"

"Do you think I would put myself 60 miles away if that were happening?" He picked up his keys and stood. "Go on, get ready."

"If you're so tired, why do you want to drive 60 miles? We have a Denny's here."

His hand on the small of her back, a little pressure worked to start moving her out of the kitchen. "I just don't think you'll want the possibility of anyone we know being around when you tell me what's going on with Angel."

She stopped and spun, so sharply they almost collided. She was barely 6 inches away, almost eye-to-eye. "That's *my* business."

"If you expect him to live here, it's mine too." He didn't back up, or even lean backwards.

"Here you go with the *my* house *my* house." She broke eye contact and blitzed past him back into the kitchen. "And I suppose it's not people *we* know you're so worried about hearing, but *your* precious friends who you won't introduce me to."

"Who might those be?"

"*Might* be? Mr. High-talk. Mr. college-educated-works-in-a-music-store."

That time he didn't stay through it to the end, whatever kind of end there might have been. He went back to the store and taught the two private students he was going to blow-off in order to go to Yuma, then stayed until 10 working on woodwind re-pad jobs, the core of his shop's income. Before Cliff locked up at 9 and left, he told Cal that Virginia had been by the store during his lessons. Just came in, looked around, and left. Didn't even say Hi.

Cal was not surprised. He had come out between students for a smoke break around 4:30 and, standing in front of the store in the shade of the awning, had thought he saw Virginia's car, not in the parking lot but on a side street beside the strip mall. He asked if Cliff remembered who else had been in the store at that time. Cliff wasn't sure, maybe one customer, also probably the parent of Cal's student. He must have been busy with someone, Cliff said, because he didn't ask Virginia if she needed to relay a message or leave something for Cal, and she was gone by the time he wasn't engaged. The fact that Cliff felt he needed an explanation of this length told Cal the surveillance had been noted. Cal couldn't remember if he had greeted the student's mother inside the store then went outside to smoke alone, or if the woman and student had gone out the door at the same time he did. It was minutia and he didn't want to have to think about it during potential alone-time, but that's one reason why he went home at 10 instead of staying an extra hour.

Why haven't you sent a card in a while? I decided it's OK even if you're married. I can't give you up entirely. Even just one of those zoo postcards, and you only have to say Hi.

Don't you have to 'have' someone in order to 'give them up'? You must mean give up ON me. Dang, Cal.

1991

Virginia had mostly stopped coming to gigs, unless it was some sort of banquet where the band would get a free meal, and the other guys' wives were also coming. But he didn't blame her for not coming to most of his gigs. Blue Sand played the same sets every gig, who could be expected to listen to the same tunes time and again. And despite the occasional foray into Average White Band or Tower of Power, the band was all jazz standards and jazzed-up Latin folk, not Virginia's taste. Which had made for gigs with a different kind of alone-time.

She may pass through once or twice a year, visiting her parents in San Diego. One trip, she's held up by construction in the Colorado mountains and hits El Centro after dark. The motels beside the interstate cost more. More suited to her bohemian sensibility, the dumpier motels farther up Imperial Ave., with fewer palm and acacia trees, no patches of water-greened lawns, no coffee makers or free breakfast. There are a few close enough to Burgers-n-Beer that, while unlocking her door, she not only can smell the food but hear that there's live music and knows that it's not a garage band or mariachi. It's jazz. A bebop bass, comping guitar, and lamenting blues licks of a trumpet and saxophone. Saxophone. Cal's ax. Cal's voice. Cal's cry. She drops a dopp kit into the room and follows the riffs across an empty parking lot full of tumbleweeds, cans, trash, cigarette butts and condoms. Burgers-n-Beer's lot is crowded with jacked-up big-wheeled pickups and lowriders alike. She feels like a shadow floating between them, approaches the building on the side at the service door, where the busboys and waitresses enter for work, where the band hauls in the amps, speakers, stands, stools, and instruments. Right inside is the long hallway with doors to the storage room and restrooms before it hits the entrance to the kitchen, then opens into the bar and eating areas. Since it's after 10, the family dinner crowd is gone. Sure a few burgers still come out with pitchers of beer, but the lights are lowered and some of the tables pushed aside to make a small area for dancing. It's not really a dancing kind of bar, and the floor space is almost always empty. When she comes out of the hallway, she's not an already-seated guest returning from the restroom. She'll have to work her way around tables full of cowboy-hatted or baseball-capped guys, women and girls with big hair and spaghetti-strapped tops, smoking and draining mugs of beer. It's not really a jazz crowd. They talk, thump mugs and palms on the tables, even shout and squeal over the music, and seldom clap after a solo or final drum flam breaking off a last shmmering chord. She makes her way to where the pushed-together tables have empty chairs. Or maybe she doesn't even sit. She's dressed for travel in the desert, a plain black t-shirt and jeans. Is her hair still short? Yes, exposing her face and neck which catch the dim amber lights. But from where she stands, the sax player is eclipsed by shadows from the speakers mounted on stands. He's wearing black too. His horn a glowing diagonal slash across his body. His eyes are closed, stay closed through his poignant solo in "The Nearness of You," through the turnaround, back to the head, and then slowly open during the playout. Open directly into hers.

No need to go farther. Not during the gig, at least. He would replay her arrival and approach through every ballad. Then, later, when he crept into the dark, breathing bedroom at 1 a.m., undressed and rolled himself carefully onto the bed, stretched out on his back on a 2-foot strip at the edge of the king sized mattress, sheets bunched around his feet, eyes once again closed, he watched her move with a pleasure she's never known all the way through how he expressed to her the magnificence of his feelings, but which he knew were going to end in desolation, after he wiped himself with a washrag and absorbed all over again that she was somewhere else with someone else and he was alone. Or, worse, not alone. The soft snoring on the other far edge of the big mattress often didn't lose a beat, as though Virginia slept soundly on a rocking boat, or through an earthquake. He might offer to take her to breakfast in the morning, if she wasn't already frying bacon when he woke. The aroma pouring *some* kind of life back into him.

But gigs that offered any kind of reverie were becoming fewer. Virginia had started going to gigs again. As well as popping into the music store in the afternoons. Did it have anything to do with Angel getting home from the Army six months earlier? However it had come to pass, Cal had given him a job, of sorts, gathering and delivering instruments needing repair from far-flung schools. While the arrangement did allow Cal to expand the reach of his repair shop to 50, 75, 90 miles away, Niland, Blythe, even Yuma, Cal had to let Angel use his car (Angel's beater wouldn't have been able to make those trips), and Cal frequently didn't have time to check the mileage before and after. If no deliveries or pick-ups were eminent, Angel sometimes hung around the music store, but Cliff asked Cal to please keep Angel's time in the store to a minimum. Angel had had his lower lip pierced and wore a stud between his mouth and chin. His military hair had grown out and he used gel to make it look as greasy as possible. The jeans he wore everyday had more frayed holes than material, and he usually stank. Once he'd been lurking by the CD rack when Cal came out from a private lesson and spoke to the student's mother who was waiting. Cal immediately sent Angel to Brawley with two flutes that could have waited until Cal finished the clarinets, trumpets and a trombone that had also come from Brawley.

Not a half hour later, Virginia came into the store. "Can you take a break, Babe?"

He didn't have another student, so Cal took her to the burrito shop at the end of the strip mall and bought two sodas. While walking there, a car out on Imperial tooted, and Virginia waved. Cal didn't ask who it was, but Virginia said, "That's Trin, so glad she's getting out again."

"Did what's-iz-name get paroled?"

"They all look alike, huh? That what you saying?"

"I didn't *see* anyone, I just assumed, since she was so loyal to—"

"She couldn't be waiting for*ever*. She's young. She met Cedric up there, he was visiting his brother."

There was a single table outside the burrito shop, between the storefront and the cars pulled into the first row of the parking lot. Virginia waited there while Cal bought the sodas.

"You should get diet coke, Cal, you're getting a little pot there."

Cal turned his chair so he was at least halfway into a strip of shade and lit a cigarette.

"I'm glad the job for Angel is working out," Virginia said.

"Well, we'll see. I haven't run any numbers to see if it's losing me money."

"Losing *you* money, that's all you care about?"

"I imagine you enjoy having electricity and water, a house, groceries, nail salon—"

"All *right*, you can stop." She adjusted her huge barely-tinted sunglasses and sipped her soda. "But you can't even try to help a young man get his leg up without making sure there's a profit."

Cal puffed his cheeks as he blew out smoke, then kept blowing, tightening his stomach and facial muscles into an embouchure until he had no more air and felt his eyes popping. Only then did he inhale and say, "As I was saying, that so-called *profit* ... well, a little prophet is telling me we're going to have to cut down expenditures somewhere."

"You could bring your whole gig pay home if you don't drink so much beer." She wiped at sweat beginning to trickle at her temples.

Wigs were hot, he knew, and this time of day with the sun pushing west, the shade at the front of the strip mall was at a minimum.

"Did you want to talk about something in particular, or just craving a watered-down soda?"

"We don't spend enough time together."

He waited until a loud motorcycle passed. "Couldn't we talk about it at dinner instead of in the heat of the day on glaring pavement?"

"I wanted to see what keeps you at the store so late."

"It's four-thirty."

"But you get here at 7, sometimes 6, and don't come home til 6. Then go back after dinner." She used both palms on her forehead to wipe moisture. "Who's coming here to meet you?"

"I *work* here, Virginia. I'm trying to keep my— *our* heads above water." He crushed his cigarette on the bottom of his shoe. "Now, I've got to get back."

"You think I don't know what's going on? I know how young they are, those mothers whose spoiled babies lug violins and flutes in and out of this store. I've seen them. You think I haven't seen them? So I'm old in the tooth, and you've got a steady never-ending supply—"

"What are you talking about?"

"You tell *me*, Cal!"

"I have no idea."

"But you have plenty of ideas when they start showing up at your gigs."

"Who?"

"*You know who.*" She stood and threw the remainder of her soda and ice, hitting him in the chest.

Dang, Cal, isn't that like—
No, probably not.

In the valley, by at least May, weddings and quinceañeras moved indoors to air-conditioning. The last outdoor party to hire Blue Sand that year was at end of April. It wasn't as though Cal had failed to notice (or reflect on with the guys via either a few code words or exchanged facial expressions) that 15-year-old birthday-girls and 20-something brides had lots of friends their age who dressed to conquer for the parties. So why should he be surprised when Virginia started wanting to come to that kind of gig as well, when previously the gigs she had been attending were at least holiday banquets or fund-raisers, where not having been invited didn't matter as much.

He kept his sax in his mouth and his eyes on his charts—or closed, but wouldn't have been able to run his nightclub chimera anyway, what with it being sunny and in the 90s, plus Virginia seated at a pirated table just off the band's right flank. Between sets he sat at the table with her and smoked, sometimes 2 cigarettes, sucking in and blowing out, telling her he needed to *veg-out* (a term Virginia had started using recently) when she asked him if he wanted to dance to the tunes played by a DJ hired to provide music during the band's breaks. More people danced *during* the band's breaks because the recorded music wasn't jazz.

There were plenty of rock, country, Latin pop and mariachi bands in the valley, why did people hire the only jazz combo? Cliff was a businessman, active in the Chamber-of-Commerce, and well-off parents of brides and 15-year-olds were frequently businessmen too. Plus, of course, jazz was *classy*. An assumption based on elitism as well as a history of white land owners, even in a town on the professional rodeo circuit and 20-miles from a huge cosmopolitan state capitol city in Mexico. *That* was part of a conversation he imagined having with someone, if that someone had asked him why a quinceañera would want jazz for music, or why people didn't dance to "How High the Moon," "On the Sunny Side of the Street" or "Ain't Misbehavin."

But Virginia didn't ask that, she just asked Cal if he wanted to dance to "Ladies Night" or worse, "Can't Touch This."

Admittedly, Cal was bushwhacked by uncharacteristic optimism when Angel—during the few minutes he was allowed by necessity to wait in the shop for the instruments he would be delivering that day—started asking questions about what made a particular instrument worth the cost of the repair. With private instruments, Cal would telephone the owner to let them know the estimate before he started the repair. *Is this worth fixing?* and *why?* then became recurrent questions. And Cal answered. "That's only a 4 or 5-hundred dollar clarinet—I'm about to put at least a hundred-fifty bucks into it. They might want to sell it as-is and upgrade to a better instrument."

It hadn't gotten to the point where he broached an upbeat conversation with Virginia about Angel taking an interest in instrument repair or running one's own business. Perhaps if he had, and if he'd been lucky enough that Trinity overhead it, he'd have gotten the wake-up call from *that* unlikely source instead of where it eventually came from.

Trinity had been furious that Angel had been given "such an easy" job but she hadn't. There'd been a shrieking scene. "I think the shit he did to get kicked out of the army should be worse than making my own decision to just quit something that was totally useless," was one of only two complete and coherent sentences he'd heard. Maybe the reason Virginia hadn't backed Trinity up and come to Cal to give Trinity a job *was* the screaming, plus the trademark flinging and shredding of objects, and this time in the kitchen so the 'objects' were Virginia's cooking tools, even her new electric griddle set up on a counter and cooking hamburgers—wrecked, as were the burgers, when it crashed off the front of the stove and ricocheted to the floor.

Afterward, Virginia, crying, had washed off the burgers and put them in a frypan. Then Cal had brought the griddle to the shop to try to repair it. The second sentence he remembered from the fight was also from Trinity, "It's so *bogus*, how can you *totally* favor someone who either fucks or steals from anything in range?" But most of why he remembered it was that Virginia had said, as she washed and re-cooked the burgers, "I just don't like how she uses the fuck-word," and he'd told Cliff because, well, maybe it was easier to share the humor in Virginia's speech-stumbles than to actually think about what Trinity had said. He realized that, but a little too late.

The cops who stopped Angel for DUI between 2 and 3 a.m. found musical instruments in the trunk. The two trumpets, two trombones and a baritone were not in cases, but each had a sticker indicating it belonged to the Calexico School District. Cal didn't hear that part until a band teacher from Calexico called the shop to tell him that the police had contacted the school about the instruments. The band director had declined to press charges because he needed the instruments back right away, but told Cal he'd been about to call anyway because the repaired instruments delivered just a day or two before had included empty cases. "I thought you'd just had a brain fart and forgot to put the horns back in the cases, but I guess you've got bigger problems than memory," the guy chuckled.

The license suspension alone meant the instrument-repair pick-up and delivery was also suspended. Cal dropped Angel from the car insurance policy he'd had to maintain because of the delivery-service. Cliff had already advised and helped Cal make his repair shop an LLC, to protect his personal assets from liability. But the blow came when private customers came looking for their instruments, and Cal couldn't find either the instrument or the invoice proving it had been there in the first place. Those complaints were still trickling in weeks, even months later, as people found their copy of the repair order lying somewhere and realized they'd never heard from the shop that the horn was ready. It came to about 8 or 9 instruments that had seemingly walked off in the night. Or, more likely, while Cal was teaching private lessons in the afternoons.

Each time he had to pay someone for a lost horn, he came home, told Virginia, then walked away before she could reply. He still watched *Home Improvement* with her, still said "thank you" after eating dinner and lunch before going back to the shop. Still said "good night" if they went to bed at the same time, or when she went in before him. Still gave her the ATM card when she went to the grocery store, still asked if she wanted coffee when he made a pot in the evening, still answered when she asked what time he might be home or when was his next gig, even if the answer was *I don't know.*

> *Dang, why don't you just leave?*
>
> *You're not the only one to say that. I don't know.*
>
> *Cop-out, Cal.*
>
> *Okay … maybe I don't believe someone should just say 'I do until I don't.'*
>
> *What a monumental pile of bullshit! Were your precious vows to stand by her criminal druggie spawn? Did you vow to let them all drain you of blood and spirit, let alone money?*
>
> *I'm not bleeding, she's never broken skin.*
>
> *You fucking know what I mean.*
>
> *Okay … yes, there's been some shit I didn't think was part of the bargain, Did I expect her to be able to hold a job? Yes, but … aren't I provided a basic comfort level, despite the chaos? And didn't I misrepresent what I brought to the table?*

I know it hurts her that I have no interest in her for … you know … I only want
that with you.

    Man , all I can say—
    I know, dang, cal.

It was October when he paid for what he hoped was the last of the stolen horns, three months after Angel's DUI. "Another one came in today. Another five-hundred." He didn't know why, maybe the smell of the oil starting to warm for tacos dorados, but he stayed in the kitchen instead of immediately withdrawing. Although he did keep moving, pacing a five-foot span behind Virginia, toward the kitchen doorway and back. "So far, I've had to reimburse over five thousand for those missing horns."

    She pushed the pan off the burner and turned. "Can't you check the pawn shops?"

    "A little late for that."

    "I've been trying to suggest it, you wouldn't listen."

    "When do you think I'm going to have time do that? Every pawn shop in a hundred mile radius? You want to help out and do it? Be my guest. Who knows, maybe a few will turn up."

    "Well …" she was tapping something on the counter, a spoon or knife. "I don't really have time either."

    "I see." Cal's pacing was at a point when he was heading toward the kitchen doorway leading to the foyer and hallway toward the bedrooms. He could've kept going and would have been out of the kitchen. But he turned and continued the back-and-forth route.

    Virginia replaced the pan on the glowing burner. "It's Angel's community service. You want him driving himself there with no license?"

    "I hear his car come and go at night while you're sleeping. Who's driving him then?"

    The oil in the pan was muttering. "He has to get to his new job."

    Cal stopped his pace. "No, Virginia, I'm not biting." He pulled a chair out from the table as though to sit, but didn't sit. "Quit the lying and covering. He doesn't have any job. Unless he's selling drugs."

"*Don't* you accuse him—" The pan rattled when she pushed it off the burner again. "You're so *selfish*, not everyone was born biting a silver bullet like you. Just because he makes a mistake time and time again?"

"*I'll* say. And this *mistake* was a doozie. You should thank me for not pressing charges."

"*Thank* you? After you fired him and didn't even pay his bail—"

"And he's got a month to find some other place to live."

"You can't do that. Where's he gonna *go*, what's he gonna *do*?"

Cal reached for a bag of tortilla chips on the table and ripped it open, splitting the bag down the side. "*Shit.*" Chips exploded onto the table, but he kept the torn bag in his hand. "Don't you realize when I have to repay customers to the tune of five thousand dollars, or more, that it's money from *our* income?" The chip bag crackled as he gestured with it. "Our food, our mortgage, our cars ... he would *do* that—steal from his own mother, he's willing to fuck his mother, you know that? Know what that makes him? He's a mother-fucker is what he is, a *mother-fucker.*"

She made some kind of sound, there was some kind of clatter, he flinched, more chips spewed into the air, and the frypan whizzed past him nearly noiselessly before landing upside-down on the rug in the foyer without hitting anything, even the kitchen doorway. A shiny spattered path of oil splotched the linoleum.

"You made me do that – *you* can clean it up."

But Cal was already leaving. He paused only a second before stepping over the pan, then veered toward the front door instead of the bedrooms. Usually when he left, he left in silence, even if walking away from a tempest. But this time, the storm continued blowing at his back, and since he hadn't bothered to close the solid door, it continued through the screen door as he got into the searing furnace inside his car. "*Sonofabitch, you come back here, don't you dare walk away from me, asshole, bastard, get back here ...*" The seal of the car door snuffed the rest. The neighbor, across the street, was sitting in the shade of a tattered tarp. Cal could often smell carne asada, eggs, beans and tortillas wafting over when that neighbor cooked breakfast outside early Sunday mornings. The neighbor waved as Cal pulled out of his driveway.

A year ago, maybe two, Cal and Virginia had been visiting Cal's parents in their new mobile home in San Diego. In the guest bedroom, which was the last room in the long square tube that made up the house, Virginia had been upset that Cal didn't want to go with her to pick up some of her belongings still stored at her brother's house. Virginia's brother had requested that she come get the boxes, which Cal suspected consisted of clothes that wouldn't fit anyone anymore, even if wearing five-year-old styles were acceptable to the former wearers, which they wouldn't be. He hadn't actually said he wouldn't go, but that if he did, he'd be stopping at the closest Goodwill to drop off the boxes. In reality he'd told his father he would help change his car's oil while Virginia was running an errand, then they had to head back to the valley. By the time Virginia was screaming, it was too late to remind her what the walls of a mobile home were made of. *Asshole* was her favorite, but there were enough *sonofabitch*'s and *bastard*'s as well. He remembered being thankful that *fuck*, and *prick* were among the words forbidden by her church, even when she was revved up and spiraling. When he'd left the room and made his way outside, he found his father watering potted plants just outside the wall of that bedroom. He'd stood beside his father for a minute, then said, "I guess I won't be able to help with your car this time."

"Gotta do whatcha gotta do," had been his father's reply.

He didn't smoke inside the music store, even in his shop, so he stopped at the park, the one where he'd found Trinity when Virginia had kicked her out. He trudged to the table Trinity and her cohorts had been using that time, still strewn with fast-food trash as though it had been untouched ever since. Early evening, late afternoon, whatever 6-ish in the desert could be called, still over 90 degrees in October, the table was in the shade, and no one else stupid enough to be using the park until after dark. But long before that, Cal was gone. He drove to a taqueria for food and a soda. That's where he saw Trinity, in the donut shop next door with her new boyfriend. Cal left quickly with his tacos in a sack. The only car in front of the donut shop was a black Impala, the back seat crammed with what looked like paper grocery bags of clothes, stereo speakers, a microwave oven, and boxes of other small items.

He ate at his shop, then re-strung the valves of a French horn, a job he hated and had been putting off. He saw few French horns and didn't feel he was a good enough technician to handle them, considering he hadn't been trained at an instrument-repair school and was uncertified.

When he got home, the light in the foyer was on and there was a large wet place in the carpet where the pan had been lying. Even after the carpet shampoo dried, the oil stain still showed. Virginia tried the rug shampoo 3 or 4 more times, but the stain barely diminished. The fund for new carpet, or even another go at professional cleaning, was long gone.

Every day, going out the door, and then coming back in, the grease spot mysteriously triggered the quandary: shouldn't he find a time to *not* avoid sex? Would it preempt her suspicions or make the two of them a more united front regarding Angel's activities? Putting it off, or avoiding, had become so engrained, that he actually wasn't having to do or say much of anything anymore. *The kids'll hear* no longer applicable, since neither Trinity or Angel was home between 9 p.m. and or 2 a.m. But since Cal didn't come home until 10 or 11 p.m., Virginia was usually already asleep. He was up before her too. She got her full 8, but Cal could take care of the lawn, sweep the sidewalk and water by 7, come in with every fiber of cotton on his body drenched. She'd be in the kitchen by then; he'd take a shower, come back out for breakfast, then off to the shop. The gears worked, and the days fell away like dominos. Except when the suspicion monster was fed (by whom? Angel? Her friends at the hand-waving church?) or another incident involving one of the kids, usually Angel (often Trinity and Virginia were barely speaking). Angel had almost totaled his beater (although he continued to drive it with no insurance), disappeared for 3 days and told his mother he'd been detained in Mexico, and one of the neighbors had made an official noise-complaint after Angel and a friend spent several hours after midnight in his car in the driveway playing a new stereo they'd spent some time installing (Cal had to park on the street when he came home, and wasn't able to move his car into the garage until the next day when he came home for dinner, even though he'd asked Angel to move his car the night before and asked

Virginia to ask Angel to move the car when it was still in the driveway the following morning.) Angel said the neighbor who'd made the complaint would be sorry. That's when Cal had finally told him he had a month to move out, and in the ensuing altercation Virginia tried to flush Cal's car keys and wallet down the toilet. That was over a month ago, and Angel still occupied the bedroom slated to become Cal's music room. His saxophones had to be kept at the shop, lucky survivors of Angel's pillage, considering the tenor alone was worth five grand. Cal thought he might have once told Virginia that number but supposed it shouldn't be something he mentioned again.

I'm sorry, I have to, pounded in his temples like a tune trapped in his head, at his workbench, after the store was closed, during *alone-time*. He said it to her postcards, which he kept there in a drawer under scraps of cork sheets. He didn't have a photograph. He didn't need one. He said it to the sideways look she might give him, and the way she would say *Dang, Cal, who are you apologizing to ... or for?"*

It feels like cheating.

Isn't it what happens when people are married? You must know I'm not a virgin.

You don't love me, so it's not cheating for you ... even though I don't like to think about you doing it with someone else. I wanted to only feel it with you. Even if you're ... even though ... even when you're ... somewhere else.

I've been tryna tell you it doesn't do anything for me anyway.

I'm sorry about that. For you. I wish I could help. I know I could help.

The sad smile, the dull glaze in her eyes before her gaze dropped away from his, the heartbeat of silence before her eyes returned, the almost imperceptible shrug. He finished before he'd slid the straps of her tank top down over her shoulders.

But felt he should apologize, again, remembering he would have to do it, next time Virginia brought it up. He tried to explain again, while he had a cigarette, outside the closed-and-locked music store:

Sometimes I can tell it's coming because she's been crying. Or if she's still up when I get home. She might have a story about one of her friends dissing her, not being invited somewhere, her sister receiving a surprise delivery of flowers while at work. She wants to be hugged. I know it. Sometimes I manage it beside her, sideways, one arm across her shoulders for a few seconds, the usual EVERYTHING'LL-BE-OKAY *bullshit. If that doesn't snuff it, the next thing will be her hand on the back of my neck when she takes my plate after dinner or my coffee mug after some TV show is over, then comes back from the kitchen and uses both hands, starts to massage my shoulders. Even though it does feel good, I don't let it go on too long. That would be too much using, too much one-way-street, too obvious. I usually get up and go outside for a cigarette. I know I should quit. But, really, WHY? Maybe it'll all be over sooner if I don't. When I go back inside, she'll be done with the dishes, if I was on a dinnertime break. I can either go back to the shop, or find some work outside. I'll be so sweaty and tired when I come back inside, instant sleep will be more honest, and defensible. I want every time to be for you. But I know I can't hold off forever. Things are getting too hot. Not in a good way. It might defuse some of the poison. Some of the rage. Some of the fear. No, I'm not afraid. Not of her. Not really. The money ... the kids ... what does it really matter? So why do I have to appease if I'm not afraid? Just so it's all at least neutral... until it's over. It's just not easy to make it easy. To do the thing required. You know? Maybe it's the same for you. If I'm reading you right, it's similar. Believe me, though, I don't want to. I have to.*

It didn't take long, which at least made the sick anticipation shorter. Virginia used a different signal, a new one. Saturday evening, before Cal went back for a stint at the shop, she told him she was making huevos rancheros Sunday morning, so plan to sleep in and let the aroma awaken him. (That's when she told him she'd been taking the cooking classes they'd bought Trinity for her birthday.) But it wasn't an aroma that woke him. Virginia put his *Stan Getz with Oscar Peterson* tape, which had been in his car, on a portable player, and came into the bedroom with it playing. When he opened his eyes, the tape player was on the floor by his nightstand. Stan was still playing the head of "I Want to Be Happy." He didn't see Virginia. But almost immediately felt the bed jiggle as she got on from the other side, then moved up against him.

"No one's home but us," she whispered. He was on his side. Her hand crept under his top arm and onto his stomach. Just muscles and nerves reacting, like an anemone, the curl of his body closed, his knees tucked up higher. She started kissing the back of his neck. Two choices were: squirming sideways and falling off the bed, or turning backwards and flailing to knock her away with an elbow. He remained static. Now the mantra was *get it over with, get it over with.* Her hand was pushing its way down below his stomach. His tight fetal position blocked access. But how long could that last? This could easily end in a completely different kind of exchange if she got her hand on him, found him flaccid, and then it stayed that way even after she started fondling. It was imminently obvious what he had to do.

He rolled slowly, dislodging her arm and hand. Then, face to face, she could move her kissing to his mouth. He opened his lips enough but didn't use his tongue—he never had with her, he knew what she would consider his m.o. in that department. Likewise there was never any touching breasts, sucking nipples, he hadn't ever even encouraged complete undressing. Probably the first time, the time that was supposed to be the only time, he'd been so horny he was raging and ready simply because of the unexpected opportunity, the shots he'd downed, the weed, the whole stranger-sex mystique. And of course he'd been more like 23. Now, what, 34, nearing 35? It's been only a dozen years of this? And his body is already like a 60-year-old?

His own hand pushed down to his crotch to do what was needed to get hard. And tried to do it without her knowing what he was doing. In fact, it seemed the rhythm, the motion *wasn't* familiar to her. Apparently she really did sleep through it, those times he'd been too lazy to get up and go into some other dark room at 3 a.m. for an alone-time session. Even odder, or maybe fortunate but he didn't feel very lucky right now, the position of her pelvis was such that the back of his hand was coming in contact, and she grinded herself there, assuming that was his goal.

She started vocalizing softly. He was taking longer to get it up than he was accustomed. He needed an image, a story to follow. But it seemed so wrong to bring X here, now, into this. Wrong to X, not to Virginia. Although wouldn't her suspicions then be *virtually*, even if not literally, true? Like that virtual reality thing some kid was babbling about in his music lesson. Virginia could put on a special headset and earphones and get the virtual sensation that he was actually making love to someone else.

This kind of thought stream wasn't helping. But his dick knew his hand, and something was happening. In his bathroom drawer he'd stashed some condoms when he'd starting knowing the time was coming. Not to prevent pregnancy—Virginia had both tubes tied now—but to prevent evidence that he wouldn't finish. He had to get a condom on without her realizing what he was doing. He gasped, "Just a sec, my bladder's bursting," and he surged out of the bed, into the bathroom. He did pee, because she would hear if he didn't, then worked a little while longer with an image of X when they were 16 that he hadn't brought up in this kind of situation for a while. That worked to get to the point where the condom went on. He added some lubricant, then returned to the bed where, thankfully, Virginia had rolled to her back, so moving to the final stage was not only accessible, it would've been too weird if he didn't.

Propped up on his arms, eyes shut, he realized he'd been counting his thrusts when numbers in the 30s were pounding in his head. He consciously counted into the 40s and decided it was enough. Breathing a little more rough, he stopped moving, tensed his body, let his head drop and hang. He stayed still, again found himself counting, and this time when he got to twelve, he withdrew. Removed himself from the bed as well, returning to the bathroom to wad the condom in some toilet paper and discard it. She had no reason to paw through the trash, but he'd had enough foresight to realize that using a condom would suggest protecting her from things picked up in the trysts she imagined. So he was still in his underwear out in the garage emptying the bathroom trash into the big container, even tying off the bag, when Virginia came to the kitchen to start huevos rancheros, which turned out pretty damn good.

~~August~~ November 1991,

Hot enough for you? Haha. (OK, wrote that in Aug and now it's now.) Shit happens, ya-know? What I didn't know was shit = life. Some people use movies to get away. True, so many movies *aren't* about the shit of life, so ... escape, right? But dang, so much menace, carnage, grief - how does that work? Even comedies, someone's getting hurt and it's supposed to be funny (except when it's so-called funny that someone's not getting any.) The world's worst "story" is that someone dies. I decided to not see any more movies where someone is mean to anyone else, especially if anyone dies.   X

Post Card

Cal Tonnessen
7512 W San Diego Ave
El Centro CA 92243

1992-1994

So after getting married, it seems not much happened. It would make some kind of blow-by-blow (haha!) autobiography, but not a memoir. Just trained the dogs, did well at shows, the dogs earned high rankings, met a few clients weekly, by reputation (and referral) attracted more of them, studied some (mostly about animal behavior) but went to training seminars, sometimes wondered why things were the way they were "at home" (i.e. Blaine went out for lunch every day and never wanted dinner). But certain things should have needed no wondering, had a lot clearer implication: The first dog was almost 12. For some dogs that isn't long enough to say it was a good life, that it was old age, that the animal used up every day it had coming. Sure there was more than one dog in the household by the time it happened, and the oldest was retired and wasn't the one that really set a reputation, but … "*just* a dog"? Really? That's how you show support to your wife? (Dang, *that* ugly word too. *Partner*? But when was it ever that?) And why didn't those three too-wretchedly-common words *just-a-dog* get her off her ass and out the door back then when it wouldn't have mattered as much, financially, seeing that he had no idea what, if anything, was important to her, since they were already sleeping in separate bedrooms, purportedly because she crashed earlier, got up earlier, and he snored. He didn't like someone else's skin touching his while he slept. While he fucked, either. (Which, needless to say, was mercifully less and less frequent, because, after all … why bother?)

She actually told her sister—the one called "Girly" by their grandfather—that she'd never had an orgasm. How would that come up in conversation? During holiday-washing-the-dishes banter, for whatever reason (not the scullery duty) "Girly" said "Enough's enough already!" So it was easy to echo that phrase and add the punch line from the Seinfeld episode where Elaine tells Jerry she faked all the orgasms she had with him. *Yeah, enough's enough and I just want to get some sleep.* So since "Girly" hadn't watched Seinfeld, the episode had to be described: Jerry is devastated (does a man actually *care*?) Elaine laughs and says it wasn't his fault, *I just didn't have them then*.

"When does someone usually start?"

"Well, it partly *is* the fault of the dumb men you've been with," sister *Girly* proclaimed.

Yeah. There was this boy. He did everything wrong. Except one night he was doing everything right. And she didn't even know it.

Chapter Five
Five Exclamation Points

November 1992
I know you wouldn't say <u>just</u> a dog.
Why do good things have to die? Like
the part of my body that's always
been dead. Damn, sorry, it was my
first time, standing there holding the
still-warm body while poison is
injected. Part of the deal, the
partnership, the 'agreement' - "you
won't die alone, you won't be in pain."
No meds for the guilt afterwards: did
I do enough, did I try, was it money
that stopped me? Is 12-years-old
enough to give up? Otherwise, news: I
have a Sat morn call-in show on
local NPR. Big whoop! (God, look, an
exclamation point. Here, have a few
more !!!!!)   X

PLACE
POST CARD
POSTAGE
HERE

D23422

Post Card

Cal Tonnessen
7512 W San Diego Ave
El Centro CA 92243

1993

As though it was a New Year's resolution, Virginia was at the shop at least once a week. She usually swept and dusted workbenches while he taught a private lesson, although he asked her to stop cleaning the work surfaces because he couldn't find screws or pads he'd set aside to put an instrument back together. At first he didn't notice her visits were during the same private lesson, a promising 7th grade clarinetist. He'd been teaching her for about two years. Lessons were only a half hour, her mother always somewhere in the store when he finished, so he walked with the girl to where her mother might be flipping through CDs, or just waiting in one of the chairs provided for parents just inside the door where brochures for new instruments or rentals were displayed. He might suggest a new method book, a new type or thickness of reed, or just tell the girl's mother how unusual it was to have a student so young practice so diligently. And then Virginia began to always be there too, saying something like, "How's the wonderkid this week?" or "She'll be ready for Blue Sand soon, won't she?"

When the student and her mother were gone, Virginia followed Cal back to his repair shop. "No smoke-break?" she asked. Her voice somewhat dry. Cal didn't get it. Yet.

"Too busy here," he said. "Look, I appreciate you coming down and cleaning up, especially the floor but—"

"Well, it's filth on top of filth, as usual."

"I guess. But could you check the dust-pan for screws before you dump it?"

"You could get a shop-vac." She picked up a trumpet mouthpiece from the workbench.

"I have one but I don't use it if I'm missing screws," keeping his eye on her hand, in case she reared back to throw the mouthpiece, "Which I almost always am since I can't keep anything straight anymore."

"OK, so don't gripe about me helping out." The brass mouthpiece pinged when she set it down, hard.

"I just thought you might have other things you need or want to do." He moved the mouthpiece to a shelf on his other side, but there were plenty of other objects in her reach. "I mean, if not, maybe someone would pay you to clean up for them."

"Are you suggesting all I could ever *be* is a maid of some sort?"

"No, but—"

"I know what could happen." Virginia's tone shifted toward the way she'd sounded in front of the student and parent. (He would call it *girlish*, except .) "You could give me Angel's old job."

He was still halfway thinking about what the term *girlish* really meant, if X never sounded or acted any of those ways, so he barely heard Virginia continuing, "It would be fun, working together, building a business as a team."

But he caught up to where this was going. "Wait, no—that wasn't a real job, just sort of an … some kind of experiment that basically went horribly wrong."

"Always so *negative.*" Her hands flew up, but didn't seize or strike anything. "Admit it, you don't want me around because you can't continue your *thing* with that woman."

His adrenaline flashed. Woman? Had she seen a postcard lying around his shop?

"Um ... what?"

"You and that woman who was just here, with the cute little girl. You know, the same way *I* was when we met."

"You can't really think—"

"Can't I?"

"I'm after little girls?"

"I don't know, *mothers* of girls? Who knows what turns you on, Cal. *I* certainly don't."

She doesn't know what turns you on, or she doesn't turn you on?

No, X would never say that ... and of course he didn't say it either.

"I saw that woman at a gig, Cal. Okay? I *saw* her. What was she doing there? Did you invite her? Didn't know I would be coming, or didn't care? Because you could secretly exchange looks, she could dance for you, you could play for her, where does it end?"

She was loud enough now, anyone shopping in the music store would be able to hear. Cliff might appear in his doorway soon, with a joke or fake message. Which might be enough to back Virginia down from whatever she was building toward. Her hands on her hips, then crossed over her chest, then up into her hair (which she could do without knocking her wig askew).

"I can't control who comes to gigs. It's a small town." His hand on the small of her back, he moved Virginia toward the doorway. "Calm down. You're upset over nothing." The fabric of her shirt was damp, as though steam was coming off her. "Maybe getting some sort of job would give you a new target to focus on." Thankfully the store was empty of customers or parents. She was allowing herself to be guided toward the front door. Cliff must have been hiding in his office.

"I'm trying to raise my kids, not that I have any *help.*"

"The kids are adults now. You've done all you could. It's up to them—"

"Never up to you, right Cal? Nothing's ever *your* responsibility."

"Running this shop, making a living, okay? Let me do it." Then, outside on the sidewalk, he even pecked a kiss on the top of her head (or her wig) as he removed his hand (with a slight push) toward her car, which was parked in the closest space, supposedly reserved for customers.

When he got home later, he waved to the elderly woman next door who frequently needed help doing anything that required two hands. The woman was on her front porch beside a dead tree in a pot. Instead of waving back, she went into her house and slammed the front door.

The following day, Virginia had an idea for a job. She showed him the *Work at Home* ad in the back of a *National Enquirer*. "Please, Virginia, why do you waste money on this trash?"

"It's one I already had. The ads are always the same. Look, all I do is buy a starter kit, then I get paid to stuff envelopes in my spare time."

"Why not go apply for actual jobs that you do in your ... prime time."

"I'm running a household here!"

"Okay, but part time jobs could be 4 hours in the evening. And you wouldn't have to *pay* to get the job."

"What about uniforms, or the gas to get there, or the right kind of shoes. People pay for stuff for a job all the time."

"Fine, spend the ten bucks to get started, you'll see."

What Virginia got back in the mail was instructions on how to place the same ad herself and get people to send her ten dollars for a starter kit. But she would have to pay for that ad, and for a batch of the instructions to mail, plus buy her own envelopes and stamps—and those would be the envelopes she would be preparing, thus technically the ad didn't lie. If someone responded to her ad to get the starter kit, that was how she would be paid for stuffing envelopes at home.

"So they just keep my ten dollars that I sent for this?"

"I guess so."

"Well, then wouldn't I be getting lots of payments of ten dollars that *I* would just keep?"

"Except you've paid for an ad, for envelopes, for Xeroxing the so-called starter-kits, for postage." He went through it three or four times, using monopoly money to show her how she would probably be spending more than she could hope to get back, even looking up the price chart for advertising in the local newspaper.

The next day she told him a friend at church was a "distributor" for a brand of candle and incense that "improve emotional health and promote mental stamina and focus " (she read from a brochure). This friend was hiring her on as a salesperson, but it would be her own business, giving home aroma-therapy parties.

"How much?" He hadn't yet put his nylon backpack down and was still holding the mail.

"Wow," she laughed, "my first customer so easily!"

"I meant how much do you have to pay *her*."

"Nothing. I just buy my inventory—what I'll be selling—and a video with pointers how to give the parties. And—" She pursed her lips.

"And what?"

"Well, some of the other equipment can wait. They have this satellite so you can communicate directly with the home company."

"But your friend is the distributor, why do you need the home company?"

"For product updates. Like you have to find out about new ... I don't know, flutes?"

"Oh Virginia, what do you have against a timecard?"

"*You just want me out of the house!*" The brochure didn't fly far despite her arm's heave.

Cal retrieved the brochure and put it on the kitchen table. He glanced toward the oven where he could smell potatoes baking. "Have you been to these parties?"

"Where do you think our candles come from?"

So that's why I'm so emotionally healthy.

You bragging or complaining?

He looked back toward the oven. "What's going to go with those potatoes?"

She was in front of the sink, looking out the pass-through at the TV in the family room, her back to him. "Roast. It's the only month I can use the oven without roasting myself."

He put his backpack and mail on the table, covering the candle brochure. Maybe if he could sneak it out into the trash with the junk mail, she'd move on to something else, although this seemed more benign than other things he could remember or anticipate. "Hey, what's wrong with Mrs. Sanchez? She slammed her door at me yesterday and today turned her back when I asked how she was and if she needed anything."

"She probably doesn't like Fill-enders."

"What?"

"Need a translation, Mr. Educated? Men who screw around. Then keep their wives as cooks and maids."

"Oh *Jeez*." He swept up the mail (and candle brochure) and went past her into the garage where he picked the bills out of the mail and tossed the rest. Whatever crashed in the kitchen before any of the mail hit the trash must have been a chair. The roast was still in the oven when he returned to the house after spending a half hour in the garage wondering how his workbench there had been obliterated by boxes seemingly stuffed with other people's castoffs.

The answer was that Virginia (still, or again) was gathering for a yard sale. People from her church who were moving had donated stuff they weren't going to pack. Another church member and Virginia's sister were planning it with her as partners. Over the weekend, she directed Cal to get a big box from the rafters in the garage—Trinity's outgrown clothes since she was 12. Many of them had been gnawed to tatters by rats. Virginia salvaged the rest and added to the growing pile in the garage. There was barely an aisle to access the boxed, bagged and stacked junk. Virginia had just started putting prices on items when a fight with her sister ended the partnership and the project.

"I'm supplying the storage space and the yard for the sale, I was supposed to get *half*, I've been running around like a chicken with my legs cut off, and suddenly the greedy dog says we'll split thirds. Like heck we will."

"So if the sale is off, what're you doing in here?" He had found her in the garage when he got home. It was March, starting to be too warm to stay in there very long.

"This is where I was talking to her, the phone's somewhere in here, it's disappeared into thin blue ice, I must've have ..."

"What, thrown it?"

"Who *wouldn't*. I had a plan, a sale maybe once a month. It might have built into my own business. But *she*—"

"Not a good idea to partner with family in business."

"But it's something Trinity could do with me. Then I could retire and turn it over to her."

Cal's shirt was already damp and sticking to him, sweat rivulets running from his scalp into his eyes and behind his ears. "I gotta get out of here. You should too."

Her hair, of course, was dry, but her neck blotched red.

He was halfway through a soda when Virginia joined him in the kitchen. She was carrying a used coffeemaker which she set on the counter beside the one they already had.

He almost said, What *has* Trinity been doing? That is, it's the thing he was thinking of saying. Thinking it, then reconsidering. After all, didn't he already know? She slept until afternoon, when she slept there at all. Then a muffler-less car pulled into the driveway. She was either already in the kitchen putting brownies she'd made the night before (after midnight) into a bag, or she bolted from her bedroom with a huge purse, grabbed something from the refrigerator, and left the screen door flapping when she left. He knew all this from the times he'd come home for lunch, which he did more frequently, especially the days he expected Virginia to show up at the store. After lunch he might give Virginia money for a manicure or a special request for dinner, to try to forestall her visit to the store—which she might do anyway, leaving groceries in the hot car, but at least that kept her from staying through a full private lesson. Virginia soon countered his ruse by announcing at breakfast what she was making for dinner. He couldn't offer a manicure every week.

The week in late June when Virginia got called for jury duty broke the maneuvering, at least temporarily. That was also when he found Trinity's journal on the kitchen table, sitting open—but not to the final entry.

May 30

Today my father calls (asked for my mom but she wasn't home) and well – he wants to find my brother!! Finally he told me why. I found out my wonderful sibling has pulled a little – wait, pretty big – fraud on my father! He was using my dad's name, address and whatever else to "swindle" about 8,000 dollars in debt!! Now my father is the one who owes!! This is fucked for my dad big time. And it's majorly fucked for Angel (if my dad decides to report it!!!). I thought I was the screwed up one. Shit! Everyone else thought so too! But there's no way I could do something that damaging to my father, mother, or even grandparents (???). I can care less about someone I don't know. I'll do something like that or even worse to someone but not to my family!!!

In a way it's almost predictable. Our parents, to be honest, sucked at it!! She wasn't a woman with a lot of knowledge about life. Unlike my father – he was handsome, outspoken, charming and a lady's man. A shovinistic, womanizing asshole and the biggest bullshitting con artist I'll ever know! He was smart, athletic, and while he was sober he was a great father! My brother grew up sheltered, protected, babied, he was mama's pride and jo.. My father didn't want any kids and she got pregnant on purpose and he didn't like that at all. So my father resented him and my brother picked up on

122

that and then it all began, he withdrew. So society saw him as a "nerd" or whatever, along with my dad telling him what a wimp he was, making fun of how he ran from bullies at school. Dad tried to make him tuff by beating him until he fought back. Then I came along and Daddy was perfect for a while, but then my parents grew apart, fought constantly, partied all the time, were hardly ever home. I was spoiled but then all of a sudden left to fend for myself. I was a pretty, smart, outspoken, lying, mischievous, violent little girl! I showed no care toward anyone unless it would benefit me! But inside I cared and loved and at times felt bad for the things I'd done. I started doing bud and meth around 9 years old and that started me THINKING. I didn't do much thinking before that. My mind went crazy for a bit and it took almost dying to find me again. But when I came back, it was a whole new "self respected" Trinity – that's me ☺ – my brother hasn't hit that point. Maybe this will open his eyes to the fact that, damn! He's been afraid to face any kind of responsibility that has to do with money. His all cocky confident "I'm all good" attitude FRONT that gets him through each day without breaking down into the shame of how he KNOWS he isn't doing crap with his life. Oh deep down inside his weak soul, there is an extremely powerful, abundant, worthy man. How else can he put on that most convincing <u>front</u>?! It's partly real!

He read standing up and hadn't touched it yet. He'd come home to see if Virginia had been taken onto a jury, and, if so, to catch an hour nap under a fan in the bedroom. The journal hadn't been on the table when he left for the shop, so Trinity must have put it there after she got up, before she left. He had thought she hadn't been home at all last night. Angel hadn't been home for 2 or 3 nights, he knew that much. Virginia got jumpy during his absences, slept lighter, made it more difficult to do anything in bed without her waking and asking what time it was and did he hear Angel come home. He closed the journal and put it into his backpack.

Trinity never demanded her lost notebook, because she was gone after that. She'd left her mother a note, under her pillow, saying she would let her know where she was living, and maybe come home to get some stuff in about a month. She would, after all, be 21 in September, no tragedy or emergency that she'd decided to start her adult life, even though the requirement that Cal had imposed for Trinity continuing to live there after she turned 18—that she would get her GED and possibly start a vocational program at the community college—had, as far as he knew (and then the journal verified), never even been started, so no one could say *abandoned*.

Virginia began planning what things to give to Trinity to help, making a pile of items from the aborted yard sale, but also listing pieces of furniture she could give to Trinity and then buy replacements. "It's the Lord's plan. She can get her start with her father's old things. It's high time *we* stopped using them. At least the bed. Maybe that's what's been bothering you."

"I sleep fine."

"*Sleeping* isn't the only thing to do there."

"Has *your* business made enough to buy new furniture? Mine hasn't after Angel—"

"Blame blame blame. I'm still getting started, I need some supplies. It's called *start-up*. Have you heard of it? Someone just *gave* you your start with that shop."

Yeah, the Lord giveth and the Lord taketh away.

Say that out loud, I dare you. Too chicken?

Yes … especially in the year since Angel's shenanigans at the shop. He was thinking about some unusually high credit card bills lately, trying to remember if he had checked each item to be sure it was really his. Had his wallet been left in the kitchen even overnight? Was the file cabinet with the old tax returns still locked? Trinity leaving the journal open, on that particular page … had she meant her mother to find it, to open her eyes to her beloved son's character? Or was it for *Cal*, a warning? The rest of the notebook was no clue to an intention. He'd been reading it when he had time, instead of a newspaper, instead of looking back at any of his old postcards. There'd been no new one for a longer span than usual, although he could easily find some similar stretches of years in the chronological stack of cards.

The journal's chronology was less certain. Not the actual journal entries, which only spanned about two months this year. But because there were much older loose pages stuck between some of the blank pages at the end. Two in particular seemed unlikely itinerants in a 1993 journal. There were no dates on the loose pages, but one was obviously Virginia's handwriting. It was an exercise from the brief sessions of "family counseling" the two had attended when Trinity was 15 or 16— recognizable *not* because Cal had ever been filled in on what occurred there (nor had he asked; his questions had allowed only for a *yes* or *no* answer, like "a good session today?")—but because Virginia's page had the name of the counselor at the top, and Cal had filled out the checks to pay him.

My Problems
1. I let her go to graduation 8th grade
2. I let her off restriction early
3. I've cleaned her room
4. Made her do dishes or chores when I was upset
5. Let her tell me things she was going to do in spite of what I wanted
6. Let her come home late about 15 mins to half hour and no restriction
7. Buying her clothes in return for my uglyness to her
8. I made her what's she's today.

Her Problems (help)

1. Lying and cursing
2. Doing what she wants
3. Selfishness
4. Lazyness
5. Spoiled
6. Over sexed
7. Thinks shes older
8. Thinks she smarter than me
9. Sad (or mad) all the time

With junior high graduation the only specific, and coming in at #1, maybe Trinity was younger than 16 when they'd had therapy. That would mean more like 14, except he could swear the counselling was just before Trinity quit school altogether, after a hellish two or three years. Trinity had failed a few classes in 8th grade and had to take summer school before she could start 9th grade, but when Cal suggested not participating in junior high graduation as an appropriate consequence, it was vetoed by Virginia. In the face of other things Trinity was occupied with from 7th grade until she finally quit school—some of which Cal had only learned from the journal—his suggested atonement for failing junior high courses was pitiful. Yet if a counselor had offered the same idea, Virginia was at least able to consider it. The rest of Virginia's "problems" could have been any time since Trinity was 12 or 13 on up to the present.

As for her list of Trinity's "problems," sex was down at number 7, but drugs hadn't made the top 10. Could it be Virginia had been oblivious? Unfortunately there was no corresponding list where Trinity provided her version of where her life needed "help." Maybe they'd been given separate assignments, because Trinity's page—equally paradoxical regarding how old she was when it was written—was a pro/con list about her mother.

Mom

GOOD:	*BAD:*
She lets me smoke	*Nags me constantly*
She buys me cigs	*Cal*
She buys me things	*No phone*
She cooks great meals	*No TV*
Lets me wear make-up	*We fight all the time*
Lets me dress the way I want	*Only lets me out on the weekend*
We talk about "almost" anything	*Scared that I'm going to hit her*
Parties ... 12:30 curfew	

So many questions aroused. After buying her cigarettes and "things," giving no complaint about how she dressed (and permission for make-up had already been granted when she was 12 or 13), what in the world would Virginia have to nag or fight about? Why was the curfew on the *good* list? And had Trinity really never managed or even tried to land a blow in any of the brawls?

Obviously, those are the things X would've said, with scratchy laughter, first pointing out that Cal had (only) made 2nd on the *bad* list. But to the rest of the journal, if he and X read it together, he let her stay silent. He didn't want to have to explain, again, why he'd thought, or maybe still sometimes thought, that helping Virginia and Trinity solve this kind of life problem was what he needed to ... what ... *endure?*

May 7

Me again, or still ... this house, this town, this life ...
It's been awhile since I've written a "Diary." Two
months ago my hopes had a total 360 and I don't know

what the hell is going to happen now after the love of my life Ced left. ☹ Well, <u>physically</u>, left town. Probably because of Cy's ex girlfriend Pansy. She lives in a trailer behind Cy's house. Too close to <u>him</u> for comfort, but, well, me and him have been friends for almost 5 years. He was seeing if he and Pansy could work things out but me and him were getting closer and closer to becoming a couple and then we did. And now me and Ced have been talking again about possibly trying to get back together, me moving up there (or him back here, not my choice but there's $$ to consider). Every day is sort of like a frickin twilight zone, but in good ways, confusing, but good. Last night was a strange one. I was high as usual. But I can't seem to explain it. I'm in love, but with who? My mind's in love with one and my heart's in love with the other. I have a decision that I don't seem to want to make. And truthfully ... I might <u>need</u> to but honestly don't <u>want</u> to. I've got to live this life for ME! Some might say I'm wrong for what I'm doing, but it's my life, I'm a sexy confidant woman – And why shouldn't I be?!! But I don't want to hurt either of them, and either way two of us gets hurt, one of them and me!! And that makes this all fucked up! There's more to all this. But that's just for me to know!!!!! ☺

May 16
Sunday 3:30 p.m. I just got back from starting my weekends with Cyrus ... C-town. It's unbelievable! He's seriously my soul mate. Okay, I still have these feelings for you-know-who. All this happened so fast! My heart

didn't have as much time to heal as maybe it should. To heal, not mend back to what I was (in love with Ced) just time to get over the 360 life has dealt me! I'm 20 fucken years old and my life that was starting to come together came apart and, well, I'm handling it the best way for ME. This wonderful "thing" has come to me and it's got me in this sort of trance that has me so happy!!! ☺ He's ALL that I want and definitely NEED! He's almost perfect! He has a few little things that I know are going to get better. Like "our" money situation. It's both our faults, we both have been lagging around getting high and not doing shit. At least he said he does want to move away. So I'm definitely NOT that image of a "all together" young woman, doing the "right thing" - whatever the right thing is??! I guess things could've been handled more responsible. To me it's whatever can make me happy, keep me safe, and put food, clothing and the necessities under my roof, and however all that is gotten, it really doesn't matter to me. I've got to look out for me and those that I love and those who love me back! Now a days you have to get what you need any muthafucken way you can!! If that means having to kiss ass or kill, then FOOL you better do it!!! And when you are as lucky as I am and find "that person," that someone who's kind and who's going to always be there and not just loving you but seriously liking you for what you are, that alone can make a person happy for the rest of their lives. I've not only got that person but an amount of intelligence so I can go out there and find a good-paying job. Not like when I had given up on life and did all sorts of immature things. Shit. I hope I don't get that way again. It's only the "I don't have it alls" that go there and never come back and I know for a fact that's not me!!! And neither is my baby!!! I learned to live mentally on my own my entire life and deal with disappointments. But all of a sudden you are falling in love and feeling helpless over this crazy emotion taking over your thoughts, and if it's the wrong person it can seriously fuck with your head, you don't look at bad things the way you normally would, day after day you feel worthless and not worthy of love, and when it's over it fucken hurts, not only because you lost the thing you seemed to cherish but because you fucked up and lost yourself. Then, damn, a perfect "everything" falls right at your toes!!! I needed to see how I <u>don't</u> need to be treated to be able to truly appreciate finally being treated the way you know you deserve to be!!! It feels so GOOD and so scary all the same time. (!?!?!) One fucken minute I'm content, smiling and Cedric (along with the hurtful memories) seems a million miles away ☺... But then something said or some look makes you feel like you know that you are going to do something to make this perfect thing go away. How can one person come in and out of your life and affect you in such a way that you might not ever EVER fully let go. He's still in my heart, but unless both of us change the way we are there is no good way for us to be happy together and make it last. He's a good person (and I don't call him C-dick for no reason !!! I'm a size C bra and he's a size C you know what!!!) and he will forever be a piece of my heart and I wish him the best, but I have a MAN that respects me, knows me and cares for me as he would himself. A man that loves me, has always cared for me and I love him, and deep inside always have! I notice the more time that I spend with him I start to feel confident again and the real Trinity starts to show more and more. And I like me!!!!! ☺

May 18

6:47 p.m. sitting here in my room, just doing nothing as usual, but thinking about All this crazy shit that has gone on in my life, and yours ... At times it doesn't affect me then at others I start thinking about all the time I spent with you, days that we shared together, everything that went on, and my heart starts to burn. It hurts, but then I come to reality and know that seriously we cannot be together. For one thing, we don't have trust. Well, you can't trust me. And I can't live with someone that doesn't trust me to even go out with my friends. And another thing, the way I want to live my life will not make you happy, and the way you live yours isn't what I want. We grow up and we change – at least I have! We were an experience in our lives, that first true one, and I do still love you, and it does hurt, and you really need to start getting yourself together. All that I'm saying, Cedric, is that I don't want you to hate me, I just want you to understand me and let me go. If true love never dies, then one day we'll be back together!!!!! Well, I hope that you have read this letter. You probably already threw it away, but if you haven't, then, Goodbye Ced, I do love you and wish you the best of luck in getting what you want out of life. If you want to call me, that's okay. But let's not ever talk as enemies, because we both know what we really are!!!!!

May 24

I've been gone since Friday. Shit, as usual. And now I sit here in my nice clean room. I have a strange feeling and I'm still trying to figure out the root of it. The only thing that comes to mind is that I haven't been doing anything. I mean _anything_, for going on 3 weeks but hanging out and getting high on anything that comes through the house or wherever I am at the time. And knowing this doesn't seem to affect me in any way. But what's going on? I'm so fucken confused lately!! And when I'm alone there it goes: This gnowing feeling that something is going wrong!!? ☹

**Cedric Watson ♥ ♥ ♥
Cyrus Washington ♥ ♥??
Sand Dunes High School 337-8900**

May 29

My mind's all spinning around with this decision! At times it's all made up, and I know exactly what I want to do! But then it changes? I miss him and want to run to him like I've done so many times!! But thoughts of the future come to me and I hate being so unsure. It could turn out bad with any decision I make! But you can't live solely for the future! Hopefully soon my mind will be made up and I'll have to live with whatever the consequences are. I need some fucken bud, drink, crypto, yeah, something right <u>now</u>. ☹ My mind may be screwed up and confused but it's definitely strong enough to handle <u>that</u> shit. Now my body, that's another thing. I'm not too sure if my body can handle all the damage I put on it?? That would be the only reason to fully stop. Or of course if - or when - I get preg. Hopefully soon. Maybe that's what I need! It's what I want. Right now I need to get my ass a job and in school before I totally give up on it. I don't want to end up a "nothing." Shit that won't happen!!!!!

Then the entry about Angel's scam was May 30 (and Cal had witnessed no evidence Trinity ever told Virginia, although he could also imagine Virginia deciding to keep the news from him). In June, Virginia's birthday had been her 45th. In the weeks before, she'd asked Cal for a new wig (which she called *a hairstyle*), and he gave her the credit card number to order one. Then she'd asked for a toe ring and ankle bracelet set, so he'd let her get that as well. She'd wanted to go dancing, but her birthday was on a Tuesday and Blue Sand had gigs both the Friday and Saturday before and the Friday and Saturday after. The gigs were a lie, but he gave her $200, which he said would be his pay from all four gigs, so she could buy sandals with leather straps that wrapped her lower legs, a mood ring and more earrings for her new additional piercings. Still, she'd cried periodically throughout that day, until, dressed in her new things, Cal took her on a drive to watch the sunset in the desert state park, and then to dinner at a hideaway Mexican restaurant.

So possibly while Cal ate real corn husk tamales, Trinity was seeking clarity, as though an explanation to someone else, before disintegrating to the usual (although surprisingly, for the most part, well-spelled) meandering blather.

June 1

Is it around time for Mom's birthday? Something a person should remember. Anyhow, I'm here, laying on my bed in my mother's and step-father's house. I just got home from spending a few days at my boyfriend's mother's house, where I go on weekends, and other days. His name is Cyrus Washington or C-town (or Chubbs to his friends), Cy or Sweetbaby to me. He's twenty-three years old, 6'9" about 300 pounds. He's half Caribbean and the other half Creole. He's really "cool," that's the perfect word for him. On Feb 7 1997 he asked me to be his girl for the third time and I finally said yes. It was only a week before me and Cyrus got together that my fiancé (at the time) left me, it seemed like all of a sudden just walked out on me. His name is Cedric Watson. He's 6'4", about 265. He's African American with green eyes and a bald head (shaved) (FINE!). I was totally head over heels in love with him. I still have this thing that lingers for this guy. He still calls me and says that he feels we are still "together." He wants me back and for me to move north and live with him. I haven't told him that me and Cyrus are seeing each other. I can't bring myself to tell him. All I can say to him is that I miss him and still love him, And at times I seriously do!!! There have been moments that I'm all ready to go!! We would be so HAPPY! I just know that it won't last. The fighting will start again. He would start wanting me to change my "attitude." And I don't want to put up with that again. I've cheated on him too many times and lied to him so many times. But I fucken LOVE him! It hurts me to tell him that I need more time to decide what I want to do. That's what's so stressful in my life right now. I have Cyrus now, and he's so good to me, compliments me, lets me do whatever I want! He likes everything about me!!! ☺ We've been friends for so long, that really helps out in a relationship. BUT ... there is one thing that I've noticed about him that I don't really like!??! I've noticed that he is LAZY. And he doesn't seem to want to do anything to "come up." He doesn't work, he doesn't go to school. And he doesn't even hardly go anywhere! Okay, now this is partly my fault!! I'm not doing anything either – no work, no school. But I'm not just sitting around NOT thinking about it. I do, all the time! I'm going back to school to get my GED. And this time I will stay with it. I would certainly respect my own self a little more and in a way that I don't do now. But don't think that I don't respect myself now. Because I do. I totally got off the subject of my two loves. Cedric, C-DICK, great in a lot of ways, he's gorgeous and he really loves me. But I constantly hurt him. He didn't understand that person. He walked out. And that same day I ran to Cyrus Sweetbaby C-Town Washington. And we've been inseparable since. He makes me feel comfortable and safe. He also makes me want to do nothing all day but party. Now what do I do about both these guys??! I don't want to stop talking to Cedric! Because if me and Cyrus don't work out I would go back to him. So I don't want to tell Cedric about Cyrus. And Cedric tells me that he wants to come down and visit me!!! But damn, what about you-know-who? I could tell him that I'm going away for a weekend and me and Ced could get a motel?!? But I'm nervous that he'll see some of his other friends who'll tell him about me and Cy!! Maybe we could go to San Diego together to see how we would get along??? I would love to make love to him right now. He is soooo fine!! Cy doesn't have an ass and his body ain't the bomb. But sex with him is YUM!! But the other day when Cy was kissing on me, it felt horrible. I felt like throwing up. I didn't want to be there. All I could think about was Cedric. I started thinking that because I was sober I got put back into reality about my true feelings, and that the only reason I seem to like being with Cyrus is because I'm high, and that made me sad for Cyrus and what I was doing to him. But the next day I thought it through again and realized that Cyrus is good for me, he treats me better!! And I should just stay happy with that and concentrate on making him start doing something with his life!!!

June 2 9 p.m. or after that

Here again, sitting on my bed, it seems all I do. I seem to have made a decision and I'm sticking by this one so far ☺! Not really a " major" second thought. He (~~Cyrus~~) oops! (Cedric) called tonight !!! It's funny, I don't seem to love him the way I used to?!? But I want to be with him <u>really</u> bad. When I think about being with him and living with him, I think it's right. Now last night with Cyrus felt right also. Why am I not there right now???!

June 4 early morning about 12
I'm sitting here on my bed tweeking and I wish I wasn't alone. Shit, ☹ I wonder if my parents are awake? It sounds like they are! It's probably just Cal. I talked to my father tonight. I guess my mother got a hold of him and talked to him about what I've been doing. NOTHING. ☺ And of course she most likely blew it all out of proportion. He told me he doesn't want me to go back to the way I used to be. I told him that it wasn't happening and not to worry. I don't know why I called him. I can tell that Cy is changing his mind about wanting to leave with me, but I want to move the fuck away! Now I think I rushed too fast into this thing with Cyrus. If I would've waited, me and Cedric could've gotten back together and then when he left I'd have gone too. Wow, okay, here comes that second thought that I said hadn't come?!!

JUNE 5, 1:43 A.M.

AND YES! I'M HOME! ALONE! BY MYSELF! SITTING HERE ON MY BED! I'M NOT MAD, IT'S NOT ONE BIG THING, IT'S A LOT OF LITTLE THINGS. I'VE GONE AND SPENT ALL

THE MONEY THAT I OWNED*!!!!!* AND I'VE GAINED SO
MUCH WEIGHT*!!!!!* NOW I'M FUCKING TWEEEKING PRETTY
MUCH ALL THE TIME*!!!* I'M NOT WORKING, I DON'T HELP
MY MOTHER IN THE HOUSE, I HAVE TONS OF BILLS (THAT
I DON'T HAVE THE $$$ FOR). AND MY LOVE LIFE GIVING
ME A NERVOUS BREAKDOWN. THEN LATELY WE HAVEN'T
BEEN TALKING MUCH LIKE WE WERE*???* BUT IT'S TOO
SOON TO WORRY MUCH ABOUT IT! THINGS AREN'T
FALLING APART, IT'S JUST HANGING ON FROM FALLING
AND NOW IT'S UP TO ME TO KEEP IT TOGETHER*!!!* BUT I
HAVE NO PHYSICAL MOTIVATION. IT'S THERE, BUT IF I
DON'T REACT TO IT RIGHT THEN, I LOSE IT. I WANTED
TO BE WITH HIM RIGHT NOW AND HE DOESN'T FEEL LIKE
HAVING ME AROUND RIGHT NOW *!!!* I UNDERSTAND
THOUGH. HE NEEDS TO BE WITH HIS FRIENDS
SOMETIMES. HE FEELS BAD ABOUT IT. I'M SUCH A NON
TRUSTING NOSY BITCH. BUT SHIT HOW CAN I NOT BE*???*
WITH ALL THE BULLSHIT I GET PUT THROUGH. WELL,
"GOT" PUT THROUGH. IF CY IS THE ONE I CHOOSE, THEN
HE BETTER TREAT ME RIGHT – LIKE HE HAS BEEN*!!* AND
THAT'S WHAT IS GOING TO HURT THE WORST, IF I
CHOOSE THE "OTHER" ONE. IT MAY TURN OUT WRONG –
AND WELL, SHIT HAPPENS, I GO ON*!!* AS LONG AS I
KEEP MYSELF AS HAPPY AS I CAN, THEN I SHOULD DO
JUST FINE, AND I CAN ALWAYS, AND HAVE ALWAYS BEEN
ABLE TO, FIND ANOTHER MAN*!!!* YOU KNOW THIS,
MUTHAFUCKA*!!!!!*

So what had been going on in June that he could have so easily
missed Trinity's drama? Although the drama part seemed to have
happened elsewhere, and her agitation into her notebook likely well after
midnight in her bed that Virginia still made every afternoon after Trinity
left for more drugs, drink and drama. Maybe he hadn't tried as much as
he'd thought to help her, to make a difference. Thinking he could help
them, and obviously failing, setting himself up to utterly fail … Was
there nothing on earth that was a credit to his having ever been alive?
That was *his* drama.

June 22

Afternoon, 2:19 p.m. !!!

Last night (or this morning about 3:45 a.m.) Cyrus got himself arrested.

And last night, me and Cyrus sort of broke-up. ☹ Things are sooooooo crazy fucked-up right now! I am out of here! He lies to me! Damn! Of all the people that could do this to me! A person I had trusted completely! Are there any descent people out there ?! I thought that this could be something 💣*! (BOMB!) But he doesn't "really love me"! If he doesn't even SEEM to want me, I'm gone!!!!!

June 22

Hey, Damn, Cyrus, Things have been crazy. ☹ I want you to know that I don't hate you for lying to me. I could never ever hate you. You are my best friend, and that also means that I look at you differently than, let's say, Pansy might. I can actually look at all that you are going through with open eyes rather than blind-folded. Because through all we shared, I always looked at you that way. You are most likely going to receive this letter way after the 22nd. But I want you to know that I've known for a while that you love her more, even now, than you could possibly love me! There are many explanations you may have for lying to yourself about who you want in your life and who you want to marry. I only hope that you did find someone who's kind, honest, all that you look for, hopefully cool and funny and great in bed!! I wish you all the luck that I can to get through this period *with a clear conscience and a strong heart. But also with a powerful will to keep doing your best once you've started. Things between us were going along pretty damn good, emotionally at least. And definitely physically!! ☺ But seriously, mentally, you were ready to <u>explode</u>. I constantly tried to do something that would make you feel better. I guess my love just couldn't be enough. This doesn't really matter now because I don't really want you if you can't/won't fully love me. Or at least give me a chance in your heart to love you. So my sweet baby, please find yourself and ultimately find yourself happy. I'm going to do the best that I can to get you out of there! Me, Pansy and Stevie are trying!! I'm so sorry that this had to happen to you at a time like Sunday with everything else (and for a while thought it was my fault!!). Anyways I'm staying here to see how I can help. Because as I'm sure you know, I love you! But after this week (maybe?) I'm leaving. For how long? I'm not sure. I'll probably be back (just to visit) in a month and I'll call or page you and if you are no longer living here, that's an answer in itself. OK!! So today talking to Pansy made me realize that if you want to not be with me ☹ then you'll be making a mistake! It may not affect you in some big way but you'll look back and know that you did!!*

A week or so after she found Trinity's goodbye note and began sorting items in the garage for the alleged apartment, Virginia remarked that Trinity and Cedric had gotten back together and were living in Oakland. Of course she didn't know Cal had access to the whole story first-hand, even if he'd never figured out which one she chose. Still, he asked "The one who went to jail?"

"You *never* paid attention to her life. That pervert's been history for a long time. *Ced.* She was dating him here, then they broke up for a while." She lifted a power drill from a bulging plastic trash bag. It had no battery. She dropped it back and took out an electric carving knife. "So now their acts are together. But we can still help. Let's help furnish their place."

He waited until the carving knife was settled into the box she was packing. "Are you sure they *have* a place?"

"She *called.* That means a *phone.*"

Like the previous one, this conversation took place in the stifling garage. He'd come home for dinner but it looked like nothing was cooking. The box she was packing was propped on top of an open trash can. Precious little was making its way into the can. Two boxes with the flaps folded closed were pushed against the concrete step into the garage, where Cal was standing, which was as far as he could get into the garage.

"So you want to ship boxes all the way to Oakland? Do you have any idea how much—"

"Okay, we could send the money, but I'd really like to help pick out things for her, or give her something from her childhood for her to feel comfortable. But apparently *you* have some need to hang onto that old bed I've slept in for a million years."

No comfort like the bed where you were conceived. X would say it, but he didn't. "I have a need to not go bankrupt, as I've said a million times. So, be my guest, get a job and give Trinity anything you can. Send a whole truckload of this crap, so maybe I can use my garage again."

"Oh, your *guest* ... *your* garage."

"I guess I shouldn't say I'd like my dinner?" And yes, he knew he shouldn't say it.

The transistor radio she threw didn't hit him, and probably wouldn't have even if he hadn't taken a precarious step to the garage floor, almost falling sideways over the haystack of garden tools leaned beside the door. The radio bounced off the top of the door frame and its plastic body splintered on the concrete stoop where he'd been standing.

He recognized it was one he'd had in high school to listen to baseball games in bed at night.

When Virginia pushed the trash can aside to make room for her to leave, the box balanced there tipped sideways into the barrel. "F it!" She kicked the trash, but it had no room to fall over (although he was pretty sure the plastic side of the barrel cracked).

"I made you a sandwich, if you could do anything for yourself, like take a plate out of the refrigerator," she said as she passed, going into the kitchen.

"Okay, thanks." He was picking up the radio and pieces of its body. Had he maybe brought it to a game with him, one he remembered attending with X?

Trinity's return in a month didn't happen. She did, after all, say *probably*. Virginia didn't seem surprised or alarmed. Five or six boxes were packed, each marked with a big T. The rest of the erstwhile yard sale remained, with paths plowed through for access to various portions of the garage, until Cal borrowed Cliff's pickup and took as much as he could to the Salvation Army. He mentioned to Virginia that she should check into how one got a job there, since they were supposedly training the disenfranchised to be able to get back into the workforce.

"I've *got* a franchise!" She'd gone back to the group with the hair-loss product, who had "reorganized," she said, "changed our name, and expanded our product." Nu-U sold beauty and age-defying commodities. "Now I'm the type of affiliate most qualified to represent." Probably because he didn't respond, she continued, "The perfect age to benefit from the products."

So the Nu-U business was launched, and by the end of August Cal had invested in the membership fee and first two months of products, minimum of $75 a month required. Actually, he gave her that amount to open her business checking account, so she was overdrawn almost immediately because of shipping and handling, so he paid the fee. Trying to sell her products should have taken enough of her time that she wouldn't be in the music store, but that's where she showed up, almost daily, in the afternoon when students' mothers might be waiting, to hawk Nu-U. She asked Cliff if she could set up a permanent table in the store. When Cliff asked Cal if that's what *he* wanted, Cal advised that if Cliff *could* say no—but benignly—he should. She ended up with a card table under the awning outside the store on Saturday mornings.

Whether or not she made enough money to ship the boxes to Trinity, Cal didn't know (OK, yes, he knew she *didn't*). But in September when he asked when she was going to get the boxes out of the garage, she said it might be a while now because Trinity was in jail for shoplifting. Since Virginia hadn't been able to send bail money, Trinity was going to serve the 30 days. "After that, she won't have an address for a while. Ced's living in his car, waiting for her. Then they might both go to Utah or New Mexico."

The bank closed Virginia's checking account in December, on Cal's request. Since Cal had co-signed, he paid the overdrafts. The evening he spread the five checks, ranging from $50 to $200 and made out to Angel, on the kitchen table, Virginia poured a pot of beef stew there, between the two empty plates. Cal jumped back and only received a few red blotches on his T-shirt. Cal hadn't even seen Angel for several weeks, although he could have sworn the beater Angel had mysteriously been able to buy had been in front of the house a few mornings when he went out for the newspaper. In December and January, even February, Cal usually stayed on the front porch until 6 or 6:30, with his coffee and morning cigarette, especially the rare days it rained. He was there the day he heard Virginia scream, and then begin to howl, and continue to wail, until he got inside to see if she'd cut off a finger or burned her face in steam. He held her convulsing body while her feet stamped, arms flailed, and tears and snot saturated his shirt. The cordless phone on the kitchen floor beeped to be hung up. At some point he learned there'd been some kind of vehicle pileup, and Angel had been killed.

January 1994

I just read this: "*Nothing was happening. It would never happen. It would never include me.*" Reading a lot, since I need distraction and swore off movies plus most of TV, except Discovery Ch. when they have an animal documentary - actually can learn basic behavioral issues which I could've gotten as an Animal Behavior major (*Ethology*, the study of ethics? Ha.). Was it offered when we were in school? How did I miss it? Like so much else passing me by. And now you can even become an animal *psychologist*. Those who can't blather their problems might be easier to 'cure.'   X

Post Card

Cal Tonnessen
7512 W San Diego Ave
El Centro CA 92243

When it seemed that going on with this history would be impossible, you don't know how close I came to calling you. Cuz of how you were there when my childhood dog was a victim of vehicular manslaughter. (*Dog*-slaughter.) No, selfish connections like that aren't the only reason to consider real contact ... a person dealing with building some kind of life sometimes wonders what's happening for people you knew before, maybe a talented person you once saw frequently while you were both preparing for adult life, and you wonder if his talent was enough to save him from... well, basically, from himself ... but that kind of wondering isn't enough to want *him* to know what's happening (or not) for you. Who cares if you win a dog show. It lasts about as long as ... dang, the dog's *life*. In the end, all she has is pain and eyes that say "help me" to the only one she ever trusted, but *that* idiot is *fucking* helpless.

1994-1997

So another life chapter (otherwise known as a suitable hunk of years) could be conveyed via another list of the requisite and the routine: meals, sleep, bills, the next dog in the height of a show career, winning enough to keep a reputation; no major illnesses, several breast biopsies but no findings, one procedure not done very well so it looked like a bite was taken out but nobody (else) noticed, (but thankful for the medical insurance and that the "it's just a dog" comment hadn't been allowed to end it) ... Trained the dogs, laughed at them, lay on the floor with them, made lists of names for future dogs (creating a context they'll respond to with drive because it means *action* and *excitement*); continued to do well at shows, heard the dog-show gossip-mill say mean things—a snob, only out to win, couldn't bother with those just having a good time with their pets, doesn't smile at anyone unless she does well—and maybe most was built on some reality. Not the reality I was feeling or thinking, just the reality that appeared when I showed up with a well-trained dog, gave that dog my complete focus and attention, made what the *dog* needed to be successful be *my* complete agenda, earned my (often winning) score and then went home. (OK, with that rant, I had to finally give up the passive voice pretense, yes, it's me talking.) The client list continued to grow, ebbed some years when the economy faltered, flourished other years, especially if the local TV station needed some "expert" to come talk about a recent dog attack incident (yes, très ironic) or coyote pack filleting backyard pets.

A lot of ass-time spent staring at screens in-between clients and their dogs—both usually overweight, thumping down the stairs into my basement. Is that really *all*? Not quite, if you count the arrival of Climax. No not *that* kind—she was a new puppy back in 1995. Someday to become the last dog. Then … became the crushing example of how powerless I ultimately am to protect, and how much havoc I actually wreak instead.

1998-1999
Two things: Climax torn up by storming rottweiler and 22-year-old oboe player comes to town. Both swooping down like doomed fate. The latter started first, then the attack, then the obsession getting weird, combining itself with the dog-attack lawsuit … Gak. As powerless to help the man as I was to save the dog, but for him didn't even try. For her, willingly took some of the teeth in my own flesh.

When Climax supposedly healed and only I knew where the scars were (those scars themselves hid the spinal rupture that would come back to kill her in the most ghastly way), she had her revenge on the world when she rocketed to her championship with all first-places. Why do I think of winning as revenge? What did it gain *her*? Or me for that matter. My scars didn't show either. (Maybe only to you.)

Chapter Six
Six Weeks and Six Years

1994

Members of Virginia's church brought the requisite casseroles and baked goods, but for two weeks Cal made his own oatmeal or eggs in the morning and sandwiches at noon. He didn't go to lunch on his own or with Cliff because he came home to bring Virginia soup and crackers. She didn't get out of bed except to use the bathroom. He moved the phone into the bedroom and she sometimes called her ex, Pete, their conversations murmured, punctuated with weeping. The same for her almost daily calls to her mother and sister. The church people called occasionally; those dialogues were shorter. Cal never lingered in the room if Virginia was on the phone. He brought her tea and clean pajamas, buttered muffins and boxes of tissue, small plates of macaroni-and-cheese or chicken salad, even changed the sheets once while she was in the bathroom, wailing, the water running, steam seeping from under the door.

Cal took the phone, or used the phone at the shop, for his attempts to get information. Virginia had said, "I just can't, Cal, I won't be able to stand to hear them say it." But she wanted to know what had happened.

"I don't have legal standing to be given information."

"Pete won't do it! He says what difference does it make, it was in the cards, waiting to happen, says Angel would've been killed over there if he'd stayed in the Army."

The Lord's plan. Cal kicked himself at the thought. He said very little to Virginia when he brought her food, 7-Up, tissues or sleeping pills. Do you need anything, are you hungry yet, maybe you'd like to watch TV?

Angel's body had been identified by a chip in a front tooth that had happened during his military stint. Angel had never explained how it had happened. Virginia had asked Cal for money to take Angel to a dentist to repair it, and Cal had declined. His back had been turned so he didn't know how a table lamp had ended up skidding across the coffee table, knocking glasses half full of soda out of its path. But now Virginia said, "I'm glad he never had the tooth fixed, or we'd never know—"

A lot of things they still might never know. Had Angel's car been chasing another car or had the cops been chasing Angel? Possibly one then the other? Or multiple parties all chasing Angel? Was anything in his car incinerated that might have been part of the story? Did the crash close one investigation and open another? Were the investigations important enough for them to process the car for forensics? Were there witnesses? Who was the last person to speak to Angel that night? Was there anything in his room that might be a piece of the story? No one ever came to look through the laundered clothes in the closet and drawers, the freshly made bed, the stained but vacuumed carpet—Angel hadn't been home for several days, maybe a week, and Virginia kept his room clean. Once, before this happened, Cal had stood in the doorway and sang a Billy Joel lyric, "Well, you're twenty-one and still your mother makes your bed ... and that's too long."

She hadn't thrown anything, just said "Shut up, it makes me feel good, being a mother was the Lord's path for me. Something *you* can't stop, even though you *tried*."

The ectopic pregnancies? He didn't ask.

It wouldn't make anything better for anyone for him to tell Virginia about the probable police involvement in the crash. Among the reasons he withheld, that she would undoubtedly turn connotations that Angel was nefarious into a conspiracy, and therefore ask Cal to search further for clues. So, without the information, she frequently sustained a whimper of *why, my sweet boy, why*, but stopped directly asking him to find out. She did ask him to see to the transfer of his body to a crematorium, which finished the job started by the crash, and Cal brought home the plain brass urn, which he put on Virginia's nightstand. She often carried on her progressively more quietly moaned refrain with her hand on the cool metal.

One day she asked Cal to stay for a minute after he put a dish of fruit cobbler on her nightstand. He was already back around the bed heading to the door, so sat on his side of the mattress, his body forming a question mark, as it had several hours ago in the moments between waking and rising to dress.

"Is Trinity coming?"

"Not that I know of." He picked up the little broken radio that had been thrown at him last summer. It had been on his nightstand for months waiting for him to try to fix it. It didn't work except the click when he rotated the dial to ON, and the other dial moved the needle across the broadcast band numbers.

"Didn't you call her?"

"Does she have a phone number?"

"I don't know. I don't remember anymore where she was or in what condition before this ... happened." Virginia was still, as she had been since he'd put the cobbler on her nightstand, lying on her side facing the wall. She wore a kerchief instead of a wig.

"Don't stress over it."

"I need her here for the ... service."

"Don't worry, nothing needs to be decided now." He put the radio down.

"Everyone... everything's leaving me. Except you. You've been so good to me."

He swiveled so he could put his feet up and stretch onto his back, head on his pillow.

"Where did this cobbler come from?" The spoon he'd balanced on the dish rattled once.

"Mrs. Sanchez brought it yesterday. She was very nice. I guess ... well, certain things that happen can ... smother that kind of ... disapproval." He was going to say *someone dying can make people friendly*.

"Oh ..." Virginia rolled to her back. "I need to tell you something. I feel bad about this, I meant to tell you. She was mad at me too, but I fixed it." She paused, but when he didn't ask *how*, she continued. "Was it last year? Maybe longer? She had fallen, out in her yard. I was in *our* yard and she was calling for help, but it sounded just like when she argues with her daughter on the phone in Spanish, so to give her privacy, I went inside."

He wished he'd turned on the ceiling fan before lying down. Getting up to do it now might seem like he didn't want to be lying there, side by side. Especially after she raised her right arm and put her hand on his left upper arm.

"A month or so after that happened," she said, "I went next door because potatoes were buy-one-bag-get-a-2nd-bag-free, and I was bringing the 2nd bag to her." Her hand slid slowly down, past his elbow, cupping his forearm like a stair rail. "At first she wouldn't come to the door, told me to go away, I couldn't figure it out, but then she opened the door to yell at me for leaving her on the ground like that." When her hand reached his, she threaded their fingers. "I explained the mistake. I don't know if she was convicted, but ... she did take the potatoes. And I've given her other things since then. When there's such a good sale but I know we can't eat that much ..."

"I thought she hated me because you told her ..." He usually extricated his hand from being held this way, fingers laced, because it made his knuckles throb.

"What are you talking about?"

"Never mind."

Her hand tightened, then loosened. As though trying to start the throb. "Cal ...?"

"Yes?" He pulled his fingers free, then let his hand stay in hers, without fingers entwined.

Her fist closed around his hand, her thumb rubbing his knuckles. "Would you ... I mean I'd really like for you to be the one ... for you to do an elegy ... for Angel."

"An elegy? Like, write a poem? Or compose music? You want me to play my sax?"

"Just be the speaker, talk about Angel, the tribute."

"Oh. You meant eulogy."

"You have to correct me and be superior, don't you? Even *now?*" She released his hand and rolled away again.

"But why me?" When she didn't answer, he added, "I mean, why not his father?"

"Parents can't do it." She was crying.

"Isn't there someone who knew him better?"

"You helped raise him!" Sobbing rising to a wail.

"Well …" He might've said he wasn't taking the blame for that, X as audience to his tacit snark, but he wouldn't want her witnessing the consequence of a reckless blurt-out. "Okay, I guess I can. I'll try … I'll … think of something."

But what to say? Angel hadn't left even so much as a scrap of paper containing anything of himself, so he went back to Trinity's journal. He wasn't thinking that a mock eulogy about Trinity, with a name swap, could pass unnoticed. Just looking for the entry where she'd analyzed Angel's character following his credit card scam on their father. But when he reread it, he realized there were only 5 sentences about Angel, other than details of the scam.

My brother grew up sheltered, protected, babied, he was mama's pride and joy, practically her best friend. My father didn't want any kids and she got pregnant on purpose and he didn't like that at all. So my father resented him and my brother picked up on that and then it all began, he withdrew. So society saw him as a "nerd" or whatever, along with my dad telling him what a wimp he was, making fun of how he ran from bullies at school. Dad tried to make him tuff by beating him until he fought back.

> *Well, isn't it possible he died running from a bully, so to speak?*
> *I don't think I should say that.*
> *Duh! But … his Mom's best friend. Sick. Now who has that honor?*
> *I really have to do this.*

Knowing how X would have turned and flounced off wasn't helping.

Even if he removed the obvious negatives, Angel was a zero for Cal. He couldn't remember a single conversation when Angel grunted more than two words, other than retorting that he wouldn't do, wear, or eat something.

And of course the journal was no answer. Could you even believe half of what Trinity said? Just a few lines later in that entry, *My mind went crazy for a bit and it took almost dying to find me again.* He had no memory of Trinity ever "almost dying." Still, the journal had made it shamefully obvious that he hadn't a clue half the things going on inside the same walls where he lived. That much made evident not only in the two months of journal, but the loose sheets of paper that had been stashed at the end, probably not with any purpose or plan. Besides the therapy pro/con and problems lists, there was some raunchy and overly syllabic rap lyrics involving dicks and pussies of various colors, a dot-matrix printout probably from a vocational course before she quit school, and a long letter that started "Dear Daddy" and was tucked in the flap of a stamped/addressed envelope.

HI MY NAME IS TRINITY AND I'M GOING TO TELL YOU ABOUT MY LIFE SO FAR. I'M 15 YEARS OLD. I HAVE BROWN HAIR AND BROWN EYES. I'M 5'9" AND I HAVE A THICK BUILD. I'M ONE QUARTER MEXICAN MOSTLY SPANISH. I'M IN THE 10TH GRADE. I HAVE ONE BROTHER HIS NAME IS ANGEL. MY MOTHER'S NAME IS VIRGINIA. MY FATHER'S NAME IS PETE. MY PARENTS GOT A DIVORCE WHEN I WAS ABOUT 7. I WAS SENT TO MY GRANDPARENTS IN NEW MEXICO. I LIVED THERE A YEAR BECAUSE MY MOTHER WASN'T ABLE TO TAKE CARE OF ME AND MY BROTHER AND MY FATHER I GUESS DIDN'T WANT US. THEN WHEN SHE CAME BACK AND GOT US WE WENT TO LIVE WITH MY UNCLE IN SAN DIEGO THEN MY FATHER WANTED US BACK SO WE MOVED TO LAS VEGAS AND LIVED THERE HALF A YEAR THEN MY MOTHER WANTED US BACK BUT MY BROTHER WANTED TO STAY SO I WENT WITH MY MOTHER BACK TO CALIFORNIA, NOT SAN DIEGO BUT HERE EL CENTRO. THAT'S WHERE ALL THE TROUBLE STARTED. I WENT TO SCHOOL, GOT BAD GRADES, GOT IN TROUBLE AT SCHOOL AND AT HOME BUT NOT THAT BAD OF TROUBLE. WHEN I WAS 10 I LOST MY VIRGINITY, AROUND SIXTH

GRADE IT GOT EVEN WORSE I STARTED DITCHING SCHOOL AND DOING DRUGS AND DRINKING. I GOT JUMPED INTO A GANG THEN SEVENTH GRADE I STARTED DOING A LITTLE BETTER. BUT I WAS STILL DOING THE DRUGS. OF COURSE MY MOTHER DIDN'T KNOW ABOUT IT. THEN EIGHTH GRADE CAME AROUND. I WAS DOING ALMOST EVERYTHING FROM SEX TO DRUGS TO GETTING INTO INTENSE FIGHTS WITH MY MOTHER AND STEP-FATHER, THEN TO RUNNING AWAY AND GETTING CAUGHT THEN RUNNING AWAY AGAIN AND GETTING CAUGHT. EVERYTHING I DID WAS TROUBLE. I GOT KICKED OUT OF SCHOOL. I DIDN'T COME HOME. I WAS HAVING SEX WITH ANY GUY I KNEW. I WAS HEAVILY INTO DRUGS. THEN EVERYTHING ENDED. I STOPPED DOING HEAVY DRUGS I STILL SMOKE WEED AND I STILL DRINK. I'M NOT DOING GREAT IN SCHOOL BUT NOT TOO BAD. MY LIFE RIGHT NOW IS WEIRD. BUT I'LL MAKE IT BETTER. I'VE GOT A BOYFRIEND WHO REALLY LOVES ME AND CARES ABOUT ME. I THINK I'LL MAKE IT THROUGH.

Dear Daddy

You have been on my mind lately. I'm wondering if all is OK for you, is there anything wrong? I know that losing your father makes life not very "OK." Losing Grandpa hit me with a loss I didn't expect. He took good care of me both times I lived there, when I was a little brat and later when I visited one time, even though we had some slightly heated conversations. He felt a bit "shocked and disappointed" in me. I explained myself the only way I could. Which he didn't quite like. But he thought about it and he came to me one morning for a talk. He said I had been disrespectful to my family, but that he understood why. He said that my parents didn't do very well raising me, and that he wished you guys should have left me with him and grandma to grow up there. He also told me that I was smart and strong and I would be alright. All this in so many words and about a half a pack of cigarettes. Now losing him has also made me think about losing you. Daddy — I want to explain to you about me. I want to apologize for the many stupid and extremely fucked up things that I have done. Let me explain a little. During the time in Las Vegas, I was this little beautiful, smart girl. You were strong and handsome, I felt like a little princess around you. I had everything I could want or need. But things changed, and changed me. Seriously, Daddy, the way I felt about my mother confused me. Mom was so beautiful-looking to me, she was so fun, she played with me and read me stories. But she would change! She would yell at me for strange reasons. Scold me one time and not the next. She would make me feel like I was always letting her down and then make me feel that I was perfect. She even _apologized_ for disciplining me. She would buy my love way too much, she still does! Her mothering was confusing, so when I looked at her as a woman, that's when I lost all respect for her. Not getting exactly what she wanted drove her to be an emotional wreck! First the bitching and nonsense yelling would start. The things she would say to you! She just kept on and it would get violent. I don't even know who started the violence, but I always felt that she deserved it. She had to make sure that the whole outside world saw a perfect family, marriage, mother and woman, and if it didn't look that way she would cover up any way she *could. I learned to be one way around Mom, another around you, a different "me" for every situation. I was smarter than all the other kids, really, I was bored with school, I had all the boys, I had the best clothes, I was the bravest. Then you left! That "bitch" that was my mother threw you out! Then she sends me away! I don't remember hearing anything from you during that time I was with Grandpa. I couldn't understand why you didn't want me. Well, after some time, back to Mom, I was 7 or 8 and my image of other people was that they were all idiots and sad. I didn't know why I was so different, but I chose to live in my own world. What I've always done to get by, what's always worked, it's my*

At the end of the second page, there was no page three, the letter jumped to a final half page, marked #4, starting in the middle of a sentence.

so much pain that I took what came my way with no care. If you didn't know, I started doing crystal meth when I was 12 or 13. If it wasn't for this drug, I think I may have gone insane, because holding in my rage and then finally letting it out and it didn't seem that anyone, including you, gave a damn ... And yet I feel that the woman I am today is a great woman! I'm still smart, beautiful and strong. I know I seem like a loser. I haven't accomplished anything worthy to anyone else, but me. I have goals, and I know that when I'm ready and able to go for them, nothing will stand in my way.

And the letter ended without a sign-off or signature or smileyface.

Trinity's paternal grandfather had died two years ago, when Trinity was 18, two or three years after the stint in family therapy (from which Trinity had apparently picked up plenty of explanations and justifications, the "rage" that had to be "let out," the therapist-assisted view of Virginia's character, as though a six-year-old could have such a perception. The counselor had managed to turn chaos into a cliché). That would make this letter around the time Trinity had agreed to Cal's ground rules for her being allowed to live in the house, like finishing her GED and getting a job, which, by the time of the journal entries from last summer, Trinity had not even started, despite the "goals" and nothing-standing-in-her-way.

But why did there seem that so much more had gone on in that black hole of time, the late 80s to early 90s, when apparently, and without his cognizance, Trinity had run away (he was probably told she was at a sleep-over), didn't come home at night (ditto), had been kicked out of school, commenced sex, drugs and gang membership (although he did recall the gang writing on the sliding closet doors in her bedroom which—after one of the "intense fights with mother and step-father"— she'd been required to paint over, but the job only half done, and now Virginia left that closet open so the painted door hid the remaining gang writing on the other door).

In a way, he'd been lucky. Trinity's willingness to "do something like that or even worse to someone" had not included a claim that he'd touched her. But Virginia had once told him that Trinity described a "dream" where Cal raped her and, therefore, Virginia left him. He had probably, at the time, misinterpreted why Virginia was telling him (and had considered that perhaps she was making it up). But he'd been smart enough to not say, "A nightmare or fantasy?" Virginia would have, perhaps rightfully so, become a cyclone of fury. But of course by that snark he wouldn't have meant the girl was perhaps fantasizing about his sexual facility, but more likely about a means that would get her something she wanted: getting rid of *bad thing #2.*

Luckier still because if Virginia had chosen to remember that dream during therapy with Trinity, Cal's ass would have been in legal hell.

But, besides appearing second on the "bad" list, wasn't it clear that Cal's presence wasn't a significant source of Trinity's trajectory? That

Trinity hadn't been the only one in the house preferring one's own world to so-called real life where one worked, breathed, ate and shat?

All these contemplations about the girl and none about the boy. Well, she'd left a piece of herself, and, like cancer or tape worms, pieces tended to keep coming back to feed. And indeed Trinity would, and he would continue to be lucky, because the house would not burn down and Cal wouldn't be handcuffed and taken away. She would steal a box of checks, try to hack into the computer, probably take cash; leave behind her cats, household junk, and of course eventually a kid, every time she cleared out to go off with who-knows-who who-knows-where until they (or he) also got tired of cleaning up after her. Maybe she wrote gang writing on *their* closet walls as well, marking every place that had given her a bed, bathroom, access to water, food (and brownies), drugs, a telephone, even a car.

March 1994

The memorial service was on their 10th wedding anniversary. Virginia had wanted to hold it in their backyard, and use the occasion to renew their vows. Cal had diverted the backyard plan by suggesting there would be too many guests. Invitations had been sent to every aunt and cousin and second-cousin, friend and extended friend on both sides of the family. The price for the postage alone, not to mention the printed invitations, was enough that Cal deleted stamped-addressed RSVP envelopes. Although an RSVP was requested, none came by mail, a few by phone. Virginia's church was available that day—a Wednesday—without charge, so he let her order several huge white flower arrangements. There would be no casket, of course. So she fussed over photo choices to display with the flowers and had his military portrait blown up to poster size for the front alter. She had not protested any of the arrangements Cal changed or vetoed.

The church was barely a quarter full, but it was a large sanctuary, seating 400—adapted from a closed-down Akron store. Cal didn't know half of those in attendance. He supposed members of the church. He didn't even know if the man, Pete, who'd called him at the shop that one time, had come from Las Vegas. Trinity had not come down from Oakland. When Virginia had finally gotten a hold of her, Trinity said she didn't have enough money. Cal had said okay to buying her a bus ticket, but Trinity said they needed money for rent and food. He was pretty sure Virginia had sent cash from the grocery money he still gave to her, especially since she hadn't done a lot of grocery-shopping and he'd been buying the necessities. Virginia was in the front row enveloped by her sister and mother. She wore a new dress, white floor length; and new wig, dark brown a little past her shoulders with heavy bangs. Somehow she was not overly pale. Her sister had done her make-up.

The banner on the biggest easel display of white flowers beside the poster—also on an easel—said "My Angel." She'd given a list to the organist for "Angel" songs, so there was a medley that moved from "Earth Angel" to "Angel of the Morning" to "Heaven Must be Missing an Angel" to "There Must Be an Angel (Playing With My Heart)" to "Angel Baby." The organist had added "Teen Angel." Virginia asked Cal to play one on his sax, "with the noodling doodling you do."

"There are other aspects of him besides his name," Cal told her.

He stood in front of the plus-or-minus 40 people—is it called an *audience* at a memorial?—his sax hanging from its neck strap like a large, heavy tie. "Although I didn't know him long …" He cleared his throat. His voice was softer and foggier than usual. "His life was too short but had the intensity we all should envy." He fingered an E, then E-flat. "It's not how he died that matters …," aware instantaneously that it was the voiceover of a TV sports movie. "His creativity, his …" He swung the sax to a position under his right arm. "He loved his mother." A few people started coughing. Reminded him he could use a cigarette. Cal closed his eyes.

In high school, he'd tried to write a political-protest song for his band. He'd asked X to look at his lyrics, and she'd said, "It's so literal, like just putting *Reagan's a bastard* to a tune. Use symbols and metaphors," and she'd directed him to Paul Simon's "Loves me Like a Rock" as an example … *my mama loves me, she loves me...* Then in their year of college together, X had shown him a tribute she'd written for a high school classmate who had been found dead, slumped over a chemistry experiment in his kitchen. She'd used the phrase "good and decent" and he'd chided her for sounding like a politician at a funeral. One of the times she hadn't spoken to him for 2 weeks.

He looked down at his mouthpiece, his reed likely drying out. But resisted the urge to put it into his mouth.

"He was … he had a lot of … obstacles in his … young life." *Dang Cal* … his turn to be mocked again, but instead of an inept songwriter, more like an evangelist who didn't know the deceased from a hole in his elbow. Somehow he was coming up with his own Virginia-isms, just marry two clichés. *Dang Cal* again, *are you trying to be ironic?* As only a walking cliché can.

And it didn't elude him that he wasn't using the boy's name. Would he hear about it from Virginia, if she noticed as well? Behind sunglasses, in the dark mop of wig hair, her face was somewhat tilted down.

The audience's—*spectators?*—coughs were more like throat-clearing. Feet were shuffling and paper whooshing. Virginia had had a program printed. Cal's eulogy listed after the first prayer, before inviting others to come up and tell their own *loving memories of Angel*, followed by a few more songs and the final prayer.

He opened his eyes. "Despite early hardship, he had an uncanny ability to …" Had he been about to say *survive?* He thought he heard Virginia sob. "There really are no words for … a young man taken … from his mother … or from his family … from life … so early." He looked down at his mouthpiece again. Then it was in his mouth, at first just air, warm air, rushing through the horn. Until the air became subtone, the fuzz of an E-flat, growing stronger and clearer as the melody for "Why Was I Born" began to swell, inflate, heave into the booming acoustics of the formerly retail auditorium, the sluggish deep dirge-y blues melody. *Why was I born, Why am I livin', What do I get, What am I givin'.* If anyone knew the words, maybe it could still somehow be suitable. X would know. Hadn't he been playing it for her in the shop, Billie Holiday, then Coltrane, then Ella … if she doesn't know by now …

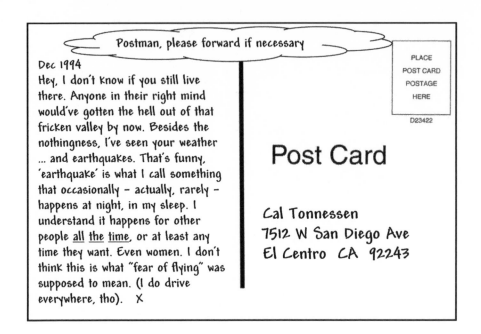

Postman, please forward if necessary

Dec 1994
Hey, I don't know if you still live there. Anyone in their right mind would've gotten the hell out of that fricken valley by now. Besides the nothingness, I've seen your weather ... and earthquakes. That's funny, 'earthquake' is what I call something that occasionally – actually, rarely – happens at night, in my sleep. I understand it happens for other people all the time, or at least any time they want. Even women. I don't think this is what "fear of flying" was supposed to mean. (I do drive everywhere, tho).   X

PLACE
POST CARD
POSTAGE
HERE

D23422

Post Card

Cal Tonnessen
7512 W San Diego Ave
El Centro CA 92243

1995

Maybe you need to have someone "drive" you. Someone else. Drive you 'til you fly.

Would he even be able to?

The address was in Trinity's journal, he went back and found it. The Sinclair Institute. Ordinary Couples / Extraordinary Sex.

No one would call us an ordinary couple.

No one would call us a couple.

His large stamped self-addressed (to the music store) envelope came back with a catalogue. The damn place still existed, wasn't some scam Trinity fell into. Well, Trinity wasn't Virginia. Maybe the videos she had listed in her journal had actually arrived at the house, had been watched in her room, and perhaps were still there, somewhere in the boxes and bags of stuff on, under and around the bed and dresser so that neither the bed or dresser was fully visible anymore. He wasn't sure what was going on in there, whether it was all Trinity's belongings packed up for her to someday come get. How could it be possible that all of that was at one time put away in the small room. Maybe some was Angel's.

When Trinity came back—showed up unannounced, unless you counted the invitation to the memorial service 6 months earlier—all the boxes and bags got moved into the living room. She arrived with nothing except a tattered nylon backpack, wearing jean shorts that her thighs mushroomed out of, and a too-small spaghetti-strap top with a rose tattooed on the topmost bulge of one breast. She left with the backpack and two suitcases, wearing an exercise outfit, pants and sweatshirt, maybe over something else. Virginia wouldn't buy the bus ticket if Trinity didn't wear more than she'd arrived in. He wasn't sure if Virginia bought her new clothes or they just rummaged through what was in the house. Virginia was the one to say Trinity had to go, after Virginia came home to find something going on that Cal never got the full story of. In the fight he came home into the middle of, Virginia used the word *whore* a great deal. The damage caused by the fight was mostly spillage: make-up, some food and sodas, the whole basket of bills kept on the kitchen ledge. Virginia took Trinity to the bus depot the next day, let Trinity decide how far and what direction the ticket would provide, came home and cried in bed for a few hours. She didn't move the boxes and bags back into Trinity's room for a few weeks.

He never went into Trinity's room, even after she was gone again. Angel's room was where Cal started to store his speakers, mic and amplifier; his file cabinet; and half his clothes that had been moved from their bedroom closet to a rack on wheels. There wasn't room for more clothes in Angel's closet either. He only went in there to get clean clothes, or his speakers and mic when he had a gig. He didn't even need the speakers at gigs—Cliff had a whole sound system for Blue Sand—but the speakers and amp plus his sax and gig bag filled his car so that it wouldn't take a passenger. This had been working for a while, but the jig might be up soon, so to speak.

He'd also put in a set of plastic shelving in Angel's room, as an auxiliary pantry, since the garage was too hot to store food, after Virginia had begged to join Price Club.

Two people fewer and an extra pantry needed.
You're not getting fat, are you?
That's why I still smoke, which I know you also loathe.
I just would've thought you're smarter than that.
If you really knew more than an address, you'd know I'm not.

Still, he didn't have a TV, much less VCR, at the shop, so what good were the tapes going to be? The plan would be to get a bigger TV and new VCR for the house, and then quietly bring the old ones to the shop. If she asked why not the bedroom … well, how much time did he spend there? Also, maybe he needed the equipment at the shop to video and play back music lessons.

Dang, Cal.

Among the catalogue's offerings was a series called The Kama Sutra Illustrated: tranquil teachings from the ancient discoverers of sensual pleasure. He ordered that one. Then took Virginia to Price Club to buy the bigger TV and new VCR. She never questioned his needing the old units at the shop. Perhaps she was too focused on stocking up on cleaning supplies. At some point that year Cal found the cache: Dow bathroom cleaner, Tilex, Softscrub with bleach, Limeaway, lime scale remover, Clean Shower, Old Dutch cleanser, Arm & Hammer, Mr. Clean, Spotshot carpet spray, Resolve carpet spray, 409, Lysol bathroom cleaner, Comet, Kaboom, Fantastik, most of them not yet opened. The house often smelled of bleach when he got home.

Virginia's church attendance had increased. Not surprising with the new friends collected after Angel's memorial service. Prayer meeting one night, Bible study another, worship service and Sunday school on Sunday, and she volunteered in the childcare room two days a week during afternoon meetings of various groups, Christian Singles and Christian Mothers.

He was able to remember the names of the groups because when she informed him of her new schedule of responsibilities, he'd said, "The singles group needs childcare?" Not a smart thing to do, considering she was ironing at the time. He thought maybe she would hold the iron down on his shirt long enough for one of those bad-TV-comedy black iron prints. He didn't notice the iron jammed into the shirt pocket hard enough to tear the pocket halfway off, at least not until he tried to put his pencil there before going to the shop.

It would have seemed that childcare would remain her choice, but on one Price Club trip, she asked Cal when they could buy a computer. She wanted to try to work for the newsletter and maybe be on the events committee, so she needed to "get onto AOL mail and surf on a net."

Right after he said, "Does all that do something a phone can't do?" he thought about the stack of postcards with no return address. He said, "Okay, I'll look into it. Cliff will know a good computer brand."

"Thanks, Sweetie!" She hugged him around the waist from behind.

The afternoon group Virginia did go to was Christian Cooks. She must have told him she was attending the group because, after dinners of beef stroganoff, shepherd's pie, chicken & broccoli divan, and Hungarian goulash, when he'd said "To what do I owe for these new meals?" she responded, "I *told* you, do you ever listen to *anything* I say?" A spoon or something like it tapped the back of his head. Maybe a little more than a tap.

A little later when she was sitting with her own meal, she said, "Christian Cooks. But don't worry, you'll still get your tacos once a week. A Christian wife feeds her man's body, soul, mind and spirit."

"Your tacos do all of the above." Was the comment really out-of-line? His dinner was taken and thrown in the sink.

But mostly, with all Virginia's scheduled afternoons and evenings, and except for the 3 or 4 weeks Trinity had holed up there before they kicked her out, Cal did have more time alone in his own house, and what he did with it hadn't changed a lot. The VCR and TV still not hooked up at the store, the videos that arrived from The Sinclair Institute still in the padded envelope and hidden in an empty trumpet case from a horn that had been cannibalized for parts. What was he waiting for, a murmur from afar?

Aug 1995
Do you still get the back-to-school
feeling in August? New classes, new
people, sometimes a new school, a
chance to start over as someone else.
Dem daze R gone, eh? (Am I talking to
you or myself?) So now Aug is a good
time for a puppy. Back-to-basics,
focused only on here and now, her little
brain developing fast and I can't let it
get away from me. Give her the right
start, avoid a lifetime of glitches. Which
includes the right name! Dang, I'm
drawing blanks. But the payoff, in 3 or 4
years, blue-and-gold ribbons, the only
ones that matter (to hell with red, yellow
and white). The feeling of that in-sync
flow of a perfect partnership working
together... as good as orgasm. Or so
they say.   X

Post Card

Cal Tonnessen
7512 W San Diego Ave
El Centro CA 92243

Spring 1996

The scene that apparently took place in the women's rest room at a gig was after Trinity's next appearance, this one coined in advance as a "visit." She'd reunited with Ced or Cy. Cal wasn't sure at first, which prompted another "They all look alike, huh?" from Virginia. How could they look alike when he had never seen either one before Trinity and the man came through the door. He was tall and heavy—muscular, maybe moving toward fat. His head was shaved and in one ear wore a diamond stud. His baggy jeans and T-shirt were clean. He smiled and shook Cal's hand. He let Trinity do most of the talking. She—also heading toward fat, still dressed so that the tops of her breasts (and tattoo) showed, now sporting a baseball cap, a short tight skirt with chunky-heeled ankle-boots, sections of her hair a cheesey sort of yellow—said she wanted to visit home before they moved to Las Vegas where Ced planned to work in a casino. Despite being a couple moving to another state, they brought only a black plastic garbage sack of clothes and Trinity's backpack. Virginia told Cal an unreasonable landlord had thrown them out.

I suppose unreasonable because he asked for the rent. Cal smiled inside at X, but said, "Maybe they can take some of this crap you've got in the garage."

She turned after kicking her shoes into the closet. "What do you mean?" No expression and her voice flat

He meant, besides the erstwhile yard-sale items, the 20 assorted packages of pasta and rice, not counting the boxes of pre-prepared pasta or rice dishes; the collection of fabric softeners, laundry detergents, skin lotions, foot powders, bandages, sunscreen, bath oil, and hand soaps. The big flat boxes of packaged ramen noodles and canned soups—each box carrying dozens of the same kind of soup—the gallon cans of salsa, cheese sauce, Crisco, molasses, and thousand island dressing; the bouquet of cake mixes.

"Just that now's your chance to help her set up a household, including some food."

Virginia's eyes brightened. "Can you lend them a car to get it all there?"

He was afraid she might jump to the bed and land on him. It was so rare for them to be preparing for bed at the same time, but sorting everything out after Trinity's arrival—clearing out the room again, moving his things out of the 2nd bathroom, Virginia's fancy "tablecloth and napkins" meal of roast chicken and potatoes Au Gratin from scratch (despite the array of box mixes for potato dishes stacked with those of rice and pasta)—had brought them up against 10 p.m.. Trinity and Ced were still home, so he knew Virginia wouldn't suggest any activity in the bed, or if she did his answer would not be beyond his past behavior.

He was still seated on the bedside. "I can't see how I can do that."

"Why?"

"I think that kind of trust has to be earned, don't you, Virginia?" Immediately realized the mistake of putting her name at the end of the sentence—for a kind of emphasis, he admitted, but it was already said— so he wasn't 100% surprised when she picked up the socks he'd just peeled off and, as though accidentally, whipped them across his face as she turned to put them into the laundry. There was no sting. He lay down and fiddled with the alarm, even though it always kept the same wake-up time.

When Trinity and Ced were still there a week later, Cal asked, over his lunch and their breakfast, when they were planning to move on to Las Vegas.

"We're waiting for some arrangements that have to be made," Trinity answered.

"They have to have somewhere to live," Virginia offered, buttering toast then putting it on Ced's plate.

Trinity shot her mother a nasty look.

Virginia continued, "I just meant why move if you'll be living in your car?" The next piece of buttered toast went to Trinity's plate. "Stay here until your dad or one of your cousins can—"

Cal shoveled a last bite of ranch beans that had complimented the Polish sausages and sauerkraut Virginia served him. He stood and left the table, pushed in his chair then touched Ced's shoulder and asked if, while he was living there, he could do some work around the house that was too heavy for Virginia.

"Sure thing, man, just let me know what's needed."

"There's a dead tree in back, needs cutting down and cutting up." Cal picked up his satchel, kept his eyes on Ced, because he could feel the focus of Trinity's scowl had been moved to him. "Work early mornings when it's cool." He moved to the kitchen doorway. He didn't know why he paused there.

"How about you *hire* him ... like you did for Angel?" Trinity said.

Virginia froze, sponging off a countertop. Cal watched her close her eyes. As though in sympathy, the refrigerator sighed and went dormant. The only sound in the flash of silence was Ced's fork scraping egg yolk from his plate.

"I'd assumed," Cal said, "this was a visit ... indicating temporary."

"You want us to leave?"

"Actually ... yes. If you're planning to get started on something in Las Vegas, I don't know why you would put it off to ... mark time here."

"Maybe we're getting ready, *making preparations*, ever fucking hear of that?"

Virginia still hadn't moved or opened her eyes. Cal left the doorway. Behind him, before he opened the front door and security screen, he heard Trinity say, "Can you fucking *believe* it?"

Virginia: "*Trinity*—"

Trinity: "Whose side are you *on?*"

In two or three days, two branches were sawed off the dead tree with a carpenter's saw. The branches were left under the tree, the saw on the patio table, hidden between several large, now dusty and collapsing boxes that had been there since the yard sale collection had swollen out of the garage. The rest of that week, Cal let his work day stretch by two hours, from 7 – 6 to 6 – 8. He had lunch with Cliff every day. Supper was left for him on a plate to be heated in the microwave. He came home early on Friday, around 6:30, parked on the street because there was a little splotch of shade from a palo verde. He started to hear Trinity and Virginia from the driveway. The event didn't include the familiar screech of chairs on the floor or thumps against the wall, nor the somewhat less familiar spatter of glass, just the voices, strident and simultaneous. He wondered what Ced was doing during this, but found out later Ced was gone, put on a bus to Las Vegas by Trinity that morning. Trinity had remained another day, Virginia said later, because she hadn't yet gotten the "help" Virginia had promised.

"How much … help?" he asked later, when Virginia recounted.

"Believe me, less than it would've been, after she speaks to me like that, using the Fuck-word and everything."

Those words – all of them – had been difficult for Cal to pick apart from the driveway. But when he got inside the door, caught Trinity's last screech, "… like he wanted to own a *slave.*" When the door closed, all went quiet in the kitchen. Cal usually went first into the kitchen, for a soda. But he took his satchel down the hall to the bedroom. The women's voices modulated, continued, footsteps thumped partway down the hall to Trinity's room, then back out to the kitchen. Maybe a half hour. Then they left. Cal was smoking on the front stoop when Virginia came home, alone. Tacos Dorados for dinner.

June 1996
I found a better address. Lots-o-shit found online these days. Search your name, you might "find yourself," like people in the 60s used to do. Look at us, we're getting close to 40! Maybe I shouldn't tell you, but I throw away more cards than I mail. I've even thrown them away already stamped. And look, I'm filling this one with a shitload of nothing. Why? Because anything that's not nothing is TMI? Maybe I should write a memoir instead of these postcards. An adventure where nothing happens. But probably could only do it if I pretended I was only telling you. Why you? Because earthquakes don't faze you? Maybe you don't even notice anymore when the "earth shakes beneath your feet." Will I mail this one?   X

Post Card

Cal Tonnessen
c/o Cliff's Edge Music
136 E Main St
El Centro CA 92243

He did finally get the TV and VCR hooked up in his shop. Part of the delay had to do with the whole unpleasant snarl of technology itself, the sweaty hours installing and programming the new VCR at home, and more recently assembling some exercise equipment he'd let Virginia order when she became alarmed at her weight gain. Even fully assembled, and with an instruction book plus VHS showing various exercises, neither of them could figure out what to do on the metal and vinyl-padded apparatus that sat mostly horizontal on the floor. He hadn't acquiesced to the Elliptical Fitness Crosstrainer she'd seen on TV, and she'd eye-rolled his suggestion of a mini trampoline. But not as much as X's lip might curl at this pitiful excuse for not watching the tapes sooner. Although ... why would she care?

At some point in the past, at some gig with bandmates who weren't the guys in Blue Sand, a guy had made an obvious pun about *licks*, just as obviously aligning it, the oral act, with ambrosia. Somehow Cal had managed a retort that produced a dialogue, one which included Cal's admission that he'd never done it, and the guy had said "God,

you're missing out, it's the best thing, makes it *all* that much better."
Could a guy really have said that? A guy in a band who could've, after all,
even been a drummer or bass player? Cal must be conflating what the
guy said with his own dissonant thoughts at the time: that his "alone-
times" with X almost always went there, but his single actual almost-
attempt had turned his stomach. (Who was that with? Probably a gig
pick-up before Virginia.)

I almost don't blame you. Yuk. Who would go nose-and-mouth there?

*This tape, this shows why I had the instinct ... but only with you ... it would
help you, allow you to feel ... make us be ... and look how he ... it says that he
should press his hand there afterwards, to help her feel secure, safe ...*

*What does afterwards mean? How do you know when afterwards should
start?*

*You'd like if it was me. If I went there. If you let me ... it would mean you
trusted me ... and you'd be able to let go of ... everything else. We both would.*

Oh Cal, how in your life as a pessimist do you still believe this?

Like the wedding season, the holidays provided multiple gigs.
Companies, from a law office to the whole hospital, having parties: these
were the gigs he brought Virginia to. (When he tried to say his car was
too small for all his equipment plus a passenger, she said, "Let's take
mine." So he stopped dragging his mic and amps to gigs. Soon they
would be permanently hemmed into Angel's room as the storage of
goods there flourished.)

He hadn't seen the restroom altercation, and only heard of it later
from the drummer whose wife was in a toilet stall during all or most of it.
So it went from drummer's wife to drummer, from drummer to Cal ...
and who knows who else. As though Virginia's wariness had been on
hiatus while she went through the states of grief over Angel (not that he
expected her to someday be "finished" with that), apparently she
followed a woman into the restroom and confronted her, told her to stay
away from Cal.

The parts Cal didn't know: What did the woman say when
challenged with this kind of possible threat? *Was* a threat included? Who
was the woman? What had she actually been doing?

Possible guesses for the latter two: She'd been dancing at the party, perhaps dancing alone, or in a group of women. And she was somehow familiar to Virginia, perhaps a parent of a student or former student. Cal couldn't remember seeing the particular student's-mother who Virginia had been suspicious of several years ago. And he also didn't remember seeing anyone dancing who he might've thought to say *hello* to later at the gig. He wasn't even sure which gig it was. He actually called the drummer a few days later to try to find out a little more, because of something that had happened a few months prior: Virginia had pushed a woman, causing her to fall to the ground in a parking lot of some store, probably PriceCostco. Virginia reported that the woman had pushed her cart into Virginia's, on purpose, and didn't apologize or even acknowledge that it had happened. "That's how they are," was Virginia's summation, to which Cal had not responded *Oh, they all act alike, huh?* He was too concerned the woman might have followed Virginia to the car and gotten her license plate number and a lawsuit notification would be arriving soon. There was still plenty of time for that to happen, and now a possible second aggressive altercation in a restroom?

The drummer didn't have any new specifics, just "she said it got pretty hot, Virginia was pretty excited," and "She didn't want to come out of the stall while they were going at it," but couldn't answer when Cal asked if both women had raised their voices or was it mostly one who was *going at it*, and by *it,* did that mean some pushing-and-shoving … or worse?

"I don't think it was an all-out cat-fight, if that's what you mean. Just … you know how Virginia can get." Said as though Cal needed to be reminded of what everyone else knew.

That's when he heard (saw?) X's teeth-barring inhalation. *Dang, what's up with her?*

She's crazy suspicious. It's almost as though we are having an aff—

Gak, stop, not that suburban 1950s word.

Okay … seeing each other.

Except you know we're not.

Oh how it feels so real, lying here, no one near, only you, and you can't hear me, when I say softly, slowly …

Jeez, You answer with Elton John?

... Now she's in me, always with me, tiny dancer in my hand ...
I'm gagging, you know that.

Jan 1997
I actually looked up to see if there's
ever a dog show where you live. Not
that I would go that far, "not the end of
the world but you can see it from here."
Why do you stay? But I guess someone
could ask the same of me, for different
reasons. As far as the place itself,
enough rich people to pay for my
services, which something tells me
would never be the case *there*. So,
another card filled with useless nothing.
But what else is there except my puppy,
who's not a pup anymore, finally
scheduled for her "alteration," PC
lingo. "Fixed." HA. Spay her & get rid
of that whole shebang, so she can focus
on her true mission. (Dang, that
sounds bad. But *I* never wanted kids!)
X

PLACE
POST CARD
POSTAGE
HERE

D23422

Post Card

Cal Tonnessen
c/o Cliff's Edge Music
136 E Main St
El Centro CA 92243

A very rare occasion, out to Saturday lunch with the guys without wives: Cal tried to say what guys say when they're out with the guys without wives. "Why do women whine, *you never make love to me,* after they've spent all day bitching your ass out?"

He didn't notice, at first, that the guys' laughter was tinged with discomfort, with knowing more than they wanted to know.

Dang, Cal ... but I know what you mean, tryin'ta sound like everyone else.
I know you know you don't have to pretend with me.

Two other members of Blue Sand had been in the store, one to drop off the lights he'd brought home from the last gig, the other already there to give Saturday morning keyboard lessons. A local school band director brought two clarinets and a saxophone for repair. Someone suggested lunch. Cal, smiling a little crazily, said, "Okay, but Ricky's gonna have some 'splainin to do."

The same kind of uneasy laughter from the guys.

Spill it, Cal.

I'm not allowed to have fun if she's not invited. Isn't it, well, typical?

Of _what_? Dang, _pathetic_.

Where _are_ you? So much I'd tell you better than this shit if I could really say

it.

Cal and Cliff in their early 40s, the insurance-salesman keyboard player closer to 50. The band director had to be somewhere between; he'd been teaching longer than the 15-plus years Cal had been in the fricken valley working at the store, still the only music store in a town with a prison but no university, a comedy club but no live theater, a weekly outdoor farmer's market but no natural food store. Now there were four high schools, six trade/technical schools, a Home Depot, Costco and Walmart, but still only one bookstore that was mostly magazines and cards, hanging on because the stationary store had gone out of business. No botanical garden or art museum but two dirt car racing tracks. No Volvo dealer or Thai restaurant, but three bowling alleys and a firing range. Quincañera coming-out parties almost every weekend at the dozens of banquet/reception halls, a stop on the professional rodeo circuit, but no ice rink or dog shows; a community choir, community orchestra, and one semi-pro (if pocket-change made them pros) jazz combo with Cal on sax, but dozens of country bands, metal bands, and hundreds of mariachi bands. A town on the wrong side of the Southern California mountains from where he and X had grown up and gone to college, only a hundred miles away from here and long before he was bald. But X no longer lived a mere hundred miles away.

Somehow Virginia already knew about the lunch. Dinner wasn't cooking when he got home at 6. He put his bag down in the dark, clean kitchen, and went down the hall to the bedroom where she was on the bed in the dark. At least not *in* bed, as she'd been for weeks after Angel died. He didn't turn the light on.

"Not feeling well?"

"You know how I'm feeling."

"Sad, I guess."

"Betrayed more like it."

Cal felt in his pocket for his cigarettes, but they were out in the car.

As though he'd asked what she meant, she said, "You can go out to eat with the guys but never with your *wife?*"

"Okay c'mon, pick someplace to go tonight."

She wouldn't pick, in fact didn't answer, so when she finally got off the bed, straightened her wig, put on her shoes and picked up her purse, he took her to Denny's because she liked their pies. She ordered a cobb salad.

"Hope you're leaving room for pie," he said.

"Oh are we here just for dessert? Did you eat your all-important man-meal with the dudes? And of course dudes don't eat *rubbage.* You need rubbage in your diet, *here*—" And off she went, each remark punctuated by a piece of lettuce thrown across the table at him.

• He would rather have fun with anyone but her. • The other guys wives were probably there. • He must've taken someone else. • She knew he was seeing someone. • Mrs. Sanchez *saw* him with someone. • It had been a lie when she'd said that whole thing with Mrs. Sanchez was a misunderstanding. • Did he know what it was like to be the only one trying to have a marriage? • The Lord was going to pay him back for what he's done to her.

The last piece of lettuce hit his head as he bent to take a bite of meatloaf. It stuck to his scalp and he had to peel it off.

Remember in college when you said my hair was like dry wild hay? Now it's like lettuce.

Sept 1997
What do you think of a guy who goes out
to lunch <u>every day</u>, but never wants
dinner? Not complaining, cuz cooking
ain't my <u>thang</u>. After all, lunches he's at
work, and no one *I* know packed him a
lunch! I'm out training by the time he
leaves. A suit plodding to & from "the
office"? Is it cruel to not try to make it
better for him? Why am I asking <u>you</u>! I
can't imagine you living that way.
Especially the suit. Unless you wear one
to spill your guts at gigs. My new dog
almost ready to start showing. She'll kick
<u>ass</u>. Almost named her Orgasm –
couldn't go through with it. So she's
Climax. I'll get some funky looks. But her
recall command isn't "Climax, <u>come</u>!" You
probably don't know what I'm blathering
about. X

PLACE
POST CARD
POSTAGE
HERE

D23422

Post Card

Cal Tonnessen
c/o Cliff's Edge Music
136 E Main St
El Centro CA 92243

What the fuck are you talking about?
    Is this a cosmic connection, or …
    Sheer coincidence, don't try to make it bigger than it is.

1998

He didn't find out that he'd been "carded"—that Trinity had found a
way to use the inspiration provided by her brother—until the debt was
close to $8,000. What she'd bought on the card that Virginia had
cosigned for at the beginning of the year was a mystery, since Trinity was
dropped off from a battered van (which backfired as it pulled away,
immediately after Trinity closed the door). She had a small suitcase full of
make-up, a laundry bag packed with clothes, sections of her hair bleached
white so it looked zebra-striped, eyes so lined in black it seemed even her
irises were obscured, and a tube top that looked like it was made of neon-
colored latex, the rose tattoo on her breast now joined by the tail of a
snake (its head under the tube top, god knows where).

    Making room for Trinity in her old bedroom—moving boxes and
bags into the garage and then spilling over into the living room—let him
realize how much more had accumulated in the past year. He'd given up

on ever using his workbench in the garage. A few times during the year, needing to clean the lawn mower filters, put a garden tool in the vise to reattach the handle, or lay out the parts to a faucet he was trying to repair, he'd had to move a box of trophies. Twice he had put the box on top of the trashcan while he worked. The third time he put it into his car, along with the closest two unmarked bags of soft stuff (one was sofa pillows of various colors and ages), and drove them to the Salvation Army. It might have been a few weeks later that Virginia called him at the shop, yelling about where had her trophies gone. When he'd pointed out that none of them had been won by her or her kids, she railed that she had planned to take them apart and rebuild trophies for the church to use at Bible Daycamp, and besides *his* trophies from high school band were in there as well, and good riddance, maybe she should just bring his saxophone to the Salvation Army and be done with his philandering at gigs. The next day he'd moved his instruments back to the music store, where he'd intermittently over the years kept them locked in the shop, but then had gotten lazy (or the shop got too crowded) and brought them home. He hadn't discarded any more junk after that, and now one wall of the living room had a double row of boxes and bags as well.

But they didn't even *have* to move everything out of the bedroom so Trinity could use it. As soon as Cal found out about the $7,834 credit card bill he was responsible for, Virginia— crying, apologizing, pleading-ignorance (and how could he argue that she wasn't)—agreed that Trinity had to go. The beater that picked her up a week later, a muffler-less sedan, was driven by none other than Ced or Cy (he hadn't gotten out to help Trinity throw her stuff into the back seat).

To try to help pay the debt, Virginia had taught at Bible Daycamp for a week, then mysteriously didn't work the 2nd week nor the additional sessions, except to cook for the end-of-camp picnics, for which she'd stocked up at Costco with more box cake mixes, bags of various-shaped pasta, and gallon-size jars of mayonnaise, pickles, relish, and mustard. Cal hadn't noticed the upsurge on the pantry shelves in Angel's old room because he'd been working until 10 or 11 every night at the shop after an outreach to schools in remote desert towns, Blythe, Calipatria, even as far west as Campo, and he'd driven the circuit to haul in all the old deteriorating horns that might now be made playable, to pay down the debt.

June 1998
How can I fit this on a card. You thot I disappeared. Some days I wish I had. Climax was attacked while I was training in a dog park. "Leash-free" must mean it's OK that some dumb-fuck's Rottweiler has never obeyed a command in its dumb-fuck life. I don't know which saved her, me getting myself ripped up by getting in between, or the hyperbaric chamber flooding her wounds with oxygen. Had to pull some strings that might not even exist to get that chamber to allow a dog – my "celebrity" on local TV once a month. Biggest HA in this pitiful so-called career. Damn fuckin damn. But she's alive and finally starting her career. 199 ½ at her first trial. Some Climax, huh? Her scars covered with fur, mine with jeans. X

PLACE
POST CARD
POSTAGE
HERE

D23422

Post Card

Cal Tonnessen
c/o Cliff's Edge Music
136 E Main St
El Centro CA 92243

1999

Two things happened before he quit playing in Blue Sand. He would've quit anyway after the first thing. The second thing just happened to come later in the day after the first thing, and before Cal had a chance to tell Cliff to find a new sax player.

They had a New Year's gig in the mountains. The drummer had a little place in Pine Valley and had booked them at a local bar & grill December 31st, 9 p.m. to 1 a.m.. He invited everyone in the band, and spouses, to stay at his place afterwards, so they could feel free to imbibe at the gig. Three of the guys, Cal included, accepted the invitation. So with the drummer and his wife, that made six people in the cabin and two in a camper parked outside. The cabin had two bedrooms, plus futon in the living room. Cal had had enough to drink during the gig that sleeping on the futon—closer to Virginia than in their bed at home—wasn't a problem, and in fact he slept until all of the others were up and already having breakfast in the tiny kitchen on the other side of the wall from where he lay. The voices, articulated with laughter, were just a rhythm, not an unpleasant one, until Virginia riffed, "I know, *so* interesting to see Cal at work on the chickadees, proves what's been driving me star-craving mad." The moment of silence wasn't the group wondering if Virginia was craving stardom. Somebody mumbled something. Plates clinked. Then Virginia's voice was even louder, "I just don't understand why one of you wouldn't have told me instead of let my suspicions run wild." A chair scraped. A low voice hummed, then a softer one pipped up. Virginia again: "Actually I *do* know. I wish Cliff was here because it extends into the music store—not the students themselves, I always trusted him with my daughter, but look how young their mothers are nowadays. I mean, if he's going to carry on like this, believe me, I'll throw my hat into the fire." The next silence was quickly broken by two female voices, but they were more likely trying to change the subject than asking Virginia if she planned to run for public office. "No, wait, really," Virginia said, "I've tried, over and over, like Jesus said, to be the one to throw the first stone. I can see he's out of control now."

Cal let his feet hit the floor as heavily as he could, walked deliberately down the short hall to the single bathroom, thankful for the creaky floorboards, then closed the door a little too hard, but not so it seemed like an irate slam. He stayed after peeing, fighting the need for a cigarette, the hot water feeling good on his hands. When he joined the group in the kitchen, the bass player's wife was remarking that they'd been circling the parking lot of the new Red Lobster ever since ground was broken, jonesing for soft-shell crab, and they should all go to dinner when it opens.

"Cal doesn't like fish," Virginia said.

"They have steak and chicken."

"He doesn't like the *smell*."

He would never know if they would have laughed or sat in another frozen moment, because he spoke up immediately, "But the coffee smells great—could I get a to-go … I'm sorry I have to get rolling, but there's a shop full of horns that need to be playable by Monday." The drummer's wife got up to fill a travel mug, and all three guys stood and shook his hand, which itself was strange, but the pianist put his other hand on Cal's shoulder, looking into Cal's eyes, and said, "Now?" Cal knew he didn't mean "you have to work *now*?"

Yeah, Cal, why <u>don't</u> you leave? Really, just because her kid died?

I suppose that's one reason.

You didn't kill him.

And I wasn't even all that sad about it. But he was part of the thing that I thought would be my … well, my reason to go to work every day. I thought if I could help, I could make some kind of life out of fixing their chaos, or at least keep it in check …

Yeah, kept it in your <u>checkbook</u>.

But would I have stuck to it, started my own shop, managed to make a living at it, if I hadn't taken on responsibilities?

Dang, did you want to be needed or just <u>used</u>?

What's the difference, if it was my choice? But I know, it just punctuates all the harder that there'll be nothing I've done or added to the world when I'm gone.

Especially now that you abandoned your ax. I warned you. Remember?

He did work in the shop that day, the music store closed, quiet and dark. The next day, January 2, was Saturday and the store would be open, expecting the onslaught of Christmas guitars, straps, sheet music and CDs brought back for exchange. He would find a moment to speak with Cliff in his office, tell him he wouldn't be playing with Blue Sand any longer, and the stones grinding in his gut might have been for that, echoing X's scratchy voice, *Quit her, not your ax.* But somehow it also seemed to be because of the other thing that marked New Year's Day, the afternoon before.

After driving down from the mountains with barely a word exchanged between them, Cal stayed in the car in the driveway when Virginia got out. She held the door for a moment, looking in at him, but he didn't move, so she slammed the door and went toward the house. Cal backed out of the driveway and went to the shop, stopping to refill his coffee and buy a breakfast burrito. He ate, then finished a cigarette in the cool quiet on a bench in front of the store, 11 a.m. too early on New Year's Day for anyone to be around, besides all the stores on Main Street being closed. It did seem strange that during the afternoon the phone in the music store rang three or four times, barely a few minutes between each call. Wouldn't everyone know it was a holiday? Yes, of course they would. He knew the calls were from Virginia. So he didn't get the news until he went home for dinner. When he came in the door, something rattled in the kitchen, and Virginia appeared immediately, before he was fully inside, propping herself in the in the kitchen doorway, a hand on either side of the jamb. Cal couldn't have gotten through into the kitchen even if he'd wanted to, so he started down the hall. Virginia followed.

"It happened, Cal, it happened!" She didn't sound mad.

"I guess whatever it is, I'm not in trouble?" He put his satchel, which usually went on one of the kitchen chairs, onto the bed.

"*You?* Everything's not about *you*. But maybe it'll make you happy."

She was still behind him. He was sort of trapped between the bedroom door and the bed, so he pushed his satchel over and lay down, his hands behind his head, eyes closed. He'd switched from coffee to soda during the day, so his pulse was jumping, but the rest of him felt wilted, sagging into the old mattress.

"Things could change, Babe." Virginia's voice moved to the end of the bed. "When all that's been said has been done, this could be what she needs, she's been wanting it for so long."

"Who?"

"*Trinity*, silly, she's pregnant!"

Cal opened his eyes. Virginia beamed, nodding. He didn't know if he even blinked or how long he would have stared at her, but a timer sounded in the kitchen, and Virginia rushed out of the bedroom, calling over her shoulder, "Just a sec—the black-eyed peas!"

A loud hissing subsided, pans clanked, water ran. She was gone what seemed a long time. Long enough for him to recover after he wept for a second. He hadn't cried in how many years? Not when X wouldn't talk to him for so long after that one night at a gig, not even when he got the postcard revealing that she had married. Not when his father had died, and of course not after Virginia's ectopic pregnancies or when Angel was killed. It would have to be undetectable when Virginia came back. He got up to wash his face, and she materialized in the mirror behind him. "Aw, tears of joy?"

"Hardly." He dried his face. Then, his eyes still pressed into the towel, "Have you even given this one moment of thought? What kind of life—"

"What's there to think about? Babies are one of the Lord's gifts. He took my Angel, but see how he gives in return? Trinity's tried for so long. She thought because of the abortion that she wouldn't be able to."

He should've said *what abortion?* but what difference did it make? "But she can't even support herself, and what money she does have—"

"She *knows*, this is her chance to start over, she has plans—"

"—and I thought Ced or Cy or whoever it is this time was in jail."

"That was just in December. She's *three months.*"

"And he'll be out, what, when his kid is 10? 15? Maybe when the kid is upholding his heritage and getting locked up?"

"A *year*, maybe two, you're so negative, so *objectionable*—"

"Virginia, what chance does any kid of theirs *have?*" His voice started to wobble again, so he shut the bathroom door, which must have taken Virginia by surprise because she backed up to let the door close. Then something hit the door, hard. Too high to be a kick. Three more thumps. Fists.

The black-eyed peas, including a whole hambone, were in the trash after he'd showered, shaved, dressed, and brought his satchel out to the kitchen. He could hear Virginia shoving stuff around in the garage.

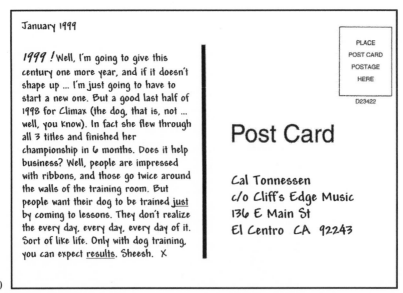

January 1999

1999 ! Well, I'm going to give this century one more year, and if it doesn't shape up ... I'm just going to have to start a new one. But a good last half of 1998 for Climax (the dog, that is, not ... well, you know). In fact she flew through all 3 titles and finished her championship in 6 months. Does it help business? Well, people are impressed with ribbons, and those go twice around the walls of the training room. But people want their dog to be trained <u>just</u> by coming to lessons. They don't realize the every day, every day, every day of it. Sort of like life. Only with dog training, you can expect <u>results</u>. Sheesh. X

Post Card

PLACE
POST CARD
POSTAGE
HERE

D23422

Cal Tonnessen
c/o Cliff's Edge Music
136 E Main St
El Centro CA 92243

You should know, it didn't always fit on a postcard.

Was that frustrating? Maybe, sort of. Suffice it say *my* frustration was my own choice, but I also chose it for you, and isn't that passive-aggressive? Manipulative? Domestic-abusive? (Well, domestic from afar.) Psycho? Why did I do it? One reason, I thought or wanted to claim, was to avoid obvious pity-seeking. If you ever did go on FB (which I'm almost 100% sure you haven't, unless by a different name), you'd see this penchant run amok. Photos of surgery scars, reports of illness, accidents, maladies, sexual harassed past sexual abuse, and I-weep-as-I-write-this reports of a parent's or pet's death. There can be no other reason to over-share! *Pity me*! Or at least *console me*. At the *very* least *think about me*. Remember that old Peanuts cartoon where Charlie Brown goes up to the group of girls and says "I know you girls are talking about me" One of the girls says "We're not even *thinking* about you, Charlie Brown." Pause - cartoon frame with his mouth just a line - then, "*Why don't you girls ever think about me?*" That's FB.

1999 - 2000
So I could've posted on FB (but didn't cuz they're all my clients and what they need from me is answers not this wah-wah bullshit) about how surgery for melanoma was deep enough to be "touching blood supply." So they removed a lymph node to test that. Blaine didn't bother to come to the hospital - drove myself in, then, since it was two days later, drove myself home. Same thing for every chemo blast. As well as for the trial (dang, was that before or after the chemo?) - the lawsuit over the macho asshole's macho monster's attempted massacre of my future-champion. And guess who testified for the defense! During his I-wish-I-was-you phase with the 22-year-old oboist. Didn't ever tell me he'd been contacted by the defense, that he'd agreed to appear on their behalf, then pronounced with faux authority that I was a trained expert in dog behavior and would have known the attack was going enough in advance. Their argument: I should have used my "expertise" to prevent it. Gave the jury just enough leash (so to speak) to find me 50% culpable - not only no punitive damages, but no compensatory damages either, and all court costs plus my lawyer's fee: *mine*. Couldn't get a loan to begin to pay down the debt (which included vet bills) because that same someone

who testified about my animal-behavior prowess wouldn't participate in a second mortgage application. No knowledge about animal-behavior could've helped me see that one coming. But *he* must have known bankruptcy (and, in fact, the debt itself) would affect him too, regardless of the separate bank accounts, can't get past that legal document uniting our property. A mess, I admit, that someone might do *any*thing to get away from. But it didn't happen for several more years. Gave me time to continue acting like an asshole. Or *being* the asshole I am.

The big picture, after all: wasn't it all my doing? The big bait-and-switch? Did I seem to offer sensual intimacy – fuck-it, I mean SEX – beyond his prurient yearning, and then flip the bargaining chip after I got what I wanted? Which was … *what*? The medical insurance? I could have sworn it was more than that.

How could you have even *liked* me?

Chapter Seven

Seven Reasons to Leave, One to Stay

May 1999 So it didn't take long for the last year of this suck-filled decade in this suckfest century to SUCK. Yes, I've been moaning that life is a stale parade of the daily obligation to eat and breathe for yet another day of the same shit. Where is adventure, thrill, fireworks? Even winning a dog show has become like I'm addicted, so winning only takes me to neutral, and *not* winning is like being buried alive ... until the next show where I can get a fix to just be ... normal. (Is this normal?) But my body <u>has</u> been hiding a surprise, just not the one that's been missing. And typical of this husk of mine, not even breast cancer, let alone anything "down there." Melanoma. My fucking <u>skin</u>. They think they caught it "in time." In time for *what*? X

PLACE
POST CARD
POSTAGE
HERE

D23422

Post Card

Summer 1999

A good season to try to quit smoking because sitting outside comfortably was limited to between 4 and 6 a.m. (earlier if you were awake). Still, for years he'd been going outside to smoke 5 or 6 times a day at the shop, and at home immediately after dinner, once again before bed, and usually first thing in the morning before breakfast, then again after breakfast (which could be combined with on the way to work). That was about half a pack a day—not counting nights of gigs—which he'd been able to tell himself was below average and therefore not something to concern himself about, he would just live until he died, and maybe it wasn't such a bad thing to get there sooner.

But he decided to quit the cigarettes, which Virginia assumed was because Trinity had given birth in New Mexico (he knew where because by the end of the year he ended up paying a few outstanding bills).

"Good to make yourself healthy so you can be here to pitch in visa-versa the baby."

The comment came during a television ad. They were side-by-side on a sofa they'd inherited when her sister bought a new one. He'd only accepted, and rented a truck to move the handed-down sofa a hundred miles from San Diego, because it was really two recliners fused together with a table built-in between the two seats. Looking sideways at her, he noticed a pouch of skin starting to sag under her chin. His hand moved to his own neck, might have felt a similar thing like a web between his chin and throat. Maybe he would grow a beard. He hadn't had one since his 20s. *If—or when—you go bald, Cal, just turn your head upside down.*

Finally he said, "You mean vis-à-vis."

She stared back in some new glasses she'd started wearing lately. "I *meant* a new innocent mouth needing food and shelter, does it matter which credit card?" and if she was clairvoyant on that issue, well, who *wouldn't* be? The baby was a boy, not named after its father, so Cal still wasn't sure if it was Cedric or Cyrus who had paternity, although in prison. And it wasn't exactly the reason he resolved to give up smoking.

He opted to do it without any gum or patch or nasal spray, because he didn't feel like going to a doctor. Just stop doing it. Which was the most difficult after dinner. If he'd still been playing in Blue Sand, gigs would've made quitting impossible, so maybe there was an upside to the fact that his ax hadn't been out of its case in 6 months.

Every time he wanted to smoke, or would have smoked, he tried to hear X: *Dang, Cal, some balls, okay?*

Or he would prompt her: *I want a cigarette.*

Blow that off, Buddy.

Other things that helped, at work, was to turn the lights off, lock the door, put on a headset with "All the Things You Are," from Bird to Sinatra, show her what it meant.

Then like Duke said, "I'll Come Back for More," but he had to get some work done between cravings.

The cravings at home were more difficult to answer, but if he didn't let himself go outside to smoke after dinner, he sat there and had another serving of food. By Christmas it showed.

Maybe a good thing you'll never see me again.

She had no answer for that one.

Spring 2000

Weird, but when the clock alarm turned the radio on his arm didn't lurch out of the sheets as usual to hit the snooze. He just opened his eyes, as though that was all he could move. The song playing was Merle Haggard's "Today I Started Loving You Again."

It was 5:03 a.m.—a time that gave a better chance the radio would come on to music and not yakkata-yak. But the country station was the only one that ran 24 hours.

As the song continued, through *I'm right back to where I've really always been*, he still hadn't stirred. *I should have known the worst was yet to come.* Virginia came down the hall, stopped in the doorway where the floorboards always creaked. *And the crying time for me had just begun.* She might have had the oatmeal spoon in her hand. His eyes may have flicked up once. Haggard sang all the way through to the last *Then today I started loving you again.* Cal reached to turn the radio off. Other than that he didn't move except to close his eyes. He heard Virginia backtrack down the hall. A lid clanked on a pot. Dishes clattered in the sink. The door through to the garage closed—maybe a little hard. He turned over and tried to go back to sleep. No cigarette craving, no hunger for the now fading scent of bacon, no erection. Mostly silence. The undertone (plus slight squeak and rhythmic tick) of the overhead fan. The rattle of the manhole cover whenever a car drove by the house, once, then another time, then a third time. The country station might have played two or three more selections by now, or five ads with catchy jingles. But the Merle Haggard song continued boring through his brain.

I never take a sick day.

No response to that. None necessary? Give her more of an opening.

I'm wallowing.

The fan ticked once, twice, three, four times. He could make himself stop mental counting if he just repeated four, four, four, four.

Are you still alive?

Four, four, four, four. Somewhere in the house water was turned on.

Because if you're not somewhere in the world, I can't … I mean … why did I bother to quit smoking?

Eventually Virginia came in from the garage. The TV came on. The noise moved from morning round-the-coffee-table chit-chat news, to game shows with almost constant applause and female whooping, to soap operas (*day lite drama* Virginia had once corrected him, meaning *daytime drama*) with their weird music-less ambiance since they'd dropped the organ background years ago. He must have dozed on and off. The daytime drama vibe was lulling, except when commercials jerked him to a hot, somewhat fetid present. As though he was decaying, but for the most part serenely.

Maybe I needed this.

But X would never reply with soothing assent.

Virginia didn't return to the bedroom until lunchtime, but it wasn't to bring him a sandwich or soup. She rolled the closet open with vigor, not bothering to catch it before it banged at the other end of the track. "What're you doing?" Cal mumbled.

"Getting dressed for Bible study. What're *you* doing, Cal?" Her voice metallic.

He could only imagine that she might be standing with her back to the closet, arms folded, because he didn't roll over or open his eyes.

"I heard that song, Cal. *Who* are you thinking about? Do you think I'm deaf, blind and dummy? I'll tell you what, I'll give you til I get home from Bible study to get your ass out of bed, shower, get dressed and act like an adult. We need to go to Costco anyway."

And if I don't?

Instead of *You're getting an ultimatum from someone going to Bible study?* it was *She might have a point with the adult part.* But it could have been his own voice. Wasn't it always his own voice, both sides of the conversation, just like it was his own hand during alone-time, and didn't he always know it afterwards, when the solution for the vacuum used to be a cigarette and now might be trying again, like when the only relief for nausea is during the actual vomiting. Except how many times an hour could a man of 42 be expected to get it up? If things had gone differently in 1980—now almost two decades ago—that question would have orbited a million light years away, never to enter his consciousness.

"Okay," he said, but it was mostly a whisper.

March 2000
Has it been a year? Can't claim I was
displaced by chemo. The cancer-shit was
over as soon as the sutures were out,
xcept exams every 3 months. If it's in
your lungs or guts, a machine looks
inside you, but I have to lie there bareass
naked. At least my PA is female. And it's
not like being examined has taken all my
time. I've just felt <u>dead</u>. Sleeping longer
in the a.m., watching too much TV.
Bizniz is OK, buys food, pays utilities. He
does the mortgage and insurance. And
thank <u>god</u> for his medical ins. I still owe
big-time for the hyperbaric chamber and
so-called lawyer (who <u>lost</u> the lawsuit
against the marauding beast's owner!)
Well ... Climax is alive and continues to
win. It's almost boring. Likewise this
card. X

PLACE
POST CARD
POSTAGE
HERE

D23422

Post Card

Cal Tonnessen
c/o Cliff's Edge Music
136 E Main St
El Centro CA 92243

Spring 2000

Not that it was unusual for Virginia to make a doctor's appointment for Cal—they went to the same G.P., so when Virginia was there, the receptionist might mention it was time for Cal to have a blood test. But this was a full-on complete physical, not something he'd planned after gaining 20 pounds the past year. *Nice that you quit smoking but now get your cholesterol down, get your blood pressure under control, eat balanced meals, cut out the caffeine, fat and sugar, get some exercise, blah blah blah* ... in a voice obviously tired of saying the same worn-out advice to a parade of men with paunches who the doctor knew weren't going to change a goddamn thing.

"I already know what he'll say."

"Maybe not." For some reason, she was sitting in the waiting room with him, had insisted on coming. He could have said no—not just *no*, but maybe that he had to go pick up some instruments at a school afterwards—but it took less effort to just let her sit in his passenger seat then read a magazine beside him in the waiting area. In the last year or so she'd switched to all short-haired hairdos—several wigs which all looked about the same to him. Plus the glasses. He had to sometimes wonder if she'd found a lost yearbook and was trying to look like X. Not that there would ever be any imaginary conflating.

"I wish we could take a trip and bring her some stuff."

"Who?"

"*Trinity.* Don't you listen to anything? I just said the baby's crawling, and they have such cute outfits."

A glance down revealed she was looking at a 2-page spread with photos of baby clothes and accessories. He tipped the pages up so he could see the name of the magazine. "So who's the *working mother?*"

"That's *enough.* She's so devoted, she has to be with that baby 20-20. But she does have trouble getting childcare."

"How often do you talk to her? Is she living somewhere?"

"Everyone lives *somewhere.* She's staying close to the prison."

Thankfully, the nurse called Cal's name before he said, *Good, so the kid can learn his legacy.*

"Cal. Good to see you, how're *we* doing?" The doctor remembered the joke initiated from Cal's first visit, years ago, when the doctor remarked that they were the same age. "More than likely su problema es mi problema, amigo," the doctor had said. He was not Latino, a slight man, shorter than Cal, still had hair but was prematurely grey. "They didn't ask us which we'd prefer, no hair or early grey," the doctor had joked on another occasion. Then he'd said the pattern of Cal's balding usually meant he'd had way too much testosterone in his teens and 20s.

They shook hands. Cal wasn't undressed. The nurse had just taken his blood pressure and weight and left him without instruction, and Cal didn't even know why he was there. But he was sitting on the examination table's tissue, his legs dangling between the two inactivated stirrups.

Seated on a wheeled stool, the doctor slid closer. "So, then, let's have a look." Peering into ears, mouth and nose seemed perfunctory.

The stethoscope slipped between two buttons of Cal's shirt a little more concentrated. Then he asked Cal to take deep breaths while he listened.

Looking at his watch while he held Cal's wrist and counted his pulse, the doctor said, "I heard you quit smoking last year. Has it helped with ... what do you play? I saw the band at the hospital benefit, but couldn't see you up there. But I know you weren't on a smoke break."

"Tenor sax. I don't know if it changed anything. I left the band."

"Oh?" The doctor lifted his head and met Cal's eyes. Cal could've asked how the doctor knew he'd stopped smoking, but he didn't need to.

"Your weight's up, your blood pressure too."

"So much for quitting making an improvement."

The doctor rolled his little stool away from the exam table, crossed his legs. "What are you doing with your spare time now, if you're not in the band. Why'd you leave? Something new in your life?"

"Not really. No. Just working."

"I hear you have a grandson. I know you're a little young, but some grandpas like to—"

"I haven't even seen him." Cal realized he'd interrupted the doctor. "But I know what you mean about doting grandparents and how it's all they think about and all they can talk about. No, that's sure not happening."

"Well, then..." The doctor looked up as though following a fly. "Virginia mentioned ..." He looked back down at Cal's chart, a manila folder on the counter beside him. Then he opened it. "I don't ordinarily tell one patient what another patient said during an exam. But she's concerned."

Cal's heels thumped softly against the exam table. He put his hands on his thighs to help himself remember to stop swinging his legs.

"It seems your sex life ... has diminished." After saying that, the doctor looked up and faced Cal again. Cal only felt it because his own gaze was on his knees. "It's normal that attraction would wane for a partner you've been with so long. Physical appeal, face it, it's a fleeting thing. Whatever attracted us in the first place, and those kinds of feelings, they're not going to continue. Especially when she's so many years older than you, her changes ..." The doctor smiled. "What I'm saying right now, I did not say to Virginia."

Cal looked up enough to see the doctor pick up a brochure that was on top of the papers in his chart.

"We don't use words like *impotence* anymore." He tapped a corner of the brochure on Cal's chart. "And erectile dysfunction – E.D. – which can be as psychological as physiological, maybe even more so, can be handled … improved with medication."

Yes, it was a Viagra brochure. The doctor opened the trifold as though he needed to review the generic information.

"It's also not unusual for a man with E.D. to feel some measure of depression. Maybe you thought quitting smoking would help this."

"That isn't—" Words lost in a foggy esophagus. Cal cleared his throat. "Isn't what it is."

"But withdrawing from life isn't an answer." As though Cal hadn't interjected anything. His voice that hazy?

Cal cleared his throat again. "These things aren't related. The band. Smoking. Sex." The last word notably softer, practically just the sound of an X. He closed his eyes. Moron. He felt like he'd barely moved a muscle for an hour, so he crossed his legs, his hands sliding to the inside of his knees. Probably looked like dick-shame, but if he uncrossed immediately, even more so.

"It's up to you." The doctor extended the brochure toward Cal. It seemed rude to keep his hands tucked in his legs, so before the doctor could place the brochure on his lap, Cal pulled one hand out and took the slick paper.

"Let me know, because I'll want to refer you to a urologist." The doctor stood, took Cal's chart, headed for the door, then turned and extended his hand again. Cal slid off the exam table. As their hands clasped, the doctor said, "Get involved with something. If playing in the band isn't right for you—or available—anymore, there must be something, besides work that is. Gardening, painting, a book club— ah maybe that's too passive. Something you and Virginia can do together? Golf?"

The handshake was going on too long. "I'll try."

Before he got to the waiting room, Cal went into the small restroom, mostly used for providing urine samples. He slid the brochure under the wadded paper towels in the trash can.

When he re-entered the waiting room, Virginia looked up from her magazine, eyebrows raised above the tops of her glasses. Cal headed straight to the exit, then stood and held the door for her. She had to tuck the magazine into her purse and pick up her sweater before she could even get up and get out the door.

"You're taking their magazine?" he said when the door was closed behind her.

"I wasn't finished. What did the doctor say?" By then they'd gotten through the foyer which had entrances to other doctor's offices, little metal boxes by each door containing blood or who-knows-what to be picked up by a lab. Cal opened the heavy glass door for Virginia, felt the hit of warm, dry outdoor air. Virginia stopped to shed her sweater, so he was in front of her when she said, "Cal, what did he *say*?"

"I'm dying."

"Really?"

"Well, aren't we all?"

"But we're not dead *yet*."

"Good to know." He was already seated in the car, which had turned into an incinerator in the unshaded parking lot. Virginia had to hang her sweater on her seat's headrest before getting in. The air conditioner was full blast, and the radio on to a powerful Los Angeles news station. *George W. Bush scored decisive victories Tuesday in Virginia, North Dakota and Washington state, curbing John McCain's surge as the two head toward a potentially pivotal March 7 showdown. Boosted by a heavy GOP turnout and support from the religious right—*

Virginia turned the radio off as soon as she'd buckled her seat belt. "So, babe, what're we going to do?"

"I'm stopping at Ace."

"I mean the *doctor*. Didn't he give you any advice?"

"Yes, I'm going to paint the house."

"But there's a medicine—"

"I don't think I'm going to paint any impressionistic landscapes but I can paint the house."

"Stop digesting! What were you two doing in there, conferring against me?"

"Sorry, I'm not really digressing, I'm *digesting* what he said, that I need some new hobbies, especially since I quit Blue Sand. It's not good for blood pressure and other things to just work. I mean work at work."

"Blood pressure, is *that* the problem?"

The Ace was just a mile down Imperial from the doctor's office. "There's no problem. I've just neglected the house too long." He parked far out in the lot where a little acacia tree made a blotch of patchy shade.

She wasn't getting out of the car. He walked around to her side. She'd never sat there waiting for him to open her door before, but in high school, before he knew X, a girl had done that, sat there waiting while he walked alone toward the movie or restaurant or wherever they'd gone on that one-and-only date, then he'd turned around and called back to the car, "Aren't you coming?" before the realization hit him and he walked back, eyes on his feet, and opened her door. X thought the story hilarious (well, it was) and had replicated his obliviousness in other situations, *Arncha comin'?* Did he wince every time she'd squeaked it out and then laughed?

He opened the door but Virginia still didn't move. She'd taken off her glasses and was wiping her eyes with a tissue.

Still, he had to force himself to start the work instead of spending all day Sunday in the closed and quiet music store. What he'd purchased at Ace was calk. He figured he had sandpaper and scrapers, but if there was any calk in the garage, it was years old and unusable. But that first Sunday he had to spend several hours finding his painting implements. The garage had three aisles in the array of boxes and bags. Some attempt had been made to get as much as possible into boxes with lids, either plastic or floppy used shipping boxes (many with logos of speaker and amplifier manufacturers). Most of the boxes were caked in the omnipresent desert dust that eventually coated everything, some less than others. One aisle went alongside Cal's workbench (and the wall it was against) back to the utility sink and washing machine. But the workbench was concealed under the boxes stacked there and beside it on either side. Plus some of the items that couldn't be boxed, like three vacuum cleaners of various ages standing in a row in front of the workbench with handles too gritty to want to touch, 8 to 10 used mops or brooms leaning against the wall—the working ends were hidden by open-top boxes of accessories for the several sets of car-washing gadgets, whose long attach-to-hose poles were leaning with the mops and brooms. Unrelated to tools, on top of the workbench were boxes containing mismatched dinner plates and easily more than 20 coffee mugs, some with the name of a business, others with supposedly cute sayings like *No Such Thing as Too Much Chocolate, Not Retired Just Tired,* and *Kiss Me I'm Italian.* Stacked but not in a carton were board games with a range of tatter afflicting their cardboard boxes—one or two classics like Candyland and Payday, a Chinese checkers and Bingo, plus others obviously based on toys or TV shows or game shows or even movies, Barbie, Rodney Dangerfield, Smurfs. When he moved the stack of games, the box they'd been on top of was filled with plastic baby toys, maybe dog toys mixed in, some faded, chewed, frayed. The box emitted rattles and musical dings and tinkles when he moved it. Everything he took from the workbench, he tried to find a more permanent place to stack it in another row. That's what took so long. He was plenty sweaty but even more dirty by the time he could open the workbench cabinets and discovered that's not where his calk gun, scrapers and sandpaper were anymore.

Working from 5 to 7 a.m. seven days a week, he got the house's wood trim and eves sanded and various spider-filled fissures calked before summer sent him inside even at those early hours. Indoors he commenced sanding, spackling and calking anywhere he could access a wall, which did not include Trinity's old bedroom or most of Angel's room. He did take Trinity's closet off the track, put it on sawhorses in the shade on the patio, and primered over the remaining gang writing. Then the closet door had to be propped upright against the window in the living room because bugs and the ubiquitous dust kept falling into the drying paint, necessitating more coats. The living room—with its sofa invisible behind the old family room hide-a-bed couch being stored there, and beneath plastic storage boxes—had a big southern window that needed to be blocked in the summer anyway. When he moved the closet door back to Trinity's room, he could at least prep 2 walls of the living room. When he finally began using paint, he used colors he found on the discount shelf, colors someone had chosen then rejected. He never took any of the shades of pink, mauve, or pastel shades of blue. But found a gallon of grey-green and did the two living room walls and the foyer with that. A darkish grey-blue covered two big walls in the family room. The bathrooms and kitchen received the basic white in a generic brand.

"That white's going to be hard to keep clean," Virginia said.

Since the cooktop was on a peninsula between the table and sink, and the sink was fronted by the pass-through window to the family room, there were no painted walls near anything that would splash. The white walls were mostly on two sides of the eat-in nook where the table sat. He said, "Then don't throw food around while we eat."

His heart beat in his ears for a second when she said, "Har-diddly-har." She cracked eggs into a pan. It was still before breakfast.

"Where'd you hear it that way?" He was on his knees, removing blue tape that had protected the molding, the smell of toast and bacon starting to roll over the clean scent of paint.

"As in you don't know Bo-Diddly."

He kept his smile aimed at his hands, slowly peeling the tape. "That's true, he's pretty famous."

"Who?"

"Never mind." He stood and balled the blue tape for the trash. "Do we have to put those cowboy pictures back up? The walls look so bright, like letting in light without the heat."

She came around the stovetop island and extended a full mug of coffee, already fixed, cream and sugar. "Plain white walls? What is this, a hospital?"

"The way there's always one generic picture on each wall, more like a motel."

"When did you ever care about the house?"

He sipped his coffee, looking at the white walls. Strangely, the plain blemish free whiteness, just like the calm grey-blue and grey-green, the smooth flat perfection (or as close as he could get it) felt a *little* like completing a series of good riffs and turnaround back to the top of a tune. Why would that be?

Dang, Cal, almost no one just lets the roof and walls crumble around them.

194

"You're not planning to sell it, are you?" The eggs were on plates, with bacon and toast, on the table. "Not that I would mind a bigger place."

"Aren't we more at the stage of downsizing?"

His mouth was full of egg, and, surprisingly, there was no explosion of choking, when she said, "No! What if Trinity needs to come back?"

Because why be shocked? It was bound to happen. Right around Trinity's 28th birthday a flurry of shifting, boxes and bags from Trinity's bedroom to the living room, boxes from living room to garage. Then Cal's rolling rack of clothes, his amp and speakers, from Angel's room to the living room to make room for a crib, which sent still more boxes to the garage, eliminating one of the two aisles in there. Cal had to move his lawn mower to the covered patio, which itself was housing a few boxes on the table, helpless against the daily dust.

Cal's locked file cabinet and the extra pantry shelves stayed behind in what became the baby's room. But he wasn't able to paint any of the walls in those rooms because Trinity was already there, had been there from the first cognizance that the rooms had to be cleaned out for her. She appeared one day while Cal was at work, a phone message calling him home for a surprise at lunch.

The baby was nearly a year, not yet walking, using few actual words, thin and less energetic than a pre-toddler might be (according to Virginia) but perked up considerably with daily breakfasts of cheesy eggs, lunches of mac-and-cheese, dinners of a ground-up version of whatever Cal was served. It was just the boy and Cal at the table most meals, the baby in a high chair at the end of the table, which kept the white walls safer (although not impervious). Virginia was there, just usually not eating yet herself because she was feeding the boy. His name was Lionel. Cal heard Trinity call him L'il-Train. Trinity didn't get up for breakfast, might be standing around or on her mobile phone during lunch, and was absent most dinners. Cal came home for meals as usual.

When he fattened up and his skin not as ashy, Lionel was brown with a few freckles. "Just like Trinity," Virginia said, "but his won't last."

Virginia had shaved his head almost immediately because he'd had lice. When his hair started coming in, Trinity said he'd be able to do anything with it, "from 'fro to braids to dreads." It was one of the few things Cal heard her say about the boy, except "OK, you can clean up his shit," when Virginia tried to give him spicy refried beans, and, "I want him to be saying *Daddy* when I go visit Ced next month." Which answered the father question, except that Cal couldn't remember if Ced was the one who'd briefly lived there a few years back.

Cal tried to stay out of the almost constant care the baby needed, which kept Virginia so busy that meals became far more basic again, and sometimes not very spicy because the boy couldn't tolerate that. But as his walking started to catch up to what was expected by his age, he was following Cal as Cal continued to calk, spackle, sand and then paint in the bathrooms, so he asked Virginia to buy a plastic set of tools because he was having to keep one eye on the kid and had already taken a file and scraper away, but not soon enough before the metal ends were in the boy's mouth.

How the file cabinet was left unlocked did incite a clash, Virginia insisting she didn't even know where the key was and would have "no unearthly reason to go there anyway," Cal countering that he wouldn't have ever left it open because he was all too aware of what might happen, and he was right, after all, because it *had* happened: a box of his checks were missing.

But he had to wonder if the file cabinet had been left unlocked all along, since the days they were shuffling boxes to make room, when Virginia slid a battered opened-topped carton at him with her foot and said, "This can't stay in the closet anymore, do something with it."

The box held his college work, essays he'd written, spiral notebooks where he'd taken class notes, a few books, some music, various folders of mimeographed handouts. He'd stayed on the floor of that room, on the heavily stained decades-old shag carpet that had never been replaced, looking through the box. His history essays fairly unremarkable, "The Truth About Lincoln's Speeches," "Benedict Arnold's Famous Words," "Imagining the Present World if the Lousiana Purchase Had Never Happened." He didn't read them. He started to read a psychology paper, "The Nature of Obsession." *Many people will claim to be obsessed but will never know the condition of true obsession. There is a difference between passion and compulsion just as there is a difference between preoccupation and fetish.* He stopped reading when his main examples became Howard Hughes and Jay Gatsby. The sheet music for musical composition his senior year was titled "The Obsession."

Who knows how long he'd already been on the floor when he found the PeeChee folder. It was strangely un-frayed, the side pockets still tight, the "all-season" athletes not colored-in, no dialogue bubbles written above their heads, as he would guess most of his PeeChees eventually looked. On the cover just one phone number and a note "2 hour reception." Likely a gig. Then inside on one of the pockets, above the box of *Useful Information* his penciled handwriting:

When a person has found the one thing or other person that they want in life, but knows that they can't have them, they are better off dead. —Cal Tonnessen

And under his printed attribution, just below the printed title *Multiplication Table* but above the table itself: *I love her but it's too late*

Directly below the table: *for me.*

At the very bottom of that pocket, below the lists of forms of measurement, from time to "apothecary weights": *My life isn't worth the pain and loneliness of living the rest of it without her. Someday soon, when I have the guts, there will be no more loneliness …*

And like every other pathetic whiny sap, he was still here, two-plus decades later. Except how many other college-aged whining losers were now regular people, whatever that meant, with families, jobs – *careers* – and couldn't even remember their wallowing self-requiem. Not that Cal did actually remember writing the lamentation on his PeeChee folder. But nor did he remember locking the file cabinet after he'd stood, stacked the college papers with the PeeChee on the bottom, and put them behind the files in the top drawer, throwing out about 20 boxes of cancelled checks from the late 80s to make room. His boxes of new checks were in the next drawer down.

Dang, Cal.

You're right, not only was I gutless, I knew you'd have been even more convinced I was weak and foolish.

At that age, who isn't? You think I had my shit together?

But nothing's changed with me.

Nothing ... and everything.

There were going to be two days when all three adults shared one bathroom, while paint dried in his and Virginia's. Instead of putting his shaver, lotion and after-shave on the other bathroom's counter—where Virginia's make-up, lotion and shampoo vied with Trinity's cosmetics for space—he put his things on top of the file cabinet in the boy's room. And saw the drawers were all slightly cracked open. He couldn't tell if the box of extra house keys was missing one, but one of the four boxes of new checks was missing the last set. He ate lunch before informing Virginia.

"Go get them back from her."

Virginia seemed to be purposely not looking at him as she wiped the highchair table and washed the boy's face. The high chair, especially when it was occupied, made it difficult for anyone else to get into the space where the sink and cooktop, drawers and food cupboards were. Not unless he went through the living room, through the family room to the other entry of the kitchen. "I can't just go accuse her of stealing."

"Why not?"

The boy began a squeal of protest as Virginia continued to wipe first one side of his face then the other.

"She's out looking for work, she's trying to do the right things." She went to the sink to rinse the washcloth.

"What's she looking for, one where the first 3-weeks are paid vacation?"

"You think she's a wolf in cheap clothing!" Finally Virginia turned around. She snapped the wet washcloth like a whip, hitting the frypan's handle. The pan jumped and crashed back on the burner. The boy froze, staring.

Just before the baby started to cry, Cal said, "Actually ... yes, I do. Except it's not so cheap." He glanced at the crying boy as he began to wail, mouth open, eyes squeezed, tears popping out onto his round cheeks, turned in Cal's direction, not Virginia's.

She swooped him out of the highchair, bouncing him slightly to free his feet, then left the kitchen with the boy snuggled against her neck, singing "I'm a Little Teapot" as she went out of the kitchen into the family room and turned on the television.

Cal surrendered the 2 or 3 instrument repairs he might have made at the shop that afternoon. He sat at the kitchen table, balancing his checkbook, paying bills by phone, looking through a pile of junk mail that had been sitting there, growing, for easily a month. He found a lost department store bill, and several credit cards being offered to Virginia. At some point Virginia put the baby back in his highchair and went down the hall toward the bedrooms. Cal put a handful of cheerios onto the tray table every time the boy squalled, forestalling the launch of full-on bawling. Eventually the boy was asleep, head down on the remaining cheerios that were glued to the table with his drool. Virginia came back. "They're not in her room."

"Of course not, she's out trying to cash them."

"Well, when she does, *if* she does, *then* you can accuse her."

"We wouldn't know that for at least a week." He jammed the pile of trash junk mail inside an old newspaper. "I just called the bank and cancelled the whole set, which wasn't free, by the way. I want her gone by Friday."

"Gone! Where's she going to *go?*"

"She's lucky she won't be *go*ing to jail."

"You bastard. For *checks?*"

The baby woke, raised his head and his arms, reaching out, yowling, cheerios stuck to his forehead and cheek. Cal flipped the newspaper back open and tore the credit card offers into shreds, then closed the paper again. "Please take this to the recycling bin, I can't get through to the garage anymore."

"Go through the living room." But she did snatch the rolled newspaper out of his hands. A few shreds of credit card offer fluttered out. Cal retrieved and jammed them into the kitchen garbage, then lifted the crying boy from the high chair. It was the first time he'd held him. Virginia was back from the garage. The high chair's feet squealed on the floor when she dragged it to the sink to wash it.

Cal sat again, the boy on his lap. He didn't know how much longer he could afford to stay home. But also knew he couldn't afford to leave. He began flipping through the current newspaper, but couldn't focus on the print when the baby wrapped a wet fist around one edge and began shaking it. Virginia pushed the high chair back into its place and cooed, "You want to read the paper with your grandpa?"

"Don't call me that."

The front door creaked.

"Well, I'm Gamma. I think he's learning to say it. What can he call you?"

The front door slammed. "You better fucking not be teaching him to call you *Daddy*." Then Trinity was in the kitchen doorway, propping herself there, hands on either side of the jamb, feet likewise spread, shoes bent up against the woodwork.

"I just painted that."

"Could I give a fuck?" She turned, dropped her knapsack and started kicking the molding.

"Oh god, she's—" Virginia was trapped on the other side of the high chair.

Cal stood. He felt a yank in his back when he had to extend the baby, crying again, at arm's length toward Virginia across the high chair. Trinity was still kicking. Then her last kick was to push her knapsack aside. She lunged forward and started edging between the refrigerator and high chair toward Virginia, but Cal caught her arm. When she whirled toward him he saw how her eyes were darting around. The pain in his back made him want to jackknife his body, but he didn't.

She used fingernails to dig at his hand. "Let go you fucking pervert," her voice vibrating, but not like an uncertain tremble, more like bad tape being played back. She kicked out and her foot got caught in the high chair.

He did let go because the chair was hopping and jerking between them. But he re-grabbed her when she turned back toward Virginia. "Take him out," he said, surprised at how flat his voice sounded, but between Trinity's cursing and Virginia's "*Oh no, oh no*," anything would seem level.

"He's mine, fucking give him to me." Trinity resumed clawing at Cal's fingers.

Virginia left into the family room. The boy's wail could be heard passing through the living room, then down the hall to the bedrooms.

Cal thought Trinity might try to bite his hand so he released her. His back yelped again when he bent and swooped the knapsack from the floor. "Where are the checks." He unzipped the top.

The high chair finally crashed sideways to the floor, pushed against his shins, Trinity with both hands on the knapsack, tugging, and once again kicking, the high chair preventing her from making contact with him. When he let go of the knapsack, she fell back against the refrigerator. Virginia returned from the bedrooms but could only get into the kitchen doorway because of the fallen high chair. Trinity took a crumpled brown sandwich bag from the knapsack and threw it at Cal. The three of them panting, separated by the downed high chair. The baby screaming in the bedroom. He could feel a tablet of checks through the brown sack. Maybe something else.

"We're a family, the Lord doesn't want us fighting like this," Virginia said. "If you could get a job, we could all live in peace. Or take care of your baby and I'll get a job. Maybe we could start a daycare here. We can work together."

"What the fuck are you blathering about?" Trinity spewed saliva.

"I'm just talking out loud."

"I know you are, but are you *thinking*?"

Cal was looking into the brown sack. "Trinity, just go. Leave right now."

"You're not thinking either, Cal, the baby!"

"Virginia—" He had to whirl sideways when Trinity made a grab for the sack. A third wrench in his back. But he had the rings firmly in his fingers. "Look what she has." His hand upturned, extended toward Virginia.

Trinity screamed, "You gave them to me!" She tried to grab Cal's wrist.

"You took my wedding rings?"

"From *Daddy*, you told me I could have them."

"When you got married! Not when you got yourself knocked up and—"

Virginia was pushed backwards into the foyer as Trinity picked up the high chair and used it like a bulldozer. Virginia came back and caught the other side of the chair. Each of them using it to push at each other.

"*Stop*, just stop," Cal raised his voice. "Virginia, she's going. That's all there is to it."

And surprisingly, Virginia dropped the chair. "Yes, I won't have a thief here. *Thou shalt not steal.*" She grabbed the rings from Cal and ran down the hall and their bedroom door slammed.

Trinity turned to Cal. He could feel from this distance how hot she was. Her face slick with sweat. Her eyes continued to flick back and forth, up and down. But he pulled her toward his chair, pushed on her shoulders, and she sat. "Nice going. You managed to scare both your mother and your baby."

"Well, everyone is out to scare *me*."

"You're incoherent." He put the cordless phone on the table in front of her. "Call someone."

She did. She had a number memorized. She spoke in lucid sentences of two or three words. "It's me." And "Come get me." And "Right now."

Cal put all the baby food jars he could fit into the knapsack. A few hours later, when a clanking car pulled into the driveway, Cal was still in the kitchen. He'd tightened the screws on the high chair, straightened a tweak in the brace for the tray table. He heard the floorboards in the foyer creak, the front door open and close softly, then she came back, went down the hall again and left through the foyer a second time, but this time with the boy chanting "*buh buh buh, puh puh puh, gimmee! Gimmee!*"

"Shut up," she said, and the door closed.

Before Virginia came out of the bedroom, he had the high chair disassembled and propped between boxes in the garage.

December 2000

He put the high chair back together, although the boy was a year and a half, when they took him. Took him *back*. Took him *in*. Took him *out* of a car—the same car that had pulled into the driveway a few months before—parked at the interstate rest stop outside of El Centro.

The owner of the car was not present when Cal and Virginia arrived. But it wasn't Trinity's car. She had called from somewhere, either with a calling card from the payphone at the rest stop or someone else's cellphone, unless she'd managed to finagle a way to get one of her own. (Cal had just started looking into cellphones because he'd read that roaming charges were being phased out. Still, he didn't know why he would want a phone on his belt that could ring wherever he was, and there'd only be a possibility of one person who would be calling.)

He'd heard about Trinity's call afterwards, when Virginia phoned the music store and left a message, handed to Cal on a scrap of paper: *Virginia—the baby's hungry*.

So an hour later they were at the rest stop. Cal had filled a bag with the rest of the toddler baby food Virginia had stocked up in September, but they took it back home with them when they took the boy. The car smelled of b.o., cigarettes and urine, plus additional unknown funk. The foot wells in the back seat area were filled with laundry or old clothes that (they discovered later at home) were being used for diapers. Virginia opened a back door and scooped the boy into one arm. Cal gathered fast food trash from both front and back seat areas and brought it to the rest area dumpster. When he came back, he said, "Let's just take him."

Trinity, lying in the back seat, barely moved or looked at him.

"What about her?" Virginia threw her head back because the boy was grabbing at her glasses. Something an infant would do, not an almost-2-year-old.

Cal didn't say, *Stay here with her if you want*. He didn't want to take a toddler home, but he *really* didn't want to do so by himself. The rest was obvious.

He dropped Virginia and the boy at home, threw two gas cans into the car, filled them and returned to the rest area. The car was still there, all four windows down, Trinity still motionless in the back seat, and a woman and man about the same age as Trinity in the front seat. Cal didn't look long enough to see how grubby they might be. He opened the gas tank flap—the car was old enough that it didn't lock. "Hey, man!" the guy said, opening the door and putting one foot on the asphalt, then stopped and shut up when Cal looked at him and did not break eye-contact while he dispensed the fuel into the car. The guy had a mustache and wore a ball cap.

"My mom's old man," Trinity muttered. "He wants me as far away as possible."

"Now you understand," Cal said. "I recommend you start this car and get going, because my next stop is the police station, regarding some stolen checks." He wished he'd had that tablet of stopped checks and could've tossed it into the car just before he left, because it was such a weak threat. And yet the engine started and before he'd gotten back to his car, the clanking, vibrating, squealing car was on its way out of the rest stop.

Oh girl, what makes you think you haven't disappeared?

Summer 2001

Was he the last hold-out to get a computer? He knew that wasn't fair, in a town full of migrant laborers. The last home-owner to get a computer? Or just the last computer-buyer who drove to work every day? Who had gone to college, owned a business, read a newspaper? The last chump? Virginia had said, "What kind of chump doesn't have a computer these days?"

But Cliff had agreed, without knowing there was a debate, when he asked Cal: didn't he want to keep track of billing and expenses without the piles of paper and old fashioned ledgers taking up space in his shop?

There wasn't room for a computer at the shop either, so it went on a new computer desk in the family room, up against a permanently-shaded window, off to the side of the recliners and TV. The dial-up service allowed one email address, so Virginia named it Virgie_N_Cal. Just as well to be sharing one, he could see what she sent, which turned out to be religious inspirational quotes, and what she received, more religious inspirational quotes as well as bulletins from the church, until ads started to pour in after she started buying stuff online. When the church switched from the calling tree to email, the phone didn't ring quite as often, even though she sent Trinity a prepaid calling card once a month.

The first time Cal sat at the computer, which was not and never would be loaded with business-running software, he muttered "what the *hell*."

"This has nothing to do with hell. *Doodle* something."

Cal twisted around and squinted at her.

"It's computer language for searching. Look." She leaned up against his back, reached over him and typed something, then remained there with her hands on his shoulders. After the hour glass dripped dots of sand on the screen for several seconds, the plain Google page appeared.

"Oh … you meant *Google*." Cliff had asked him to chip into a Google advertisement program that got specific businesses to show up when someone looked for something broad, like *music store*. He'd asked Cal to chip in and he would feature instrument repair on the store's

205

website. It had turned out Cliff couldn't afford to buy the advertisement, even with Cal's help.

"Doodle is what you *do*," she said, "like when you're doodling on a piece of paper, so an idea comes to you."

"Where did you hear that?"

"Do I have to hear it somewhere to know it?" She shoved on his shoulders with both hands as she stepped back. "It was in Pastor Hemmings sermon a few weeks ago. Stop the vanity of doodling your own name. You know, like girls will doodle their name with some boy's last name, hearts and flowers. That's not the kind of doodling that serves your moral ascension."

Cal blew out a deep breath. "Okay. I'll figure out how to avoid moral decline."

"Only *you* would have to *figure out* how to not be immortal."

No, Cal, don't answer, don't say anything.

Yeah, I won't be lucky enough that she would disappear. Sorry, bad joke.

'S'okay.

Are you? Okay, I mean?

I'm busy. Just wanted you to shut up while there's still time.

What could I have said, anyway? That being immortal is the last thing I want?

Virginia called through the wall-opening above the sink, where she could look at the back of his head if he was at the computer while she washed the dishes, "While you're hooked up there, the phone will be busy if anyone calls. Don't get any ideas about porn."

"Are those supposed to be related?" He didn't say it loud enough for her to hear.

"In case you're still *figuring it out*, I know about the blondshell at the music store."

He typed *immortal blondshell* into the Google box, then just disconnected from the phone line.

"Did you hear me?"

He powered-down the computer. "Yes, dear."

No, Cal, goddamnit, shut up.

Virginia came quickly around from the kitchen into the family room, and Cal swiveled the computer chair to face her. "Are you trying to make me sound like a ... *fistwife?*" She was holding a dishtowel stretched between her hands as though it was a rifle or horse-whip. More the latter, because she brought her hands together then snapped the towel tight two or three times.

In his peripheral vision, he saw the computer monitor go dark. "I promise, I'll only use the computer while you're at church. You won't miss a call because you'll be with all your friends." He stood and pushed the chair under the desk.

"You're deflecting from the topic!" She whipped the towel at him and he caught it, wrapped his hand another time around it. She held her end in both hands, jerking up and down. "Let go, you—" She kicked at him, the usual m.o. One of the recliner footrests was up and was between them. She used her foot to slam it down, then kicked again, striking his shin. So he let go of the towel, stepped back and held both his hands up.

"What's that supposed to mean?"

"I'm letting you fly, Virginia. Whatever you feel you need to do. And you can let another generation learn by exposure. But if you break the computer, there won't be a replacement."

"He's asleep and I'm not anywhere near the computer."

Instead of passing Virginia to get to the kitchen where his satchel was, Cal turned and went through the front—now storage—room. If he'd been able to put the computer there, he could have maybe used it even while Virginia was home. He hadn't even thought about that, privacy, when he set it up. Hadn't thought he might—

If I searched for you, would I find anything?

It was a lot shorter to get to the kitchen directly from the family room, so Virginia was already there when he came in through the foyer. "It must mean something, you not answering about her."

Cal startled, then stared at Virginia.

"Your eyes are bulging, Cal. Did I strike a guilty nerve?"

"Over what?"

"The blond I saw in the music store. Did you help Cliff with interviews?"

"For god's sake, Virginia, he hired an 18-year-old part time."

"Why someone so pretty and young?"

"Why don't you ask him?"

From his bedroom, the baby began a protracted moan—really not a baby, closing in on 2 years, too old to cry when waking from a nap. His wail crescendoed as he padded down the hall toward the kitchen. When he got to Cal, he clutched the leg of Cal's pants and buried his head into Cal's thigh.

He did the search at the music store on Cliff's computer, and got his answer, which he'd already realized would be the most likely possibility: Her business must have a different name, and if there was a website, it didn't have her name on it, so nothing with any contact information appeared. In fact nothing came up. Not even her lawsuit, which it seems would have at least had a paragraph on the city pages, considering it concerned a public leash-free park. But it hit him: she'd changed her name. She went by something different. Everyone she now knew knew *her* as someone else. Thus the X, for only him, for whom she would always be who she'd been, and, of course, because she knew *he* would know who wrote the card. But that *he* even thought of her as *X* now, whose idea was that? As though keeping anyone who might read his mind from knowing … ? Knowing *what*, exactly? That she was always with him, yes. But also, that *she* kept him in some secret place as well?

I'm right, aren't I? About the X?

Whatever, if it makes you happy.

208

2001-2004

Did it ever make you wonder what individual people thought and felt after Pearl Harbor, in terms of everyday like continuing to collect stamps or go skiing or fishing or take quilts to the county fair—hobbies, and pretty far afield from each other, but, in a lot of ways, training/showing a dog could be viewed that way (although my rep is my *business*), and I wondered: How can I go on training and hoping to win a ribbon at a local weekend show when this *thing* has happened? I know what my father would have said. He was in his early 20s in 1942, and what he did was immediately enlist. In our 40s in 2001, *not* a first impulse—speaking for both of us, but I actually wondered if the military would put together bands to send around for entertainment, à la Glenn Miller. Back then, Pearl Harbor, you had to stop driving as much or eating as much or buying as much. If you made quilts or canned fruit or baked, you might start making shit for the USO or Red Cross. If you trained dogs (or horses or pigeons), you might start doing it for the Army, including donating your own animals. Nothing like that in 2001. Just the helplessness. And back into recession again. The terror-thing happened after Blaine had disappeared, and probably, when it happened, they might have still been looking at me as their "person of interest." But I think 9/11 made his elaborately planned escape not a priority to solve. That's probably why I had to do it myself. How did I hire a detective being well into bankruptcy? Glad you asked ...(ha) ... one of my sisters ("Lily") made the loan. Actually a loan against inheritance, as my dad was still alive but barely, in one of "Lily's" spare bedrooms ... "Lily" the executor and also power-of-attorney, paying his bills, so wrote a check from his account. True, when it was finally over—my Dad's estate, not the detective's work—the inheritance, even with the advance given me, paid down a lot of the debt, which was considerable because of the divorce attorney and not finding much cash stashed after Blane pulled incognito splitsville.

What Blaine did could be called clever, resourceful... but also it spoke the depths of his unhappiness and so ... my complicity. He had a brother I'd never met (the *why* of that notwithstanding) who was out of work due to the 9/11 recession. Conveniently also an accountant. So a deal was struck: Blain assumes the bro's identity, including name and SS#, so he can disappear and resume life as "Curtis" (how ironic is *that*? You know, the 22-year-old went to Curtis Institute of Music).

Gets a new job, new state, etc. The bro benefited in that the payroll taxes and Medicare contributions went into his account for future use. Blaine was that desperate to get away ... from me. What else could it be? *Possibly* his sexual identity was a problem, but to this date in 2009, I've heard nothing about him coming out or transitioning or even partnering up with anyone, M or F. That whole "might be gay" thing ... also my complicity. Lesson: don't use someone else's life to escape your own mistakes or disappointments or fears. The divorce became an easy process of giving him as much as I could afford. Thankful he never did do jail-time—of course his bro didn't press charges for identity theft—but I think he had a hell of a time getting a job as himself, if he ever has.

The mess made me glad both parents were gone. And also wonder: what would you have said or thought? I don't know why, but it mattered. And made me return to this dream ... wait, *was* it a dream? I remember it now as though it was a dream I'd had, but it can't be a dream since I used it as go-to-sleep imagery. Anyway, it was a dream where I suddenly remember there was someone living in a tiny house built in my back yard and had been living there all along. (That's why it's seems like it *was* a dream, because that particular recurrent nightmare where you've forgotten to feed or water a dog for months or years, a dog put down in the 90s—you know the "just a dog.") But back to this other dream-that-might-not-be-a-dream: the only tiny houses built in backyards I've ever personally experienced were in San Diego, and *I* was the one living there. So the usual dream-conflation gave me this: you lived in the house built in the backyard, built during WW2 when the yards typically ran all the way to an alley and maybe someone kept a chicken coop back there but then housing was needed for the influx of war-machinery workers, and by the 60's-70's so many backyards had little houses with addresses that added a ½ to the front house's number, and almost everyone living in one was a college student, former hippie or musician. And in the dreamy scenario you were all three. That long hair and beard! Playing your sax all day. A tenor sax in the backyard so much preferable to an oboe in the bedroom. But why? Scales, arpeggios, the reedy tone, exactly fitting the clicking metronome. Whereas you took a scale and bent, wrapped, pretzeled it around a tune that was in that key. And suddenly, in a cyclone of dog training and dog shows and TV appearances and picking a new puppy, then husband disappearing and bankruptcy and detectives and lawsuits ... I realize (or remember) you're back there in that little house! There I am on your square front stoop, knocking on the door, turn my back and look at my own house— windows blank-eyed, shades all pulled—while I wait for you to answer ... and hear the door open behind me. What will happen, what will I do when I turn around and see you ... for the first time in ... how many years ...?

Chapter Eight
Eight Party Invitations

November 2001
I don't mean he just disappeared
from <u>me</u>, as in changing his
address and phone (OK, I know ...
guilty) ... I mean a real missing
person — abandoned car,
abandoned apartment, abandoned
job — and *I* was the first place
they came looking. They = police.
Yes, that happened a while ago,
before the thing last month that
changed everything. It <u>seemed</u>
changed everything. Or was
supposed to. How 'bout you ...
anything change? Or everything, but
you just can't name anything?
X

PLACE
POST CARD
POSTAGE
HERE

D23422

Post Card

Cal Tonnessen
c/o Cliff's Edge Music
136 E Main St
El Centro   CA   92243

If <u>only</u> something would change.
> *Who's gonna make that happen?*
> *No, I can't give you up.*
> *Or is it give up on me?*

Winter 2002

One difference was his weight. A continual, steady difference. The little boy was also chubby now. Several times a week Cal took him for hamburgers and fries and to play in the room full of plastic balls that kids slid down slides into, burrowed through, and threw armfuls of. The child got frequent colds, so Cal and Virginia did as well. The plastic balls were probably germ incubators, but the kid needed exercise. Cal sat and watched with a soda and second order of fries. He was aware that people looked at him, at the two of them, with curiosity. One day, just after the boy had left the table for the play area, a guy about Cal's age—who'd been glancing over, unabashed, as Cal tried to tell the boy the difference

213

between an apartment and a house—said, "Little brother?" Cal knew he meant the program pairing fatherless kids with volunteers, but he responded, "That would make my mother pretty amazing, to have two kids 40-plus years apart."

Cal immediately turned his attention back to the play area, didn't even wait to see the guy's response, except he could hear the guy gather up his trash and leave. He didn't feel especially proud of displacing the community-good-will ambiance the guy was probably trying to exude. But it was better than the time Virginia had said, "he's my grandson, you racist," in a similar situation. Right after that she'd started talking in watered-down Ebonics when they were out in public, "You be ready to play, L'il-Train?" Which was one reason Cal took the kid and left without inviting her. Another reason was the way the child ran crying to Virginia for every perceived bump or scratch, missed turn or lost toy, a trait that didn't seem to exist when it was only Cal watching him play.

Cal called him Leo—sometimes Leo-the-Lion-Hearted, until he rented a copy of The Lion King and they watched it together (three times, in fact), then he was Leo-the-Lion-King. That was the first poster in his room, the lion, chest-puffed, standing on a cliff, his own image recreated in the clouds above. His room was now the one Trinity had used, with a full-sized bed that Leo wet two or three times a month. Virginia put a plastic protector over the mattress, under the sheets. It was difficult to find cartoon-themed sheets in full size, but that was one of her online purchases, imprinted with characters from the Disney Tarzan cartoon. The child had been afraid to get into bed when he saw the monstrous eyes of the boy-Tarzan, so Cal rented that movie as well, which they watched numerous times in the week they had it. But Virginia decided the sheets were wrong, saying "Tarzan was a columnist," as she stuffed them into one of the bags for the Goodwill (which grew in number but never left the second bedroom, also becoming a 2nd storage room). She said Leo—she started to call him Leo with Cal, then did so all the time except on the phone with Trinity—needed Black heroes, that her Christian Motherhood group was helping her attend to his heritage as well as his religious nurturing. "Nurture vs nature," she said.

"*Versus*? They're antithetical?"

"Only *you* would think it's not ethical."

214

"I actually think—"

"They told me at church I don't need to give him a Black Jesus or Black Santa Claus, it's OK if he respects famous white people, but I can show him famous Black people too, to let him know he can be someone."

"I agree, I think that's great."

One day at work, Cliff handed Cal two rolled-up posters, saying, "Here, Virginia called and asked for these." They were Jay-Z and Ice-Cube.

"She asked for them by name?"

"Just for some Black singers. She might have said Rappers. I was only half listening. She was going off on teaching the boy his heritage, and how it was hard, with you as white as you are."

"Get me a Coltrane, okay?"

He put the two posters up on either side of The Lion King, opposite the bed, which now had sheets with hot air balloons or race cars, depending on which were in the laundry.

About the posters, Leo asked, "Who are they, Papa?"

"Ask Nana."

Being at the music store all day, Cal didn't hear much of Virginia's religious/cultural coaching, except last fall, in the month after the attacks when Leo was only two, when Cal stood in the doorway of his bedroom while Virginia tucked him in. Once she said, "There are people in the world who hate us because we're Christian." Another night it was, "They hate us because we're American."

So Cal asked her if they should be scaring him like this, with talk of someone hating him.

"I don't know." Her back was to him. She was bent over the bathtub, gathering the plastic toys that had been bobbing around Leo during his bath. "They say his brain is spongy right now so we have to get this right."

"Maybe we should take a parenting class?"

She turned, still kneeling, 8 or 10 boats, dinosaurs and alphabet letters glistening on the bathmat beside her. "You go ahead. *I've* done this before, remember?"

Don't you think he's with us <u>because</u> of the magnificent accomplishment of parenting Trinity? No, he knew enough to only say that for X's benefit, for her snort of appreciation.

"Then why take advice from church hens?" Knowing what he shouldn't say only went so far.

"You think no one who believes in the Lord is educated?" She stood with an armload of bath toys. Cal was in her way if she intended to take them out of the bathroom. "Why shouldn't I take advantage of a wealth of experience and knowledge? If Mohamed can't go to the mountain, the mountain can go to a molehill." Some of the toys squeaked or gurgled softly as her arms tightened. "*Damn!*" She flung them back into the tub. The front of her blouse was soaked. She already changed out of a wet shirt after she'd bathed and dried Leo.

"Just tell me what your plan is so I can—"

"You can what, tell me how dumb it is?"

"... help you. You just admitted you weren't sure—"

"I told him his ancestors came from Africa and mine from Ireland or somewhere like that, but now it doesn't matter. We're Americans and the enemy of my enemy makes my enemy my friend." She pushed past him, unbuttoning her blouse.

"When were African-Americans your enemy?"

"You know what I mean." She was in the bedroom. The lid of the plastic hamper smacked shut. "We're all in this together now, no need for this racial infighting."

"I think infighting means within the same group."

"Like in a family, like right now, like you with your channel vision questioning everything I want to do for him. But *I'm* his grandma."

When the Coltrane poster arrived, Cal also bought a plastic saxophone. It was red with black keys. He got on Cliff's case for not stocking yellow sax toys so they looked a little more authentic. But he had students coming in with plastic purple clarinets, so what *was* authenticity anymore? He tried to play a little bit of 'Trane on a cassette after he put the poster up on Leo's wall. Leo was more interested in hitting the stop button, the fast-forward button, the rewind button. So Cal took out his own sax and felt his way through Leo's favorite song,

"Scooby-Doo Where Are You," with some riffs. That made Leo reach for Cal's sax, so he gave him the red toy.

The plastic sax would actually play 8 notes until Leo broke enough of the keys that it tooted in monotone. And then, mercifully almost, was forgotten in the box of broken toys in his bedroom.

That winter, around MLK day, Cal added a poster of Martin Luther King to Leo's increasingly teeming wall decorations, which now also included posters of Shrek, Ice Age, and Monsters Inc. They took him only to cartoon animal movies. The MLK poster showed King from the side, one arm raised, hand open, paper in his other hand, addressing the throng in Washington.

"Here's someone else named *King*," Cal said.

"Lion King," Leo said.

"That's right, The Lion King, and this man named King, both heroes."

The boy sucked his index finger and stared at the poster, his brows furrowed. Then jumped up and ran down the hall and into the kitchen, bellowing.

"What's he crying about?" Cal asked when he got there. Leo already had a cookie in one hand. Virginia was making dinner, several pots steaming, a pile of something on a cutting board.

"He wasn't crying, he's asking to watch *Clifford*. He watched it this morning. Go see if *Sponge Bob* is on. I keep meaning to set the VCR so I don't have to keep up with the schedule."

"How long til we eat?"

"About an hour. I shouldn't've started tamales so late."

Cal pushed *The Land Before Time* into the VCR. Leo sucked his finger and clutched his cookie, even as Cal lifted him over the back of the sofa and settled him to watch. Cal considered going back to the music store to finish a trombone he'd left in a bath. An hour later he woke, slumped on the sofa, the movie still playing, most of Leo's cookie crumbled in his lap, no longer a warm presence against his ribs and thigh. "C'mon, Cal. Supper," Virginia called. Leo already kicking the underside of the kitchen table from his booster seat.

Summer 2002

Leo was almost three. Too young for summer Bible schools, but the church had a daycare. Cal almost asked if the daycare was supposed to be for women with jobs. But Virginia was seldom home when Leo was in daycare—her various groups, plus shopping—and the church wasn't charging them for it, so he let it go. He braced himself for doctrine Leo might start to repeat during his growing schedule of time with the boy, evenings and Saturdays. But other than one "God made the world," Leo was not distracted during cartoons or movies or fastfood fieldtrips or any of the stories Cal would try to tell when Leo asked for one—not reading but pulling fragments of fairy tales out of his ass of a memory with the boy squeezed beside him on his recliner. Virginia had either bought or borrowed an array of Bible stories for children, but Leo never brought those out of his room when he asked Cal for a story.

Saturday yardwork became "mantime," Virginia's catchphrase the first time she told Cal to take Leo with him because she needed to vacuum and wouldn't know if he got into something. To keep Leo out of danger while he pushed the mower, Cal let him ride on his back. It got so the sound of the engine being pulled to life brought the boy running. They had recently watched a nature show about baby animals, so Cal instructed, "Hold on like we saw the baby orangutan do," then winced at his comparison, although *he* looked more like an orangutan, with his pot belly and profuse auburn body hair, than Leo did. Leo squeezed his arms around Cal's neck and often brushed Cal's wide straw hat askew with his head, or knocked it completely off, so Cal had to kick the hat out of the way to save it from being mulched. Once Cal stepped in a hole, jarring them both, and Leo's brow knocked against Cal's hatless head. Leo cried, but hung on, until the mowing was finished. When Cal squatted so Leo could slide to the ground, he was still moaning, which Cal had felt as stereo vibration against his neck and back while he'd gone back and forth with the mower. As soon as Leo's feet touched the grass, his crying ramped up, and he was going to take off toward the house, but Cal caught his arm. "What do you think happens when the baby orangutan's mom has to suddenly climb a tree and the ride gets a little bumpy?"

"Gives him a cookie."

"Yeah, I don't think so, bud."

Once when Cal took off his gloves to use the pruners, Leo worked with an absorbed industry Cal didn't think possible in a three-year-old until he had both gloves on, the cuffs practically to his armpits. He had to hold his arms up or the gloves would drop off, but he completed donning his gear quicker every week. Cal started leaving his straw hat on the table beside the gloves, and watched the process, pretending to be wiping down the mower or pruning the only tree still alive in the backyard. The first time, Leo tried to put the hat on his head after he'd accomplished getting both hands into the gloves. But of course he couldn't hold the hat because his fingers were lost in the gloves' stiff canvas. So he had to remove the gloves, position the hat on his head, then repeat the process of getting both hands into the gloves but with the added problem of the hat coming down over his eyes and the brim touching his knees as he sat, legs extended, bent over his task.

Cal bought a miniature plastic rake that Leo dragged around behind himself (and too often swung in the air, once hooking Cal's glasses) while Cal gathered debris. He told Leo they were preparing the sports field for athletes to practice. A few weeks earlier, a partially deflated soccer ball had been left in the gutter, down the street two houses. He'd sent Leo to see what it was, and Leo had trotted back with the ball in his arms, falling once (and crying). But now, after weekly yardwork, and any other day Leo was jumping from one seat of the reclining sofa to the other, they kicked the ball around the backyard. Mostly Cal kicking and Leo chasing. When Leo kicked, the ball went two or three feet, sometimes sideways. They would play until something made Leo cry. He fell or the ball bounced off him. By that time it was 9 or 10, so hot Cal was glad to follow the wailing boy into the house. Virginia would give Leo cookies and juice (and Cal a beer). Then the two of them slept an hour or two in the darkened bedroom under the fan, the boy's breath on his cheek or against his scalp. When Cal woke, alone, he would hear cartoons coming from the family room. He spent the afternoon at the shop, and had to work more efficiently while there because of how his schedule had changed, no more being done with yardwork by 8, before breakfast. He had to forego some alonetime Saturday afternoons after the music store closed, because he'd lost too many hours in the morning. He still had Sunday when Virginia took Leo to church.

Sorry I've been so busy. Maybe something <u>has</u> changed and I'm afraid to admit it.

You think I look forward to you jacking off? Sheesh.

You would if ... Damn.

Fall 2002

Virginia announced that preschool is for learning, not earning, and, despite Leo being a little too young for it, Cal had to agree, there wasn't going to be much early education at home. So if he learned to read on Biblical cue-cards, it was better than ... well, it *wasn't* better than Sesame Street, but maybe Leo did need to play with other kids instead of only with Cal. It wasn't cool to be resorting to the TV for either babysitting or education, an option Cal now thought of as *channel-vision*, even though when Virginia had accused him of that, she wasn't referring to a TV at all, but to his relentless worry about money.

The new endeavor was different than the church's daycare, now it *was* preschool. And it was no longer free. At least Virginia got a discount by agreeing to bring a snack twice a week—from oatmeal cookies and juice to carrot cupcakes and milk to peanut butter and jelly sandwiches with the crusts cut off, more than one snack resulting in allergic emergencies. Cal didn't try to figure out if the cost of the snack was less than the amount of the discount. Leo came home and napped and Virginia wasn't getting into any earn-money-at-home schemes, so it had to be worth something a balance sheet wouldn't show.

But more times than Leo came home with a picture book to read to Cal (which actually never happened), he came home early (which Cal didn't know until later) because he'd hit or even bit another kid. The third or fourth time—the last time, it turned out—Virginia admitted she had a "dragged down knocked-up fight with the teacher because I know, I *know*, Cal, she's singling him out cuz he's black."

"But don't you think he needs to be taught—"

"Oh you too? Don't you mean *train*? Train him like an animal not to bite?"

220

"But every child is taught right and wrong ... *we* don't bite." Although he wasn't sure there hadn't been a bite or two, somewhere along the line, in a shrieking skirmish with Trinity. And now that he'd thought about her, did these episodes at the preschool happen the day after one of the phone calls to Trinity that Virginia insisted upon, once a week if Trinity could be located?

He settled Leo in front of the latest *Land Before Time* movie they'd gotten from Blockbuster and might be overdue for return, since Leo had watched it 3 or 4 times already. For a while Cal had nicknamed Leo *Leofoot*, after the dinosaur character in the series of movies cranked out after the Disney original. This particular episode had Littlefoot, orphaned a decade ago but still a school-aged dinosaur living with his grandparents, in trouble for causing his teacher to run into a tree. Grandpa Longneck has to explain to Littlefoot why he should be more respectful.

Dang, Cal, can you get her to sit down and watch it?

The heavy moral themes about whether one belongs with their adopted family or their own kind would confuse her.

Whatever. Wouldn't she predictably lose interest?.

Cal went back to the kitchen. Hamburger patties and bacon sizzled on an electric griddle. Fresh-cut French fries seemed to shimmy under boiling oil in the black skillet. "Is Trinity encouraging him—"

"To stand up for himself?" She was moving the potatoes around with a metal spoon in the hot oil. "What self-respecting mother *wouldn't?*"

"How can she be a self-respecting mother when—" Cal was edging behind Virginia so he could go to the far side of the kitchen, maybe sit at the table until the food was ready.

"Stop right there, buster. She's getting her life in order." Virginia held the spoon up and used it like a conductor's baton for emphasis. "She's thinking about what's best for him. Like her rule to not let Cyrus talk to him, if he calls and tries."

He looked at a drop of oil that had flown that far and landed on the table. "How'd *he* get on her shit-list?"

"He thinks he's the father."

"Don't they *know?*"

"Well, apparently, one was in jail when the other wasn't, and visa-visa." The spoon was safely down on the counter while she flipped the burgers. "Anyway, she's not seeing either of them anymore, so it doesn't matter."

"It doesn't matter who his father is?" He dabbed the spot of oil with his napkin. "Maybe we should apply for legal guardianship."

"*What*, and take away his *mother?*"

"At least we'd get a dependent tax deduction."

"Money money *money.*" At least it was the spatula that smacked the counter for every emphasized word, not the hot oil spoon. "Trinity will be *back*. She wants to raise her *son.*"

"It might help us to know when that might happen."

"What do you think, I have extra-century perception?"

"Let's just concentrate on this century."

The only reason he'd said it out loud was that she was in the family room getting Leo for dinner. As Virginia settled him onto the booster seat and pushed him up to the table, Leo said, "Papa, Lil'foot get like— *crash*, fall all over every*one*, he a bull in Chinese store."

"Where'd you get that?"

"It's a common saying," Virginia said.

Leo chanted "*Chinese, Chinese, Chinese*" as he slammed both hands on the table, until Cal clamped a hand over his wrists and held him still. So he started to cry and kick the table.

"Sorry, Bud," Cal stood and gathered a few kicks when he pulled Leo from the chair. "Not acceptable. You can come back when you can be good company." He went down the hall, still being kicked in his legs but avoiding several near head-buts as the boy lurched, screaming louder. He continued kicking, yelling and added arching his back when Cal deposited him onto his bed.

Virginia had put the hamburgers and French fries into the oven. "We're not eating without him. I won't make him feel unwelcome."

"He's not welcome while he's pitching a fit."

"Sez *you.*"

Cal picked up two hamburgers and large fries on his way to the music store. The next morning he was served a fried egg on top of a rewarmed hamburger patty, and chopped up French fries made into hash browns. "Not bad, huh?" she smiled, "after what's done is said." Leo banged a spoon on the table. For a moment Cal considered getting him a drum set for Christmas.

The times Virginia did take a no-tolerance stance, the transgression had not happened away from home. As though he could only be disciplined for what he did in private, where no one else knew. A week later when Cal came home for dinner, he could hear the crying from the driveway. As he came through the front door, he heard thumping. But Virginia was alone in the kitchen, putting saran wrap over Leo's untouched dinner. Cal only glanced into the kitchen on his way to investigate the racket. Leo was in his room, lying on his back sideways on his bed, his feet kicking the wall.

"What's up, bud?"

When Cal took Leo's ankles and swiveled him, then tried to lie down beside him, Leo's whole back arched for a moment before the crying became a steadier vibration against Cal's shoulder. "Nana got mad!"

Virginia was already in the doorway. "Did you forget *why*?"

Leo's answer was only a louder wail.

Later, without Cal ever learning what Leo had done or what discipline Virginia had wielded, she said, "I know it's wrong. I won't do it again."

December 2002
It would help if I remembered when I last sent a card and what I said. Of course the spouse (better word than *wife* in this case), no matter how estranged in the same house, is the first suspect. (Actually maybe because estranged. Or just strange.) But it only took a complete search of the house and computers to find the evidence that he did this himself, planned it, did a damn good job. Since also no sign he's Muslim, they're not so interested in finding a depressed oboe-playing accountant. They already found the morose dog-trainer and don't care much about that either. They didn't even ask if Climax can sniff out ... better not write bo-bs! (ha!) X

PLACE
POST CARD
POSTAGE
HERE

D23422

Post Card

Cal Tonnessen
c/o Cliff's Edge Music
136 E Main St
El Centro CA 92243

I'll find you if you're ready to be found.

     Thanks, but I am well aware of where I am.

     And, I guess, you don't want me to know.

     Isn't it better this way? A virtual hideout where we're both safe.

     And, of course, you're safe from me.

Old enough to be excited about Christmas, to want the house to be decorated not only with lights but a blow-up plastic snowman and candy canes, to know (and explain back) who Santa Claus was and how he flew to every house on Christmas Eve, at 3-1/2 Leo was turning the holidays into more time outside and more time away from the shop. The new requirements were not categorically unwelcome.

It also wasn't as difficult to be outside in December daylight hours. Cal had been deflating and re-inflating the yard blow-ups every evening and morning, respectively, and every morning there were more and more leaves from the mulberry. At least it was fruitless and didn't drop purple-staining berries for Cal and Leo to track indoors. But it had been several years since he'd pruned the thing, or even raked the leaves it dropped—being, eccentrically, both drought-resistant and deciduous, which was the reason almost every yard had one. So while Leo played with his little rake (every five or so brandishes actually hit the ground and moved some leaves), Cal was on a ladder cutting branches. Every time a group of kids came jostling and squealing down the sidewalk from school, some bundled as though it was a mountain climate, Leo stopped and stared. Hidden in the branches, Cal listened for taunts, so he could jump to the ground and catch them off guard, shut the little bastards up, but heard nothing except half their chatter was in Spanish. Sometimes Leo remained frozen and gaping as a group of older kids, definitely more animated than usual, was already three or four houses down the block. Cal realized it must be the last day of school before Christmas vacation. Leo hadn't been back to pre-school for several weeks.

"Hey bud," Cal called (and had to do so several times before Leo broke his trance), "Let's get finished here, then when it's dark after

224

supper, we'll go out and look at the Christmas lights. Everyone's got their decorations up by now, and we'll go see how we measure-up, okay?"

It was dusk by the time they (well, just Cal) got the leaves and branches stashed in the garden waste receptacle. After a New England clam chowder supper, which Virginia got them to eat by reminding them she'd baked Christmas cookies earlier in the day, Cal filled a baggie with cookies and travel mugs with coffee (hot chocolate for Leo) while Virginia put Leo into his hoodie. "Just us guys," Cal said as they went out the door. In the car, he pulled Leo's hood down around his neck. "Gotta be able to see everything. We'll make this our tradition."

There were plenty of cookie crumbs and splotches of hot chocolate (and coffee too) on the seats when they came home an hour later. After they'd spotted several lighted or plastic blow-up sleighs with reindeer, Leo remarked, "Santa-Claus, he go to town."

In January Cal located a used rooftop sleigh for sale and somehow found a place to stash it in the garage rafters.

Spring-Summer 2003

A few afternoons a week, Cal came home from work so Virginia could get her nails done and do the grocery shopping. Leo really had been too young for pre-school last year, she explained, but they would be allowed to try again in the fall. Meanwhile, she could use a daycare or at least a babysitter. "For all intensive purposes, raising kids is a *job*."

"Ask Trinity if she'd like to apply," Cal suggested.

"She's trying to do better than minimum wage."

"I didn't actually consider paying her—" *Wait, is mooching off one loser after another considered better than minimum wage?*

Watch out, Cal.

"I mean I'm not going to pay anyone. I'll come home if you really have to go somewhere without him."

At first there were many times Cal couldn't come home when Virginia called, so Virginia got groceries with Leo in the cart. She came home with a bounty of cookies, cupcakes, fruit roll-ups, and sugary cereals. Cal understood what was going on. Once, Leo in tow, he'd stopped in a carniceria for some carne asada and, after he'd told Leo he couldn't have a churro, he had to put the screaming boy back in the car

225

before he could finish his purchase. The chastisement was for how Leo had demanded the snack (and showed the early-warning of a tantrum), not in Cal's discipline against treats. He certainly assisted in consuming the Ding-Dongs and Mallomars, and often grabbed a Twix at a time he formerly might have smoked. There was some added expense in having to buy new, larger-sized jeans.

But, as long as Cal was around, Leo didn't combust that way again, especially after another time when, the three of them at a kid movie, Cal had hoisted the screaming child and left, up the dark aisle, past the doors to other theaters, through the butter-popcorn infused lobby into the glaring sunlight, Virginia 20 yards behind likewise yelling something he couldn't understand until she got to the car. "You're making him an escape goat because you didn't want to see that movie."

At least, not being in daycare, Leo was sick less that spring. Except the time a stomach virus hit in the middle of the night. Cal could hear him retching and crying before consciousness made him aware what was going on. Virginia likewise awake by then, clutching her nightcap to her head. "Cal, go … I can't … I'd have to put my wig on …"

Cal sat up, put his feet on the floor, his back bent, as usual, into a question-mark. Leo was still crying, unmistakably now out in the hall.

"Go *on*," she said, pushing at the small of his back.

"Okay, I'm going." But first he went to the dresser.

"What're you doing? Go *on*."

He picked up her wig stand and brought it to the bed. "Put it on." He didn't stay to listen, although she was sputtering something about *your turn* as he left the room. It was true, when Leo first came to them, Virginia had done most of the night-calls, but she'd slept in her wig until Leo was no longer calling out at night.

He found the crying child standing in the dark in the hall, his pajamas soiled with vomit. Cal stripped him right there, went into the bathroom and wrapped him in a bath towel, then just sat on the toilet until the boy's sobs turned into wet hiccups. Then he brought Leo into the still-dark bedroom where Virginia was sitting up with the comforter gathered around her, wearing both her wig and robe, so she must've gotten up then returned to bed. She lay down with the towel-wrapped boy and cuddled him while Cal stripped the soiled dinosaur sheets and took them with the pajamas out to the garage to start a wash.

He put Leo's alternate sheet set on his bed, then brought a clean set of pajamas down the hall. But the boy was asleep in Virginia's arms, the two of them taking up two-thirds of the mattress, so Cal went back to Leo's room, which still smelled faintly of meatloaf vomit, and slept there on the clean race car sheets.

June 2003

You think it's only on TV, and then one day you're hiring your own private dick. But, ya-know, enough is enough, it's hard to file joint taxes without his W-4. Am I making it into too much of a joke? My Cobra ran out (he disappeared from his job over a year ago). So skin exams less often than doc advises. But turns out he wasn't hard to find. Working a new job under bro's SS#. I didn't know he had a brother. Nor that the bro had a few guns. (Note: the bro not dead, agreed to assist!) Dang, what a mess. Have to sue for stashed $. It's marital property, should be mine. Actually it's suing for divorce. A lawyer will get most.   X

PLACE
POST CARD
POSTAGE
HERE

D23422

Post Card

Cal Tonnessen
c/o Cliff's Edge Music
136 E Main St
El Centro CA 92243

I wish there was some way I could help. It would mean everything to me if I could fix things for you. How selfish does that sound?

I need a lawyer not a sax guy. Are you still a sax guy?

Summer 2003

Almost getting too far into the summer for the drive-in movies, but with low beach chairs in the back of a borrowed pick-up truck, it was tolerable after sundown, even though sundown was so late, Leo would be up til 10 or 11. Cal still took Leo to the indoor theaters if it was just the two of them, but when Virginia suggested a family movie night, Cal chose the drive-in. Being in public with Virginia still incited Leo's bleating, howling, full-bodied-frenzy approach to badgering for candy, toys, rides, video games, or whatever temptations the outing included. At the drive-in, temptations were fewer and Cal could discipline him, if necessary, without putting on a show to rival the film. The Motor-Vu was hanging on, when larger cities couldn't sustain drive-in theaters. Land elsewhere was valuable, but who wanted several city blocks of desert, especially when you could find empty lots galore in the middle of the city. Still, other cars were more sparse when the Moor-Vu featured kid movies like *Ice Age*, tonight's feature. Even so, they'd gotten there early to get a good spot. Sodas in a cooler, a kitchen trash bag full of popcorn, they were set for several hours. While they waited—Cal already a soda down and handfuls into the popcorn, listening to oldies pop music on the window-mounted speakers ('oldies' was now the 80s)—Leo could play in the sandy dirt with his toy trucks.

Before Virginia had gotten the toys out, Leo was jumping up and down in the truck bed, repeat-yelling a two syllable word that sounded like *barrday*; Virginia telling Cal he was going to eat himself to death and his teeth would fall out; the tinny speakers buzzing when Cher got loud in "If I Could Turn Back Time" (which was most of the song); and Cal anticipating Leo's next nose dive that would switch the chant to crying.

"Hey, slow down, bud." Cal caught Leo's arm and drew him between his knees, offered him a sip of soda, and asked Virginia, "What's he yelling about? He can talk better than that."

"His birthday. He wants a party."

"He's never been to a birthday party, how'd he think to ask for one?"

"Well, he's *seen* them at Chuck-e-cheese, hasn't he?"

"No, I leave if one of those comes in." Cal took his now-empty soda can back from Leo and held the popcorn bag open for him. Leo took a fistful of popcorn in each hand.

"Well, maybe, on the phone…" Virginia leaned over to dig into the popcorn bag, "Trinity asked him if he was having a party on his birthday."

"*Maybe?* Maybe *she'd* like to throw him a party. A reunion party."

"You're always trying to get rid of him."

"I'd be satisfied to just get rid of *her*."

"*What*? You *want* me to lose another child?" Virginia spoke with a mouthful of popcorn, and at the same time actually took the arms of her beach chair and made a jumping motion, bouncing the whole chair with her body in it on the truck bed.

Both Cal and Leo startled, then Cal said, "Relax. I meant the way she stirs him up."

Leo was standing very still, no longer chewing, staring from Cal to Virginia. "Okay, Pal," Cal said, "we'll talk about it later. But I think probably next year for the party. You're going to go back to school this year and make some friends to invite."

"*Barf*day," Leo said, and laughed, spewing bits of popcorn.

"What's that?"

"I think that's how Trinity says it," Virginia said as she opened the grocery sack holding the toy trucks. "A joke."

Cal dropped the tailgate, lifted Leo to the ground, then handed him the trucks, one at a time. He left the tailgate down so he could see where Leo was, but when he resumed his seat in his beach chair, he could only see the top of Leo's head, and then only when Leo stood up. He took another soda. Virginia repeated something about his teeth falling out. Leo yelled "Papa, Papa, watch!" The song had changed to "She's Always a Woman to Me."

SHE CAN KILL WITH A SMILE.

"Papa!"

... SHE ONLY REVEALS WHAT SHE WANTS YOU TO SEE ...

No, Cal, I'll counter with It Ain't Me, Babe.

How can you say that when—

SHE HIDES LIKE A CHILD ...

Maybe that much is true.

"Papa! Watch!"

"Cal."

... SHE'S ALWAYS A WOMAN TO ME.

You know how much that word bugs the shit outa me? Wooooooman?

... SHE CAN WAIT IF SHE WANTS ...

"Papa! Papa, watch!"

But how long are you going to wait?

I didn't know I was waiting. How will I know when I've waited long enough?

I wish you could tell me. Will it be never?

… SHE JUST CHANGES HER MIND …

Will you change your mind?

Will you?

No!

… SHE'LL CARELESSLY CUT YOU AND LAUGH …

"Papa, watch! Watch me!"

"Cal!"

"Ow! What the fu—" He stopped the word by clamping his teeth on his lower lip. Virginia was pinching his arm, twisting, digging in with her nails. He clamped his free hand over her fingers, then looked at Leo, standing just below the tailgate, a metal truck held with both hands on the top of his head, staring.

… SHE'S AHEAD OF HER TIME …

Cal had loosened Virginia's fingers from his skin, transferred her hand to his other one so they were harmlessly holding hands between the two beach chairs. "Whatca got for me, bud?"

… THE MOST SHE WILL DO IS THROW SHADOWS …

"My truck a tran-former, turn into airplane." Leo raised the truck above his head.

"That's pretty cool!"

Virginia squeezed his hand.

… A WOMAN TO ME …

Leo threw the truck to the ground.

Fall 2003

When Cal agreed to pay for another try at preschool, he stipulated it would not be Virginia's church's preschool. The costs of independent preschools were beyond his means, and his income was too high (and Virginia's non-work hours too plentiful) for public education preschools. But he found one at the community college that was used as a training ground for students in the early childhood education program. He speculated that the reason they agreed to take Leo, when he didn't even begin inquiries until mid-August, was because Leo was Black and the program was striving to make *culturally-diverse* claims. Otherwise it didn't make sense why the director of the college program would contact him and say he'd noticed Cal's music education on his application and had checked with the music department; they had a music major who needed private saxophone lessons, if Cal would agree to teach lessons—which could be done at the music store, the college paid the store, the store paid Cal—Cal would be listed as the instructor and would qualify for use of the preschool.

"The Lord has provided a way," Virginia said. "The church school wasn't meant to be. There's a larger plan. We need to follow it."

"Right now we don't have a choice."

Luckily the student wasn't a girl, but a gawky 19-year-old boy who must have assumed it made him a jazzman if he wore a fedora cocked to the side while he played. He cancelled his lesson as often as he sat for one, and in mid-October stopped coming altogether. Meanwhile the preschool requested weekly meetings with Virginia concerning helping Leo "fit in with a group."

"They mean turning him white," she said.

By the time he was hearing any of this, Cal was brushing his teeth before bed. He spit, then asked, "What's he doing that's considered 'black'?"

"What other reason could there be? It's not a pigment of my imagination."

"That's a good one."

"What?"

"*Pigment* … never mind. Are you sure he isn't acting out again?" He stripped to his underwear, t-shirt and socks, dropped his jeans on top of a chair beside the hamper where his clean jeans and a few t-shirts were folded because there was no longer room in the closet for them. "What, exactly, did they tell you when they called?"

"Adjustment issues, they said." She'd switched from her wig to her nightcap while he was in the bathroom.

"Have you asked *him* how he likes it?"

She went into the bathroom for her turn at the sink. "I think he loves it. When I pick him up, he's sweaty and excited. I can hardly get him down for a nap."

Cal got into bed. He could feel how the mattress had a permanent indentation from his weight. "Well, I could be sweaty and excited for a lot of other reasons than having fun."

"Yes, Cal ... I *know*."

By now, if Virginia had said they hadn't done it in years, she wouldn't be exaggerating.

He waited while he heard her toothbrush. "Are you sure they didn't tell you anything about what adjustment *issues* he's having?"

The water ran, then was shut off. "Probably standing up for himself, which they think he shouldn't be doing."

"Then they did tell you something?"

"How do we know someone didn't call him a name? There're a lot of reasons for him to defend himself." He bathroom went dark. The hamper lid slapped.

"Just how did he defend himself?"

"Don't you care *why*? What someone else did to *him*?" She came around the bed and whipped the bedspread down, half uncovering Cal. "Want him to learn to be a weenie ... like someone else I know?"

Cal called the school himself the next day from the music store and was told Leo had been pinching other kids.

During an evening when Virginia had Bible-study, Cal got one of the *Land Before Time* movies, and afterwards talked to Leo about how Littefoot never hurt any of his friends on purpose, and that's why he and his friends were able to go on so many adventures together, even sometimes saving the grown-up dinosaurs from problems caused by not learning to cooperate when *they* were children. He wasn't sure the concept of adults at one time being children meant anything to a 4-year-old. Just before he got up from Leo's bed to put the light out, Leo said, "Nana gets mad."

Leo was able to stay in preschool because Cal offered to come sit in the room the first hour for a few weeks, then, because it seemed effective, the teachers allowed him to switch it to last hour before the kids were released to their parents. He went on his lunch, which was a break he hadn't always routinely taken, depending on the number of repair orders stacked up. Virginia was using preschool time for an Asian cooking class at the community college. About once a week, Leo cried when it was time to leave preschool.

It took more than one weekend in December, starting right after Thanksgiving, to ornament the house with Christmas decorations, those stored from last year in addition to others acquired by Virginia or discovered in the boxes in the garage. The sleigh he'd put in the rafters last January did not have its own lights, so even if it could have been mounted on the peak of the roof, with extension cords to supply power, it couldn't have been lit up. By the time Cal finished painting the sleigh glossy red and stationed it in the brick planter box—which never supported plants through the hot summer and fall—then installing two mini floodlights, Leo had long ago run crying into the house. Cal picked up his tools and didn't try to bring Leo outside to view the finished decorations until after dark. He had put some of Leo's old stuffed toys into the sleigh to complete the picture, but as soon as Leo saw them, he took them all out and returned them to his room.

"What's Santa going to give the kids who were expecting those toys?"

"He go to the machine that gives money and buy new ones," Leo said.

"Santa doesn't use money, bud."

"Santa go on *roof*," Leo replied.

"Maybe next year, okay? We'll attach a string of lights to it, so it'll show up."

In another few weeks, they went on their hot-chocolate-and-cookies light-viewing tour. Virginia asked if she could tag along, but Cal said, "It's our tradition, just us men—you know how we are, measuring how big our lights are compared to everyone else."

"Right, yours will probably be shorting out."

Dang, how'd she carry off that dig without fucking it up with the wrong word?

It does seem strange, considering she won't even say fuck.

233

But in two seconds he wished he hadn't said it, not because of Virginia's taunt, but because he remembered that Trinity had told Leo to "be a man" when he'd breathlessly hiccupped his way through a tangled recital about playing Littlefoot at preschool, the last time Virginia had gotten Trinity on the telephone, easily a month ago.

Feb 2004
Amazing as it seems, there was no "half" to recover of the $ he took, but no prob digging "half" from <u>my</u> accounts, the house, etc. Even a possible paltry jail sentence for fake identity didn't prevent it. Had to sell the house. Climax and I now in an apt. She can't train anymore anyway – ruptured disc in her neck, can't afford surgery, just keeping her quiet. Dang, and the mean letters, the only one suitable for a public card: "Dried-up asexual not-female-enough-to-be-a-bitch" ... what did he care, he's gay, or I thot so. Maybe he can't admit and that's his problem, but c'mon, it's 2004. Dang, I have to decide something, do something, not just be a victim. X

PLACE
POST CARD
POSTAGE
HERE

D23422

Post Card

Cal Tonnessen
c/o Cliff's Edge Music
136 E Main St
El Centro CA 92243

What can I do for you? How could I help? What can I do <u>now</u>?

Now's a lost cause.

You know I would've done anything, given you anything, provided you the chance to do or make happen what you wanted to achieve. That would've been enough for me, my mark on the world could've been to make it possible for you to leave yours.

Weren't <u>you</u> going to leave a mark? Or a sound? What the fuck did you choose instead?

I didn't choose, you did. I had to take on something, <u>anything</u>, because the only thing I wanted was ... Well, now maybe if I can help him to grow to make <u>his</u> life have some meaning, it will be <u>something</u>.

Winter 2004

In the spring preschool term, Leo started coming home with pictures he'd drawn that contained a few words at the top. Usually the words were just labels for what he'd drawn, and usually copied from the whiteboard where the teachers wrote big words (and assigned what the kids should draw). House. Dog. Tree. Mommy and Daddy. The refrigerator door was wallpapered with Leo's drawings, the corners curling, until the strain was too much for the number of magnets and one would fall, get stepped on, and need to be replaced.

The one where Leo used his own words, Cal didn't ever bring out of the car when they got home. He told Leo he needed one to put up at his shop, even though Leo cried, "It for Nana," and tried to get it from him. The drawing part was tiny, an orange figure, either a person sitting in a chair or an animal on all fours. The words were huge. *Sory Nana you wre mad.*

Before he made Leo cry by telling him he was taking the picture to the shop, Cal had asked "Who's this?"

Leo, finger-sucking, had shrugged.

"Is it you? Cuz it also looks like our friend Littlefoot."

Still finger-sucking, Leo put his other finger on the tiny figure. "Littlefoot doesn't have a nana."

"Okay … we'll call him Leo Littlechap. May I have this one?"

"No."

"Please, I need it, I don't have any pictures for my shop." That's when Cal had started to put the picture into his nylon attaché, and Leo had erupted. He was still wailing as he followed Cal into the house. He would have fallen prone on the floor if he hadn't caught Virginia's blouse in his hands, his voice muffled against her, she couldn't possibly have understood the buzz of blurry words. But she said, "Papa took your picture?"

Cal said, "I think he's upset because they didn't have drawing today." When Leo's voice rose to a scream, Cal said, "C'mon, Littlechap, let's go to McDonalds."

August 2004

He had an unfortunate birthday month in the first place. Kindergarten wouldn't start for another few weeks. The preschool population shifted in the summer (another semester requiring another "tuition" payment), and didn't extend into August. Plus August was the unofficial vacation month for anyone who could flee the worst of the summer heat. Even some food stands closed for two or three weeks while entrepreneurs visited family in Mexico. There were so many good reasons not to have the party then. Other reasons, it turned out, not to have one at all.

With Leo in tow, Virginia found a matched set of paper products—plates, napkins, invitations—decorated with dinosaurs wearing party hats and carrying balloons. Not Disney dinosaurs, which incited an in-store ruckus Cal heard about later when Virginia asked him to go to Calexico, or even all the way into Mexico, and find a dinosaur piñata that matched the T-Rex or stegosaurus on the plates and napkins.

The paper set came with a dozen invitations, but Leo could only identify eight names of friends from nursery school over the past year. So the eight were dispatched, after Virginia got the school to write the addresses on her stamped envelopes and mail them.

"How do you know they'll send them?" Cal asked.

She thumped something onto the table. "You know, the level of your distrust is unparalyzed."

Cal turned. She was flipping through the yellow pages. "It's that all right."

"Okay, here, the party shop at the mall. They have helium balloons."

"Can I talk to the kids in a helium mouse voice?"

"If it gives you jollies." She wrote the address and handed him the scrap of paper. "Here, this'll be your job, the morning of the party. And don't worry, the invitations got sent. One of the teacher-aides is in our church."

"*Our* church?"

"You're welcome to be saved anytime."

"I'll wait for the Coast Guard."

"Some of your self-defecating humor?"

When he muttered "Bingo" he was already moving down the hall toward the bedrooms. He stopped in Leo's room to watch the fight Leo was facilitating between two stuffed animals, a giraffe and a zebra, both obtained on their last trip to the zoo in San Diego, where the store did not carry stuffed dinosaurs. Leo informed him the animals were fighting because the zebra didn't want to eat tapioca pudding. Virginia had made tapioca the previous week. Cal hadn't liked it and some had ended up on the wall and ceiling.

When Cal returned with the balloons on the Saturday of the party, the house—at least the kitchen and family room—was festooned with purple and yellow crepe-paper streamers. A cake with purple frosting and five candles sat in the middle of the table, set with the plates and napkins, wrapped party favors on each plate. Virginia had found a bag of plastic dinosaurs at Pick-n-Save. Cal could hear cartoons coming from the TV that Virginia had put in Leo's room as a birthday present, on his actual birthday several days before. (Cal didn't know where she'd gotten the TV—it wasn't new.) Boxes had been cleared from the family room a few days earlier so Cal could mount the piñata there. It would be 110 outside. By the time Cal had tied the balloons wherever he could, mostly chair backs and cabinet knobs, it was after 2 p.m., the start time for the party. Virginia was in the kitchen, looking out the window behind the table, which was almost always completely shuttered to block heat. She turned with an expression he'd never seen before. Her upper lip held in her teeth, her eyes buggy. Slightly deranged, as though dementia had hit and she didn't know why her house looked this way. Then she said in a faint flat voice, "I don't think anyone is coming."

"Maybe they're just late. Or lost."

"*All* of them?"

"Are you sure those invitations got mailed?"

"*Yes, Cal* …" then her voice moderated, "because … I did get one RSVP—a *no*." She turned for another look out the window. "When I got it, I was going to invite someone else, maybe those little girls across the street, but I figured, well, the table only really holds eight."

"Nana?" Leo had come quietly into the kitchen. The cartoons still rollicking in his bedroom. "When's my party?" He edged past Cal to stand between them.

"Soon, my big man."

"Virginia—" Cal tried.

But she continued, crouching so she was eye-to-eye with Leo. "Grown up boys have their parties later. We'll take a nap first. Then you'll put on your new party clothes." She began ushering Leo out of the kitchen and threw a look at Cal over her shoulder, mouthing, "*Do something.*"

Then he was outside, still not knowing what he could do. Yes it was Saturday, but *August,* as quiet outside as … as anything he could imagine, because there wasn't even any breeze moving leaves, not a single yard tool rumbling or puttering, not a baby crying, not a hammer tapping, not a dog, not a bird, not an insect using precious energy to produce a communicative sound. Across the street where the two little girls lived, no one answered his knock, a noise that seemed to reverberate up and down the block, although he rapped on no other doors. He stood there, *do something, do something,* like a tune stuck in his head. Suddenly he couldn't retrieve the melody of "How Insensitive," his go-to song in order to remove such annoyances. When the melody finally came to him, the words were still *do something,* which needed to be extended over 5 notes.

A car passed behind him, the manhole clattered. As though the familiar rat-a-tat shifted his gears, he turned and went back across the street, no running possible in this heat, even in an emergency. The inside of his car had to be 150 degrees. Without waiting for the a/c to have any effect, he opened the windows and took off.

Where the hell are you going?

I don't know. What should I do?

I don't know butkus about kid parties. Or kids, for that matter.

Like I do? I've been flailing around for how many years?

But didn't you settle for this tidy arrangement to avoid flailing around, as you call it?

Another kind of flailing. Yes. But this isn't helping right now!

He was at the mall, where he'd already been earlier to get the balloons, but the party store was stand-alone outside the mall, convenient to all the birthday parties held at Chuck-e-Cheese, plus a ring of other restaurants tempting him with perfumes from bar-b-que to tacos. There used to be a party store on Main Street near the music store, before the mall had sent many of the downtown stores down the drain in the 90s.

As other counties' indoor malls themselves began to struggle, this one still drew crowds to its free air-conditioning, and if anyone wondered where was the population of the area from El Centro southward to past the border, a good proportion of them were here, their cars turning to pottery kilns in the parking lot.

When the quarantined cold air hit, it was simultaneously sweet and rigid. His sinuses seized. Standing, blinking, the crowd ebbing and flowing past him—every adult had two to six children, older children hanging onto younger ones in chains, one crying in every third or fourth unit, many of the others eating or licking or spilling food, candy or soda.

Enough Christmases had happened, he knew the Toys'R'Us was down off Route 111 in Calexico, next to the equally toy-laden WalMart, some corporate research suggesting the two boxes could syphon off traffic coming north from Mexicali before reaching the mall on I-8. Thoughts doing him no good right now—what was *here* besides clothes? And he'd completely forgotten the box discount stores he'd passed in order to be standing here: Marshalls, Ross, Burlington, and how did he even know their names? Because they were cheaper and he'd allowed Virginia to have credit cards from one or two of them, before the cards had morphed into all-around Visas or MasterCards and he'd had to cut them up.

Right around the corner from the entrance where he'd randomly chosen to park, his attention seized by a gigantic character from *Finding Nemo*—he knew the title because he'd gotten the video from Blockbuster for Leo, and they'd watched it two or three times. The vibrant smiling fish was properly horizontal, but two human legs in the same plush orange fabric extended out of its belly, typical clodhopper Disney-character feet likewise covered in the fish's orange skin. Cal plunged into the Disney Store past the evolving fish and found a bin of excited sea creatures and grabbed the only Bruce-the-shark left—almost as tall as Leo if held upright, its mouth joyfully rimmed with soft felt teeth. Bruce had invited Nemo to a party, through a minefield of bombs mistaken for balloons, where they performed a bizarre 12-step ritual—one of the nuances above the heads of most of the kid-audience—until Bruce cried over never knowing his father.

Cal almost put the shark back. But checked his watch and quickly went to the counter to pay the hideous price on the tag.

Nothing had improved at home. Leo was still on his bed, crying, not the frenetic thrashing of a tantrum, just elongated moans of grief. The room was dark, the television off, Virginia coming out the door as Cal approached.

"He almost fell asleep."

Cal didn't respond. When he sat on the bed, Leo rolled to his back. Like an anemone, his arms rose and sucked in the soft shark, although the crying intensified. So Cal was able to lift both of them, held crossways across his chest. He headed back out the door. Virginia, mouth opened, had to step back. "Where are we going? Let me get my purse."

Again, Cal didn't respond.

"Cal, *wait*."

Then he stopped and said, "No."

Akimbo in front of him, "What-the-fudge do you mean *no*?"

Cal felt Leo grow quieter. "Sorry, it's better without you."

"It? *It*? What, Cal, *what's* better? The party? Marriage? Parenting? *Life*?"

The hallway was narrow. He had his back to the wall, the bundle of child and toy between him and Virginia. It occurred to him he was using a human shield. So he moved to get beyond the standoff, and said, "Settle down. This isn't about you."

"You're *blaming* me for this. How's that *not* about me? As though I did this on purpose! He's not even *yours*." By the second sentence she was shrieking, and Leo was crying again. Cal could hear the boy, underneath the shark, blubbering "Nana, no, Nana, no." The boy couldn't know that Virginia was pounding on Cal's back with her fists, and he doubted Virginia could hear Leo's calls through her own screaming. Then somehow she didn't maintain contact with his back when he pushed through the screen door and it hissed closed. He heard her kick the door more than once, punctuating her "*Bastard, back-stabber, don't bother to come back.*"

What good would it have done if he'd stopped to clarify that be meant *easier*, that for whatever reason he could calm the boy better alone?

He was on the ramp from Imperial Blvd. to the freeway when Leo, buckled-in together with his shark, had quieted enough to say, "We can't leave, what if they come?"

"Nana will tell them where we are."

"Where?"

"Chuck-e-Cheese."

"Did Esteban and Tito go there by mistake?"

"I don't think so, bud."

"Will Nana bring the cake and piñata?"

"Tell you what, we'll get cake there, and then *more* cake when we get home. And you'll hit your piñata."

"ChuckyCheese doesn't have cake, Papa."

"Well, your old Papa doesn't know anything then, does he? We'll just have to go across to Denny's for the cake after we have all the pizza we want for a change, right? So who'd'ya think is gonna break the piñata open, me or you?"

"Me!"

It was dark when he carried Leo back into the house, this time because the boy was asleep, despite the cake at Denny's and the sodas (plus more pizza and French fries) at the bowling alley—the final stop after Denny's which was after Chuck-e-Cheese—where they'd played three rounds of laser tag, $20 of video games and even a few lanes of bowling (Leo a perfect score of zero for 20 gutter balls). And dark in August meant after 9.

Even the kitchen was already unlit. The door to the master bedroom at the end of the hall was shut. After he put Leo into his bed, only a sheet covering him and Bruce, Cal returned to the kitchen, turned on the dim fixture over the table, and found, to her credit, Virginia had cleaned up all evidence of the doomed party. The living room was likewise dark, but he could see through the pass-through that the balloons and piñata were also gone. He heard a whispered, "Thank you." It was his own voice. Then he found the note from Virginia on the counter.

I hope you had a good time. Im sorry for yelling. I thank the Lord for how your trying. I been thinking about this party 20 for 7 a few days. I called Trin. I left a message, but not even sure its still her number. I told her about this. Me and you need to get back to loving each other, like the Lord has told us to. I'd do anything for my grandson but your my man.

*   XOX Virgie*

Oct 2004

My Halloween costume: sadder-but-wiser chick. But _not_ a deceived fool. I didn't live my life blithely and then have this thing "happen to me." I made the choice to offer him a marriage that I knew was a sham (or should have known). Doesn't that make me the *victimizer* here? Hard to look at. Why did I do it? Anyway, despite the apt-living, I tried but couldn't get another puppy. What constitutes *trying*, anyway? Just cuz I had the thought once or twice? What constitutes *couldn't*? Not sure. Another word for losing heart. Climax is like a part of me. Maybe not ready for another part. Incomplete as we are, even together.   X

Post Card

Cal Tonnessen
c/o Cliff's Edge Music
136 E Main St
El Centro CA 92243

Somehow, I wasn't enough of something to make completeness for you either, and not even enough to make a difference for him.

So maybe we both know what it feels like to lose all meaning and power.

Wow, kinda dramatic.

November 2004

It happened in less than half a day. Probably no more than an hour. But long enough for people to come out of their houses, or to their doorways, hands shading eyes without any attempt to disguise their gawking. And long enough that afterwards, when Cal's body crashed backwards into his recliner, depleted as though he'd spent an August day painting the badly peeling patio cover, the furniture gave out its first ominous *squank*.

The only physical exertion had been near the beginning when Cal had to chase Leo into the street and carry him home. Leo hadn't been running away from anything (from what he didn't know was happening to him), but just zipping jubilantly into the world, whooping *"I gotta Mommy, Hey, I gotta Mommy!"*

Indeed, his "mommy" was still in the van at that point. The van's exterior so oxidized, the fake wood siding was the same color as the formerly green metal. Splotches of rust giving it a bovine character. Like the car they'd taken the boy from almost exactly four years ago, the back of the van, behind the passenger seat, was stuffed with paper grocery bags of clothes, bedding, household items, plus, this time, an animal carrier with a yowling cat. Virginia had answered the phone, then gone to the front door. "It's Trinity," she called to Cal, who through his own karma was home for lunch because Virginia had made a Tri-tip roast the night before and there were leftovers. Still carrying the phone, she came back to scoop Leo from his stack of phonebooks on a chair.

"It's your Mommy!"

Cal's "Oh, shit, Virginia—" was lost as the screen door snapped shut.

Trinity got out of the van by the time Cal had swung Leo to his back for a pony ride home, the boy's face cheek-to-cheek with Cal's, so the last few *I gotta Mommy* squeals pealed into his eardrums.

He was probably huffing a bit as he approached the van. "Packed on a few pounds, I see," Trinity said, although she herself was clearly more meaty, a tight scoop-neck top displaying ample and slightly freckled cleavage, a bicycle tire roll around her waist exposed by the short shirt. "I'll take him off your hands now. I'm taking him."

Virginia was moving in to hug Trinity, but stopped. "Taking him *where?*"

"With me. He's my son. I can't stand being without him."

Cal headed toward the house, the boy still on his back.

"Bring him back here," Trinity called.

Cal didn't stop until he was in the shade of the front awning. Leo was twisting in a familiar motion of wanting to get down, but Cal clamped his arms around the boy's legs.

"He's my *son*," Trinity shouted. She started for the house herself, Virginia holding one of her arms and coming along, as though escorting her. Two other people—a pipecleaner-skinny woman and an African American man easily 10 years older than Trinity—had gotten out of the van as well.

"I gotta pee," the woman said as she approached the house. She went past Cal and let herself into the house. An aura of cigarettes and just plain sour stink followed her.

Virginia tugged at Trinity's arm. "Trinity, he's doing so well, we have him in school, he has friends—" Both claims virtually true, at least the school part, although not without being sent home a few times, mostly for pulling hair. And Virginia had managed to arrange one afternoon trip to the McDonalds play zone with the little girls across the street. After that their mother had let them come watch Leo's videos a few times, while she sat with Virginia in the kitchen holding a cup of coffee she never drank.

Trinity shook herself free of her mother. "How many black kids at his school? He needs to know who he *is*."

"Hey, Li'l Trane," the man said softly. He had come up to the shade beside Cal.

The way Leo said "Hi," Cal could tell he was sucking his finger.

Cal didn't recognize the man, and he was sure he'd seen both Cedric and Cyrus enough to know this wasn't either of them, aged and hardened by jail. He nodded; the man nodded back and said "Wassup."

"Give him to me," Trinity said.

"Are you sure you're thinking of his best interests?" Cal asked.

"You sound like a fuckin' social worker. I'm his mother. Give him to me."

"Do you have a place to live?"

"We'll *get* one."

"T, we could come back," the man said. He was holding one of Leo's sneakers.

"No, D, I *tol'* you, I'm not comin' back here, and we're a *family*."

"We're his family—" Virginia started.

"You *stole* him. I never signed off. They tol' me, my caseworker said unless you got legal custody, I can take him any time." Trinity had not yet gestured to receive Leo into her arms. Leo had stopped moving.

"We said you could visit, any time you wanted, but he's secure here."

"Bullshit, Mom, that fuckin' party you had for him was security? I knew I had to do whatever to get him out of this hellhole where you always have to do whatever some man says to make sure he'll still sleep with you. You're so *pathetic*."

Both Trinity's and Virginia's voices had crescendoed. That's when Cal first noticed a few neighbors on their porches. Leo turned his head and tucked his face against the back of Cal's neck.

"Can you try to calm down, Trinity?" Cal said. "We got through that bad moment. Just like many we had with you."

"My point *exactly*, it's a shitpile here and I got out—just in time, I might add—and I'm taking my son."

"Does he even look like he wants to go with you?"

That's what impelled Trinity to step forward, reach around behind Cal and grab Leo around the waist. "C'mon, li'l man."

"Papa," Leo murmured. But Cal didn't tighten his grip on Leo's legs when Trinity slid Leo from his back.

"He ain't your papa. We'll be visiting your real daddy. This here's D." She pushed Leo into the man's chest.

"Trinity, no, you can come back and live here, you can take care of him, but stay here, he needs a home, school … a church." Virginia's voice, shrill, breathless, was also starting to wobble.

"Jesus-*Crap*, Mom, what have those things done for *you*? Want him to end up like Angel?"

Cal said, "What we don't want is for him to end up like you."

"How about ending up like *you*, fat-slob bald white man whose wife kicks his *ass*?"

Virginia was simultaneously sobbing and screaming, "No, don't take him. Oh my Angel. Please …"

"I either take him now or he's yours for the rest of your life cuz you're never seeing me again!"

"*Leo*," Virginia screamed, grabbing for Trinity.

"His name is *Lionel*. You *bitch*, you changed his *name?*""

Cal heard a clatter in the house. Since Leo was safely in the man's arms, he left whatever scuffle was going to start between Trinity and Virginia. When he entered the house, the computer chair squeaked. As he came through the kitchen, the skinny woman rushed past him the opposite direction. The computer had been dialed and connected to the internet. His email login page was on the screen. He had no bank account information or anything else, not even a cagy message from X (because, of course, that would be impossible to even hope for), that would have rewarded a hacker with anything of value.

The van backfired as it pulled away. He found Virginia crumpled on the front porch bench, her wig askew so it looked like her head was upright although her face was buried against her knees, which were tucked to her chin. When Cal slid his hand into her armpit, she rose. He didn't hug her straight on, but turned sideways and put an arm around her.

She howled, "All three of my babies have left me, all three are gone."

"I suspect two of them will be back when they need money."

"I'm in the land that time forgot," her voice wet, thick, bubbly. Cal doubted she knew she was using the familiar movie title.

They later discovered Virginia's wallet had been taken from her purse. It meant replacing her driver's license and a loss of the week's grocery money, but Virginia had no credit cards or checks. She was in bed, still sobbing, when he told her. She muttered so he could barely understand, "Thank the Lord."

December 2004

When Cal dragged the boxes of blow-up Christmas characters out of the garage, Virginia, from the doorway to the kitchen, said, "What the heck are you doing?"

"Can't you just say *hell? Hell.* Isn't that more appropriate?"

"I won't speak un-Christian no matter how much anything hurts."

"I thought this might help."

"You're sick, Cal. It's OK, I understand. The trauma of it gave you a weekend immune system. Let me make you a nice breakfast. Waffles?"

After breakfast he used an air-mattress pump to blow up the snowman. Then he hung the icicle lights. By afternoon, he was on the roof mounting the santa-and-sleigh. Last January, as promised, with Leo at his elbow, he had outlined the sleigh with a string of red lights.

When Virginia came out of the house, he was still on the rooftop, prone, his body bent over the peak because he'd gained enough weight to feel like Sisyphus's boulder. He thought Virginia might he holding a knife, but if she was, she didn't use it. She went to the air valve on the snowman and opened it. Cal sat on the roof watching the snowman melt.

"The future can flop when attention is on yesterday." Who said this? How did it get in my head? (Always so full of pithy truisms.) But I wonder if you became a forward-thinker ... in self-defense against ... *moi* ...? Have to send myself back to that Peanuts cartoon: "why don't you ever think about me?" cuz I may be making a lot of assumptions about you ... it's just that, somehow, even though we were so young, I knew you. But so many things I don't know since that could've changed you. Like: Have you ever lived alone? I think way back when, that last time, you were still with your parents, and I had that strange religious roommate. (Dang, the born-again roommate and the Jehovah's Witness boyfriend at the same time, why didn't I join you on the front porch and close that door behind myself as well, instead of ...) Okay, anyway, I did live alone, briefly, when I first went to Boulder, but how long did it last, three years? Should've been enough time to find out something about myself. How soon into the thing with Blaine did I start staying overnight? Even then, Blaine had a guestroom for me to go to "afterwards."

Sex: it wasn't "never" at first. Not every day, but ... I thought I *should*. I thought I was supposed to want to. I kept track and (at first) tried to make sure no more than 2 or 3 days went by, but sometimes easy to find an excuse to skip a week—menstrual period or head cold (tried to avoid the cliché headache), early work hours at the groomer (which was actually dog-training before the shop opened), or even a sub-early alarm set for weekend dog shows. Got easier and easier. He could've complained, but didn't. So I wondered about *him* ... That's an excuse, a distraction (for myself) to be plenty ashamed of. Except I knew about that principal oboist guy he'd fixated on. When did that happen? Right around the time of the dog-attack and melanoma and then the lawsuit trial, which I've already covered, but time is so scrunched up now, and all the things that happened since ... but I have to go backwards again, around the time I was having chemo, cuz I seem to have (conveniently) skipped something in the goddamned past. Was I *jealous*? Why did I do that horrible thing I did? And I don't mean when I emptied the water from his Humistat every day for a week, helping all the reeds he'd just made to dry out. (Why did I do *that*? And would I do it to your sax reeds? Why would anyone attack a musical instrument?) But it was *Jeremy, Jeremy, Jeremy* ... was I a possessive fool? WTF! I never gave you a mercy blow, and maybe you'd be glad, if you knew how I forced one on *him* - while he was practicing no less! And kept saying, through the dick in my mouth, *is this how Jeremy does it? Is this how he helps you get the high notes at lessons? Does he wrap his lips under like an embouchure? Or is it you kneeling in front of <u>him</u>?* So of course he went limp, tried to push me away, but I had him with my teeth, plus the bell of the oboe in one hand. A dog who won't give up her tug toy! And when I did, finally, I wasn't finished: still holding the oboe and wiggled his dick around a little, showing off how limp. Next thing I knew, he let go of the oboe and it was only in my hand, drawn back like a club. But I didn't hit *him* with it. Is that supposed to make me a better person? I saw his scrunched-closed eyes, the tears on his face, then turned and swung the thing like a baseball bat. Clipped the music stand. Yeah, I paid for repairs. But ... why didn't he leave *then*? Maybe he decided to make leaving as bad as possible for me, financially, plus all the delightful shit his disappearance brought in a package deal.

2005 - 2006
So now back to 05-06, just three years ago, not only resumed living alone, but a fucking *apartment*. At least no religious roommate. Unless I could claim Climax had joined a cult, but truth is, she was injured and I had to retire her. She was my only dog by then. I wasn't even sure of the injury back then. She would repeatedly go lame. Shoulder? Elbow? Turns out the spinal cord in the neck—an injury there can manifest in lameness. Likely hanging around, building, since the dog-attack. Could've been diagnosed easily, and earlier, with an Xray ... which I'd decided was too expensive when retirement and living quietly might be as good a remedy. Not that I could retire alongside her. Craigslist ads kept the number of home-obedience clients adequate.

    A kind of training I could have afforded myself.
    Basically, bro, I got mean. Got? Maybe always was.
    Not that you would argue that.
    I deserved all of it.

Chapter Nine
(At least) Ninety Boxes in the Garage

Feb 2005

I <u>don't</u> miss him. Not one of those denials where the opposite is true. Neither is that. I'd better stop denying. What I miss is not feeling guilty, but guilt is one thing I should've felt all along. Can't blame him for running (not even his spiteful method) – I used him. Mainly for insurance. Was there ever a hope for a kind of partnership? He had his own issues, besides my selfish notion of what hole he might fill. Ha, innuendo NOT intended, but won't bother to re-write this card – who <u>else</u> could I tell this to? Just making the rent & utilities. Amazing enough clients stay with me when it's so obvious I don't care. Should work for a groomer where caring isn't required.   X

PLACE
POST CARD
POSTAGE
HERE

D23422

Post Card

Cal Tonnessen
c/o Cliff's Edge Music
136 E Main St
El Centro CA 92243

Amazing as it seems, I know what you mean.

> *Yeah, you're like a band instrument <u>groomer</u>. Precision and success without ego.*

No, I mean all of it. Using someone.

Really? She has something to <u>use</u>?

Well ... she's a good cook. And now I'm fat.

> *<u>You</u>? The skinny sax player? Bald AND fat? How could a body go so wrong?*

You always could look reality in the eye without flinching.

Can't you tell an act when you see one?

I thought I could, especially ... that one night. But, look how that turned out.

> *Just be careful, Cal. There's an edge to that cliff. Ha—the music store's name! Freudian?*

March 2005

Freud had nothing to do with it. Wasn't that all sex and parents? By now, his late 40s, Virginia's 50s, sex could be put off for double-digit months, and the parent tragedies had started a while ago. Virginia's father went during the time Leo was living with them. Nothing like losing a child, and something almost everyone else faced and recovered from, if you had a father who at minimum stayed around and kept a job through his alcoholism, as hers had done. Virginia had gone to Nevada for the funeral alone; Cal and Leo relishing pizza and burgers with fries for three days; Cal with three whole nights of alone-time. Cal's dad had been diagnosed with advanced prostate cancer before that, before Leo, the twice-monthly drives over the mountains to San Diego to visit him while he dwindled away became part of the life landscape, a bend in the road you were supposed to be able to see for miles across the desert. Virginia had insisted on going along. Except the last time, when he'd said his goodbye, then drove to a particular neighborhood, a particular street, where he parked in front of a particular apartment building ... which he could tell had been razed and replaced with a set of townhouses. He didn't know how he would have told her without her realizing he'd done that: gone back to the door that was closed on him.

Virginia's request that they send money to Trinity was not the first time she'd asked, his blunt "no" not the first time he'd answered. But the edict had always been tenuous. Like a screw that kept working its way loose. And every time he retightened it, the metal fatigued more. There would be a snap.

Of course this time it *started* with a snap. Maybe only because it was *that* day, a day he'd told her years ago "let's not make any decisions on this day," probably at the graveside, her talking about a monument or commemorative bench for the zoo.

Last year, when Leo was with them, the ten-year anniversary of Angel's death had been marked with a day and night of only candles lighting the house. Thankfully she hadn't had to buy them. Well, yes she had, but it had been years ago when she had signed up to sell them at candle-parties, but not a single candle had left the boxes of product she'd been required to invest in. So, the still-sealed boxes were opened and dozens of candles, maybe close to a hundred, burned in bedrooms, bathrooms, kitchen, family room—no TV, not even a burner on the stove. Leo had tried to play cave-of-the-wicked-queen, until Cal hustled him out to the car for a trip to McDonald's play zone, before Virginia recognized his irreverence. When they got back, the house was filled with waxy smoke, some of it scented, two smoke-alarms sounding, and Virginia sitting in the dark backyard.

This year the date was marked again, as usual, with Angel's favorite meal—chile rellenos, Spanish rice, and refried beans cooked from dried pintos simmered all day with spices—and, as though timed for Cal's mouth to be as full as a greedy pig could get it, her question came: "If we'd just supported Angel more, he'd be alive. Can I send some money to Trin?"

His mouth too full of the cheesy infusion of battered fried peppers, he shook his head.

"She needs some help to get off her feet."

Muffled in his mouthful, "I figured she was working lying down." He swallowed, the huge lump bringing tears to his eyes.

"*What?* Just a sec." Water hissed into a hot empty pan, a plume of vapor erupted. Why was he already eating when her chair was still empty, her plate steaming across from him? He put down his fork and waited for the soda she was getting from the refrigerator. While she poured it into a glass, she said, "Look, I know she said she would never speak to us again, but didn't you know that's just a child crying out for help?"

Then he was drinking, looking at her over the rim. He could hear the *glug* she sometimes complained about when he drank. He counted five of them, all the while Virginia was still talking. "Maybe because it was close to the anniversary of Angel going to heaven that The Lord brought her back to us. I kept faith, even though when she called you could have knocked me over with a fender. But I see how The Lord provided a way for her—"

He put his glass down and said, "No."

"No? Just *no?*" She still hadn't started eating. In fact she was back at the stove, taking something from the oven. "Do you want the boy to be hungry when we have plenty?" The oven door boomed. Then she came to the table with a third plate of the chiles, rice and beans. She sat at the end where Leo's highchair used to be.

"I'll buy transportation for her to send the boy back here." He packed in another huge forkful. Was he eating with serving utensils?

"She's got herself convicted that it's bad for him to be here."

He swallowed, drank again. He knew what she meant, but couldn't resist. "She's in jail?"

"Just once, overnight, for—"

"I was kidding." He liked to mix some of the rice and beans together.

"Why would you joke about *that*?"

"Well," through another mouthful, "sometimes there's only … make a joke … or cry …."

"When have *you* ever cried?"

"Now you're getting it." His plate was almost empty. He looked at the full serving across the table from him. "Does Angel mind if I have his chiles?" He asked every year. But usually later, and rewarmed them in the microwave.

"Why should he share with a tightwad like you who never gave him anything?"

"Because," he touched her wrist with his index finger, "now he's *truly* an angel." Which was something *she* usually said every year.

"Hmmm." Her chin in her hand, elbow on the table. "Oh fudge, I forgot his candle. This has got me so upset." But she didn't get up to fix the omission.

"The beans are excellent, hun, don't let them get cold."

Dang, Cal … Hun?

Why not, the least I can do.

Virginia didn't say anything as Cal slid the cooling chiles from the extra plate to his. She might have eaten a few small mouthfuls of beans or rice. She never ate much at Angel's 'ascension dinner.' But he knew she always sampled and nibbled while she cooked. The longer it took to prepare a meal, any meal, the less she ate at the table.

She stirred the beans on her plate with her fork. "Look, Cal, I know our affluence over her is very small, but we could say she has to go to school or—"

"Who's going to pay for that?"

"Dunce—*that's* what we could pay for!"

"*We?*"

"*I work too!*"

It wasn't as though he didn't know there would be blowback. He also knew it could someday be worse than a Kleenex box hurled at him—so hard the box corner broke skin near his eye. It was almost as though she was fighting with someone else, the way it went on and on with so little rejoinder from him. In fact, all he'd said was "You need to calm down," and "You're going to hurt yourself" (during a squall of ferocious splashing and clanging in the sink), and "I wish you could hear yourself." Although vaguely aware the repeated use of *you* was retort enough. It had gone on for hours and he'd wanted to get an early start at the shop in the morning. Preparing to spend the night on his recliner, it was mostly dark by the time the box was launched through the kitchen pass-through. Cal's eyes already closed so he hadn't been able to duck, unable to do more than flinch at the barely perceived and silent projectile.

If he vocalized on impact, he wasn't sure she was still in the kitchen to hear it. The bedroom door slammed. But she was back in minutes, saying he shouldn't get to rest or sleep after he'd made her this furious. She slammed herself into her recliner beside him.

"You hit me in the eye with that box."

"Good."

She didn't move and he may have dozed. But was awake when she said, "Are you okay?"

"How long was I asleep?

"I didn't know you were. I don't know how you can."

"Maybe you can too, if we go to bed." He went down the hall. It took several minutes, and maybe he'd even been asleep again before she followed.

Cal, I been tryna tell you ... there's worse things than be'n alone.

I know, I hear you, and then I do something so stupid.

"... and then I go and spoil it all by say'n somethin' stupid like ..."

That too.

May 2005

The next time he said something even more stupid.

I think I'm channeling you.

Snark? Are you sure that's even who I am anymore?

You're right: I don't know.

Her church had started offering Christian self-expression classes. Virginia signed up for poetry-writing. "… learn to express personal human emotions like sadness, yearning and romantic love in a Christian context …" Other offerings were Christian painting, Christian drawing. Virginia said the poetry might lead to a little business for her, hand-made greeting cards. She could take the painting and drawing classes next, then she would need some supplies from a craft store, the closest one in Yuma.

"We'll see."

"Your new way of saying *no*?"

"My new way of saying one-step-at-a-time. Isn't that a Christian concept?" He was in the kitchen getting a soda after mowing the lawn as early as he dared run a motor on Saturday morning (although the party-house behind his had no problem daring to ratchet up the music after midnight Friday nights).

"It's an *AAA* concept."

"The Auto Club says one-step-at-a-time?"

"*Substance abuse*, dumbskull." Virginia was seated with her blank notebook, after she'd cleared the kitchen table as much as she could—always a stack of mail as a centerpiece. Several years ago a water bill had been accidentally thrown away, so Cal had told her to just leave the mail on the table and he would take care of it. He always fished the bills out and put them into an equally overflowing basket on the kitchen pass-through ledge. The junk accumulated on the table, although the mound of it seemed to stay about the same size.

That night she had the notebook with her in bed, propped on her knees. Only her nightstand light was on. After he came out of the bathroom, Cal left it that way, semi dark. Sometimes he even closed his eyes when he undressed, half surprised when he raised his lids that the bed, dresser, hamper and closet doors were so close on all sides of him.

"How does this sound, Babes," Virginia said. "Your heavenly song / I've listened to for so long …"

Cal closed his eyes again and didn't move.

"*Well* …?"

"I was waiting for the rest."

"It's just so far. Your heavenly song / I've listened to for so long …"

"Do you want it to sound like you're tired of hearing the same old song?"

She puffed a sigh. "I never said anything about it being *old*."

"Okay." His fingers tapped silently against the side of his leg. "Aren't there too many syllables in the second line? How about: … blah-blah-blah song / I've loved so long?"

"You can't even say *heavenly*?"

Cal turned on the overhead fan. He usually liked to not use the fan until June, so when the warm weather first started there'd still be some improvement to look forward to. He put the fan on medium instead of high, then sat on his side of the bed.

Virginia murmured, "Your light is pure / of that I'm sure …"

Cal lay on his back, then turned to his side, facing away from her lamp.

"No …" Her eraser scrubbed then her hand swept the paper. "Angel, my child / you're safe and … what … Wild? Mild? Smiled?" Her pencil tapped.

"Beguiled," Cal mumbled.

"Huh? What's that, something nasty?"

"It means … never mind. You can't be both safe and beguiled."

"Angel my love / you're safe up above."

Cal tried to relax his tongue, something he'd read helped sleep come quicker. He heard the pencil scrape, the eraser scuff, the hand brushing, the pencil again. Whispery white-noise, not unpleasant.

"I dream of the day / I dream of the night …"

The fan clicked, three, four, five times. He could have just drifted off, not said another word. But … "Stand up / sit down / fight – fight - fight."

First the notebook slapped against her knees, then it fluttered across the room and onto the dresser, several items clattering, scattering, at least one thing thumping to the floor. Or was that Virginia's feet thumping when *she* hit the floor? Difficult to differentiate through the eruption of barked displeasure: He was *always* negative, *never* supportive, didn't *care*, was *so* selfish, couldn't *share*, left her in this marriage *alone*, was probably off didling his students' mothers, maybe even the students themselves, *laughing* at her, keeping her from *becoming* something, from starting her own business, holding her *hostile* as his cook and maid …

All the while, he could hear hangers rattling, feet pounding, more hangers, more bumping. He sat up. Virginia was stomping and kicking on top of a mound of his clothes on the floor. There was a cloud of something in the air, as though his shirts and pants had been full of dust. Then he saw she was dumping a container of baby power as she hopped, booted, and twisted her feet in the pile of fabric. He recognized the bizarre dance—including the next phase as she picked up pieces and tried to tear them—as something she'd done a few times in fights with Trinity, whose clothes tore more easily than his jeans and t-shirts, and who cared about her clothes a lot more than Cal did. He thought about his two saxophones, but at least they were somewhat hidden on the floor between the bed and the wall in Leo's old room. He didn't have a lot of room for them in his shop at the store. He lay quietly in bed in the semi-dark while the cotton skins he wore in the daytime were victims of a beat-down, not more than 10 feet away. The next victim was the notebook. The bed shuddered and the light went off.

In 24 hours, his clothes had all been re-washed and hung, the khakis and a few sports shirts ironed, maybe even lightly starched, although they'd previously been considered wash-n-wear. Did anyone use that term anymore? Did he ever say *tinfoil* or *oleo* or *icebox*? Those were his parents' words, not his. He actually *did* use *case knife* for a pocket knife, because that's what his grandfather said. Pretty soon he'd be using Virginia's *kleeneck* for a single tissue (not a droll rag on French plurals, but assuming it to be the literal correct form). These kinds of things got stuck up there and couldn't easily be replaced or updated.

That's for sure.

I didn't mean you.

Still … Am I only a word now? Or just one letter?

Cal's response—not to the laundry, because he'd shaped this idea at his shop the next day—was to offer to buy Virginia some useful education, something that could lead to a job. Meaning a paycheck, not some flighty business where all the money went *out*.

"I know, they make those plans sound so *good*."

"That's *beguiled*."

"Isn't that how someone looks when they get up in the morning?"

"Maybe you'll learn the difference at this school." He smiled—because she'd chosen a beautician school.

She cocked her head and looked quizzical.

"Bedraggled," he said.

The beauty school had a new class starting in the fall. It wasn't at the community college so it was far from cheap. After seeing the tuition at the beauty school, he checked the community college, which, for fast-track careers only had early childhood education, welding and nursing. He suggested the former, but not only did it require a high school diploma, Virginia pointed out she could start immediately in the church's pre-school (as a volunteer, of course), so he flicked the computer screen back to the private beauty school.

So the impending day classes tipped them into the cell phone era, late as usual. Virginia pointed out that they may need to stay in touch, if she needed him to pick up something at the store while she was at school. There were stores on her way to and from the school, but he didn't make that argument. He got the smallest account, with shared minutes and the 2nd phone only an additional $10. The phones were identical, so Virginia chose a shockingly overpriced pink case, which he paid for despite pointing out that she could put a splotch of nail polish on her phone to differentiate.

Then he remembered his reason for not keeping a landline phone inside his shop and relying (too heavily) on Cliff answering repair-related calls: Virginia called several times a day, especially in the few minutes at the top and bottom of the hour between 3 and 5 when he would be teaching half hour private lessons. If he'd left the phone on his workbench and it went to voicemail, even if he had it on his belt but didn't answer immediately, she asked what he was doing, sometimes "Hey, babes, whatcha do'n?," sometimes "What are you *doing*, Cal, that you can't answer your phone?" Her reasons for calling, after that question, were usually to tell him the trash truck had come by, or the choices for what she would prepare for dinner, or to list for him (or open and read aloud) what had come in the mail. He said to just leave the mail on the table, nothing needed his attention as much as the particular sax or flute or trumpet he had taken apart all over his workbench and he didn't even have a hand free to hold the phone.

"Your hands will probably be free when the little girls come in wearing their hotpants for so-called lessons."

"Oh for Chrissake."

"Stop using His name for *your* sins!"

Once he accidentally-on-purpose left his phone home after lunch, so if Virginia called, she would hear it ring right there on the kitchen table. But that prompted her to visit the store to bring him the phone. When he came out of one of the private lesson rooms, Virginia was filling out an employment application. "What was I supposed to say?" Cliff asked later, I'll just file it in case you drop over dead and I need her cell number."

A postcard came uncharacteristically in only 5 months, and he almost threw it away with his business junk-mail (which he was better about dumping than the perpetual pile on the table at home) because instead of the usual generic photo of some wildlife or landscape on one side, it was a blank postcard with his address on one side and the writing on the back.

July 2005 -- Take a person who thinks a postcard has to have a picture on one side and only half the other side for writing, and I'll show you a superior intelligence. And yet here I am with more room and precious little to report. Sometimes Climax doesn't want to get up. Not a euphemism - my dog. ← also not a euphemism. (Nothing to euphemize about.) I lift her into the car, keep her in a crate at work. Maybe didn't tell you I found a grooming shop where I groom part-time and can teach all my lessons in a little area they have for training. So, since in-house, I have more clients. Of course, only the worst kind - the dumbest-fuck people who think their beasts should learn not only to stop biting or shitting or chewing or barking or running away, but also fancy tricks... all without them ever spending a minute training. The parallel is obvious to me (remember, the ex was a so-called musician), like music-lesson students who never take the ax out of its case between lessons. Anyway, the rest of the time I fill in with reading ... of the most escapist kind without being fairies-and-goblins, spaceships, zombies, or murders. "Does that leave anything?" you might ask, (as the grooming shop owner did). These stories seem to all require pithy truisms about life, which I have obviously been failing to do here in telling my "story" to you. So I'll steal one from the last book I read: "They will say to themselves, 'I was heartless, because I was young and strong and wanted things so much. But now I know.'" But Cal, what did I even _want_? X

I know what you mean. There's only one thing left of what I ever wanted, and I'll never have it. I wonder what's the point.

Can a _person_ be what you want? Not that kind of _want_, cuz, well, you know ...

I don't mean that either. I mean ... if we'd been together, how much more worthy stuff I would've wanted and worked for, not just digging out enough each month for a mortgage and bills, but ... something that was proof I'd been here, something I added to the world besides ...

Wow, now who'z giving pithy truisms about life?

That's just a truism about _my_ life.

Checking to see how many of their shared cell minutes were being used on Virginia's calls to the shop, Cal discovered the extra phone. Incredible that Virginia would think he wouldn't read and understand a bill. But wasn't that the whole problem? Someone hands her something in a store, and that's the end of it, somehow the consequence on an account didn't exist for her, as though she had a broken synapse in her brain specifically having to do with *credit*.

She'd apparently gone into the phone store and added a phone to their account and their allotted minutes had been run through so the bill not only had the extra $10 but an additional $600 in overage charges. The calls made from that 3rd phone a blizzard of different numbers, including Virginia's phone, and several other repeated numbers, but also a staggering quantity of individual numbers. *No* one had that many friends. He could have done a forensic examination and made a hypothesis of whether the blizzard of calls was to sell drugs or prostitution, but either way, it was not a mystery: Virginia had sent a phone to Trinity.

When he cancelled the phone, he also got the cell company to reduce the bill (technically, did those minutes cost the phone company *any*thing to provide?). Then he almost cancelled Virginia's tuition to the beauty school. But that would mean telling her about discovering the phone and cancelling it. Since he made sure that the phone account was only his name and he would be the only one allowed to add a phone or change the account, he wasn't sure discussing it with Virginia would accomplish much. He did, however, ponder opening an innocent dialogue about looking into providing a cheap phone to Trinity solely for the purpose of allowing Virginia to keep better contact with her. Or was that move too *beguiling*?

Oh, Cal, do it. It'll be fun.

You used to tell me to be careful.

Yes, but … what do we have to lose?

We?

Aren't you both sides of this dialogue?

C'mon, don't ruin it now. It's all I have.

Still want me to walk into a nightclub? Ya gotta be playing in one for that to work.

Yeah yeah.

Cliff had recently mentioned that the trombone player they'd gotten to replace Cal in Blue Sand was probably moving out of the Valley soon. Did he say it because he'd just gotten an email from the guy and Cal was passing through the store on his way back from the restroom, or was it an inferred invitation? Cal hadn't stopped to make a comment.

Was he turning into a robot, some kind of monster? Well, it was the height of summer and that's usually what happened to everyone.

The next postcard was just before Virginia's beauty school classes started.

p.s. just mailed that last card but wanted to write this down or I'll forget (late night pensive meandering). The pithy truisms have to be realized by a character. Which we real people so rarely actually do. Real people don't realize. That's this month's pithy truism ... let's change that to laconic axiom. I have a thesaurus. Just remember "...and suddenly everything became clear to him." [or her.]
X
Now it's August ... almost September ... it always feels like a new year should be starting now. How many years out of school does it take to make September stop feeling like it should be the start of a year, including all the good intentions, new resolve, resolutions and ... well, hope a new year should bring? Did you ever sit in the first day of a class with a clean new notebook and vow you'll take notes faithfully, and listen, and read all the assignments ... and not sit there brewing in your own vile stew of teary self-absorption? Jeee-zus!
X (again)

September 2005

She didn't often come home from beauty school in a lovely mood, so Cal learned to put meat and vegetables in a crockpot at noon. This helped avert microwave TV dinners. Early mornings while he slurped his oatmeal, Virginia made them each a sack lunch, into which she usually put an apple, an orange, chips and a candy bar, with a ham or salami sandwich (lettuce, mayo, tomato). If Cliff wanted to go out to lunch (that is, didn't have a lunch with a supplier or chamber-of-commerce crony), Cal snacked on his bag lunch and drank sodas throughout the day, then after the Sizzler buffet with Cliff, stopped at home to get dinner going. He knew he would have to start losing weight soon. That thought first came to him the same time, almost the same moment, that he realized he no longer craved cigarettes.

But three weeks in, Virginia was humming a hymn in the kitchen when he arrived to start dinner. She was wearing a wig he'd never seen before. The color much lighter, and streaked. Shoulder-length with a flip.

"No more need for the daily crock-pot," she said, smiling. "And I have such great news!"

"They're letting you have a new hair-do?"

"Well, everyone else gets to have their hair styled by the girls who are graduating." She was tearing lettuce into a salad bowl. "I think this was a sample left there by a dealer."

Before this school, Virginia might have thought the word *dealer* only pertained to drugs. She was chopping carrots into disks by simply rocking a cleaver back and forth on a board and feeding the carrot into it. "That's amazing," he said.

"Wait, that's not the news. They said they already have a job for me." She scooped up the pile of carrot disks and dropped them into the salad. "I can leave school for this job right away!"

"What are we having with the salad?"

"Did you hear what I said?" Her voice grew an edge.

"Yes, you're graduating early. You're that advanced compared to the others?" He sat and pulled the stack of mail over in front of himself.

"I must be! Somehow I was made for this. I'd always thought my biggest skill was cooking, and didn't like that delusion." She'd unwrapped something that looked like a steak and started pounding it with something that looked like a hammer.

"Your cooking's not real? Is that why you're doing construction work with meat?" He extricated two bills from the pile, then pushed it away again.

"You're so funny," her voice returned to a lilt. "This is how I always make carne asada. And now, I should always be home in time to make a *good* dinner, you must be so tired of stew."

"What's your…ahem, *allusion*? That cooking's not *my* talent?" He ripped open an envelope.

"Silly," she giggled. "They said it was time for me to carpe diem."

"What?" He could have been (although he wasn't) talking about a bill he was staring at. When did he get a JC Penny credit card?

"You know, *cease the day*! I'm starting Monday as shampoo girl at a salon in Imperial."

The dates of the purchases were before Virginia had started the class. "What's a shampoo girl?"

"She washes clients' hair before they get styled."

"But weren't you going to become a stylist?"

"It's practicably the same thing." She was pouring something from a bottle into a shallow pan that held the meat. "Like how sometimes you can't tell the difference between a busboy and waiter. They both serve, and they split the tips. And I'll get discounts on getting my nails done."

"What about that grotesque tuition I paid?" Now he could smell the lime.

"Oh, I forgot, we're getting half of it back."

"Only half?"

"They said it's like a fee for job placement." The knife now rocking up and down over a pile of something green, and the sharp dirt-smell of cilantro misted the air.

"I don't remember that on the brochure."

"Well, remember I'm a special case—an exhilarated student."

Suddenly he realized. "That you are." He was a real person realizing. "So … I guess they really did tell you to cease the day."

"Yes, and …" Her voice trailed. She turned to fiddle with the knobs on the stove. "Sorry, we'll be having canned frijoles tonight cuz I didn't have time, but I bought homemade tortillas. I should've taken up Pete's mother on her offer to teach me to make them, but at the time, you know, I was so …" He watched her lift a lid from a pot, steam clouding over her. Then she suddenly clanged the lid back onto the pot and rushed past him out of the kitchen. Had everything suddenly become clear to *her* … that she was so hopeless they figured out a way to get rid of her? He got up and went to the stove, lifted the lid to smell the frijoles, his eyes closed. Then he would follow her down the hall to try to mitigate the belated wallop. Footsteps approaching—not too fast, not too heavy. He opened his eyes. Virginia, beside him, smiled and took the pot lid from his hand. She was wearing one of her older short-haired wigs. "I suddenly realized I might be ruining the new hair-do in the steam. That's only for wearing to work. The best part is now I can help Trinity and L'il-Trane. The Lord has shown us all a way!"

Cal left the kitchen into the family room and went to the computer. His email was rarely anything but jokes sent by Cliff.

"I wanted to tell her I would save up to send her to this beauty school, if she came here to live … but her phone's not … "

He waited, but apparently she wasn't going to finish the sentence with either *on* or *working*. "That phone's gone," he said. The computer was going and he was staring at it, but hadn't started the dial-up yet.

"What do you mean?"

"It's de-activated. I'm not paying for it anymore."

"How much could it have possibly been? Couldn't you go without a few sodas a day, or your morning donut—I know all about it, Cal."

"So we're even. I snuck a donut, you snuck a phone onto our account."

"How dare you! It hardly compares! More pounds on your waist visa-vee my *only* way to be in contact with my *only* living child and grandson."

He turned. She was glaring out the pass-through, her face shiny, of course her wig hair still dry. In her hand a metal spoon. He kept his eye on the utensil while he said, "It was a way your only living child could make me pay hundreds of dollars for the overhead on her … nefarious doings."

Instead of being hurled at him, the spoon was used more like a baseball bat—his basket of bills was the ball on a T. Only the two new ones were unpaid, and they weren't there, so the chaos when the envelopes scattered was largely symbolic.

When Virginia got her first week's pay (plus tips), she asked Cal if she could pay him $10 a month to re-activate Trinity's phone. He said no, and showed her the last statement before he'd removed it from the account: the hundreds of calls.

Virginia only glanced at the paper while she took a pan of cookies out of the oven. "Maybe she has a lot of friends."

"Good try," he said. "You know good and goddamn well what it is." He reached to take a cookie. *Dang, Cal, such bravado.*

Virginia swatted his hand with a hot pad. "You don't have to besmooch the Lord's name."

"Besmirch."

"La-de-da to you too." She began sliding the cookies from the pan to a cooling rack. "You can have *one*. These are to put out for customers at the salon."

"I'll tell you what you can do." He took a cookie. "Go to the phone store and open a new account for Trinity. A separate account. Then you try to pay for it." A hot chocolate chip burned his tongue. "Are you opening a new checking account for your money?"

"I hadn't thought that far ahead." She was spooning out another pan of unbaked cookies.

"Time you started learning to do that."

"Don't start bringing up my age. You seem to remember it every day of the year except on my birthday which you can't seem to remember with even so much as a card."

"Didn't we discuss how that beauty school tuition was your birthday present?"

"That's mute."

"I'll tell you what should be mute." He swallowed his last mouthful of cookie. "When you talk to Trinity, I want to hear nothing. Not a word. Do it when I'm not home and then I don't want to hear anything about it. Or her. Not anything she says. Even about him."

The toys had finally been collected, bagged, put in the garage. Even if the boy ever came back—even if they could be discovered and excavated from the garage's inventory—he'd be too old for them.

Her work hours were midday, 11 a.m. to 3. She said after she got more experience, she could be moved to the busier afternoon/evening slot when the business-ladies came in, and they tipped better than the blue-roller-sets and soccer-moms. She said she was waiting for that schedule switch before she got Trinity a phone. So Virginia was always home when Cal had his breakfast and again when he came from the music store for dinner. He didn't even know when the job had ended, and only heard *why* third-hand.

Granted, he actually was going behind her back—since she'd been expressing interest with an offensive frequency in seeing *The 40-*

Year-Old Virgin—and that's where he and Cliff were stealing off to mid-day, midweek, after lunch at Sizzler. When Cliff came to the shop's doorway, Cal stood up from a sousaphone that would be needed by a junior high for a parade that weekend, then said "just a sec," and went to his drawer to get his phone.

"Expecting a call from home?" Did Cliff smirk? Probably.

"Virginia's at work. That's why I *am* taking it." He thought Cliff cocked his head a funny way, so added, "I want to tell Donny to let me know if anyone calls about a horn they need tomorrow. I'll have it on vibrate."

"He could text you."

"I'm not sure I have texting on my phone."

Cliff laughed, "Cro-Magnon Man."

"Pro-*Mignon* man!"

"Hey, did you hear about the guy whose boat was going down in the … well, near Germany. He gets on the radio, 'SOS, SOS, I'm sinking, I'm sinking.' The radio crackles then a voice says, 'Vat are you sinking avout?'"

After steaks and salad-bar (which included tacos, soups and chicken), on the way from lunch to the theatre, Cliff asked, "Are you going to have to come up with a story?"

"What do you mean? About lunch?"

"Where you are now." Cliff either adjusted his rear-view or checked himself out in the mirror. "Why you're not answering the phone."

"She won't call … until around three." He turned the A/C vent so it was blowing directly at his face. "And I'll tell her the truth: I saw a movie. I'll just learn the plot of a different one, one she wouldn't want to see, and describe it in detail … or as Virginia says *ah-museum*."

"Careful, man," Cliff laughed, "she'll get the real truth out of you!"

"Nah. When I get Jones'n for a kid-movie, she never insists on going. I'll just memorize one and give a blow-by-blow."

Dang, why set yourself up like that, isn't he the kind of dude to react with something like 'too bad you're not getting any blow-by-blow'?

To us … it means playing our horns. Remember those?

Oh, yeah, Your ax. Blowing your ax. Not your ex. Hahaha.
Girl ... don't.

Cliff said, "But you won't be able to *blow* with your usual guts. She'll smell a lie. She can get you to talk. She's been reading the Prez's torture handbook. Maybe you can stand up to her previous interrogation tactics, just don't let her give you a shampoo!"

"Why would she shampoo ..." But it didn't sound like a bald-joke. "*What?*"

"You don't *know?*" His hand through his hair, eyes intently forward. "I thought maybe you meant she'd gotten *another* job, after ..."

"After *what?*"

"Oh, God, you *don't* know."

Cliff was able to tell the story before they got to the theatre. Cliff's wife was a client at the salon where Virginia worked. *Had* worked. Had been let go 3 or 4 *weeks* ago. She talked too loud, Cliff's wife had reported to him, they kept telling her to use a "salon voice." That wasn't the culminating event. It was her shampoos. But why had it taken a week for the final shampoo-bowl incident to take place? Was it the height of the client (short), the length of her hair (also short) that had made the final shampoo more difficult? Cliff's wife hadn't even seen it; she heard about it from the salon owner, and neither Cliff or his wife had asked the questions Cal would've. So this was actually *fourth*-hand news, and yet there was no reason to not accept it as true, considering the salon owner had included the detail about the client's short stature and short hair. Virginia had already had a problem, a few complaints, with tangling then pulling clients' hair during their shampoos. But with the tangling and pulling issues already raising the caution flag, Virginia experienced a particular problem rinsing a short-haired client. The woman started to sputter because the sink hose was splashing both the client's blouse and her closed eyes, so Virginia put a towel entirely over the woman's face, then proceeded to soak the towel while she sprayed the soap out of the client's hair.

"So ... she ..."

"Waterboarded some poor woman!"

"I was going to say ... hasn't been working for a while. A long while." For some reason he held onto the dashboard while Cliff pulled into a parking slot and stopped. "What is it now, almost November?" And what was with those cookies? There had also been brownies and walnut candies. Had she been trying to coax her way back to being employable? An apology for the drenched client? Or just making cookies at home? Cal actually remembered eating at least a dozen of them himself, never wondering how many she'd brought to the salon. That first week's pay ... of course, the only week's pay. People usually got paid every two weeks, not every week. That was why there was no new checking account. She'd likely already been let go when she told Cal she was waiting for the better shift before starting Trinity's phone plan. The initial offer to pay him $10 a month to add a phone to their account?—something only the biggest dupe in the history of suckers would fall for (and why hadn't he fallen, wasn't he now the champion?).

Dec 2005

Nuttin happen'n, just thought I'd write. Maybe we need another insight. Something new to get this story going. Not just something to react to, like we're sea anemones.

I want to clean out my apartment, but I did that purge when I had to sell the house. A good go-to way to avoid the real clutter in my head.

Some of it pure-ass resentment. When he cleaned me out, I was saving for an underwater treadmill for Climax. A way to strengthen and maintain muscles without stressing anything (like her cranky neck), which she didn't even have when I started saving. So now, it's off to the K9 hydrotherapy spa as many times a week as I can afford. I quit my own gym. She needs it more.

January 2006

The most perfect weather on earth, for two months. More than one location made the claim. But still, parks bloomed with family picnics, towns booked outdoor festivals, businesses scheduled outdoor sales and parties (Blue Sand likely getting plenty of gigs). The county fair had its week in February. It was the time of year a body could endure being in an un-insulated garage all day. No need even for a fan. Cal had made a decision. He called it a New Year's resolution. And one he wouldn't have to maintain forever, if he could succeed in getting the garage cleaned out, and do so without the extravaganza of a real yard sale. That is, the work itself wouldn't last forever (hopefully could even get done in two months of after-work and weekends), but could he "decide" it would never get this bad again? Could he decide for two? Was it a familial disorder? DNA or just proximity? One thing that had helped lead to this decision was finding at least a dozen candy wrappers stuffed in a hole bored into the plaster wall of Leo's room.

He did not ask for Virginia's help. In fact, did not even announce to her what he would be doing. Strangely, she didn't ask, not even when he started putting things out on the parkway with a sign that said "FREE / GRATIS." She was spending a lot of time cooking and baking, another thing that could be done more easily in the two months of winter.

He kept a mental inventory of what he sorted into piles of trash / recycle / put-on-parkway. Some in categories:

- Leo's clothes, toys, and VHS movies (bought when Blockbuster was changing over to DVDs). Last-in, first-out. Picked up off the parkway by young Latina women with strollers. (To be safe, he took care of Leo's items the first Sunday he worked in the garage, while Virginia was at church.)

- Food, canned and otherwise, from Costco that must have been, at one time, stored in the garage instead of the living room where the plastic shelves for surplus food were now set up in front of a china cabinet. (He tried a tortilla chip from an unopened bag. It was rancid. The soda he gulped to get rid of the wretched taste was flat).

- Furniture: a king sized bed headboard made to look like a wooden gate, from when Virginia was married to Pete; an unfinished wood TV/stereo stand he'd had in college, (the several TVs being warehoused were lined up along the wall in the storage-slash-living room, to preserve them from the heat), a crib, two bar stools with ripped orange seats, and up in the rafters a mattress that was now only the metal outline and coils. (It had been there when he bought the house, the only item in the garage at that time, and he'd never discarded it).

- As-seen-on-TV exercise equipment, never used, only partially put together: ab circle pro, leg magic X, a few other pieces to things he couldn't figure out, curved chrome frames ending at plastic hand-holds and/or vinyl padded places.

- *But-wait-there's-more!* kitchen products: vegetable peeler, hamburger stuffer (although he wouldn't've minded taking that one inside to use), grilled sandwich maker (to use with refrigerated tubes of biscuit dough), a Fat-Magnet (freeze it then rub over the surface of food), Meatball Magic (for homogeneous meatballs), Egg-stractor (it peeled hard-boiled eggs), plus colored plastic pieces of unsolved gadgets.

- My-Own-Business leftovers: melted and partially-burned candles from the candle business, fat loose-leaf notebooks of instructions and product descriptions from the hair-growth-cream and weight-loss-powder businesses. None of the actual cream or powder, nor the before-after photo book Cliff had sworn Virginia showed him. How had some things managed to be discarded?

- Electronics (not necessarily together in boxes or bags, and more than one of each): rotary phones, corded push-button phones, cordless phones with retractable antennas, radios from transistor to boom box, cassette players, car radios and cassette players (remarkably no 8-track, that denizen of any good garage stockpile) and something that he thought was supposed to be the satellite device for direct communication with "the manufacturer" of one of Virginia's "products," but looked more like CB radio gear.

Some he just tried to remember by tub-, bag- or box-loads.

- Numerous containers of pots, pans, dishes, silverware, lamps, small appliances and tools they'd never owned.
- One with framed pictures of V's children, nieces, friends' children etc.
- Several of Angel's personal effects, including baggies from a time he'd been arrested and from the night he was killed (perhaps where Virginia got the idea to use zip-lock baggies for storage, like the gallon-size zip-locks of snapshots jumbled together, several in Angel's boxes as well as here and there in boxes of other miscellany).
- One box containing his college textbooks plus water-damaged h.s. yearbooks—only Virginia's, Angel's and Trinity's. (And where'd the water come from? An old water heater had broken many years ago ... maybe that.)
- Young adult romances Trinity had read, fashion magazines, a year or two of *Playgirl* and *Rolling Stone,* and too many linen, gift and clothing catalogues to count.

From boxes in the rafters that simulated explosion on impact with the garage floor (the cardboard instantaneously disintegrated into shreds), sending roaches and silver fish scrambling:

- Trinity's schoolwork from elementary (every paper she brought home? In the days when she would actually put a pencil to paper in school), likewise decaying and blown to pieces on impact. For several weeks, broken pieces of brittle paper fluttered and settled again on the small front patio between the brick planter and bench.
- His high school band uniform pants, stored with Trinity's clothes from when she was 8, everything in the box rotting and used as nesting for mice.

You never turned in your uniform? They're probably still look'n for you.
At least someone would be.

Wait .. d'you want to be fffound or lost? Didn't my ex's scheme give you any ideas?

Only for a second. I'm too big a chickenshit.

You? Really? I thought you had your shit so together ... I thought you'd go on to be ... so many things. Like ... well, a jazz musician, for one.

I could've only been that if I was with you.

That's what's chickenshit, Cal.

There were two other things he found. The first not buried very far because it was a currently accumulating stash: He found the reason why the pile of mail on the kitchen table never got any bigger. Apparently, every week, Virginia gathered the junk and closed it in a gallon ziplock bag. There must have been 40 or 50 bags in the garage. That wouldn't even be a year of weeks, but he didn't find any others elsewhere, and some of the dates on some of the coupons and sales were several years old. In all those ziplocks, was there a postcard he'd somehow missed? He looked at everything, one at a time, before flipping each item—flier, unopened insurance or credit card offer, appeal for donation with free return-address stickers, or folded newsprint circular— into the recycle bin. If there'd been a lost postcard, it had been found by Virginia. He doubted there'd been one because Virginia wouldn't have been able to stay calm. Although weren't there certain weeks when her alert system moved from green through yellow to orange? He also thought there was probably a reason his yearbooks weren't among the garage's loot.

The mail ziplocks were piled on top of a cardboard box—limp and creased, not really able to hold weight on top of itself. That particular box was another hoard of old magazines he'd never known to arrive in the mail. *Glamour, Working Woman, Cosmopolitan, People* ... most taken from doctor and dentist offices and nail salons. Some subscriptions to Virginia's sister, some just purchased (no address label). The whole box would of course go into the recycling bin—one reason this job took so many weeks was the limit on the capacity of the recycle bin—but when he dumped it, a manilla folder dropped in among the magazines. Inside the folder, black-and-white drawings of sex positions, one per page, with a title and brief explanation. The first few were obvious, in name and

274

position ("missionary" was notably missing). Then they got (or tried to get) mischievous:

Woman on Top (already part of his alone-time repertoire.)

Kneeling Fox (aka doggy, ditto his repertoire.)

Standing Up (how would this even be possible unless X was standing on a stool? Wasn't she only five-feet tall?)

Speed Bump (doggy, except lying down over a pillow. "You'll be orgasming for England before you know it." What did that mean?)

Sexy Spoons ("… for slow intimate sex" … yes, he could occasionally slow alone-time down.)

The Scissors ("easy to do, complicated to explain." In the drawing, they looked like they were lying facing each other, just talking in bed. *Dang, Cal …*

Sultry Saddle (sideways sex, "it might take practice, but who's complaining?" In this drawing, like a few of the others, the only items in color were the two pair of underwear, his and hers, lying casually cast-off beside the couple, plus the picture frame on the wall was askew.)

Manhandle Her ("he gets to play with you" … but another standing position, with X so much shorter, would their parts line up?)

The Spider (ouch, his dick would be bent the wrong way. "Slow, wiggling movements to keep each other aroused for a long time." Is that what she would want? Does he think about himself too much?)

Edge of Heaven (same as her on top only sitting upright in a chair. "Great for female orgasm."

Really … has he been too selfish?)

Melody Maker (she's arched backwards over a hassock, he's kneeling. In fact, if her legs were lifted and hooked over his shoulders, she'd *be* his saxophone, and the melody would be …)

Not that he didn't understand it was Virginia who had saved these drawings. Not just saved them but at some point went looking for them, or was given them by someone to whom she confided about her troubled marriage, her suspicions as to why it had turned out this way. And then never shared them with him. Waiting for the right time. A time which he had, without realizing his success, successfully kept from happening. He needed an incisive quote to indicate his realization of a searing shame for something he, nevertheless, wouldn't stop doing.

Feb 2006
It's funny how I don't know what you think when you read these. If you even do. Maybe one look at the handwriting and it's lying on top of the chicken fat in the garbage.

Sorry to be so boring. In a life where you have a missing-person spouse (in such a dramatic scheme), not much more than that a girl can expect. Got to be some routine nothingness. Work to pay the rent, pay the rent then work some more. New clients come for two sessions then give up, let the dog lie on furniture, chew walls, dig up gardens, bark at neighbors. Wet fur, lather, rinse, repeat. Shave out mats and burrs. Lecture on tick prevention. Grind down the eagle-talon nails that made the dog ice-skate on sidewalks. New clients come for two sessions then give the dog to the shelter. Too much trouble. The trusting/forgiving dog will willingly accept another version of the human asshole who just abandoned it ... if he's lucky enough to be chosen. F this. (Does the USPS care if I write FUCK on an open-faced card?)

You would know what I think if you let me answer.

    Atta boy, Cal, get angry!

    No, I can't. Not really. I don't even blame you for not wanting to have to hear my mess.

    But you're hearing <u>mine</u>.

    That's just it ... it's <u>yours</u>. That makes me want it. And want more.

    You poor sick bastard.

April 2006

I wonder if you kept these cards. I'd love to see them again, to see the timeline, the points in my life I put on half a 6x4. Like if I wrote a book where each chapter was only that moment (maybe what led up to it and the aftermath) ... then I could write my own pithy truisms that other people wrote on postcards.

Like this one: "Maybe it was, after all, the adrenal gland that loved, and not the heart." (See the quotation marks ... it's not my own line. Stealing lines. Why'd you even like me?)

X

Like you? LIKE you? Listen, there's nothing on earth that I've accomplished or will leave here. So it seems all I really wanted out of life was to be with you ...

How would that have changed it?

Because you made me feel I should be and that I could be more than I was ... that I would keep improving, developing, becoming ... with you in my life doing your thing at the same time ... that's what I thought life was supposed to be. Like that.

You know I don't even hear all this stuff you say

Whose fault is that? You chose this. One of your decisions ... I've always lived by your decisions.

Dang, Cal ... you've lost meaning ... assurance ... worth. Life is a piling up of loss ... for me too.

Except you're you.

June 2006

I've been saving this one:
"The world just goes along. Nothing much matters, you know? I mean really matters. But then sometimes, just for a second, you get this grace, this belief that it does matter, a whole lot."

Note to self: can't force the grace. In any context of the word! Remember "grace under pressure" from high school English, the whole Hemingway bullshit code? For men only, of course. That must have been a different grace, though. This quote written by a female ... one few have ever heard of.

Why did I save it for exactly now? Dunno. Not that I had that moment of grace or anything. Still waiting to feel that something matters. Something besides this sweet little dog, more and more inactive. Must run in the family. haha

All men automatically have it better? Make better choices, handle problems perfectly, never struggle or feel alone or ... Either that's feminist bullshit or I'm ...

    No, Cal, not all males, all *men*. Of course some are just weenies.

    Oh, I see.

    Joking! Can't you hear me laughing?

    Yes, always. That sublime scratchy sound stowed in my head. Like a lot of other things ... like a stuffed garage I wasn't able to completely clean out.

    What, you're a poet now?

August, (now also Sept) 2006

Quote of the month: "People's lives... were dull, simple, amazing and unfathomable—deep caves paved with kitchen linoleum." –Alice Munro

Maybe I still have some "deep caves" to explore? Ha, no sexual innuendo, I assure you.

Kind of was the quote of last month cuz I wrote ↑ then didn't have anything else useful or interesting to say.

Do you do Facebook? I know you don't cuz I looked. (I do FB for biznuz.) If you were there, don't know if I woulda poked you. You must think me such a ... well, I don't call people bitches cuz there's nothing wrong with a bitch, spayed or intact. Some trainers won't train bitches, say their hormones hamper consistent working attitude. Jeez, why can't these hormones just do what they're supposed to do and leave work out of it! Do I still have work to do, some "amazing unfathomable" accomplishment yet to come? ←Gak, not a sexual innuendo either!

Okay, this Facebook thing ... I looked into it. Unless I "join" I won't see anything. And if I do join, people can either "accept" me or not, and if they don't, I still won't see anything, can't say anything. What's so different from ... this?

Touché, bub.

My mom used to call me that.

Don't do that to me ... pleeeeez.

Okay. Just that she was so disappointed, I could tell, when I got married. With you she would've ... She would've known why.

Explain it to me. (I know, you keep trying.) Because the span of time is beyond incredible.

Your 'span of time' is my lifetime.

Well ... bub ... why don't you leave?

I think it's been too long. After two years, three, five ... yeah, I should've. But now, after over 30 years? After she's proven over and over again to be incapable of holding a job or managing a budget ... or after I've allowed her to become that way.

And apparently she's allowed you to get fat. Not to mention learn to duck.

I wasn't going to mention that again. I heard how disappointed you (would've) sounded. Also not sure I should say she's gotten me fat. Is that fair? Who's the one shoveling food into my piehole? I'm disgusting. I can't say she's making me disgusting. Or mean. Or ...

279

But you could leave. Couldn't you leave? Why don't you leave?

I don't know. Yes I do. I don't want you to see me like this. But what makes me think leaving would allow me to see you?

I dunno, bub.

Nov 2006

"She thought of being launched out on a gray, deep, baleful, magnificent sea. Love."

What must that feel like? (I know, it says <u>love</u>, not <u>sex</u>.)

Looked up *baleful*. (It doesn't mean you're baling out water in a leaky boat on your magnificent sea ...)

Wow ... malevolent, spiteful. Yeah, my ex for sure. But didn't he have sort of a *point*? That it was complete bait-and-switch, not "love."

Or does it apply to me? Not me-to-him, me-to-*you*. Just cuz of ... well, you know. I barely remember the details, tell you the truth.

Also *menacing, sinister* ...

Grey I can buy.

X

When that client said "no one loves you like this," meaning his dog—
but with a hostile context that *I* would never be loved like that—it
ultimately, at least a few times, despite being something I deserve,
wasn't true. Climax must have "loved me like that." And, at one point,
so did you. Haven't all the postcards and more recent doodling on
these word docs (you could call all of *this* letters I never sent) been
because you are who I should've had to hear me, to listen to, to know
me all these years. More than that: who I should've been answering
for. In its meaning of atonement.

See, I was always running away from a feeling. A tangled ball
of a feeling, in some ways based on immature misunderstandings that
I built into a huge story of betrayal to justify running away from you.
Now I know it has to do with a collision between what I didn't want to
want, and what I would never be able to want. Way back in 1980 … I
guess I was still just unfathomably afraid, and I ran. But didn't run
without looking back. And tying a thread, or leaving bread-crumbs.
The breadcrumbs were for *me* to follow back, since you couldn't (or
didn't) use them to find me. But the way you wanted me … I knew no
matter how I felt about you, you'd never get what you needed from
me.

See, I am pretty sure, now, that I was asexual. Am. It's the only
explanation. *Look it up, meathead*, as Archie Bunker would say. On
the ultra slim possibility you even remember me, or think about me, let
alone still have those same feelings … once you know *this*, would you
want me now? I thought about putting this on my last postcard, but
didn't. Not a thing to announce to your work colleagues at the music
store. Yes, of course, I could've used a sealed letter—I did do that once
when I was spewing about the worst day of my life … or at least this
century. Why I didn't do letters as a rule was probably a check rein on
myself: just say what you can on a card. Short and public, two useful
inhibitors.

The asexual thing… it's no excuse … but maybe at least partial
explanation for my foibles (including getting married to try to blame it
on something or someone else). But it can't be avoided that it's part of
what happened between *us* … besides the usual horn-dog 16-year-old
male and his heat-seeking penis. (That's bad too, that girls have to

survive *that* and then actually start to like sex themselves. And amazing that so many of them do.)

It's getting explained all out-of-order, with so much we both already know ... except you *don't* know certain things.

See, I wrote you a letter back in 1981. Over a year after that night I went to your gig. (I write that as though you would remember exactly what night I mean.) And over-a-year was, I knew almost immediately, about a year too late.

So I'm going to force myself to keyboard it into this doc (in old typewriter font, incapable of italic) without changing anything, like it's some kind of ... well, penance.

Hey, just so you know, I'm still doing the same shit, accounting school although wondering why. Rudy, remember him?, finished the end of last year and got married to someone he'd pointed out to me at his churchy-thing (they don't call it church). Why was I there with him? Good question. Maybe one last test to see how committed he was, and I could tell it was set in stone. What I couldn't tell is why he'd wanted to bring me, since it was so obvious he had no interest in converting-then-marrying me. (Maybe he could tell I was unconvertable.) He pointed out this woman he'd never met and said she was who he was going to get to know then marry because some "brothers" -- no he said "elders" -- had recommended her for him. Then he let it drop that the elders also thought he needed to log more door-to-door miles and start scoring some converts (which of course he did not convey in that vernacular), so settling down with a "sister" might help. I was able to deduce that converting then settling <u>for</u> me would not accomplish the same, since I'd also been the worldly dirt he'd had to resist. I was able, because of that, and partly because of you, to incise the Rudy episode out of my life with clean edges. I barely ever had another thought about him, except gratitude that I was so unconvertable.

But you're going to notice the "partly because of you," which is the main reason for this letter. I know you didn't hear from me for so long, and maybe I can also say that it's "partly because of Rudy" that I took so long to write this -- in that I needed to find out what I found out then kick myself in the head a few hundred times for wasting so much time on him. Shall I get to the point? I can make a bunch of excuses for being so mean to you that night.(Remember that old comedy sketch about Nixon: "I take full responsibility … but not the blame. Let me explain the difference…") So … why did I close that door? It's not that I hated it, with you, that night. I was scared. But it's been hard to explain even to myself what I was afraid of. Another reason it's taken so long, since if I didn't know, then how could I tell you?

Which one was stronger, more prevalent: being scared or not hating it? See, I can't even say "liking it." And that's, I think, what I was scared of. But it's been tugging at my mind that maybe you're the one who could change it from "not hating" to "liking." Even if it's not possible, I wonder if "not hating it" with you would at least be better than being afraid of it alone.(Why was I not afraid of it with Rudy? Maybe I knew there never would be anything to be afraid of, just like you said. Obviously he didn't like me enough.)

Anyway, so I was thinking, maybe we could get together now and then, and not have to call it anything. Just have some laughs, take me to a gig every other month … and whatever … If not you, then who …?

And I know that's a pile of steaming hypocrisy or contradiction, to say "if not you, then who…?" considering what happened when we were sixteen. I still don't understand why you would do that to comfort me. But who says I was entitled to comfort? Then or now. But … what do you think about this new idea?

Well … I never sent it cuz I got your card, whatever it was—an address-change notification or wedding invitation … although I think not a wedding, did you ever get married? Probably. But I was about to send this letter when I heard about the woman-with-children you hooked-up and moved-away with. So I sent a glib postcard instead. At that time you *did* know my address, but you never answered. That sort of changed how I went about it: moving and never giving you my address.

But, Cal, if I could ever someday explain to you … about that night in 1980 … and also that time when we were sixteen. I know I was a mopey teenager, and even tried to tell you why, having to do with not liking things I was supposed to want. And you *listened*. And usually tried to joke me out of it. Then that one time, you … well, you tried something different than a joke. And you wanted to call it love. A 16-year-old human male can't *love* any more than a feral wolf. And if love is expressed by jamming your finger inside someone— Dang, Ca!, I know one of the ten-thousand times you apologized, you said you knew it must be wrong cuz I wouldn't stop bawling. I don't remember crying, before *or* after. But if I was, it was because it was the same day, or the day after, my dog was mashed by a car. I'd had Shep since I was FIVE. Anyway, understandably, our friendship had been getting more and more awkward since that time, but I always needed someone to talk to after my pointless non-relationships. With men, I mean, not dogs. A *few* men. Very few. Two. The real relationships with dogs so outnumber the men. The night in 1980 in that club with you … I hadn't yet gotten another dog. Yes, I needed to talk to someone who already knew me, but I didn't want you to know I was still a virgin. That's a paradox. And it's all what *I* needed and what *I* wanted. Has that always been who I am?

Here's the whole deal: Dammit, you went too far, too fast, add in that I didn't *like* sex, never *wanted* sex … all of it made it impossible for me to know or admit I felt anything for you: The admiration I had for how you expressed yourself in music, how much I loved the way you could make me laugh, how gregarious and friendly you were, how you thought things were *possible* for you. I hope none of that has changed.

Meanwhile I was stern. I was antisocial. I was humorless. I was lonely. I hated everyone. I hated myself. I was mean. I wanted to *be* something. I wanted someone to see through that to *me* and still want that, like a dog does, not even realizing …. I should have just wanted for you to be *you* and to be near enough to enjoy it.

Chapter Ten
(Not Even) Ten Postcards

Feb 2007

Jeez-louise, what can I say ... if noth'n to say, why'm I say'n? Hey, a country song. Folk-rock would have better pithy one-liners ... whereas jazz ... says it without words, right?

But know what? ... certain things are because of <u>choices</u>. We <u>do</u> determine our fate. Let's list some of mine, in reverse order: married, moved out of state, dropped out of accounting school, that night in 1980 ... Nothing changes without a decision.

Forgot to include the dog ...(s). Decisions to start a relationship. Eventually a decision to end it. Not yet though.

Know what, this isn't helping, sorry ...

∨

Dang, girl, I can't spend all my time talking to you.
Who you gonna talk to instead. Let me <u>guess</u>. Ha!

March 2007

Do you think it's cheesy when a book uses song lyrics? It's cheating —too easily triggers a certain feeling for a swath of a generation. (Maybe you don't even read books. Do I even know you?) So isn't it equally tacky for me to use quotes from books to represent whole swaths of ... WHATEVER ... on a postcard? I suppose I could be tweeting this ethos into the ether instead, altho if you're not on FB, you're for sure not on Twitter. And actually, neither am I cuz I have nada really to say and no one who wants to hear — you're kinda forced unless you toss this with the junk mail. I have to have FB cuz of my alleged biznez. OK, now there might not be enuf room for the quote-of-the-month: "... two people who love each other can be saved from madness only by the things that come between them — children, duties, visits, bores, relations — the things that protect married people from each other." Arrgh, can I change children to dogs?

Girl, if only it worked that way. Oh, right, you said two people who <u>love</u> each other
... not ... oh well.

Got no answer for that one, bub.

He asked Cliff what this thing called Twitter was. Cliff said, "Fuck, what guy wants to go around saying he *tweeted* or *twittered*. Shit." Which of course wasn't an answer, and was why he asked Cliff those kinds of questions. He'd also asked Cliff if he should get new cellphones when his first contract was up. Cliff had said, "Will you get better calls from more interesting people?" Cliff didn't know about X, but knew Virginia.

Cal got Virginia a phone that could get and give text messages—only 10 per month. She would, of course, go over that, but only twice before he changed the account to allow unlimited texts. He never looked at her texts. It did seem she actually talked on the phone less (she used the landline for that). He wouldn't have known how to get a text to show on her phone. But he heard about people "finding" texts from a secret affair on their spouse's phone. He sort of fantasized about that— obviously, unearthing a cache of intimate texts to *Virginia,* since he had none of his own for *her* to discover.

What he did find on Virginia's phone, and not something she tried to hide, was a photograph. Almost postage-stamp sized on the screen of her phone, a tiny figure, strangely posed, resembling the way athletes used to pose for action-shot trading cards. The front of her phone stayed lit for a minute whenever she used it then put it down. And she frequently seemed to pick it up, open it, then close and put it back down without doing anything, even though some kind of noise would have told her if there was a call or text. The thing was a noise-kaleidoscope. His just lay there like turd most of the time.

What else would they be doing in the same room, and what other room would it be: the kitchen, while she prepared a meal. Cal sat at his place at the table. She was making chicken a la king, which she said was basically beef stroganoff with chicken and milk. He asked what was the opposite of the dots of sour cream on beef stroganoff, and she answered, "dumplings." She had piles of prepared slices of chicken, sliced mushrooms, chopped onion and celery. "Don't worry, it's a fancy cousin of your fav, biscuits-n-gravy. An anecdote for what nails you."

"Jeez, I guess I need that, or its red-headed-step-child."

He might have regretted the jibe, but it was one of the times she had come to the table to open her phone and put it back down. She didn't seem to hear him, returned to her preparations, and Cal saw the photo. He turned the phone upright and pulled it closer. Then the screen went dark. "Hey ... what's this picture. Where'd it go?"

"Didn't I show you that?" She came back, flipped the phone open, snapped it closed, then handed it to Cal. He thought he knew what it was but retrieved his reading glasses from beside the pile of mail.

"He's growing up!" Virginia said, back at her sizzling skillet, browning chicken.

"He's ..." Cal held the phone until the screen went dark again. It was Leo. Wearing baggy pants, bare-chested, posed in a standing slouch, his arms held at drastic angles, elbows bent, his hands sideways with two or three fingers extended. "Are these gang signs?"

"He's just playing. Experimenting. Kids have to imagine."

"He's not going to think *this* out of thin air. *Trinity* had to—"

"So he's not living in a bushwa bubble." Something hissed when she slid the next pile of ingredients into the skillet.

"You think this is ... okay?" And *bushwa*, what was that, a cult? Oh ... *bourgeois*.

"It's better than being locked in a closet."

Cal thought for a moment, until a faint trace of sweet basil dissipated. "Is that a saying, like *it's better than being poked in the eye with a sharp stick*?"

"I'm saying it's what happened, at first. Didn't I tell you? Not listening as usual." She looked up at him through a thin veil of steam. "It was racist childcare. Or, wait, maybe I'm mixing it up with ... I'm not sure, her boyfriend's mother and step-father? It was three years ago ..." She wiped her brow with the back of her wrist, then pulled her wig forward. "A seniority moment." Her knife clocked on the chopping board a few times. "Okay, I remember ... The babysitters had jobs and couldn't watch him all day. So they put him in a closet with a bottle and blankets and crackers and a few toys."

"What the hell—"

"Don't curse at me. Trinity found out." The next addition to the skillet quieted the sizzle. Almost immediately the food started a soft thick popping. "I think she had a fight with her boyfriend and went early to get L'il-T." Virginia covered the pan. Too late to prevent the thick scent of something like chicken potpie.

"Why wasn't he in *school*? And what the fuck was Trinity doing during the day?"

"Don't use the fuck-word with me. Trinity is … doing what she has to do. She's … out rustling …"

"Oh? Rustling cattle? Or *hustling*? While Leo was locked in a closet?"

"I *said* she found out! She's got … better help now. More like a family." She unwrapped a stick of butter, put flour on top of it in a bowl, then started working at it with the familiar (and disturbingly welcome) circle of wires—biscuits from scratch. "And he does *so* go to school. He's in first grade." Milk added to the bowl. Off-script for biscuits, but she'd said dumplings.

"He should be in second grade."

She scraped spoonfuls of dough into the bubbling skillet with her index finger. "What makes you the expert?"

"Counting. On my fingers if I have to." Then he did. He tapped four fingers on the table over and over, counting 5-6-7-8, 2004-2005-2006-2007, kindergarten-first-second-third … but the fourth finger hadn't happened quite yet. In November it would be 4 years since Trinity had taken Leo. He should be starting *third* grade in September. He wouldn't be 8 until August. The scrawny bare chest in the photo confirmed that. Virginia's phone was still lying in front of him, but he resisted opening it again to look. When she put a steaming plate of food in front of Cal, Virginia picked up her phone and moved it to the pass-through window ledge.

He was still silently tapping his fingers. His eyes moved to the plate. The food had a creamy texture, the pale color of chicken-based gravy, a family of cooking Virginia hadn't done much until more recently. Angel hadn't liked milk-based food. Virginia had said he was *lack-toes intolerant* and that it was the same condition causing diabetics to sometimes have toes and feet amputated. She said the same of Leo, even though she gave him pudding and ice cream and chocolate milk. Once she'd made Linguini Alfredo and Cal had eaten his plate plus Leo's, then had seconds.

Meanwhile the dumplings had puffed up in the steam to make floating islands of biscuit amid thick gravy. She'd put flecks of parsley in the dough. Softened mushrooms had a heady sheen. Onions and celery were translucent, infused with chicken broth. Similarly, he was swathed in a deep fragrance of rosemary and sage. His heart throbbed in his gut.

Dang, don't go into a trance, bud, it's just food.

No, it's not a trance … just thinking …

Vat are you sinking avout?

Yes, that too. See, when I smoked, it was just me, alone. Truly alone. More alone than even … I never even talked to_you while I smoked. The opposite of playing my sax, when sometimes, in a solo, I was … begging you … And, of course … you know … alone time. Not the same kind of alone as smoking. I knew what you thought about my smoking, so I don't know why it was the only time I could stand being alone with myself. A damn good thing I could never afford cocaine, and weed made me so paranoid.

Is this your pithy truism?

Maybe. But realizing it, and realizing also that eating was … became something tangled mostly with Virginia. If there is partnership in this thing, it's that she cooks and I eat … and it's good. And for that, I feel I need to apologize … to you.

What the fuck—?

Remember, no fuck-words.

Ha. Especially if we remove the original meaning of fuck.

Anyway, what I mean is … I do share something with her. I participate, and it's … how to say it … a physical thing. Does that seem … right? It doesn't to me.

Dude, I was married too.

But you're not anymore. And … there's something else. I've now eaten myself into … a swine. I'm fat. I'm disgusting. You never thought I was attractive anyway, and now … Now of course you'll clam up. Of course, what could you say—agree that you always found me unattractive? Well … So it seems that, even though it's not her fault I've eaten like such a pig—and of course I also do eat without her around, but not nearly as often as most guys do, or would, if no one was cooking at home … But it's like she's been able to make any chance of you ever thinking I'm ... well, if there ever even was a chance ... how could I let you see what I am now?

"Hey." Virginia snapped her fingers between his plate and his face. "That's the longest I've ever seen you sit and stare, especially over a plate of food. Maybe you're the one getting old-timer's disease."

"Funny. Where'd you hear it said that way?"

"What way?" She put her own plate down and sat across from him.

Cal dropped his eyes to his food, picked up his fork and shoveled in a whole dumpling with surrounding gravy and vegetables. With his mouth still full, he said, "How many calories does this meal have?"

"Since when are you a calorie counter?"

"Since ..." He swallowed. "It's good. You can add it to the repertoire."

"The what?"

When he didn't answer, she added, "Do big words make you better than me?"

He chewed another huge mouthful slower than usual. Soft and rich, mild but flavors remaining distinct. "Talk with your cooking. It's full of big words."

Dang, Cal, what the hell?

What should I say instead? I don't want constant friction.

You could've said, Like I talk with my sax. But you don't anymore. How'm I gonna hear you if you're not talk'n? Can't you even find a piano player and go play somewhere for free?

Which Mexican cantina is going to add me to their mariachi line-up? Which Italian restaurant is going to replace their piped-in Frank Sinatra? Which Sports Bar is going to turn off football and the other "football," and baseball?

None, if you don't ask. How about a coffee place? I know they're not dark, but a sax playing in the corner... Imagine: I'm wearing a ballcap and reading the newspaper, around the counter from where you're set up. I don't need to see you to know it's you, to hear what you're saying. Not fair, you say? Okay, there's a series of photos on the wall opposite where you're playing, big poster-size B&W photos of the street and the Valley back in the 40s and 50s Main Street robust with shops— stationer, bookstore, drugstore, diner, bakery, JC Penny's, the Hotel Barbara Worth, all long before there was a music store struggling to anchor the hairstylists, bars, jewelry, thrift stores and boarded up empties that are there now. The photo shows the big Studebakers, Buicks, Pontiacs and Chevys filling the diagonal-parking along the street, nose-up to the wide shaded sidewalk flowing under cantilevered roof extensions. You like to look at that photo in particular and daydream while you play, because being an adult back then might have been simpler, you think. But it's in the darker photo of the groves, orange, lemon or grapefruit, that the Valley had once sustained and nourished—rows of 30-foot tall and wide trees, room between for a flatbed pulled by a team of mules or a tractor, but in the photo only a lone man in bowler and suit reaches to pluck fruit from the foreground tree—that you can see a reflection of the person in a crop-pickers ballcap sitting around the counter from where you play.

I hope you realize how field workers don't have time, inclination nor resources to be sitting in a coffee bar listening to a slothful saxophonist's fantasy.

That's how you know it's someone else. And you know who it is. And she'll take the hat off before you're finished with "Sabor a Mi."

How about "Ghost of a Chance."

Sure, okay, we can pretend we're imagining this together. How long will "her" hair be when "she" takes off the cap? No, not one of those 'surprise-it's-a-girl' clichés when a helmet is removed and lush locks tossed side-to-side. Her hair was always short. Well, not always. In high school it was long and straight, like everyone else's, and it was all gone by the second year of college, short and sassy like the shampoo of the same name, until she permed it once when it was a little grown out, then let that grow and cut the frizz off the ends just before that night in 1980 … so now … now … she hasn't changed it at all? Straight and boy-cut … Is there any grey? Has she pierced her ears (or anything else)? Are her lips darkened with lipstick or her brows arched with shaping and penciling … no, no, no, and no. Although the reflection in the photo of lemon trees wouldn't be able to tell you. You play for her— what's the next tune, "What's New?" … no, "You Don't Know Me"—until she lifts her chin, turns, you can see her profile, and slowly she runs all ten fingers through her hair, face tilted up, eyes closed, and she starts to rise from her table …

Wait, no— Let's just leave it here. So you can talk to me, and I can look at you.

I uzta still come through on 1-8 couple times a year, but not anymore. It woulda been around now, usually. The parents are both gone now. Have you noticed how we use words like <u>passed</u> and <u>gone</u>. How about <u>no longer with us</u>. I also don't think I even bothered to mention it, either time, in a postcard. And no F'n way on FB. Just something to grapple with, partly with a family, partly alone. I'm sure you know. Some life story I've compiled here ... as though I had asked you to keep the cards, file them by date, make a book. I think early-on I wasn't say'n much about anything. For that matter, too little about not-much being said here. Climax is so slowed-down ... ok stuff the laughter about how <u>that</u> one sounds.

X

April 2008

Someone must have needed money because Virginia's aversion to a cooking-based income cracked. Not that she filed applications at restaurants or catering companies. Another my-own-business for which the planning started and ended with the name, *The Lord's Meal Plan*. But it looked like:

The Lord's *Meal* **Plan**

Actually she did have an additional plan, which must have come from somewhere, although he suspected it hadn't been divine. Someone at her church must have suggested that she have a big party, and do it as though catered, except have people come early enough that she could give some demonstrations (fresh ingredients, speed of preparation, certain special touches like cherry tomatoes carved into roses, asparagus spears standing straight up along the edge of bowls of dips to look like trees), and not only have business cards and fliers on hand for guests to take home, but a guest book asking for email addresses so she could send coupons for services—everything from the cookies for your kid's class Valentine's Day party to full family Easter or Thanksgiving dinners—and referrals.

The invitations included church people, of course, but also neighbors, and then Cal saw Cliff and even hourly employees at the music store opening the hand-addressed embossed invitations. Already the business—i.e. Cal—was in the hole for the cost of those.

Not that they were the only initial expenses. The business cards also embossed and full color, an image of a cake in the shape of a cross, stars of light emanating from it. Her new website, he discovered, would be a page on the church's site, and the church webmaster (who also designed the business cards) would design and maintain it. In exchange the church would get free catering services.

"That's actually ... shrewd," Cal said, "but not including the food, I assume."

"Let's not be calling names and expecting failure."

"I didn't call ... never mind. The food, though, do they get free food when they have a free catering?"

"I don't know, we never discussed the details."

She chose a taco and salad bar for her demonstration party. Both Cal's favorite, tacos dorados, plus soft shell options, chicken and carne asada, fish and shrimp, two kinds of beans, complete array of taco toppings including guacamole, three kinds of cheese, three choices of salsa, sour cream; and ample salad array including more avocado, olives, homemade croutons, bacon bits, sunflower seeds, and three made-from-scratch dressings, plus bacon-wrapped cheese-stuffed jalapeno poppers and fried mozzarella for appetizers, and home-made flan for dessert.

Meanwhile, the RSVPs, mostly from church people, started stacking attendees into a 15 to 20 range. Virginia was disappointed, but thought she would probably have to have more than one demonstration party. She would follow up, she said, with a 4th of July barbecue and then maybe even a Thanksgiving dinner.

Taco bar groceries overstuffed the refrigerator. Some time ago, on her request, Cal had taken in a used refrigerator left on a neighbor's parkway, now installed in the garage. Sometimes the garage got to 125 degrees, making the refrigerator work its ass off in the summer, and he'd been about to get rid of it when it also filled with supplies for the party.

He begged Cliff to come to the party, but Cliff only laughed, then admitted Virginia's tacos dorados were good enough to make the church people less insufferable. The best he would do is say "I'll see."

It would be difficult to do much food preparation in advance, with so many fresh ingredients. He watched, without hovering but with understandable interest (besides the usual mouth-watering), as the salsa and salad dressings were prepared the week before, cheese shredded and packed air-tight zip-locks, croutons baked, jalapenos halved and cleaned, beans soaked and cooked—black beans left whole with onions, peppers and chili, the pintos refried—then frozen to keep them from going rancid. Still, was one person going to be able to cook marinated chicken and skirt steak on a charcoal grill, shrimp and fish on another grill, fry some taco shells, shred lettuce, cut carrots, cucumber and radishes, make guacamole not so soon that it turned brown, and bake a flan? Virginia hired a helper. But Cal never saw her. He could only hope she hadn't been paid in advance.

The morning of the party when Cal went to the music store, the kitchen table had already been moved to the living room and spread with a paper tablecloth, with plastic plates, drinkware and napkins on a folding table nearby. The tablecloth, napkins and plastic-ware had been broken, shredded and wadded, then heaped in the foyer where he would walk right into them when he came home at noon. He'd come in expecting to deliver some welcome news: that Cliff had finally agreed to attend—on Cal's report that preparations seemed coordinated well enough that the whole idea actually seemed able to materialize—and Cliff was active in the chamber of commerce, did a lot of networking with other businesses so could be a valuable source of referrals.

"Virginia, what the *hell*—" But once he turned into the kitchen doorway, no need to finish. On the counter, where she should have been chopping or stirring or seasoning, there was a single white card. A postcard.

"That's right! I found out your little secret!" She was standing in the TV room, on the other side of the pass-through window, maybe had even been hiding below the window and popped up when he picked up the card.

Why had he not put it in the shoebox at the music store with the others? Obvious. It was one with a picture on one side, an orangutan, the card bought at the San Diego Zoo. The message was not the usual wistfulness nor life-update, but scrawled, only a few words, *Visiting the parents, thought of you!* Sure enough, the postmark was from San Diego, not Boulder, and a smeared date, probably 1990. The X signature took up most of the writing space after the six words. He almost felt the same blood-loss feeling of disappointment he'd had at the time, to have waited so long for the next installment, only to receive a fatuous joke.

"This is almost 20 years old."

But no, he knew the swooning sensation was also something else.

"Which means you've been carrying on with her for over 20 years?" Virginia came around from the TV room and up into the kitchen, the kitchen being two steps higher. She became taller, her voice louder.

"Carrying on? What even makes you even think it's a *her*?"

"She's seen you naked!"

He recoiled and backed up as she plunged forward. "Where are you getting this? It's a fucking postcard from the zoo."

But she was lurching for the refrigerator, not him. "Where you always wanted to go, every time we were in San Diego, zoo zoo zoo, you and that zoo. Is that where you've been meeting her?" She started tossing items for the party onto the cooktop counter.

"Meeting *who*? I haven't been to the zoo in—" Bags of cut salad vegetables slid off the cooktop to the floor. He tried to catch it then picked one up. "This is … I don't even know who sent this, it was 20 years ago, it's something *any*one could've … a guy in a band, a guy from college, Cliff, dumb guy-humor, *hey you look like an ape, man*." There was no kitchen table to put the bag onto. The cooktop counter was filled, she was tossing food toward the sink now, in bags, in Tupperware.

"She knows about your body hair, the kind of joke you would only have with … with *me*." Virginia brandished a flat sealed Tupperware. "That you have body hair, that you're huge with a big gut—*I'm* the only one who should know this about you."

"Thanks, I never knew you thought so much of me."

The flat box skidded on the counter, ricocheting a few other containers into the sink. "Have I ever said anything about it, rejected you or— In fact, it's *you* who—" Now the main course in her arms, four two-gallon zip lock bags of chicken and steak, marinating in lime and carne asada spices. "That's why it's been so long, it's been over ten years, Cal, all my friends say if he doesn't want it at home, he's getting it somewhere else." She held the four bags up in two fists, as though courtroom evidence, the raw meat awash in red liquid some kind of damning forensic substance.

"You're fucking crazy, it hasn't been ten years."

She raised the bags over her head, then stomped on the foot pedal to open the trash.

"What the hell are you doing?"

"Just keep cursing and you'll see. This is all going in the trash, the garbage, just like our marriage has turned out to be, *garbage.*"

"Oh no you don't." He kicked the trash aside and reached to take her by the wrists.

Virginia backed away, raising the bags higher. "Keep your hands off me! I'll throw them, I will! Then you'll be cleaning the walls!"

"You need to calm down."

"Just admit it and I will."

"There's nothing to admit."

Suddenly she brought the bags of meat in to her chest, hugging them, face to the ceiling, wailing, "You never loved me. Now I know why."

"I'm here with you, aren't I?" The words seemed to freeze her. So he said, "What do you want me to do?"

Her eyes back on him, narrowed and glaring, and no tears on her face. The bags dropped to the floor. She kicked them toward him. "Cook it. Cook it all, right now. Or I'll throw it away."

"Okay. Are your guests still coming?"

"You know who's going to eat all this food? *You.* All by yourself. Go ahead. Get fatter. No one will want to sleep with *you* either." As she pushed past him, she stepped on one of the bags. That one broke, but nothing oozed onto the floor. They'd been double-bagged, he saw when he picked them up.

The first searing heat had come early. It hung near 100 degrees while Cal stood outside over the two gas grills (one had been borrowed but he didn't know from where). He cooked all the beef and chicken, and even did the fish and shrimp even though the smell of shrimp made him nauseous. He kept piling cooked meat on a tray on the desert-dusty picnic table near the grills. Between 4 and 4:30, someone called from the gate beside the trash cans. It was Cliff, wondering why no one was answering the front door. Cal's shirt was sweat-drenched and his neck was sunburned. He opened the gate for Cliff, then just turned and returned to the grills. When he felt Cliff join him, Cal said, "You know, my grandson used to say *grills* when he meant *girls*."

Cliff handed Cal a beer. "I didn't think she would have a liquor license."

He and Cliff ate almost all of it, locating the taco fixings in the sink or on the countertop, some still in the freezer—they had to nuke the beans to eat them—assembling everything on the table in the living room. Cliff remarked, "We're like a coupla fucking kings gorging on everything in the castle." Then after a few more bites, "Or you ordered the whole menu for your last meal." Cal wasn't sure if the muffled hammering he heard from down the hall had a brassier response to Cliff's word choice, but he knew his sax was not in harm's way.

Cliff took left overs, including *all* the fish and shrimp, back to the store for his other employees and music teachers. Cal had cancelled his own afternoon lessons, but said he'd be in later. He arranged the unused salad fixings and left-over cheese and meat back in the refrigerator, in case he needed a meal tomorrow. He didn't know why not a single one of the other guests who'd rsvp'ed ever rang the doorbell.

The thudding and other construction-like noises were explained when Cal went down the hall to shower and change for an evening session (maybe a session of alone-time as well) in his repair shop. But the shower, the instrument repair, and the alone-time had to wait, as he spent the evening putting everything away. *Everything* being the contents of most of his drawers, the shelves above the closets, his clothes (all over the floor with pockets turned inside out), and his locked file cabinet had been tipped back and forth enough so that even though the locks had held, the folders had jumped and spilled portions of contents inside the drawers.

Virginia was straightening her "business" hairdo in front of the dresser mirror, standing between drawers dumped on the floor and drawers still hanging out of their slots. He said, "Find anything interesting?"

Passing him in the doorway as she left, her elbow made a furtive jab into his gut. There was simply no room for a guy as big as he'd become to be able to avoid it.

Do fat people buy bigger houses? Bigger cars? Bigger beds? I still drive a Yaris.

Interesting leap over the bed when you got down to providing an example.

Queen. I sleep in a queen. How does that sound?

Exactly like what you fear.

A king wouldn't fit in the room. Apparently doesn't fit in the doorway either.

Haha! So lose weight, jackass.

That would mean giving up the only enjoyment or times of contentment I have.

No more music?

He'd moved his saxophone to the shop for safekeeping, but it did take up valuable room there, especially over any school holiday when the shop filled with instruments needing repair. That evening he brought it back home and put it under the bed in the extra bedroom. He had to throw away several empty Amazon shipping boxes first. No mystery who'd hidden them there, and no mystery why.

May 2008

You can tell ... I printed this. Was going to glue to a card, but too long. What a chickenshit I am. Besides being a fucking betrayer, SHE was try'n to tell me ...

Cliché alert -- not sure can say this without them. A nightmare of colossal magnitude. OK, just the facts, ma'am. Those had to be listed over and over: to front desk, vet tech, ER vet, neurologist, next ER vet, next vet-neuro. Can't see keyboard through pooling swollen eyes, typos in every word. Fix later. Digressing so the words won't get typed. If it's not written, maybe it's not real, didn't happen -- that's shit, it did, she's gone, best friend, partner, soul mate. Just say it: she collapsed, 48 hours ago, middle of the night heard her plod toward the water dish, maybe dragging feet -- a telltale sound probably started days ago -- then the ka-thunk. Thought just down to sleep again, Fucking selfish bitch, didn't check til my own need to pee, then she's in the way, wouldn't move ... couldn't move, swam on the tile floor. Lifted her but legs like noodles, crashed back down, chin hit hard. Luckily small enough, could pick her up to race to the car. But couldn't do without her serrated wail - will never un-hear it. But she never stopped recognizing me, knowing me, needing me, my hot bloated slimy face. 8 a.m., the 24-hour clinic's neuro doc already in emerg surg on day-off then will leave, so we have to go 50 mi farther to Denver, gurney to the car, load her floppy body, anoth screech, fainter, anoth check-in, anoth ER doc, anoth vet-neuro, now hours later ... Xray, pros and cons of MRI, there's something there, in her neck, have known about the disc for years, pred for pain ... but it turns off immune system ... that shadow there, could be tumor, could be infection. Limbs floppy, fully paralyzed, but pain, savage pain ... surgery has 50% success prediction ... try antibiotics, intravenous, leave her, cold metal cage, fluids, opioids, closes her eyes as her face is stroked, me kneeling on the floor for an hour, bent forward, a fetal pod people step over and around, the noise of the hospital blurs, glaring lights dim with my face against her shoulder, but an occasional whimper means she's hurting, I'm hurting her - hell I killed her. 24 hours of antibiotic proves an infection, legs can swim again, but that's all, would take days more, a week, in the hospital, and probably wouldn't work, surgery still the only hope, and still little hope of success ... When I return in the morning, she hears me, jerks and heaves her head up, yowls, but just a squeak, her chin lands in my lap and doesn't move from there again, heavy warm weight, trusting me, needing me ... decision had to be made but the wait several hours until the doc can kneel beside us and help me let her go ... fucking let her go ... fucking damn as though that's what she wants ... she wanted me to help her, take care of her, and I couldn't, didn't, my fault, I didn't listen, wrapped in my own woes, just let her physical malaise be the evidence of mine. I suck and she found out and you should know too ...   x

I don't know what to say.

    I know, Bud, no one does.

It wasn't as though he thought he had anything to apologize for, and it wasn't as though Virginia's blanket coldness worried him, made him lonely or unwanted. She still cooked meals, although more frequently out of cans or boxes, with pre-prepared sauce or spice mixtures. Her time at the church had probably increased—he couldn't tell because it wasn't time he was at home, except Sundays (a traditional *alone-time*)—but the ATM card at the grocery store still drained the bank account, and there was always soda in the fridge and crackers or chips in a basket on the counter. So it wasn't as though he was impelled toward conciliation by any recent specific discomfort or privation he could name. Still, he asked Virginia, as she prepared to leave for Church one Sunday, what household odd jobs she could think of that needed to be done. He figured he could have alone-time before or after the task, but as it turned out, *that* would have to skip a Sunday.

"Clean the screens," she said briefly. "And get rid of that freakin bird."

There had been a bird pecking at the windows of the house, sitting on the sill, tap-tap-tapping, painting the sill with purple shit. Two, three, four different windows, all day for several days, rat-a-tatting. Drought-resistant mulberry trees used by early developers in residential landscaping had a prolonged fruiting season, explaining the color of the bird's crap, but not its deranged obsession with the windows.

The task of cleaning screens wasn't a punishment-invention— they were almost always congested with desert dust, and he did usually spray them out once a year, twice if he had his shit together. He was almost sorry he'd had to ask and be assigned the chore. It was already too warm to open windows. Usually he could do the screens with the windows closed, but since he also needed to wash the sills of the plum-colored splotches, he opted for a complete air-exchange: let the house breathe dry air for (dust notwithstanding) an hour or, and wash the sills inside and out.

The screens were drying propped against the garage door, the windows cranked open while he washed the sills, so the bird achieved its life's wish. It was finally in the house. And, inside, realized this was not what it wanted at all.

Cal caught the bird in a sheet, put it in a cardboard box and drove it 20 miles away, into the state park. When he opened the box, the bird, despite its tattered wings, flew instantly, gone in a fluttering second. The force of its departure knocked the box out of Cal's hand. Gone so fast Cal could barely follow the directional line of flight. But thought, perhaps, it was—by accident, just fluke—the route back to town.

Later, the screens back in place, the windows shut, the bird returned, tapping, not knowing why it so fixatedly wanted this thing it wanted, this thing that has frayed its feathers and bewildered its instinct, this thing that upon achieving led to imprisonment, darkness, and miles of flight, only to return and want it again.

He looked it up. It was a male brown-headed cowbird. Instead of spending its time with a mate, building a nest and making hundreds of trips back and forth with bugs to stuff down the pre-fledglings' throats, the male cowbird had time to spend pecking at windows because the female, producing up to a dozen eggs a season, laid them into the nests of other, usually smaller, birds. Industrious sparrows, dove, towhees, catbirds. The cowbird hatchlings grew faster, frequently crowded the bio-kids out of the nest and occupied the step-parents' time and resources. Why wasn't it the duped, dutiful sparrow or dove pecking with aberrant wretchedness at his window?

Aren't I mister irony today?

No answer achievable. How could he even expect to invent one. *Yeah, bro, haven't you learned from this one-way discourse, it's never going to be about you.* No—that's *him* being a passive-aggressive bastard. Had even the hypothesized voice in his head been snuffed?

Even though there might have been enough time left for alone-time, he went instead to the extra bedroom, formerly Leo's room. Slid the sax out from under the bed, put it together and strapped it on, then turned and sat on the mattress. Down by his feet in the open case, he saw a roll of charts. Charts he'd kept in his case and not in his gig bag of music. The tunes he had used to cry out to her. *How Insensitive, You Don't Know Me*, Tower of Power's *You're Still a Young Man*, standards *The Nearness of You* and *Ghost of a Chance*, offbeat classics *Something Stupid* (better as a duet a-la Sinatra and Sinatra), and *Windmills of Your Mind*. The charts were too permanently rolled to stay open propped against the case like a music stand, and even if they would stay, he could no longer read music from that distance, something he'd done in countless rehearsals for various groups, even the most recent. By memory, he fingered keys for the harmonic minor scale that opened *What Are You Doing The Rest of Your Life?*

I can't even pretend you can hear me ... I can't think of what to say when you're so gone. You've been gone for longer periods before, but I always knew you were out there building your life, doing something, putting it all together ... now ... I can feel how gone you are.

Later in 2008, he put the charts into his frayed file of gig music, prepared the sax for long-term storage and moved it back to the music store again. He idly considered offering it on the store's used-instruments-for-sale bulletin board.

It remained that way with Virginia for a while. He initiated driving to Yuma for pie at Denny's, even though there was a Denny's in El Centro. "Better than driving 8 blocks down Imperial and recognize a few too many people in other booths," he said.

"Meaning you don't want to be seen with me."

"Not at all."

But whatever he was doing, for whatever reason he was doing it, continued. Several times he brought her with him when he got up at 4 a.m., made a thermos of coffee and drove out into the desert to watch the sunrise. They sat side-by-side in beach chairs and didn't say anything. The third time she brought homemade coffeecake.

He started taking her to the movies once a week, maybe every-other week, depending on what was showing. Superheroes like *The Dark Knight, Hulk* and *Iron Man*, aging adventurers like Indiana Jones, other elderly top guns like Clint Eastwood. She chose a few light comedies, after going on Fridays became a *thing*. The day before Christmas, when Virginia suggested *Benjamin Button*, he agreed, then read a synopsis and pretended to be coming down with the flu.

January 2009

Of course I've had to pay the rent, utilities, feed my own gut. I couldn't just sit and stare until the consciousness of what I'd done evaporated. Altho maybe I tried-- went to an isolated static place. As I start to come back, flashes of unnamed fear ... that I'll let feeling OK or "normal" cause me to let her fade back into the usual vague, distant yearning. Any peace of mind (now) is fragile. I'm afraid of it - because I don't *want* it to be OK that she's gone. Where did I hear this, the TV numbing white noise blathering in the background or a book I'm staring at w/o really reading: Happiness = Something to do, something to love, something to hope for. Looked it up. Chinese proverb. Can't be argued. And by "do" I'm sure it doesn't just mean ... pay the rent, utilities, feed your gut.

X

Glad you're still there. I was ... worried.

> *Try scared.*

OK. Good truism—thanks for that. SOMETHING TO DO, and by that it means besides whatever job keeps the roof from blowing away? And SOMETHING TO HOPE FOR ... can it be something to dread? Of course, not the same thing.

> *You're get'n it bud. Hard to fill in all three blanks.*

How about alone-time on Sundays ... can that count as something to love, something to hope for ... something to ...?

> *That's some<u>one</u> to DO. Hahaha—asshole.*

Under the category of it's easier to laugh than cry.

> *So go ahead and cry if that's what you consider funny.*

But haven't I had something to love for ... more than thirty years?

> *Some<u>thing</u>? Maybe that's all its been.*

No. <u>You</u> wrote these cards. You licked the stamps. Who even does that anymore? Something to <u>hope</u> for? Sometimes it's so faint, so shadowy, it's not there, it's nowhere. Except when I've been holding the cards. You don't know how my pulse gets hot and fast when I see one in the mail. Especially this time. And I sweat. And sometimes feel the fluttering of being over-caffeinated. Ok, yes, and sometimes a hardon, or the beginning of one. So if my body, my nerves and blood and muscles, think something's there, isn't something <u>there</u>?

> *Who're you tryna convince?*

The house was again growing a collection of boxes and swollen black garbage bags. The seldom-used living room furniture—2 chairs, a sofa and coffee table, china cabinet on the far wall opposite the fireplace, all from Virginia's first marriage—had been pushed toward the center of the room (except the china cabinet), a tighter, more intimate conversation area, but the reason for the seating arrangement huddling closer together was the rows of boxes stored against two walls. More were stashed in the supposed guest room, and in the room where now most of his clothes hung on the portable rack because there was no room in the bedroom closet. He counted back: it had only been three years since he'd tried to clear out the house and garage.

When he mentioned he might sell the amplification system he used to use at gigs, Virginia said he could donate it to the big annual sale held by the church. She'd been volunteering there, organizing and pricing items, a few afternoons a week, in addition to Bible-study Wednesday nights and choir practice Tuesdays.

"Is that what all this stuff is for?"

"What stuff?"

"Whadda you mean *what stuff*?"

"It's for Trinity. She might be getting a house."

"You mean she might start mooching off someone who lives in a house instead of their car?"

The swift kick to one of the bags probably resulted in some breakage. A jangle of glass or metal pieces. The bag even seemed to double over, clutching its gut after a blow to the solar plexus. Which was better than the time a few weeks back when Virginia had whipped a belt at a wall in the guest room and left a buckle-sized gouge in the plaster. For some reason, one Sunday afternoon, after alone-time, he moved everything away from that wall, repaired the plaster, then painted it with an almost empty can left over from when he'd last painted, when Leo was a baby. There were flecks of dried paint and rust in the can, and the wall was a slightly different shade than the rest of the room, but it didn't show much when, before the paint was even fully dry, additional boxes and bags were moved in.

"So *how* is it you're getting all this stuff for Trinity?"

"From what people are donating to the church sale."

"You're stealing it from the church sale?"

"Not *stealing*, dumbnut, they *donate* to people in need, why not donate directly to Trinity?"

Despite the trips to Yuma for pie, the sunrises, movies, dinners out, cards and flowers on birthdays and Valentine's, Virginia didn't waste opportunities to bring up the wayward postcard. From "Seventh commandment, Cal, *He* doesn't forget so why should I?" to "What did you send *her*?" to the best one: "There's no statue of imitations on adultery." He wasn't even entirely sure of the triggers. Maybe on days he ever got the mail instead of her, which happened remarkably, but not unexplainably, less and less often.

Finally, in late spring, he told Virginia he was calling the church to pick up all the donations she had amassed for their sale. "It's a win-win," he said, "They'll see how tirelessly and successfully you are able to work for their causes, and we get this stuff moved out for free."

"But *Trinity* …"

"How the fuck would she ever be able to transport any of this stuff anywhere, even if some miracle happened and she had a permanent place to live?"

"You jerk, you infidel, go ahead and call, I told pastor about *you* and what you've done."

"Well, rest assured, I won't tell him what you've done."

The Pastor did seem to know a little about him. After an overly hearty greeting, and then informing Cal that Virginia knew how to arrange for a donation pick-up, the pastor went on, "We hear you're a musician. How would you like to make some joyful noise with us on Sundays? We do call our group Joyful Noise." The kind of guy who didn't pause to let you answer after a question-mark, the kind which maybe made the best preachers. "It's a pretty good little combo. I play some electric piano and a little guitar. We're starting to *rock*."

"Well, I haven't played for a while."

"Come back, brother, music might be a good way for you to come back."

"There's no *back* for me, Reverend—"

x

"Call me Rick. I was going to contact you about joining our combo, but also something else, it might be beneficial for you and Virginia to come in for a conversation. She's been pretty upset about something and we think we can straighten it out. Can you come in on a Monday evening? Our groups meet every other weeknight, Mondays are when we do family counseling."

"She asked you to call?"

"Not exactly, no, but of course our mediated conversation can often nip little issues before they flower and spread seeds."

"No issues, maybe a misunderstanding."

"Then why not come in and get it straightened out, don't let it fester, brother, that's what we're here for."

Cal couldn't think of a way to throw the plural first-person pronoun back at the pastor without it meaning himself and Virginia. While deliberating that problem, the pastor set a date.

The church had moved some time in the last five years and now occupied the old Kmart store on Imperial. The other storefront that had been attached to Kmart had become the daycare through kindergarten, and housed children's Sunday school as well as summer Bible camp. The interior of the old Kmart had been partitioned to allow for offices, a kitchen, an adult classroom, storage areas large and small (the old "in the back" that every store supposedly had now housed the donated items for the parking lot sale), and of course the large auditorium area with pews, lecterns, choir risers, even a smaller stage with amps for a band. Cal actually started to gravitate toward the band stage, just to check out the set-up, but Virginia's hand went to his arm long enough to redirect his momentum to align with hers: toward the office doors, one marked Pastor Rick.

"No last name?" Cal said, after Virginia had knocked.

"He's everyone's brother."

"Are you sure this isn't—"

But then the door opened and a man with fluffy blond hair falling over half his forehead and covering his ears was shaking Cal's hand.

Strange that it took noticing the Pastor's fisherman's sweater, cargo shorts and Birkenstock sandals before Cal realized how much Virginia had dressed up for this appointment. She was wearing her best hairdo, a down-to-her-shoulders job with unobtrusive streaks of a lighter color, but maybe she always wore it on Sundays so had to now in order to appear to be the same person. She'd also chosen an above-the-knee secretary-ish skirt and sleeveless silk or satiny top, two or three bracelets on each arm, high heels, (but not fuck-me shoes—a term Trinity had used once when Virginia was wearing them, which might have resulted in one of the heels putting a scratch on Trinity's face because the combat had been in the tiny bathroom). Cal's jeans and pocket-T weren't anything other than what he always wore.

"So," the pastor began, after they were seated in a triangular arrangement in chairs around a coffee table, "we understand there's a disturbance on the homefront."

"Why are you soft-buttering it? He's cheating!"

"Let's calm down, Virgie. Remember, Grace conquers." The pastor's voice ... Virginia had it right: buttery.

"But he—"

"Let's listen to what Cal has to say."

"Are you really taking his side?"

The pastor touched her arm—her wrist—with one finger. "Cal?"

Cal looked at a coffeemaker on a side table behind the pastor. On a TV talk show, they'd each have a cup, but would they really be drinking? Would this be when he should lift his mug and take a big gulp? "If we were on Dr. Phil, one of us would have our back to the camera."

"Good one," the pastor said, smiling, his finger back on Virginia's wrist, but looking at Cal. He raised his eyebrows.

"Okay, but I don't know what I'm supposed to be trying to come up with here."

"You don't know what's upsetting Virgie?"

"She ... Virginia seems to think—"

"I *know*, Cal."

"Shhhh." The pastor touched her wrist again, or the back of her hand, like there was an off button that needed to be refreshed. "We want to hear your version."

"My *version*? You mean how she found a 25-year-old postcard from a friend? Which in our house should hardly be surprising."

"What's that supposed to mean?" Virginia actually moved her hand and arm out of reach of the Pastor's finger.

"Nothing ever gets thrown away. I should back a dumptruck up the driveway and fill it."

"You're carpetbagging."

Cal possibly didn't wait long enough before he said, "I'm not even *sand*-bagging."

The pastor was probably hiding a smile. He coughed.

"*See?* See how he thinks I'm stupid? He can't claim he hasn't—"

"Virgie," the pastor recovered his neutral Mr. Rogers expression and tone, "We all will have a time to speak and a time to listen. Cal? Is that really all there is to it?

A time to be born, a time to die / A time to plant, a time to reap, / A time to kill, a time to heal, / A time to laugh, a time to weep ... Maybe he hadn't really sat there long enough without answering to resurrect all the lyrics as his mind played the *Turn, Turn Turn* melody. Cal said, "What else could there be?"

"More sideswiping. He won't even say if it's—"

"Virgie, how can we talk this out without hearing what Cal has to say?"

"Why are you on his side?" She stood up. "You won't let me finish. You're letting him *deny*."

"Sit down," Cal and the Pastor said simultaneously, with the Pastor adding "Virgie." Cal wasn't looking at her but could feel her spotlight gaze on him.

"It's just some postcards," he said. His own gush of alarm came just before her response.

"*Some?* See? I told you! He's been carrying on for years." She was still standing. Her purse was on the floor by her chair, so no danger of it becoming a club if she started to flail. The pastor got up, put his hands on her shoulders and guided her back into her chair.

"I don't even answer them." He did finally look at her face. She was wearing make-up. Maybe she always did, so he was used to it. But it seemed her skin surface looked both impervious, and also ablaze in a startling way. "You can't really call it 'in-contact.' Let alone carrying-*on*."

"How is it *not*—"

Still standing behind her with his hands on her shoulders—the position of a husband in a staged family photo—the pastor must have delivered some kind of compression to shut her up so he could say, "Could you tell this … friend to stop sending the cards?"

"No, I couldn't … even if I wanted to." Cal felt his head drop, as though his neck had reached the end of durability for the day.

"Thank you for your honesty, Cal. I know this must be difficult." In the moment of silence, the pastor was moving back around to resume his place in his chair. "Now, Virgie, it's your turn, we have better information. Perhaps, with prayer, we can determine a direction."

"The only direction is for him to stop."

"Virgie … Sister, we can only decide our own behavior."

"I can decide to get a lawyer and take everything."

"I think some prayer might help us recover the grace needed to make positive or constructive decisions."

"Does grace mean I just *take it*? That I have to stay with him while he *cheats*?"

Cal looked up. "There's no locked fence around the house, I'm not forcing you to stay if it's so intolerable."

"I'm not the one—"

"Virgie, we'll pray together. Remember we hate-the-sin-but-love-the-sinner, and we also have to remember that human frailty is weakness, not sin. Yes, we fight against temptation our whole lives, it's god's way of helping us become godly, but we *know* it's a lifelong quest."

Virginia, miraculously, did not respond.

Cal cleared his throat, and stood. "Father, I mean Reverend … *Pastor* … I hope her membership in, or her belief in this church, or the whole thing *it* believes, can help her."

She was staring straight ahead without expression. Maybe he could leave her here and pick her up in an hour, let this guy have a go at her.

But the pastor also stood, extended his hand. "Thanks, Brother. And by the way, we play that one in Joyful Noise."

Cal squinted. "Did I miss something?"

"You were humming it. The Byrds rendition of Ecclesiastes. See? The Bible's cool, Brother. You're welcome to join us, anytime."

It was only a 15 minute drive home, including time spent at stoplights. He could have walked and given her the car. But they went side-by-side back out through the church and into the parking lot to the car. She went to her side and he to his. They buckled their seat belts and he turned the A/C to high. Before the car was out on Imperial Ave., she said, "We need coffee. We're almost out."

"That's a catastrophe we can't let happen." So he pulled into the grocery store a few lights down. They went into the store together. No one waits in the car in El Centro after April 1. She took a shopping cart from the supply outside the door. He didn't say, don't we just need coffee? After she put bananas, cereal, milk, and ice cream into the cart, she asked, "What do you want for dinner? Nothing's defrosted."

July 2009

I'll just call it 'the dead year.' But now I know it was always sort of there, the potential to happen. Think way back to ... whenever the hell it was ... I got into a marriage – chased him, pursued him – because I wanted to get as far away from *that* feeling as I could. Muffle it, distract myself from it. It didn't get put away because of *him*, but cuz of 'something to do, something to hope for.' Both of those have fallen apart. But why was the confusion there in the first place? And why do I usually think of writing a postcard when I ask myself that question? A client the other day was arguing about a correction I suggested (cuz in a human-canine pack, the canine can't be alpha) ... he actually said, "how would you know, you don't even have a dog, nobody loves you like this." I thought, Oh *yeah*? But maybe it's true and I'm just afraid to find out.

X

September 2009

When he came from brushing his teeth to get his work satchel and head to the shop, Virginia had a long grocery list on the table, sitting beside her purse, indicating she was preparing to go shopping. It included turkey, marshmallows, wheat bread, celery, yams, pearl onions, butter, asparagus, various fruits, nuts, and dates.

"A little early to shop for Thanksgiving." He didn't pick up the list, but could read her block printing from where he was standing.

"I was going to tell you, I'm having a big early-Thanksgiving dinner." She turned, smiling, from putting the breakfast bowls into the cupboard.

"Having? For who?"

"For us, of course."

He almost turned to leave, but didn't. "Why do we need to have Thanksgiving early?"

"Everyone's always so busy with their own, they've never been able to come to ours." She approached the table, drying her hands on the dish towel.

"Have we ever invited anyone?"

"Yes, Cal, time and time again, and have they ever come?"

"You invite people every year?"

"Who wants to invite when they say *no*?"

Again he almost shrugged and left. Almost. "Who are '*they*'?"

"My sister, her kids, *their* kids—"

"I thought she—"

"—and Trinity."

"*Trinity!*"

"You act like I just said I was inviting Charles Manson." She snatched her purse up from the table.

There'd been a documentary on TV the other night due to the 40th anniversary of the Helter Skelter killings. He didn't think she'd been paying attention since she'd been folding laundry, going back and forth to the machines in the garage, and setting up an ironing board.

"You know," he said, "I realized the other night that Trinity would have been perfect fodder for him, exactly the type of girl who would've—"

"What, murdered a bunch of people?"

"…I was going to say *joined*."

"Because she's such a loser?"

Now the grocery list was balled in her fist. "Because some of them were directionless or coming from broken homes."

Some were middle-class cheerleaders. I can see the parallel!

Okay, I know, I should've left 5 minutes ago.

"So our home is *broken* now?"

He picked up his satchel which he must have picked up and put down three times now. "I'm not her father, you know."

"And you never tried to be, that's what's *broken*."

"Oh for chrissake, Virg—"

"Stop cursing! They *said* you'd try to isolate me."

"What the ffff ..." Then the rest came out in an exhalation of air with puffed cheeks.

"Don't roll your eyes at me—can't I have my family around my table for a Sunday dinner? Can't I have that? My family? My *grandson*?"

"Did she say she's bringing Leo?"

"She hasn't answered yet."

"Then why are you buying food?"

"She will. It's also for her birthday. Combining Thanksgiving and her birthday. I told her we'd like to give her a gift."

"You bribed her then. I hope you mean some of the junk in the garage and living room."

"That too."

"*Too?* What, pray-tell, are '*we*' giving her?"

"Do you want your grandson to have a *home*?"

This time he turned, took two steps. Paused in the kitchen doorway. Kids chirped on the sidewalk, going to school. It had gotten that late. Over his shoulder he said, "No money. She's not getting a cent. Load this stuff into whatever beater she mooches to get herself here."

She must have followed him as he moved toward the front door, because it slammed behind him and he hadn't touched it.

The week of the dinner, Virginia told Cal he wouldn't have to clear away the boxes in the living room and move the big kitchen table in there after all. Virginia's sister and all her family had decided not to come. "They all decided the same thing at the same time?" he asked.

"My sister decided *for* everyone, as usual."

They were talking through one of the pass-through windows. Virginia at the kitchen sink, and Cal at his desk in the TV room, which put his back to her. He'd dialed up to check his email, which of course there wasn't any, not even bill notifications since he hadn't ever set up online payments for anything. He'd thought about doing so several times, but the speed bump that stopped him just in time, every time, was the persistent possibility that Trinity would visit—unannounced, usually— and of course have some sponging, pilfering friend who knew his/her way around a computer. Not that Trinity couldn't sponge and pilfer with the best of them by herself.

He knew that the groceries were all purchased, including a 30-pound turkey. "What's going to happen to all that food?"

"It just won't go to waste on *bossybutt*. I'll invite her again when the North Pole freezes over."

"You mean … never mind. It's an awfully big turkey. Can you donate to a food bank? Does your church—"

"Can't you even say *our* church? Aren't we married?"

Does deciding for everyone make her a bossybutt?

Yes, but shut up.

His email did have a group message from Cliff to the members of Blue Sand, notifying them about an upcoming gig. For some reason Cliff had put Cal on this email group, even though Cal, on several occasions, asked him why. Cliff had said so Cal would see what he was missing.

"I just wonder if maybe we shouldn't cancel the big shindig."

"*Trinity's* coming."

"Did she say so? Is she bringing Leo?"

"She didn't say about that." A spoon screeched, scraping a pan. "She's looking for a ride. Can't we send her some—"

"No."

"It's *my* money too, we're married, community-bylaws."

That makes marriage sort of like communism.

"So what am I, Hitler?" She ripped foil from the roll.

"Ummm…" Had he really said the thing about communism out loud? He powered down, sat staring into the greenish screen of the obsolete cube-shaped monitor. "Well, Fuehrer, I could use some dictatorial help losing weight." That time he just muttered under the sound of the kitchen faucet, but she turned off the water just in time.

"Are we in the same conversation?"

"I just thought, if I decided to, that you could ..." He held the edge of the desk, his fingers underneath the surface, tapping, "you know, help, be supportive?"

"By what, not inviting my daughter to visit?"

"We could meet them at a restaurant."

"What is *wrong* with you—you *just* said what're we going to do with all the food? And muttering over there like a lunatic."

"As you said, could be old-timer's disease." He swiveled around and stood, then approached the pass-through window. "If so, you have my permission to set me out in the desert somewhere."

"Unlike you, I wouldn't kick you to the curve."

By noon the day of the Sunday/Thanksgiving/birthday dinner, when Cal got home from four hours in his shop—not all of which were spent repairing the trombones with tweaked slides—Virginia had the turkey out of the oven. She'd skipped church and started it at 5 a.m. while he was eating breakfast because she needed the oven for the casseroles (some made days before), pies and birthday cake. When he'd responded "Pie *and* cake?" she'd said he didn't have to eat both, he didn't have to eat *any*thing, it wouldn't hurt her feelings. But she'd only prepared half as much oatmeal so he wouldn't be too full. He wasn't, and he managed to not leave the shop for a burrito.

The aroma of the turkey, and the muggy hot kitchen, was like entering a room-sized cornbread-and-onion-stuffing-filled carcass. Virginia wasn't in the kitchen at that moment, but he did not break off a piece of gold, crispy skin from the turkey. He stood with his eyes closed, imagining the pilfered morsel on his tongue, grease melting, saliva increasing. He wondered if his whole upright body was swaying, and he felt huge, as though, like his shower stall, there was a wall inches away on all sides of him. When he opened his eyes, Virginia was squinting, or grimacing at him via the pass-through window.

"Smells incredible," he said.

Her face reorganized into a smile. "Everything will be ready by two."

"But ... nobody's here."

"She will be."

But she wasn't. The turkey, covered in foil, was returned to the oven to stay warm three more times, rotating with the yam-marshmallow casserole and mashed white potatoes, the macaroni-and-cheese (Leo's favorite), the lasagna (another of Leo's preferences), green-bean-and-pearl-onions-with-breadcrumb-crust, and a berry pie. The pat of butter on the asparagus had completely melted and oozed into a yellow and congealing film under the green (but fading grey) stalks. Gravy was becoming gelatinous. Other than its frosting glistening in the damp warmth, the cake wasn't in imminent danger, nor the pie. But there was no room for them in the refrigerator which was stuffed with sodas and cheese, dips and cut vegetables. When the timer sounded around 4 after another rotation in the oven, Cal was watching a football game with the sound on mute, finishing a rum-and-coke, bag of tortilla chips and jar of salsa, mopping his sweating forehead with paper towels because the salsa was habanero, because the prolonged oven use was overwhelming the A/C's sway, and because Virginia was in the bedroom weeping. He was heading down there—noticing for the third or fourth time the table set with her grandmother's china and crystal from the living room cabinet, cloth napkins, florist carnations and daises, and metallic confetti sprinkled across the tablecloth in between the plates—to offer to call Cliff and maybe the other guys from Blue Sand to come over and enjoy the feast, when a vehicle with no muffler turned the corner, accelerated and crescendoed, then gunned into the driveway, a metallic bang and scrape indicating one tire had gone over the curb.

The dude Trinity brought through the front door was huge, even dwarfing Cal in height and girth. The house's 1950s dimensions in the foyer, doorways and kitchen could not have anticipated two men over 225 (because Cal was aware of how much *he* weighed, and this guy was a good 25 pounds more) shaking hands across the stained kitchen trashcan between the table and refrigerator, and the delay as the big dude had to extricate his hand from deep in a baggy-jeans pocket, while a plus-sized Trinity, who had squeezed past to look for her mother in the TV area, squeezed back through to embrace Virginia when she appeared in the kitchen from the bedroom hallway after she had hurriedly (he could tell) affixed her wig. Cal backed up and sat at the table, sifting the confetti through his fingers, as Trinity introduced the man, Clarence, "but call him Big-C." Not the same man she'd brought home last time. (Cal hoped he hadn't said "good to see you *again*.") This man's head was shaved, but Trinity was sporting dreadlocks, actually just tiny thin braids. Her lips looked bigger than he remembered, but he overhead her say *injections* to Virginia. Actually she said "No, not Botox, idiot-mommy. That's for wrinkles. I hope to die before I have any." Then again, everything about Trinity was bigger than he remembered. But weren't they all? He realized Virginia, the smallest of them, also had thighs each as big as the turkey that needed to, once again, be reheated before they could eat.

As they spoke—about injections and wrinkles and botox, spot-removal cream, how good a dreadlock wig might look on Virginia, Virginia's new nail girl, Trinity's new tats, Virginia's participation in a Christian women's chat and how that's where she was getting pointers for her new business—Trinity and Virginia were transferring dishes from oven to counter, counter to oven, and the microwave kept humming. He couldn't hear every word, but he didn't hear Trinity mention Leo, or even if Virginia asked about him.

Of course he'd noticed, without much surprise, as he watched only the two big adults get out of the 20-year-old Chevy in the driveway. Not a *where's Leo* question, but a *Leo's not here* reality.

"Man, Ima get out'da way," Clarence said, moving past the outside two chairs to sit opposite Cal at the table. "Girls gotta lotta say'n to do."

Cal felt his head swivel in slow motion, turning to look at the man, and was surprised when their eyes met for a second. "Say'n to do," Cal echoed.

The *say'n* accelerating to Virginia's suggestions for where Trinity could look for work, Trinity's hooted rejection of fast-food employment, then her honks of laughter when Virginia said something like beggers can't be losers. "Can't be no loser when I know I got game," Trinity said, trying to pinch Virginia's cheek. Virginia swatted her hand away.

"She do indeed," the man grinned.

The microwave stopped, beeped, dishes came out, new ones clanked in. Virginia was painting the tops of rolls with melted butter. "I got everything under control," Trinity's tone changed, one arm around

Virginia, the other lifting a glass lid and releasing a cloud of steam from the mac-n-cheese.

"I know you do, baby."

Cal's delayed echo, a whispered "indeed," was shrouded in the next round of microwave reheating. The yams and crusted green beans put off a mingled sweet-savory aroma that almost made his stomach hurt. Virginia was using a big syringe to squirt grease over the turkey, then she put it on the table. The bird was dark brown, wrinkled, maybe a little wizened.

"Look like my granny's bare ass," Clarence said, after Virginia was back on the other side of the cooktop island. Also over there in the steam, Trinity asked, "what's with the pasta, Mom? Have we become honky 'burbanites?"

"Those were Lee— Lionel's favorites."

All noise evaporated—had the microwave finished again? Water turned off? Spoons stopped stirring? Foil stopped rattling? For some reason Cal's eyes went back to Clarence, and for some reason Clarence's eyes met his.

Trinity said, "Shit, *that* ain't happ'n. He get that shit in juvie."

"What the hell—?" Cal's chair scraped back then caught on the back of his belt and bounced as he stood. The wall behind kept the chair mostly upright.

"Settle down," Trinity mumbled. She approached the table with a bowl of mashed potatoes, looking a little stiffer and browner than Virginia's reliable variety. "I jus' said everything under control."

"What kind of control is not having your own son?"

"The kind you wouldn't know about, now, would you?"

"What is that even supposed to mean?"

"It mean min' yo' bidness." She slapped a serving spoon into the potatoes causing a white spatter on the tabletop.

Cal looked at Virginia. "Do *you* know where he is?"

Virginia didn't look up from a drawer she'd opened. Utensils rattled. Her hands and arms, mostly hidden from his view, looked like a pianist going at it. Her lips tightened, getting to the difficult cadenza.

"You're not going to answer?" The utensils continued riffing, the kind of drum solo no one wants to hear when a jazz combo passes the adlib spotlight around. "What the holy fuck—?"

"You stop!" Virginia slammed the drawer. "There's nothing *holy* in—?"

"Oh *god*." Trinity dropped herself into a chair beside Clarence. She was tearing off a turkey drumstick while Virginia wailed, "It's not about God!"

"Okay, Mom, we agree, get that knife over here."

The drumstick was on Clarence's plate. Cal's eyes must have been following the turkey leg because when Clarence picked it up and took an enormous bite, his eyes again met Cal's.

"Where is he?" Cal said.

"Hey man, she din tell'ya?" Clarence chewed and swallowed. "He in the system."

"What?"

"Foster, man."

"Why would he—?"

"Shut up, C." Trinity swallowed a mouthful of turkey. " OK, nosey— cuz they put him in a group home when he got out."

"Out of what?"

"Fuck! *Juvie*," Trinity sneered. "Does *she* even tell you anything, or have you stopped do'n that *too*?"

"Trin!" Virginia's voice squeaked at a higher pitch than Cal had ever heard.

"Just cuz he dressed and talked his home culture," Trinity continued, "play'n like d'boys."

"He's *ten*." Cal looked from Trinity to Virginia, neither meeting his eyes. He couldn't see what Virginia was holding, whatever she'd taken out of the drawer. Trinity, standing again, was stirring the potatoes. "There must be more to it than that. How does he know how *de-boys* play?" Finally Cal looked at Clarence again.

Clarence's mouth had been refilled. A pile of the potatoes sat on his plate beside the half masticated turkey leg. He swallowed and said, "She dress him gangsta."

"*Fuck* that," Trinity screamed. The potato spoon, backhanded and released, banged into the refrigerator then fell to the floor. Virginia startled, maybe flinched. Trinity actually went and retrieved the spoon while she announced in a near-bellow, "I wanted him to know his culture … he started talking about a *saxophone*. That's *HIS* fat white ass." Pointing the spoon at Cal.

"Sista, you gonna blow everthang over nutt'n."

As though the floor had opened beneath her, Trinity plunged back down into her seat. "Sheee-it," Clarence muttered. Cal righted his chair, but hadn't yet sat down again when Virginia came from around the kitchen island with the turkey-carving knife. There was still nothing on the table but turkey and potatoes.

"Angel dressed and talked his culture and he never went anywhere except from his own home to heaven." She poised the knife as though to slice off the second turkey leg, but the limb tore off in her hand without any assistance.

Clarence's "hoo-eee" was barely a whisper.

"Oh mother, stop worshiping him." Trinity's face tilted to the ceiling, eyes closed. "How many years and still I get Angel-love, and on *my* birthday. He even failed being a d-boy."

Both Cal and Virginia stared at Trinity until she might have felt the spotlight in the growing-warm silence—not even Clarence chewing—and opened her eyes. When she took the knife from Virginia, Cal could see that both of them had similarly manicured nails, but very different colors, Virginia's intense red, Trinity's almost black purple. Blood spilling then drying. "Angel was dealing, Mom. Where d'ya think I got mine?" She poised the knife to cut a hunk off the turkey, then put the knife down on the platter and took the second drumstick from Virginia.

"Is that why he's in foster?" Cal said, keeping his voice monotone, "your drugs?"

Virginia actually flinched again when Trinity gestured with the drumstick. "Cuz I couldn't work and take care of him both."

"Work? You selling in front of him or just using? This your pusher, or your pimp?"

"Hey, man," Clarence said, "be cool."

While Trinity said, "Pusher? What're you, 80-years-old? Oh, yeah, vanilla bird-shit."

A timer sounded. Something sweet was burning. Virginia was about to collapse into her still-empty chair, but Cal put a hand on each of her shoulders, gently moved her aside so he could leave the table. He stopped on the other side of the kitchen island to turn off the timer and the oven. A glance back at the table showed Virginia now seated, her plate still empty, her face blanched and frozen. The other two, from the back, appeared to be eating. There might have been some low muttered conversation between them. Still in the microwave, the asparagus was no longer warm. The scorched scent was from marshmallow topping, plus the rolls were now blackened on top. Foil-covered on the stove, the pungently-cheesy casseroles blended with the burnt-toast smell to evoke grilled-cheese with Virginia's specialty: a hint of parmesan. Cal broke off a piece of over-cooked lasagna noodle exposed on the edge and put it in his mouth on his way out to the TV area, all the blinds closed against afternoon sun. He picked up the phone receiver but kept his finger on the button, then punched 9-1-1. The dinner table in the kitchen had gone mute. Not even a tink of silverware. Cal let his voice resound. "Yes, I need some drug-users, possibly dealers removed from my home." He didn't know if he'd ever used the word *home* instead of *house* like that.

The tornado of Trinity and Clarence clearing out of the kitchen, out the front door, and out of the driveway was not prolonged and left no destruction in its wake.

When the cops got there, they found the TV room furniture a little askew with dirty dishes and food scattered on the carpet. In the kitchen, carnage of the turkey was strewn on the floor, with more dishes, even one of the crystal goblets—from broken to chipped to downright rubble—and the poultry-knife standing upright, its point buried in the wooden serving platter. They also found Cal on the front lawn, locked out of the house.

Kicked to the curve.

Dang, Cal, still joking?

As we like to say, easier to laugh …

Virginia had made the real 911 call, after booting the turkey around on the floor and chucking dishes at him via the pass-through window while screaming about family and god's plan to share loaves and fishes, *don't stoke a mother bear*, Cal's cheap cheating selfish soul would burn for eternity, *you won't even feed a hungry little boy you once claimed to love*, and some random words and phrases like *respect*, *battle-of-the-exes*, *abuse*, and *concurring against me*.

The officers, male and female, took turns, one inside, one outside, asking him the same questions that they asked her. "Are you okay? Are you hurt anywhere? Do you want her [him] arrested?"

Yes, no, and no.

"How'd she get a 200 pound man out the door against his will?"

"I didn't fight back."

"Good idea."

"Yeah, I just went the direction she was pushing me. I knew she'd calm down."

"What was the fight about, sir?"

"I won't send any more money to the … kids."

"You can decide not to press charges, but if it got worse, you can't stop us from arresting her."

"It was just food, and … I moved my horns down to the shop."

The cops, of course, didn't understand that.

He walked around the block, 8 p.m., temperature still in the 90s. Chihuahuas and small poodles shrilled as he passed nearly every other yard, like he was the domino in a chain of sound circling the block. When he got home, the kitchen was cleaned, the garbage taken out to the cans at the side of the house. Virginia was making ice cream sundaes with root beer and had cut big pieces of the birthday cake.

"A mother's instinct is fierce," she said, "but I don't mean the things I called you."

"Yeah."

So, aren't you ready to leave yet, or <u>why</u> aren't you ready? When will you ever be ready? What're you clinging to, that old cliché promise you made?

Shut up for a while, just …can't you just shut up for a little while?

Careful what you wish for.

His butt was in his chair at his workbench at his shop in just 12 hours. Nothing unusual in that. And only moderately unusual that he was there before the employee who got to the store hours early to sweep, check stock and list what inventory would need to be ordered. So there was no hum of air-conditioner or extra fans. No swish of pages as the guy read through the newspaper. And, most thankfully, no satellite radio tuned to classic rock. September wasn't known for bringing sea-change weather, but the night air had spit a thin mist of uncommon dew, and the slightest fog of vapor was rising from the alfalfa fields. The day felt like one that suggested everything would be different now and nothing would ever change. Similar to the way he felt after a day of roiling stomach virus, you could feel empty and clean but look in the mirror and still see a monster. He sat with his coffee in the quiet. He still hadn't started on any of the tweaked trombone slides when Cliff arrived. The door chime rang and lights flickered on in the main retail area. Cal swiveled in his chair to grab one of the trombone slides and get it onto his workbench. Not that Cliff was his overseer; it was Cal's shop, Cal's customer, Cal's business whether or not he ever repaired another mishandled, mistreated instrument.

In fact Cal's lights weren't even on yet, so when Cliff opened the shop door he twitched a bit, as though startled to see that Cal would come to work at all.

"Hey, man, turn the lights on why doncha." Cliff dropped a stack of mail on Cal's workbench. "Sorry, this is Saturday's mail. I picked it up on my way out to a gig."

Cliff paused on his way back out of the shop. Cal was staring at the card on the top of the stack of mail. "We missed you, as usual," Cliff said.

"Yeah. I missed me too."

January 2010
The dogs - they loved me more than a person deserves. At one time so did you. It hasn't been fair, the one-way communication. Not sure what I was trying to prove, that I didn't need you? I'm ready to admit it & change that, if you care anymore:
nonamegirl@gowebway.net
Maybe you thought it would take something big: abuse, addiction, foreclosure & homelessness, rape, terminal illness, miscarriage, abduction, family annihilation ... But it was the smell of my fear. I'll likely disappoint in ways you don't yet know, but if you still want to, we can try to get back to what we were about, friends first...
X ... I mean ... *Lexie*

Post Card

Cal Tonnessen
c/o Cliff's Edge Music
136 E Main St
El Centro CA 92243

Sorry I told you to shut up.

    You didn't tell me, bud, you told yourself. Now I'm giving you the chance to tell me. Tell me anything. If you're not too covered in your enormous monster and all dead meat inside that husk. I told you not to abandon your ax!

    How did you know? About the monster?

    Cuz, bud...you would've never hidden anything from me. I abandoned you.

His saxophone was under two of the damaged trombones. The Key Leaves he'd attached to help the low keys stay dry had effectively prevented the pads from getting brittle. The reed saver had been less successful preventing the reed from warping. He tightened the ligature that held the reed to the mouthpiece then wet the reed in his mouth. He might have had the reed against his tongue for 3 or 4 minutes, eyes closed. When he opened his eyes and looked down at the open sax case, he remembered the rolled-up charts were no longer there. The keys under his fingers made their familiar popping sound, empty of music. Without removing his lips from around the mouthpiece, he inhaled, then the first strain of a melody slipped into his small workroom, thin and tentative at first, *You give your hand to me / And then you say hello* ... He let his subtone fizz, then his sound thickened, fuller, more meat ... *Oh I am just a friend / That's all I've ever been* ... His tone rich, dark, the adlibbed garnishes a nuance that did not overpower the essence of the elemental ingredients.

> *"Well you don't know me."*
> *Dude! Now ask me what I know ... and tell me what I don't. For real.*
> *What you don't know, girl ... how much time do you have?*
> *Cal, we're over 50.*

There was a computer behind the cash register counter where all employee email accounts started with *Cliff's Edge*. He supposed that was, now, exactly where he was. And ready to jump.

Cris Mazza's latest book is *Yet to Come, a novel*. Mazza has seventeen other titles of fiction and literary nonfiction including her last book, *Charlatan: New and Selected Stories*, covering her 20 years of authoring short fiction. Other notable titles include *Something Wrong With Her*, a real-time memoir; her first novel *How to Leave a Country*, which won the PEN/Nelson Algren Award for book-length fiction; and the critically acclaimed *Is It Sexual Harassment Yet?* She is a native of Southern California and director of the Program for Writers at the University of Illinois at Chicago.